"I WAS JUST THINKING THAT DOMINIC AND JULIE ARE PERFECT FOR EACH OTHER," MAGGIE SAYS. "DON'T YOU THINK?"

"Yeah, I think they have a lot in common," Charlie tells her. "For example…"

He trails off, distracted by the piercing blue of her eyes. He's known some striking blue-eyed blondes, and some drop-dead gorgeous dark-eyed brunettes, but this combo—blue eyes with black hair…

She clears her throat. Loudly.

He tears his thoughts away from ~~her~~ ~~back~~ to the matter at hand. "Julie makes ~~the best~~ ~~suggested~~. And I heard Dominic ~~telling~~ ~~her~~

"Yes, Dom ~~~~ ~~~~ m, cherry. He loves cherry, ~~~~

"Pie?" he sup~~~~ ~~are~~ precisely the shade of ripe cher~~~~

"Yes, cherry pie~~~~ ~~agrees~~. "Dom is crazy about cherry pie." And Charlie is crazy about those cherry-red lips.

For an insane moment, he wonders what it would be like to kiss her.

PRAISE FOR WENDY MARKHAM'S
THE NINE MONTH PLAN

Also by Wendy Markham

The Nine Month Plan

Once Upon a Blind Date

Wendy Markham

NEW YORK   BOSTON

Copyright © 2004 by Wendy Corsi Staub
Excerpt from *Hello, It's Me* © 2004 by Wendy Corsi Staub
All rights reserved. No part of this book may be reproduced in any form or by any electronic or mechanical means, including information storage and retrieval systems, without permission in writing from the publisher, except by a reviewer who may quote brief passages in a review.

Cover design by Diane Luger
Cover illustration by Andrew Condron
Book design by Giorgetta Bell McRee

Warner Books

Time Warner Book Group
1271 Avenue of the Americas
New York, NY 10020
Visit our Web site at www.twbookmark.com

Printed in the United States of America

First Paperback Printing: March 2004

10 9 8 7 6 5 4 3 2 1

For my guys, Mark, Morgan, and Brody, with love . . .

And for my precious newborn nephew,
Dominick Alan Corsi,
who is waiting patiently for Aunt Wendy
to meet her deadline . . . so that she can meet him.

Once
Upon a
Blind
Date

Prologue

"I am *not* your wife, Dom."

Dominic Chickalini blinks.

Maggie O'Mulligan continues, "I'm your friend. Your confidante. Your tennis partner. But I am *soooo* not your wife."

"Hello? Did I *say* you were my wife, Mags?"

"You asked me if I could pick up your dry cleaning," Maggie points out, as, standing shoulder to shoulder, she and Dominic inch another step forward.

Now only three human obstacles lie between the two of them and the falafel pushcart. One is a businessman toting carry-on luggage; in a rush to catch a train or plane, no doubt. Guaranteed he'll order, pay, and run in ten seconds tops. But behind him—and in front of Maggie and Dom—are a pair of obvious tourists, complete with down parkas, cameras, and a subway map.

Maggie sighs. Tourists are the dial-up connection in New York's broadband world.

Hot dogs would have been faster—there are a dozen hot dog carts within a two-block radius of the midtown ad agency where they both work. But Dom insisted on falafel for lunch, and arguing with a headstrong and hungry Dominic Chickalini about food is about as effective as trying to convince him to find a nice girl and settle down.

"Come on, Mags. I need you," he pleads, his breath puffing white in the February air.

Oh. Right. The dry cleaning.

"Dominic, I have a million errands to run after work. Like picking up my own dry cleaning. And getting some groceries into my apartment. And getting my butt to the gym."

"That's not an errand. Can't you skip it for a night?"

"Not after seven days of lounging on a beach with fattening rum drinks. And anyway, you don't need me. You need a wife. And I need lunch."

They take another baby step forward as the businessman at the head of the line departs with his paper-wrapped falafel. *One down, two to go,* Maggie reassures her rumbling stomach. She hasn't eaten since the pack of peanuts on the flight home to LaGuardia last night.

Which is probably a good thing, since she definitely gained weight on vacation. All that snorkeling and swimming and hiking worked up an appetite, and there was no shortage of delicious food at the resort.

But Maggie didn't spend months sweating and starving off the twenty pounds she gained in college just to pack it on again. She's as disciplined about her weight as she is about—well, about almost every other aspect of her life.

Okay, *every* aspect. Control. It's all about control.

Maggie's rumbling stomach chimes in with a chorus of taxi horns and the jackhammer at the construction site on the opposite side of Forty-sixth Street.

She checks her watch, wondering whether she'll still have a chance to pick up her vacation pictures at the kiosk over on Lexington Avenue before she has to be back at her desk. When she dropped off the film this morning before nine, they promised it would be developed by noon. Just another one of those Manhattan ironies: that in a city where everything from conversation to erecting a new skyscraper is accomplished at lightning speed, the one-hour photo place takes three hours.

Dom rubs his chin—the famous Chickalini chin with its perfect cleft, right below his perfect lips.

"One would think," Maggie observes dryly, "that an appealing male specimen such as yourself would be capable of finding some other willing female to do all of his dirty work."

"If I had a wife, she'd definitely be doing all of my dirty work, Mags. But since I don't—"

"And I think in that telling statement we've just nailed a possible reason *why* you don't—"

"Funny. You're funny, Mags. Who says only a wife can run errands? Like, what? You think you have to be wearing a wedding band before Wong Lee Chin will release my dry cleaning to you? Because, believe me, he'd give them to anyone with cash. Just last week he almost threw some lady's sequined ball gown in with my blazers."

"Time to switch dry cleaners."

"Nah. My family's been going to Wong for years. He loves me."

She doesn't doubt it. Everybody loves Dominic, despite his faults. Store clerks, old ladies, kids, animals, heiresses, traffic cops . . .

The man can charm anybody. Including one Margaret

Mary O'Mulligan, when she's in the mood. But luckily for both of them, she's utterly immune to the animal magnetism that tends to turn other women into lustful fools. Besides, she already has a boyfriend—one who happens to be out of town—heck, out of the *hemisphere* at the moment, but a boyfriend nonetheless.

"Please, Mags? There's no one else I can ask."

She heaves a weary sigh. They've been through this before. Almost on a daily basis, in fact, before she left for Jamaica with two *other* friends; self-sufficient friends; *female* friends: Carolyn and Belinda.

The thing is, she's willing to be Dom's friend, hang out, play tennis at the health club—but she's not willing to cater to his masculine helplessness when it comes to anything the least bit domestic.

"Come on, Dom."

"Come on, Mags," he returns, his black eyes twinkling at her. "You live right around the corner from the cleaners and from me. What's the problem? I really need you."

"You really *need* a wife," she repeats, forcing herself to look away, lest he cast his spell on her. Not that it's likely she'll fall for him. She'd have done so long before now if it were at all possible. She continues, "Or at the very least, you need a personal assistant."

The businessman is now hailing a cab with falafel in hand, but the tourists are asking the vendor questions. Lots of questions. About everything from the ethnic origins of falafel to a complete list of ingredients and nutritional value.

Maggie rubs her tired eyes, wishing they would shut up and hurry.

She notices that her cheeks still feel sore from the nasty

sunburn she got on the first day in Jamaica. With her jet-black hair, you'd think she wouldn't be so fair-skinned, but she inherited a healthy dose of freckles and a tendency to burn from her mother's side of the family, the Harrigans. That, and the famous Harrigan blue eyes. And, according to her easygoing, redheaded father, the notoriously quick Harrigan temper.

Daddy likes to quote his Great-grandpa O'Mulligan, who survived the great Chicago Fire and liked to say, "Remember, it only takes a single spark to start a raging inferno." According to Daddy, that's all it takes to ignite the Harrigan temper as well.

"Look, I have to go right from work to Pop's restaurant," Dominic is telling her, still fixated on his dry-cleaning dilemma.

Pop's restaurant would be Big Pizza Pie over in Astoria, Queens, where Dom grew up and where Maggie now lives in a rental apartment around the corner from the Chickalini home.

He goes on, "I won't have time to get my suits, and the cleaners will be closed by the time I close up for the night. And I need my dark suit for a client lunch tomorrow."

"Can't Nina pick it up for you? Or Rosalee?" Lord knows his older sisters have done more than their share of coddling their motherless kid brother.

"Nina can't. She's the reason I have to work at the restaurant tonight—she's away. She and Joey are on their honeymoon, remember?"

"Oh, right. I forgot." Dominic did mention a few weeks ago that the eldest of the Chickalini brood was finally going to Europe with her husband—*and* their two toddlers. Nina and Joey Materi have been married for a couple of years now.

Dom continues, "And Rosalee—"

"Forget it, I know. She's too pregnant to move. Okay, Dom, you got me. I'll get the dry cleaning for you. On one condition."

"What's that?" he asks absently, checking out a supermodel type who's sauntering by in a fur coat. The woman flashes him a flirtatious smile, obviously not immune to Tall, Dark, and Handsome incarnate.

"The condition that you let me help you find a wife," Maggie says, adding, with a gesture at the supermodel's back as she disappears into the sidewalk throng, "and not *that* kind of wife."

"Huh?"

"You need a real woman, Dom. Not one of those lightweight *blondes du jour* you've been dating ever since I've known you. You need a woman of substance. Somebody like me."

"You?" He looks more closely at her. "Mags, you're not—"

She swats his arm, realizing what he's thinking. "No! I'm definitely not, Dom. I said somebody like me. But somebody who's actually attracted to you, *unlike* me."

"Gee, thanks a lot," he mutters dryly.

"You know what I mean, Dom. There's nothing between you and me, and there never could be. But somewhere out there is the future Mrs. Chickalini." She gestures at the towering skyscrapers around them. "And I'm going to find her for you."

He shrugs. "Fine. Whatever. Just as long as you don't forget my dry cleaning."

Meanwhile, Somewhere in Greenwich Village . . .

"What a woman," Charlie Kennelly declares around a mouthful of molten chocolate something-or-other. The dessert has a French name that he wouldn't be able to pronounce even if he tried—and he wouldn't try. Not when Julie Purello wouldn't let him live down his butchering of *bûche de Noël* two months ago.

"You really like it? It's not too rich?" she asks, looking up from the egg she's separating. Her round face is smudged with flour or baking powder.

"No, it's amazing," Charlie says, trading his fork for a paper towel and handing it to her. "Here. Wipe. You've got something white on your face."

"Again? Where?" She crinkles her nose.

"Left cheek, right below your glasses. Here, I'll get it for you."

She tilts her face up, and Charlie dabs at her cheek, wondering, as he has countless times before, why he can't make himself fall in love with Julie. If the way to a man's heart really were through his stomach, he and his fair-haired, blue-eyed neighbor would be registering at Michael C. Fina right about now.

Not that Charlie's interested in marriage in the near— or even distant—future. He won't be going down that road again. Not after what happened with Laurie.

Okay, so technically, they weren't married . . . yet. And technically, she didn't leave him at the altar. But close enough for him to be saddled with a never-worn Brooks Brothers tux and two unused tickets to the French Riviera.

He still has a few weeks left to use them, according to the airline. They were supposed to be nonrefundable, but

Julie's travel agent friend, Dana, who booked the trip, pulled some strings and the airline gave him a twelve-month grace period.

Even if he were interested in marriage, Julie just isn't his type. He's always gone for sultry, sensual, willowy, well-bred brunettes. Women who grew up in the same circles he did up in Westchester County. Back in high school and college, the girls he dated thought his literary leanings were charmingly romantic. But few grown women he knows are interested in living on love—or a full-time free-lancer's salary. And he doesn't dare tell them about his trust fund, having dealt with more than his share of gold diggers in the past.

"Did you get the white stuff off?" Julie asks, rubbing her cheek.

"Yup. All clean." He crumples the paper towel and aims it toward the garbage can beside the counter—all of two feet away, given the size of Julie's Manhattan galley kitchen, identical to his own across the hall.

The paper towel lands on the floor. Oops.

Julie promptly bends to pick it up.

"I was going to get that," he protests guiltily.

Bachelor Slob. That's what his sisters call him.

Julie merely laughs as she deposits the crumpled paper towel into the garbage can.

A talented chef, easygoing, pretty . . .

"You know, you'd make an awesome wife, Julie," Charlie declares, picking up his fork and digging in once again to the plateful of chocolate whatever-you-call-it. She's using him as her oh-so-willing guinea pig while she tries out recipes for the Valentine's Day dessert menu at the bistro where she works.

"Did you say *wife*?" She's trying to pluck an elusive bit of eggshell out of the whites in the bowl.

"Yeah. Wife. You need to get out there and start dating again. Just because it didn't work out with Gene—"

"Not Gene. *Jean.* J-e-a-n. Jean-Louis."

Figures. As pastry chef at Chez-snooty-somebody on Park Avenue South, she's more likely to cross paths with a Jean-Louis than with a Regular Joe from the boroughs. And what she needs, Charlie is convinced, is a Regular Joe.

Somebody like Charlie himself. Only, somebody with whom she shares sparks, because there are zilch between the two of them.

"Jul', just because Jean LaFoot broke off your engagement—"

"Lafitte, not LaFoot, you dork!"

"Just because Jean Lafitte broke off—"

"No!" Julie laughs. "My fiancé's name was Jean-Louis. The pirate's name was Jean Lafitte."

"Pirate? What pirate?"

"Never mind."

He shakes his head. "Look, Jul', the point is, Frenchy wasn't your one chance for happily ever after, you know? It's been months."

"Not months. Weeks."

"How many weeks?"

"Seven," she says, after doing the mental math. "It's been seven weeks. He dumped me in December, right before I met you, remember?"

How could he forget? He found her in the laundry room down the hall, sobbing into a basket full of unsorted whites and darks. He comforted her well into the fluffing and folding stage, having been in her shoes himself not so long before.

"I remember," he says now. "So it's been two months next week. *Months.* No more wallowing, Jul'. You've got to get back out there."

"Out where? Work is the only place I go, and the managers at the restaurant are all married, the waiters are gay, and—"

"You need to do something other than work. Do you realize you have no life besides the restaurant and hanging out with me?"

"Well, when am I supposed to have a life? I have to be at work when the rest of the world is asleep, and I'm sleeping when they're out socializing—other than you . . ."

"I *work*," he protests, bristling with the customary work-at-home, self-employed magazine columnist indignation.

". . . so anyway, unless Mr. Right pops up in my kitchen someday . . ."

"I'll help you," Charlie declares around another delectable mouthful of chocolate.

"Help me what?"

"Help you find Mr. Right. You know . . . I'll weed out the frogs and find you a prince."

What are you saying?

Spewing clichés about frogs and princes?

Promising Julie a husband?

Have you lost your mind?

But he can't help it. Maybe some part of him feels guilty because he isn't snapping her up himself—sort of like he's letting the perfect woman go to waste.

"You're not going to set me up with one of your friends?" she asks warily. "Because Charlie, your friends—"

"No! Hell, no." He cringes at the very idea of siccing Pork or Butts or, God forbid, Prairie Dog, on Julie. He's known them since high school and loves them like the brothers he never had, but . . .

"They're animals, Jul'."

Even if they weren't animals, they all have fairly serious girlfriends these days. But he doesn't tell Julie that. No need to give her the impression that the ratio of single women to available men in New York is shrinking by the moment—even if his reader mail tells him that it's true.

"You need a nice guy. Somebody who wants more than . . . well, what my friends want."

Hell, what *most* guys want, he admits to himself.

So what the heck is he doing, promising this sweetheart of a woman a too-good-to-be-true specimen of noble and gentlemanly marriage-ready masculinity?

Obviously, this sweetheart of a woman is wondering the exact same thing, gazing up from her egg whites with a dubious expression. "Uh-huh. Sure. And where are you going to find this nice guy?"

Yeah, where, indeed? This is New York, land of gorgeous, available single women and nary a potential husband—at least, according to Charlie's sisters, his editor, and just about every other man-hunting bachelorette he's ever met. In fact, the notorious shortage in eligible local men is a frequent theme in his monthly Bachelor at Large column for *She* magazine.

Okay. So he might have to widen his search horizons to the boroughs, the suburbs, Jersey, even . . .

But what makes him think he's going to find Julie a husband here, there, or anywhere?

"Forget it, Charlie," Julie says, seeing his expression and shaking her head. "I'm perfectly content to be the old maid across the hall. Maybe I'll get a cat. I'll name it Romeo, or wait . . . Mr. Romeo. Or I'll get a *few* cats. I'll need a bunch of cats if I'm going to be a lonely old maid, right?"

"You are not going to be a lonely old maid, Julie. I promise," Charlie assures her.

"I'm not?"

"No. I promise," he says again, wondering why he can't just shut up. "I've got a plan."

"You do?"

Hell, no.

"Hell, yes. Just leave everything to me. Okay? Have I ever let you down?"

She shrugs.

"What? Are you thinking about the oven thing again? You're thinking about the oven thing, aren't you?"

Another shrug.

"Jul', I told you, I fell asleep," he says, cringing inwardly. "But I ran over here to turn it off—"

"When you heard the smoke alarm ringing from across the hall," she points out.

"Right, but at least I saved your apartment. In about two seconds the whole place would've gone up in flames. And you said yourself that your dad didn't mind the store-bought birthday cake."

"I know."

"And I am sorry. I'm really, really—"

"I know, I know. You don't have to keep apologizing,

Charlie. And you don't have to make me any promises. You're not a promises kind of guy."

That stings. Really.

Is it true?

Probably, Charlie admits. Julie isn't the first woman to tell him as much. But it still stings.

"Let me do this for you, Jul'," he says. "I've been wanting to make that whole burnt cake thing up to you . . ."

"By finding me a husband?" she asks, amused.

"By finding you love . . . and you know, according to my favorite author Erich Segal—"

"I thought your favorite author was Clive Cussler."

"He's my second favorite. Anyway, love means never having to say you're sorry . . . so when I marry you off, I'll stop apologizing. Deal?"

"Did anybody ever tell you you're a goofball, Charlie Kennelly?"

"You won't be calling me goofball when we're dancing at your wedding, Jul'."

She throws up her hands, laughing. "You know what, Charlie? If you want to find me a husband, go for it. I put my love life entirely in your hands."

"You won't be sorry," he vows, wondering what the hell he just got himself into.

Chapter One

One Week Later

"Eeeww! What is she *thinking* with that hair?"

Maggie looks up from her computer monitor and leans toward her friend Belinda's computer.

"I don't know . . . I think she's kinda cute," Maggie protests, gazing at the woman in the photo on the screen.

Belinda—dubbed Bindy by her finishing school roommates, a nickname to which she clings as ferociously as her waning youth—announces, with a wrinkle of her cosmetically altered nose, "Her hair is pink."

"She can't help what she looks like, Bindy."

"Trust me, there is no pink hair in nature. This is deliberate." Bindy clicks the mouse, and the picture vanishes. "There. I'm done."

"You've been through all the Metro Women Seeking Metro Men listings?" Maggie asks in disbelief.

"Yup."

"Including the boroughs?"

"Brooklyn and Queens. The Bronx is too dangerous—"

"Not all of it," Maggie protests.

"—yes, all of it, and Staten Island is too inconvenient. But I went through everything else."

"And you didn't find one potential date for Dom?"

"Nope."

"What about that pediatric musical therapist who directs the church choir in her spare time? She said her hobbies are tennis and the Yankees and that her favorite food is pizza. She'd be perfect for Dom."

"She had a huge space between her teeth."

"So does Lauren Hutton."

"She's *Lauren Hutton*. She can get away with it. Didn't this chick ever hear of braces? If you're going to put yourself out there in a matchmaking service, you do a little basic maintenance first."

Maggie again regrets bringing Bindy along to Matchmocha, Matchmocha—a cozy little exposed brick-and-rafters Bleecker Street cybercafe catering to spouse-shopping, frothy-java-concoction-sipping singles. She might be one of Maggie's closest friends, but she's notoriously picky and judgmental when it comes to— well, okay, just about everything.

Not that Maggie isn't picky, too—at least, in choosing a potential date for Dom. She's got to find the kind of woman who wouldn't mind taking care of a man who can't take care of himself. An old-fashioned woman who isn't already married to her career—and who wouldn't be opposed to rolling up her sleeves and pitching in with Dom's family restaurant on occasion. That's an absolute must in the Chickalini family. Even Maggie has boxed her share of fresh-out-of-the-oven pizza pies.

So far, she's only found two women who might fit the

bill, and neither struck her as particularly appealing aside from the fact that they stated that they know their way around a kitchen.

"Look, Bindy, I'm going to keep browsing. Why don't you check out the guy listings?" Maggie suggests.

Bindy's salon-arched eyebrows disappear beneath a swoop of sprayed dyed-blond hair. "Are you kidding? Why would I do that?"

Maggie shrugs. "You're available. Maybe you'll see someone you like."

"I wouldn't date somebody who has to advertise himself," Bindy says, as though Maggie has suggested that she strip naked and do a pole dance for the two Wall Street types at the next computer terminal. "I mean, this is barely one notch above taking out a personal ad in the *Post*."

"Get over it, Bindy. Everybody does it these days."

"I don't. You don't."

"That's because I have Jason and you . . ."

"Have class?" Bindy gives an airy wave of her shiny plum-colored manicure. "And anyway, you don't have Jason right now. You might as well be advertising yourself as available, too."

"A long-distance relationship doesn't make me 'available,'" Maggie protests.

"It does if it doesn't come back."

"He's coming back."

"Mmm hmm." Bindy shrugs. "Anyway, you said you were both allowed to see other people. What if he found somebody else?"

"I'm sure he'd have told me if he had," Maggie says with a confidence she doesn't quite feel.

Three months into their relationship, Jason Hendrix

flew off to South America to provide medical care for poor, underprivileged, native children.

Bindy isn't nearly as impressed with Jason's noble life-saving mission as she was with his East Thirty-eighth Street town house, his family's Bedford estate, and his unmarried colleagues. In fact, with her thirtieth birthday looming and nary a potential fiancé on the horizon, Bindy accused Maggie of sabotaging both their love lives by telling Jason not to stay in New York on her account.

But what else could she do? He had made arrangements for the mission long before he and Maggie locked eyes across a crowded elevator in Saks that rainy October Saturday. And he *did* offer to stay.

So why didn't she ask him to?

Everything about him is right. He's exactly what she—and every other woman in Manhattan—has been looking for. Wealthy, handsome, professional, athletic, fun-loving, adores kids. He's even Catholic, a quality that's a prerequisite in all marriage candidates, as far as Maggie's parents are concerned. Not that they have any say over whom she marries . . . but it will make it a heck of a lot easier to get them to pay for the wedding, that's for sure.

How could she let him slip away?

Maybe Bindy is right about her having been a fool to let him go. She was probably a fool to agree to seeing other people, too. He's probably taken full advantage of that, while she hasn't so much as glanced in another man's direction.

Well, Jason will be back next month, and, presumably, they can pick up where they left off. In the meantime, she's got plenty to keep her busy, what with her job as media planner on a cosmetics account, working out at the health club, hanging out with her friends—oh, and finding Dom a domestic damsel.

"Can we go now?" Bindy asks, checking her Philippe Charriol watch. "We've been here forever."

"Just give me another fifteen minutes. I want to answer a few more women for Dom."

"Don't you think he should be answering them himself?"

"Are you kidding, Bindy? He's a great guy, but he's not exactly the most eloquent person I've ever met. Besides, I promised him I'd take care of all the details."

"Is it really fair to these women that you're pretending to be Dom? I mean, first you fill out his questionnaire for him, now you're writing e-mails pretending to be him."

"Of course it's fair. It's not like Dom doesn't exist."

"Yes, but Eloquent Dom doesn't exist. I think you're cheating."

This, from a woman with an illegal sublet and socks in her bra. Maggie rolls her blue eyes.

"You want another coffee?" Bindy asks, rising and picking up her red velvet Kate Spade bag.

"Sure . . . but make it decaf this time, or I'll be up all night. And make sure it's skim, okay?"

Maggie watches her friend sashay toward the barrista, then turns back to the computer screen, twirling a length of shoulder-length black hair around her forefinger as she concentrates.

Hmm . . .

Alison Kramer looks interesting, but according to her questionnaire, she's the single mom of a five-year-old.

Baggage. Dominic definitely doesn't need baggage.

Maggie clicks the mouse on the NEXT button, and finds

herself gazing down into a pretty, all-American face. A face, she sees, scanning the accompanying questionnaire, that belongs to a woman named Julie P.—no last names at Matchmocha, Matchmocha.

Julie P. is a pastry chef who lives in the Village and, according to her questionnaire, is an old-fashioned girl at heart. She says she's ready to settle down and start cooking for two. Eating for two, too.

Perfect for Dom. He's ready to settle down, too—even if he doesn't know it yet.

Maggie's always been one step ahead of him when it comes to his life. She was the one who suggested that he major in business so that he could take over his father's pizzeria. When his sister Nina decided to take over the business instead, it was Maggie who suggested that Dom follow her into the advertising industry. She got him the interview at Blair Barnett, the agency where she's a media planner, and the next thing she knew, he'd been hired as an assistant account executive.

"Sometimes I think you know me better than I know myself, Mags," Dom likes to say. "You know what I need before I do."

True. She does pride herself on being a take-charge kind of person. Plus, she's known him for six years now, having met him on her first day of freshman year in college, and if there's one thing she's figured out about Dominic Chickalini, it's that he likes to be taken care of. He had all the girls in the dorm competing for the chance to help him with his laundry, his English Lit papers, even his Christmas shopping.

It's the same at the office. The other day, Maggie actually caught one of the female account coordinators bringing Dom a cup of coffee. Not even coffee-cart coffee that you get down the hall, but the kind you have to leave the building to get from Au Bon Pain.

He's the eternal motherless little boy, soaking up the nurturing affection of women like a paper towel in a Bounty commercial.

He needs to be showered with love, especially now that his sisters are married and caught up in families of their own. He needs a wife. Not so that she can fetch his coffee, but so that she can take care of him.

That's why she needs to be a certain kind of woman. An old-fashioned kind of woman.

Like this Julie P., who comes right out and says she enjoys cooking, cleaning, and sewing.

"Here's your decaf," Bindy says behind her.

"Thanks," Maggie murmurs, lost in Julie P.'s questionnaire.

Reading over her shoulder, Bindy snorts. " Is this chick for real? '*I also know how to darn socks and churn butter, and in warmer months I grow fresh vegetables on my fire escape . . .*'? Maggie, this is just—"

"I know! She sounds almost too good to be true, doesn't she?"

"What is she, Amish?"

"She's just old-fashioned. I think she's perfect for Dom. I'm going to reply to her."

"Whatever. I still don't think it's right."

Her fingers poised over the keyboard, Maggie wonders if maybe it is deceitful, pretending to be Dom, even with his permission. Maybe he should be selecting his own women, writing his own e-mails . . .

Maggie's gaze shifts thoughtfully back to the questionnaire. Her intuition is saying that this is the right woman for Dom, and when her intuition speaks to her, she listens.

It's for your own good, she tells the smiling Julie P. *Yours, and Dom's. You'll both thank me someday . . . you can name your first daughter Maggie.*

Her mind made up, she clicks the mouse on the SEND E-MAIL button and begins typing.

"Ooh, look, Charlie, I've got mail!" Julie says cheerfully, leaning over his shoulder as her sign-on screen pops up at last. Matchmocha, Matchmocha is busy tonight; they drank two mochaccinos each waiting for a free computer terminal.

"Yup. You've got a lot of mail," he replies, after clicking to open the mail icon. His eyes widen at the long list of responses that pop up. "I told you I did a great job on your questionnaire, Jul'."

"I still don't think you should've put in that thing about darning socks. I don't even know what darning socks means."

"Which means there's no chance you'll ever have to actually prove that you can do it, Julie."

"I guess, but . . . what about the part where you wrote that I can't wait to start a family and I want at least four children. Don't you think that's going to scare off most guys?"

"Not the kind of guys you're looking for. You want family man types, Julie. And there must be a bunch out there, because look at all these replies."

"Great. Let's start reading them." She plops into a chair beside him and leans in, her chin balanced on his shoulder as he clicks on the first e-mail. The faint scent of vanilla sugar wafts beneath his nostrils.

"Okay, here we go. 'Dear Julie: My name is Neil and I think you're totally hot . . .' "

"Yuck. Next."

"Don't you want to hear what else he has to say?" Charlie asks, scanning the rest of Neil's e-mail. "Actually, no, you don't." He presses DELETE, sending Neil and his lewd plans for Julie into cyberpurgatory.

The next response isn't much more promising. Somebody named Theo has never dated a pastry chef before and wants to know how creative she can be with whipped cream and melted chocolate.

"I feel like I need to take a shower," Julie says with a shudder. "Delete him, please."

"Already done. Don't get discouraged, Julie, you've got over thirty responses here."

"If they're all from oversexed losers—"

"They won't be."

Yes, they will. At least, that's the way things are shaping up after the first dozen or so responses. Apparently, there's something about a woman who creates desserts for a living that brings out the kinky underbelly in a small segment of the male population.

"I can't believe I let you talk me into this," Julie says, pushing back her chair as Charlie deletes yet another response.

"Where are you going, Jul'? We can't leave yet. What if Mr. Right is in here somewhere?" He gestures at the remaining responses on the screen.

"I doubt that." She glances restlessly around the crowded cafe. "I'm going to wait in line and get another

mochaccino and one of those sugar cookies. I bet you anything it tastes like sawdust, but I love the way they piped
the icing around the edges of the heart. I want to get a
closer look. You want one?"

"Nah, I'm good. I'm going to go through the rest of
these guys. If anybody looks promising, I'll holler."

"Yeah, I won't hold my breath."

After Julie walks away, he clicks through another couple of losers. One has a foot fetish and wants a close up
photo of her toes; another is in his midfifties and lives
with his mother, who, in the space of one short e-mail, is
mentioned way too often for comfort. A third is married
and looking for "good clean erotic fun" on the side.

Charlie is starting to feel like he needs a shower, too.

Then he opens the one from Dominic C.

Dear Julie:

*This is crazy, isn't it? I mean, it would be much easier
for an old-fashioned guy like me to meet an old-fashioned
girl like you in the old-fashioned way. Welcome to the
twenty-first century, huh? Here we are at Matchmocha,
Matchmocha—so here's the link to my questionnaire so
that you can see for yourself that I'm not some leering
two-headed lunatic.*

Charlie clicks on the link. A photo appears.

Nope, not a leering two-headed lunatic at all.

In fact, Dominic C. is a good-looking guy. Unaccustomed to giving a fellow male more than a quick glance,
Charlie forces himself to analyze the candidate, trying to
see him as a woman might . . . whatever *that* means.

Dark hair combed straight back from his forehead,
good build, and dressed almost the same as Charlie is right

now, in jeans and white sneakers and a long-sleeved polo shirt. Good. He looks natural—a Regular Joe.

According to Julie, Frenchy the Ex enjoyed wearing custom-made suits, and wore polished loafers with his jeans. In Charlie's opinion, there's just something *wrong* about that.

Dominic's shirt is dark green, as opposed to the navy one Charlie has on; and his hair is a few shades darker and not as shaggy as Charlie's.

There's only one drawback. He looks like the kind of guy who wears cologne, Charlie concludes. He, himself, is not that kind of guy. Not since high school and the dawn of his shaving days, anyway. Not that he's opposed to it; he just doesn't pay much attention these days to how he smells—as long as it isn't bad—or to visiting the barbershop more than once every couple of months.

That was one of the things that bugged Laurie. One of the many things, as it turned out. Who knew she had gone from being charmed by his little idiosyncrasies and seeming perfectly tolerant of crumbs and dust to apparently wanting to grab his collar and shake him every time he left the seat up?

But Laurie is history, and this isn't about Charlie, it's about Dominic C. and Julie. At least, it might be, if Charlie determines that he's a potential spouse for her.

The picture of Dominic C. was apparently snapped on a rooftop, Charlie notes. He can see the river and the Manhattan skyline in the background. The distinctive slant-topped Citicorp building is on the right, and the classic spire of the Chrysler Building is on the left, meaning the photo was taken in Queens.

Pleased with his geographical detective work, Charlie

clicks over to Dominic C.'s questionnaire and discovers that he's an avid Knicks fan, his favorite food is veal Parmesan, and he's a college graduate working in an advertising agency.

Satisfied with that, he returns to Dominic's letter.

I liked what you had to say, Julie, and I want to get to know you. So let's meet and talk, okay? I'm thinking Valentine's Day, and I'd suggest the top of the Empire State Building, but I think that's already been done.

Huh? Charlie frowns. What the heck does that mean?

"What, another freak who thinks I'm his perfect match?" a voice asks, about two inches from his ear.

He jumps, startled.

"You shouldn't sneak up on people, Julie!"

"I wasn't sneaking. Here, have a bite." She holds a half-eaten cookie under his mouth. "It's not sawdust, exactly. More like . . . foam board."

"Sounds delish." He waves it away. "Sit down and check out this guy, Jul'. Dominic C. He looks pretty good, and he's literate. No typos, even."

She's reading over his shoulder. "Empire State Building," she murmurs, and he turns to see her smiling.

"Yeah, that, I didn't get."

"What? Didn't you ever see the movie *Sleepless in Seattle*? Or *An Affair to Remember*?"

He's never heard of the second one, but he and Laurie watched *Sleepless in Seattle* one night on cable. It was pretty good until he dozed off, but it was definitely what he and his friends tend to call a Girl Movie. And he still doesn't get the Empire State Building thing.

Julie has gone back to the letter, reading aloud. "'*I also considered the skating rink in Central Park, but that's been done, too. And anyway, you might not be comfortable meeting a strange man alone in the park.*' You're right! I love this guy already, Charlie!"

"You do?"

"Yes! Not only is he sensitive enough to know that I'd be nervous meeting a stranger alone, but the whole skating rink thing . . . I love it."

Charlie shakes his head. "I don't get it, but whatever."

"Duh! He's talking about the scene in *Serendipity*."

"The restaurant?"

"No, duh. The movie. *Serendipity*. With John Cusack."

Oh. Another Girl Movie. He saw it with Laurie, too, and he does recall something about a skating rink, but . . .

"That was one of my favorite movies ever." Julie sighs, clearly enraptured. "The scene at the end, with the snow falling down all around them . . ."

Charlie is starting to wonder if he might have been wrong about this Dominic C. being a Regular Joe.

"I want to meet him," Julie declares abruptly. "On Valentine's Day. As long as it's Valentine's Day night, because there's no way I can get out of work that day until the bistro closes at three."

"Okay, fine. Here's what I think we should—"

"He said he'll leave it up to me to pick the place," she interrupts, giving him a nudge. "There's a great little trattoria on the East Side, and I'm pretty sure my friend Paolo can get me a reservation if I—Charlie! Come on! Move over!"

When he doesn't budge, she gives him another nudge, one that feels suspiciously like a shove. "Charlie, I can't reach the keyboard. Would you *please*—"

"You don't have to reach the keyboard."

"But I want to answer him."

"No way. I'm doing this, remember? You said you'd leave it up to me."

"But it's *my* love life."

"And you're the one who almost married a guy named Jean who doesn't even know that you're supposed to wear sneakers with jeans."

She looks exasperated. "His name wasn't Gene, it was Jean. J-e-a-n."

"And jeans is spelled j-e-a-n-s, and you don't wear shiny loafers with them."

"So what's the problem? Dominic C. wears shiny loafers with jeans?"

"No. He wears sneakers, see?" He clicks on the link.

Julie gapes at the picture.

"Okay, he's gorgeous. You need to move over right now so that I can type, Charlie, because I want to meet him."

"And you will. But you have to do it my way. Remember? You let me fill out your questionnaire."

"Which I'm starting to think was a huge mistake . . ."

"Why?"

"Why? Because it was a perv magnet, that's why."

"You think this guy Dominic is a perv?"

"No! He's the only one who isn't. And I don't want to screw this up, Charlie, so—"

"So let me answer him. I'm a guy. I know what guys want. Just leave it up to me, okay?"

"I want to meet him on Valentine's Day," she says stubbornly.

"And you will." He clicks the SEND E-MAIL button, his mind already whirling with ideas.

"I want to meet him someplace romantic. And I don't want to meet him alone because—"

"You know what I want, Jul'?"

"What?"

"One of those cutout sugar cookies with the pink frosting."

"Here." She hands him the remaining half of the one she was eating.

"Not that one. It looks like a broken heart. Throw it away. It's a bad omen. Would you mind getting me a fresh one?"

She sighs and stands. "Okay, okay, I get it. You want me out of here while you type the reply. Fine. But I'm warning you, Charlie, if you screw this up, so help me—"

"I won't screw it up!"

She sighs heavily.

"Go, Julie," he says, already typing.

"Hi, is there an envelope here for a Dominic C.?" Maggie asks the barrista, a bored-looking college girl with multiple piercings from the neck up—and most likely from the neck down, too, but thankfully, that part of her is concealed behind the high copper counter of the coffee bar.

"There is an envelope here, but . . ."

"Great! I'll take it!"

"Your name is Dominic?"

"No, his is." Maggie points toward Dom, who is just now walking through the glass-paned door of Matchmocha, Matchmocha. "I'm his friend."

"I'm not authorized to give the envelope to anybody but Dominic C."

Authorized? Somebody takes her job way too seriously.

"Dom, move your butt, will you?" Maggie calls. "The envelope is here, and she's only authorized to give it to you. Come on!"

"I'm coming, Mags, sheesh." He pauses just inside the door to unbutton his wool overcoat, clearly not in any hurry. He poked along lower Broadway and then along Bleecker the whole way here, stopping to buy an old Bruce Springsteen CD, roasted nuts from a street vendor, and a pair of gloves because he forgot his at home. Finally, Maggie pretty much grabbed his arm and dragged him to the cafe.

She couldn't help it. She—unlike the maddeningly imperturbable Dominic—is dying of suspense. Julie P. e-mailed yesterday that she was leaving an envelope today with instructions on where to meet her tomorrow night.

As Dominic shuffles over, the barrista retrieves a white rectangle from a bulletin board behind the counter.

Maggie glances at Dom's face. "Aren't you the least bit curious and excited about this, Dom?"

"Not the least bit," he returns flatly. "Not only did you screw up my plans last night by making me miss Battle-bots to come all the way down here yet again just to use the damned computer—"

"I told you it's on an internal network so this is the only place you can check your Matchmocha, Matchmocha e-mail account. That's how it works—"

"—but," he goes on, ignoring her, "you screwed up my plans for tomorrow night, too. I told you I had a ticket to the Knicks-Lakers game."

"So?"

"So you made me tell Eddie and Rick I couldn't go."

"Dom, it's Valentine's Day. You're meeting the woman of your dreams someplace totally romantic. How can you even compare that to some stupid basketball game?"

Dom rolls his eyes.

Maggie rolls hers, too.

They both turn to the barrista, who is eavesdropping and also rolling her eyes beneath multipierced brows.

Maggie reaches for the envelope in her hand.

The girl pulls it out of her grasp. "It's for him," she says snottily.

"I'm with him," Maggie says, just as snottily.

"But you're *not* him, are you?"

"No, she isn't," Dominic says, "and thank you for reminding her."

"No problem." The girl's earring-studded lips curve upward.

He smiles back: the charismatic Chickalini smile.

The barrista all but melts.

Terrific.

Maggie snatches the envelope out of her outstretched hand and puts it into Dominic's.

"There," she says. "Open it."

He opens it, grumbling.

Maggie holds her breath as he pulls out a folded sheet of paper.

He just stands there holding it, his gaze flirtatiously flitting back to the metal-studded girl behind the counter.

She grabs his arm and pulls him into a corner.

"Read it, Dom!" she barks.

"Stop giving orders, Maggie!"

"Okay, okay . . . read it," she says, sweetly this time.

He unfolds the paper. Something flutters to the floor. Two somethings, actually.

Maggie bends to retrieve them.

They look like tickets.

Her breath catches in her throat as she flips them over, wondering where Dominic is going to be meeting Julie P. for their romantic date. The opera? The ballet? The—

"The Knicks game!" Dominic proclaims. "I'm in love!"

Maggie blinks.

"Let me see the tickets, Mags." He grabs them out of her hand. "All right! These seats are better than the ones Eddie and Rick have!"

Madison Square Garden? What kind of setting is that for a first date on Valentine's Day?

"She says she's bringing a friend, and I should do the same," Dom says, reading from the note again. "She's thanking me for knowing she wouldn't be comfortable meeting her alone. I said that?"

"Yes, you did." Maggie sighs. "You were being sensitive. You knew that women aren't comfortable meeting strangers alone in this day and age in the city."

"Oh. Good thinking, Mags." He slaps her on the back. "Sorry I doubted you. This is great. Wait'll I tell Ralphie."

"Ralphie?" What on earth does Dom's kid brother have to do with this?

"Yeah, he's coming home from college in the morning. He's on February break this week. And you know how he loves the Knicks. He's going to—"

"You're not bringing Ralphie, Dom."

"Huh?"

"You're bringing me."

"But you think the Knicks stink."

"They do stink," she points out.

"Yeah, well, Ralphie loves—"

"Does Ralphie know anything about women?"

Dom raises an eyebrow at her. "He knew enough to get one pregnant."

How well she remembers that. Dom's kid brother was barely eighteen when his girlfriend gave birth to a baby boy. Little Nino was adopted by his aunt Nina and uncle Joey and Ralphie went off to Saint Bonaventure as planned, a happy ending for everyone.

Which, incidentally, has nothing whatsoever to do with Dom, Julie P., and tomorrow night.

Maggie tells Dom as much.

"So you're saying, what?" he asks. "That you're coming with me instead of Ralphie?"

"Dom, if it weren't for me, you wouldn't be going in the first place."

"How soon they forget," he tells the pressed-tin ceiling. "I already *had* a ticket with Eddie and Rick, remember? And you made me—"

"I didn't forget, Dom."

"Whatever, Mags. I don't get why you want to horn in on this game if you're not even a fan."

"Because it's not about a basketball game, Dom," she says through clenched teeth. "It's about romance. And I'm a big fan of that. And you need all the help you can get."

"Yeah, right. I've never needed help getting women. I've had plenty of—"

"Not *those* kinds of women. Marrying kind of women."

Although she's beginning to wonder about this Julie P.

What female in her right mind considers a Knicks game the perfect place to meet the man of her dreams on Valentine's Day? Dominic did insist on writing that he was a Knicks fan on his questionnaire, and Julie P. did say she was athletic on hers, but this is pushing it a little, in Maggie's opinion.

Then again, one glance at Dom's ecstatic expression, and she has to wonder whether Julie P. knows something more about men and romance than Maggie does.

Either way, she has no intention of letting Dom go on this date without her to guide his every move.

Finding him a wife is Maggie's project, and once she puts her mind to something, she sees it through in the end.

That single-minded drive, after all, is how a Midwestern farm girl got to Manhattan in the first place. Growing up the youngest of four kids—the oldest three strapping boys—on a dairy farm, she had no intention of spending the rest of her life in her mother's shoes, surrounded by cows, fields, and people whose idea of a good time involved beer, sausage, cheese, and the Green Bay Packers.

Mom, who also grew up on a farm, had dreams of escaping to a big city, too—only, in her case, it was to the West Coast. Hollywood. Mom wanted to be an actress— but the closest she ever got was a starring role in the Green Corners Central School production of *The King and I*. The summer she graduated, Daddy gave her an engagement ring, and she chose him—and marriage—over her own dreams. Though she often told Maggie she didn't have regrets, Maggie didn't miss the occasional sweep of wistfulness in her mother's gaze.

Certain there could be no fate worse than a lifetime spent wistfully yearning for what might have been, Maggie vowed early on that she would never be left wondering about the road not taken. She set her sights on the road that led out of Green Corners—and she never looked back.

Nor did she ever doubt where it would lead. She knows precisely what she wants out of life and she's going to get it. So far, she's right on track.

"All you have to do is focus all that energy, Maggie," Daddy used to say, teaching her how to ride a bike, throw a perfect pitch, drive a standard transmission. *"Focus your energy, think about where you're going, and you'll do okay."*

At the moment, of course, the focus of her energy is one Dominic Chickalini, who is still clutching the tickets and marveling at his good fortune.

"Come on, Dom." She tugs his coat sleeve.

"Where are we going?"

"To log on to one of those computers and e-mail Julie P. a response."

"Can't we just show up at the game?"

"You're romancing her, Dom. You've got to think about what she wants to hear."

"I'll leave that up to you," he says, one eye on the blonde barrista's denim-clad backside as she bends over to get a quart of milk from a crate on the floor. "Meanwhile, I'm going to get us a couple of mochas. If we're staying here, we should order something."

Maggie sighs, watching him sidle up to the counter, a familiar gleam in his eye.

She certainly has her work cut out for her this time.

"I've got mail, and it's from him!" Julie squeals,

clutching Charlie's arm an hour later. "I'm so glad you made me stop in here to check!"

Five minutes ago, as they headed home from an early movie, she was yawning and protesting that all she wanted to do was crawl into bed. Now, seated at a computer terminal in Matchmocha, Matchmocha, her eyes are sparkling and her cheeks are flushed redder than the exposed brick behind the espresso machine.

"What does he say?" Charlie asks, leaning over her shoulder.

"He got the tickets, and he's quite pleased."

"He said that? 'Quite pleased'? The guy gets tickets to a sold-out Knicks-Lakers game, and all he can say is that he's quite pleased?" Charlie shakes his head. "Do you know what I had to go through to get those tickets away from my friends? Do you know what I had to promise Prairie Dog to give up his seat for that game?"

"Well, it was worth it, whatever it was. You were right. The game really was a better idea than the trattoria."

"No shit, Sherlock. I told you so."

"And look"—she's back to reading the e-mail—"he says he's counting down the hours until we meet. He even quotes a poem by Laura Lee Randall—"

"Who's she?"

"I have no idea, but listen: *'The west wind's sighs are of love, not sorrow, and the sunset sky is the sign for tomorrow.'* Isn't that beautiful, Charlie?"

"It's . . . yeah. It's great. It's just a little . . ."

Her eyes narrow. "Just a little what?"

"I don't know. I mean, I was an English major, and even I don't go around quoting sappy poetry."

"It's not sappy! It's romantic."

In Charlie's opinion, it's also overkill. But it's too late now. Tomorrow night at this time, he and Julie and Dominic C.—and whoever Dominic C. chooses to chaperone the date—will be sitting together in Madison Square Garden.

"Thank you so much for suggesting that I give this matchmaking thing a try, Charlie," Julie says. "If it weren't for you, I'd be sitting home tomorrow night trying to get the chocolate fudge out from under my nails. You're a great friend. And if it works out with this guy, you have to let me find a wife for you, okay?"

"I don't want to get married, Julie."

"Yes, you do. If you were with the right woman, you'd want to marry her."

He considers that, rubbing his five o'clock shadow. Considers his barely furnished studio apartment and his empty fridge; the tux in his closet and the two unused tickets to the French Riviera.

Nah.

"The only promise I'm willing to make is to find you a husband, Julie. Other than that—I'm 'not a promises kind of guy,' remember? You said it yourself."

"I remember. But I think I might have been wrong about that. I think only a guy who believes in marriage would be trying so hard to find it for somebody else."

She shrugs, looking back at the computer screen and Dominic C.'s e-mail.

Charlie shakes his head.

Julie's wrong.

He's had his fill of women, between his mother and sisters and ex-fiancée and his friends' nagging girlfriends and his prickly editor at the magazine—not to mention having been raised by a single mother in a houseful of sisters.

Yes, he thinks, quite satisfied, the last thing Charlie Kennelly needs in his life is yet another fickle female to drive him up a wall . . .

Chapter Two

Valentine's Day starts off cloudy and steadily progresses until a freezing rain begins to fall at dusk.

Maggie would give anything to be home in her small Queens apartment with the television remote in one hand and in the other, a mug of steaming hot chocolate—not the powdered mix from the package, but the kind her mother makes on the stove with milk, sugar, cocoa, and vanilla.

Instead, umbrella aloft, she's hurrying along West Thirty-third Street toward Madison Square Garden, dodging icy puddles, scurrying pedestrians, and the ubiquitous rolling racks of plastic-draped clothes that garment workers perpetually shuttle between trucks and showrooms in this part of town.

When at last she reaches the corner of Seventh Avenue across from the Garden, she looks around for Dominic's Burberry black trench coat in the sea of businessmen scurrying toward Penn Station.

Naturally, he's late.

Maggie scowls, wondering how long she'll have to—

"Mags!"

"Dominic?"

No wonder she didn't see him. He's wearing a Knicks cap and a bright blue hooded Knicks parka, jeans, and sneakers.

"Where's your suit?" she demands. "And your overcoat? And your briefcase?"

"At the office," he tells her. "I changed before I left."

"Why?"

"So I'd be comfortable," he says, as though that actually makes sense.

"Comfortable?" She swats his nylon-swathed arm. "You're not supposed to be comfortable. You're supposed to be making a good impression on Julie P."

He looks at her like she's crazy. "By wearing a suit to a basketball game?"

"Please tell me you're at least wearing a dress shirt and tie under that," she says.

Wordlessly, he unzips his parka to reveal a bright blue-and-orange Knicks team sweatshirt.

"Dom!"

"Maggie! It's a basketball game. Relax. You should've changed your clothes, too. You'd be a lot less uptight if you weren't wearing panty hose and high heels."

She looks down at her feet. "These aren't high heels. They're low heels."

She isn't about to tell him that these aren't panty hose, either. They're silk stockings—real ones—the kind you wear with a garter belt. Bindy got her into the lingerie habit, convinced that it would do wonders for Maggie's lackluster love life with Jason. He left the country a few weeks after she became a Victoria's Secret convert, but Maggie figures one thing has nothing to do with the other.

She's starting to enjoy the feel of silk and bare upper thighs under her skirts. There's something very retro about it.

Yes, or very porn star.

"So what now?" Dominic asks.

"Now we go in and get our seats," Maggie informs him as a gust of wind off the Hudson River a few blocks away sends a fresh blast of icy rain beneath the rim of her umbrella.

They cross Seventh Avenue and make their way through the throng of commuters, sports fans, scalpers, sidewalk vendors, tourists, vagrants, and an army of cops.

Again, Maggie thinks longingly of her quiet little apartment. Her warm, dry apartment. But this is important. She's determined to find Dom a wife, and she has a good feeling about this Julie P.

"The game doesn't start for forty-five minutes," Dom tells her as they step through the glass doors and are swept along with the crowd toward the escalators. "I bet the beer line is still short enough to—"

"We're not getting beer," Maggie breaks in.

"What do you mean, no beer? What fun is a Knicks game without a couple of—"

"This isn't about the game, Dom. It's about meeting your future wife."

"Cripes, Maggie, you're so into this it's scary. Why?"

He's right. She is into this. But it's not scary. It's just . . .

"It's how I do things," she tells him. "I said I was going to find you the perfect woman, and I'm going to follow through. I'm goal-oriented."

To put it mildly. She was named Most Likely to Succeed in the Green Corners High School yearbook her senior year, and was the first person in her family to graduate from college—not to mention, the only person in her family to have left Green Corners since her ancestors arrived via covered wagon in the 1800s.

"Okay, so you're telling me I should be wearing a suit, and I shouldn't be drinking beer. Am I allowed to have any fun tonight?" Dom asks, as they pause at the security checkpoint, where a uniformed guard sweeps over them with a metal detection wand and checks the contents of Maggie's black leather shoulder bag.

"Of course you'll have fun. That's what it's about. We'll watch the game and after the Knicks win—"

"How do you know they're going to win?"

"I feel it in my bones," she says, borrowing a phrase from her Grandpa Harrigan, who always says that intuition runs in the family. "And then afterward, we'll go out to eat."

He brightens. "Great! There's a good steak house a few blocks downtown from the Garden and they have really good—"

"You're not going to a steak house, Dom."

"What do you mean I'm not going to a steak house?"

"That's not part of the plan."

"Okay, what's the plan?" he asks, and she can tell he's not loving this. Sheesh. You'd think the guy hadn't willingly agreed to let Maggie handle all the details of finding him a wife.

"If it works out between you and Julie at the game—which it will, because she's perfect for you—I'm going home, and I'm sure she'll feel safe enough to let her friend go home, too. The two of you can go to a romantic dinner together."

"Yeah, fine, but where are we going?" he asks, scowling, as they board another escalator.

"To a cozy little French bistro a few blocks uptown from the Garden."

He makes a face.

Maggie sighs. "What's the problem?"

"Well, to start with, I don't like French food."

"How do you know? Have you ever had it?"

"No. I just know. And I'm in the mood for red meat. I wanted steak at the steak house."

She shrugs. "You can order lamb at the bistro."

"I don't feel like lamb, and I don't like bistros."

"Don't be a clod, Dominic. Everybody likes bistros. Especially women. And tonight is all about charming Julie P. I've given a lot of thought to this whole thing, so just do what I tell you and everything will fall into place."

"You're not goal-oriented," Dom grumbles. "You're bossy."

"I just like things done the right way."

"No, you like things done *your* way."

"Same difference," she informs him, wondering why he can't see that.

They ride in silence up several escalator flights before Dom says, "What if I'm not crazy about this Julie person? Did you ever think that I might not even like her?"

"Or that she might not even like *you*? Of course I thought of it."

Clearly, Dom is taken aback by the notion that Julie might not like him. Has he ever met a woman who didn't? Maggie hasn't.

Then again, it *could* happen.

Still, she assures him, "Chances are, Dom, you're going to be crazy about each other. After all, she looks great on paper—"

"What paper?"

"You know what I mean. On her questionnaire."

"That's on the computer."

"Whatever."

"You said on paper."

"I meant virtual paper. You know, computer," she tells Mr. Literal-Minded through clenched teeth. "What's the difference?"

"I thought you might be holding out on me."

"What do you mean?"

"You know, I thought maybe you and this Julie girl were maybe in cahoots or something."

"Cahoots? What is this, a *Brady Bunch* episode? And she's not a girl, she's a woman. Make sure you don't call her a girl to her face."

"What am I, an idiot?"

"No, it's just that you tend to be a little . . . unpolished sometimes."

"I've managed to have a love life without your help until now, Maggie. An active one, in case you haven't noticed."

She rolls her eyes. "I've noticed. But you said yourself you're ready to settle down, and this is the kind of girl you need if you're ready to take that step."

They step off the escalator on the seventh floor. Pulling Dom aside so that the upward-bound crowd can pass, she says, "Hand me the tickets. I think our gate's on this level."

Dom pats his jacket pockets, then his jeans pockets. "Uh-oh."

"Dominic! Are you kidding me? Did you lose the tickets?" she shrieks.

"Nah, I'm kidding you," he says with a grin. "They're right here. See?"

"Give me those." Maggie snatches them out of his hand.

"Geez, Mags, it was a joke. What happened to your sense of humor?"

"This isn't funny, Dominic. This is serious." She examines the tickets, then looks around at the gate numbers.

"There," she says, spotting theirs. "Let's go."

He glances longingly at a beer concession as they pass it on their way to the gate. "Are you sure I can't just—"

"I'm positive." She pats his arm. "You'll thank me when we're dancing at your wedding, Dom."

"I hate beer," Julie says, sipping from the foamy cup.

"Just drink it and stop complaining," Charlie tells her. "Or at least, pretend to drink it and stop complaining."

From his aisle seat in section 79, he looks around the Garden, admiring the view of the court and wondering if he has time to go grab a couple of hot dogs before Dominic C. and his buddy get here. He hopes whoever Dom's bringing will be a Knicks fan.

What if he's not rooting for the home team? That would suck. As a rule, Charlie doesn't associate with Lakers fans. Just like he doesn't associate with Mets fans. Or, God forbid, Red Sox fans.

With any luck, Dominic's buddy will be a Knicks-Yankees-Giants fan, and the two of them can drink beer and talk sports until the game starts, while Julie and her date get to know each other.

"Shouldn't we move in and let Dominic and his friend sit on the aisle?" Julie asks, gesturing at the two vacant interior seats beside her. "Our tickets are for the inside seats."

"Yeah, but if we move in now, I won't be able to flag down the popcorn guy when he comes by."

Julie frowns and adjusts the Knicks cap he insisted she wear. He watches her attempts to tuck a stray strand of blond hair back up beneath the brim. It promptly tumbles back down to her shoulder again.

"I feel funny in this getup," she informs him for the hundredth time since they left her apartment, with Julie wearing the brand-new cap and Knicks fleece pullover he bought for her.

She wasn't even planning on wearing jeans, to Charlie's horror. When he got there, she was all dressed up in a skirt and high heels, looking like she was headed out to dinner at some fancy French bistro with Jean LaFoot.

Charlie immediately hosted a one-man intervention, and here she is, looking like an adorable Knicks fan from head to toe.

"Want some popcorn?" he asks, catching sight of the vendor a few rows away, calling *Popco-awn he-yah, popco-awn* in quintessential New York vendor cadence.

"No thanks." Julie shakes her head. "It looks like that prepopped kind with the fake yellow butter that isn't butter. It's, like, melted chemicals."

"What do you expect, Jul'? Gourmet stuff? This is the Garden. You have to eat Garden food."

"I'm not even hungry. This is my first blind date since high school. I'm too nervous to be hungry."

"Well, that's okay," he tells her. "Afterward, you and Dominic can go out to eat someplace. I have a great burger joint you can suggest."

"Burger joint? Charlie, you know I don't eat red meat."

"Ever?"

"Never. You know I'm a vegetarian."

Does he know that?

Maybe. He can be forgetful, especially when it comes to things that are out of his realm of expertise. Like elective vegetarianism, which makes no sense to him whatsoever.

He asks, "Can't you try meat, just for one night?"

"No." Julie folds her arms and scowls at him. "Pretending I'm somebody I'm not is a lousy way to start a relationship, Charlie."

"I don't want you to pretend you're somebody you're not, Julie. I just want to help you relate to this guy on his level. Guys like to eat. They like to eat burgers and steaks and—"

"Not all guys."

"Name one who doesn't."

"Jean-Louis is a vegan."

"Jean-Louis is a freaking nelly," Charlie shoots back. "Listen to me, Julie . . . I know what I'm talking about. You need to relate to this Dominic guy on his own level. Show him that you aren't one of those girly-girls who's only interested in perfume and salad and yoga."

"I like perfume and salad and yoga."

"You know what I mean."

Julie sighs.

Charlie pats her arm. "Just be real, Julie. Real, and approachable. That's all you have to do."

"I'll try."

"Don't worry. I'll give you more pointers as we go along."

"Yeah, I'm sure you will."

"Excuse me," a female voice says, from somewhere above him on the crowded aisle.

"Just a second." He balances his own beer cup on his knee and bends to pick up the cardboard drink holder containing the two beers they bought for Dominic C. and his buddy.

"Excuse me . . ."

"Hang on, lady," he snaps, turning around to glare at her. "Can't you see I'm trying to move my stuff so you can get by?"

"I don't want to get by. You're in my seat."

Charlie blinks. She's not Dominic C.

She's a petite brunette wearing a business suit and trench coat.

"I think you've made a mistake," he tells her. "This isn't your seat."

"Oh, I think it is." Her blue eyes flash at him as she holds out a ticket and stands her ground despite the jostling people behind her making their way up and down the aisle.

Charlie examines the ticket and curses under his breath.

He's definitely in her seat.

But . . . who the heck is she?

And where's—

"Hi, I'm Dominic."

Charlie looks up to see a face peering over the strange woman's shoulder. He recognizes the guy instantly from the pictures on Julie's e-mail at Matchmocha, Matchmocha and is relieved to note that Dominic looks every bit the Regular Joe. He cranes a neck to sneak a peek at the guy's shoes, just in case . . .

Nope. No dress shoes. He's wearing Nikes with his jeans. Perfect.

"Hey, Dominic, I'm Charlie, and this is Julie." *And who the hell is the pushy brunette?*

"Nice to meet you," Julie says perkily, leaning across Charlie's lap to shake hands with her date, who has not so subtly elbowed the brunette out of the way.

"Hey! Dom, I'm getting trampled here!" She reappears, sticking her arm past Dominic to grab Julie's hand. "I'm Dom's friend Margaret."

"Hi, Margaret!" Julie's all friendly in that maybe-Margaret-can-be-my-new-best-girlfriend way of hers.

Margaret looks at Charlie. "Hello."

"Hello."

No love lost there, he thinks, half-amused, half-irked.

"So you're a big Knicks fan?" Margaret asks, turning back to Julie.

"Not—"

Julie breaks off when Charlie elbows her in the ribs.

"Not just a big Knicks fan—a huge Knicks fan," Julie declares.

Good save. Charlie sends her an approving glance.

"I'm kind of new to it, though," Julie says, sounding nervous. "It's, you know, my new passion. I never knew much about sports until recently."

"Really? Where I grew up, everybody was obsessed by

sports," Margaret says with a roll of her blue eyes. "You couldn't exist without being an expert, whether you wanted to be or not."

Even a Lakers fan would be better than this, Charlie thinks.

"Where'd you grow up?" Julie asks, all interested. Typical. Get two women together—any two women—and they're oblivious to everything around them. All they want to do is chitchat about inane things.

"Green Corners, Wisconsin," Margaret says, as Dominic stands silently beside her, admiring the view of the court. "I bet you never heard of it, right?"

"No," Julie admits, "I never did. But it sounds nice."

"Yeah, it is nice. To visit. I just never—"

"Why don't you two sit down?" Charlie interrupts, losing patience with the small talk fest.

"Good idea," Margaret says promptly.

Charlie turns in his seat to get his long legs out of the way so that they can scooch past. Dominic starts to, but Margaret pulls him back.

"Can you two move in?" she asks, all brisk efficiency once again. "Charlie, you take the farthest seat down, and Julie can sit next to you. Then Dom, and I'll take the aisle."

Charlie bristles. "How about if we stay put in these two seats and you two take those?" he suggests. "I want to stay on the aisle so that I can grab a popcorn when it comes by."

"I can grab it for you if you want," Margaret tells him. "I'll have to go to the ladies' room any second, and I hate to make everyone keep letting me squeeze by, so I'd better take the aisle seat."

Yeah, she does look like the type who'll constantly be going off to the ladies' room, probably to apply and reapply lipstick, the way his ex-girlfriend always did.

Charlie takes in Margaret's pearls, her stockings, her makeup. Talk about uptight. Where does she think she's going, to a business seminar?

Then he spots a liberal smattering of freckles that are visible beneath the layer of makeup. Huh. That's surprising. Ms. All Business doesn't look like the freckles type.

She doesn't look like the sports fan type, either. She's wearing the same slightly bemused expression Laurie always had when he dragged her to a basketball game. Charlie's willing to bet it will transform into all-out distaste by the third quarter.

"So are you a Knicks fan?" Charlie can't resist asking.

She shrugs. "When they don't stink."

Then she motions at his seat with a swing of her dark pageboy, an impatient *I'm waiting* gesture if ever he saw one.

"Come on, Charlie," Julie says, tugging on his sleeve. "Let's move in."

Reluctantly, he gets to his feet. He thrusts the drink carrier into Dom's hands, saying, "We got you guys a beer."

"Excellent."

Charlie is fairly certain he sees Dom shooting a triumphant look at Margaret.

Hmm. What's that all about?

Oh, let me guess, he thinks wryly. *Margaret doesn't like beer. Surprise, surprise. She's probably into white wine. Or blush.*

Laurie drank blush wine . . .

And that has what to do with Margaret? he asks himself, irritated.

Why does he keep comparing his ex-fiancée to this woman? They don't really look alike. Laurie has dark eyes, not bright blue like Margaret's. And she's so paranoid about her skin that if she ever caught sight of a freckle on her nose, she'd rush to a dermatologist and have it lasered off, or whatever it is that dermatologists do to remove freckles. Simply covering it with makeup wouldn't suffice for Laurie.

"Charlie," Julie prods, tugging his arm.

As he sidles past her, she whispers, "Very cute."

For a second, he's taken aback.

Oh, right. She's talking about Dominic.

Dominic, her date. The whole reason they're here in the first place.

She isn't talking about Dominic's companion, about whom there's nothing—okay, aside from the freckles, maybe—the least bit *cute*. And Charlie shouldn't waste another second thinking about her, either.

Julie thinks *Dominic* is cute. So far, so good.

And now Dominic, as he sinks into his seat beside her, is grinning at her as though he thinks she's cute, too.

Yes, so far, so good. This evening, after all, is about the two of them.

With any luck, the irksome Margaret will decide to hold her freckled nose and chug the beer she's staring at with an expression of distaste, then spend most of the game waiting in line for the ladies' room.

Chapter Three

He's a guy's guy.

That's the problem, Maggie concludes, as she returns from her second trip to the ladies' room to find Julie's friend Charlie monopolizing Dominic's attention. They're engaged in an animated conversation about the game, just as they have been for the past hour and a half, talking across Julie's lap.

You'd think that a huge Knicks fan like Julie—as evidenced by her choice of first date attire, with Madison Square Garden as the setting—would at least be able to pay attention to her team on the court.

After all, having grown up in a family of rabid Green Bay Packer supporters, Maggie learned early on that nothing can distract an avid sports fan when their team is winning.

But Julie isn't even following the Knicks' stellar performance on the court. She seems to be staring blankly into space, looking as though she'd rather be anywhere else, poor thing.

As Maggie settles into her seat, she gives Dom a meaningful jab in the ribs.

He breaks off from whatever he was telling Charlie to say, "Ow!"

"Sorry," she says sweetly, wondering if he got the message.

Apparently not, because he shrugs and promptly turns back to Charlie. "Anyway, like I was saying, back when we had Sprewell—Ow!"

Her elbow has made contact again.

Dom scowls and rubs his side. "Watch it, Mags. Geez, you're on the aisle . . . you have more room than the rest of us. Keep your arms to yourself, will ya?"

How thick is he?

Maggie grabs his head, pulls his ear next to her mouth, and snaps, "Pay attention to your date."

"Huh?"

"Julie! She's your date," Maggie hisses. "Not Charlie."

Dom glares at Maggie, who glares right back at him, and at Charlie, too.

Charlie sees her and flashes an irritatingly pleasant smile, as if to show her that he's unperturbed by her evil eye.

Not only is he a guy's guy, but he's also maddeningly self-confident, Maggie concludes. Several times since they all sat down, she felt his eyes on her and realized he was checking her out. Clearly, he's the kind of male who sizes up each female he meets as a possible conquest.

If he weren't three seats away, she might tell him that he needn't bother. That she's spoken for—by a doctor, no less. A doctor who spends his time saving underprivileged children and not watching overpaid, overgrown men wearing shorts in the dead of winter and endlessly passing a ball back and forth.

Clenching her jaw, Maggie turns her attention back to the matter at hand—Operation Marry Off Dominic—just in time to see Dominic glance over at Julie at last. She looks so bored Maggie finds herself looking for a dribble of drool beneath Julie's lower lip.

"So, uh, Julie . . . you're a pastry chef, huh?" Maggie hears Dom ask.

She brightens and looks at him. "Uh-huh."

Okay, good. If they can just strike up a conversation . . .

"So you make pies?" is Dom's sparkling effort.

"Yes. Pies, and um, other things."

"That's great."

"Oh, man . . . did you see that? They just tied it up!" Charlie bellows from Julie's other side, effectively curtailing the fledgling conversation.

What the heck is the matter with him?

Testosterone, Maggie concludes, settling back into her seat and folding her arms across her midsection. That's Charlie's problem. He has too much of it.

She's seen the type before. In her own household, growing up. Her father and her brothers went tromping around the house in their boots and jeans, roughhousing and tossing balls and seemingly oblivious to the finer things in life.

Like fashion. And culture. And romance.

Maggie slides a glance at Charlie, noting the square-cut jaw, the hair that desperately needs a trim, the five o'clock stubble. This might be Manhattan, but in that plaid flannel shirt and those washed-out jeans, with that plastic cup full of foaming beer in his hand, he could have stepped right out of Green Corners.

Maggie left home to escape spending the rest of her life with a man like him.

While all her childhood girlfriends were getting engaged to their high school steadies, she was studying communications on a leafy New York campus.

Then, while her friends were settling down on farms of their own in the Wisconsin countryside, she was getting a crash course in street smarts and navigating the urban classifieds, learning what No Fee and Floor-thru and Rent Stabilized meant and scouring the ads to find those golden phrases. She was making herself over into a sleek urban businesswoman with a closet full of clothes and a standing manicure appointment.

"No! No!" Dominic bellows beside her, as a Laker steals a pass from a Knick.

"Yes! Yes!" Charlie hollers, as the Knick reclaims it and dribbles down the court to score on a bank shot.

Maggie glances at Julie, seated between the two leaping, whooping lunatics.

Julie seems oblivious to the score and to Dom and Charlie high-fiving over her head.

She must be so hurt that Dom is paying attention only to Charlie and the Knicks that she can't even muster the ability to root for her team.

"Dom!" Maggie grabs him and whispers in his ear, "Aren't you forgetting something?"

He looks puzzled, then catches her drift.

"Did you see that?" he asks Julie. "Some shot, huh?"

"Yeah," she says, brightening.

They exchange a few words Maggie can't hear over the roaring crowd.

But she can tell Dominic is keeping one eye on the game and that Julie seems oblivious to it. She's looking at Dom, and around the arena—everywhere but at the court.

After a few seconds, she spots Maggie watching her. For a moment, she looks taken aback by the intense scrutiny. Then she smiles.

Embarrassed, Maggie smiles back and pretends to return her attention to the game. At least, at first she pretends. But as the clock ticks down and the action heats up, she can't help being caught up in what's going on down on the court.

When, with five seconds remaining in the first half, the Knicks' forward scores an impossible three-point shot, Maggie bolts out of her seat with a cheer.

Exhilarated, she turns toward the others. She finds Dominic bending over to retrieve the cap he apparently just knocked off Julie's head in his zeal, Julie busily rubbing her scalp and straightening her mussed blond tresses, and Charlie watching Maggie with a disconcerting expression.

"What?" she asks, narrowing her eyes at him.

"You were cheering."

"Well, duh. They tied it up again."

"I didn't expect you to notice."

"What, did you think I don't know anything about basketball?"

"Yup," he says with annoying aplomb. "You spent the whole first half running back and forth to the bathroom, so I just figured . . ."

He trails off with a shrug.

She shrugs right back at him, saying, "I have a small bladder."

Which, of course, is a total lie. The first time she barely had to go, and the second time, she didn't have to go at all. After a long day at the office behind a paper-cluttered desk, she just couldn't resist the restless urge to get up and wander . . .

Wander away from Charlie and his provocative little glances, in particular.

Does he think she hasn't noticed him checking her out?

Does he think she'd actually be interested in turning this into a double date?

Because there's no way in hell she'd ever want to be alone with a guy like him.

Dominic taps her arm. "Julie and I are going to the concession stand for hot dogs. You want anything?"

Left alone with Margaret—if one can be alone with somebody in a crowd of twenty thousand or so—Charlie wonders if he should bridge the two-seat gap between them and attempt to make conversation.

He steals a glance at her and finds her stealing a glance right back at him.

She's just full of surprises, he thinks, smiling to himself as she pretends she was looking at something behind him.

Then again . . . maybe she was. Maybe he's just feeling overly cocky tonight, kind of like the Knicks.

He turns to look over his shoulder and finds nothing but a pole and a trio of diehard basketball fans.

Okay, so either Margaret is fascinated by loud and sweaty fat guys, or she was looking at him.

On the off chance that the latter is true, he shifts over to the seat beside her.

She looks up at him, startled.

"So . . . what's up?" he asks.

She shrugs. "I was just thinking that Dominic and Julie are perfect for each other. Don't you think?"

Actually, he doesn't think.

Not that, anyway. But if Margaret is convinced their two friends are a match made in heaven, he might as well agree with her, because something tells him disagreeing with Margaret could be futile, if not downright dangerous. And he's not in the mood for an argument. Not when the Knicks are winning and he made this month's column deadline with a day to spare.

"Yeah, I think they have a lot in common," he tells Margaret. "For example . . ."

He trails off, distracted by the piercing blue of her eyes. It's so unexpected, seeing blue eyes with black hair. He's known some striking blue-eyed blondes, and some drop-dead-gorgeous dark-eyed brunettes, but this combo . . .

She clears her throat. Loudly. Pointedly. As in, *what the heck are you looking at, bub?*

Charlie tears his thoughts away from Margaret and back to the matter at hand, which is . . .

Oh, yeah. What, specifically, do Julie and Dominic have in common?

"Julie makes the best pies I've ever tasted," he informs Margaret. "And I heard Dominic telling her that he loves pie."

Pie? That was the best he could come up with?

Talk about lame . . .

But Margaret, whose blue eyes are staring at him,

jumps right on it. "Yes, Dom is a huge fan of pie. His favorite is, um, cherry. He loves cherry, um . . ." She licks her lips.

"Pie?" Charlie supplies, when she trails off. He notices that her lips are precisely the shade of ripe cherries and wonders if that's merely the shade of her lipstick or if her mouth can really possibly be that luscious on its own.

"Yes, cherry pie," she agrees. "Dom is crazy about cherry pie."

And Charlie is crazy about those cherry red lips, lipstick-tainted or not.

For an insane moment, he wonders what it would be like to kiss her.

His wondering heats up to fever pitch when she leans closer. Is she actually going to—

No.

No, she's not.

She's merely saying, conspiratorially, "Listen, I think we both need to ditch the two of them after the game. Dom wants to take Julie to a little French bistro he loves, and I know he'd like to be alone with—"

"Bistro?" Charlie cuts in, shaking his head. "That's no good. Julie works in a little French bistro. She won't want to eat at one when she's off. She told me she was craving burgers and fries, and she was going to suggest—"

"Burgers and fries? That won't work."

"Don't tell me Dominic moonlights flipping burgers."

"No, he moonlights at a pizza joint, actually," she says. "But that's not the point."

"What's the point?"

"Burgers and fries are not romantic. It's bad enough

that they're starting the date here." She gestures at the cavernous sports arena.

"What's wrong with here?"

"It's not romantic," she says in an aggravating *duh* tone.

"Who says Julie's into romance?"

"Who says Dom isn't?" she shoots back. "And anyway, he's an old-fashioned guy, and she's supposedly an old-fashioned girl, so he should be deciding where they go."

He wants to ask her what *supposedly* means, but instead he says, "It sounds to me like you're the one who's deciding where they go."

"I am not. The bistro was Dom's idea."

Yeah, sure it was. He checks her hand to see if she's crossing her fingers behind her back.

She isn't. She's clutching her three-quarters-full beer cup.

"What's the matter? You don't like beer?" Charlie can't help asking. There's just something about her that gets under his skin. Not just in a bad way . . .

Which isn't a good thing. Which is why he feels compelled to needle her about every little quirky quality of hers. Luckily, there are plenty to choose from.

"Beer? Not really," she says. "Not anymore."

"You used to like it?"

"More than I do now."

"And then . . . ?"

"And then I grew up," she says simply.

He rolls his eyes.

"What?" she asks.

"I'm a grown-up, and I happen to like beer."

"Yeah, well . . ." She mutters something.

"Did you say *you would?*" he asks her, bristling.

"No. I said good for you. What does my liking beer or not liking beer have to do with anything?"

"This is a basketball game. What were you expecting? White wine?"

"They serve it here. At least, I know they do in the box seats."

"You've sat in box seats here?" he asks, filled with newfound respect despite himself.

"Once or twice. On business. With clients."

"What do you do?"

"I'm a media planner at Blaire Barnett advertising, on a packaged goods account," she recites, then adds the obligatory, "What do you do?"

"I'm a writer."

He expects her to turn up her freckled nose at that, but instead, glimpses a flicker of newfound fascination—and maybe even respect—in her eyes.

"What do you write?" she asks.

"A magazine column."

"Let me guess. A sports column?"

"No. A relationships column for a women's magazine."

She bursts out laughing. "Good one."

He laughs, too. At her. But of course, Miss *I Know Everything* doesn't know that.

When she stops laughing, she says, "I was serious. What do you write?"

"I was serious, too. I write the Bachelor at Large column for *She* magazine." There. Take that, sistah.

Her eyes widen with recognition.

"You read *She*?" he asks.

"I read all magazines. I'm a media planner, remember?

And I'm on a cosmetics account. I know a lot of people who work at *She*."

Okay, Margaret isn't Laurie, but Charlie recognizes the familiar gleam in her eyes. She's all set to play Do You Know—?

That was one of his ex-girlfriend's favorite games. One minute, they'd be casually introduced to a newcomer at a party or dinner; the next, Laurie the-Name-Dropper was engaged in a fierce round of corporate networking.

Charlie decides to head Margaret off at the pass, saying, "Yeah, well, I'm a freelancer, so I'm never in the office. And I've only been doing it for a few months now—" *Ever since my ex jilted me and an enterprising editor convinced me to make lemonade out of my soured love life.* "Plus," he adds, "I don't really know many people there outside of my editor and her assistant."

"Most of the people I know are in ad sales."

He nods. "Yeah, well . . . that's the opposite end of the spectrum. I just write."

"About relationships." She's not even trying to mask her incredulity.

"Yup."

"Why do I find that so hard to believe?"

"What, you don't think I know anything about relationships?"

"Well, do you?"

"I know enough to make a living writing about them."

"From experience, or . . . ?"

He waits.

"Or what?" he asks when she remains silent, looking awkward.

"I don't know . . . I just meant, are you married?"

"Me? Married?" He laughs. "I'm never getting married. I don't believe in it."

Maggie rolls her eyes. "So have you had a lot of relationships, then?"

"A few."

"Do you have a girlfriend?"

"Nope."

"Have you, um, had one recently?"

"Nope."

I had a fiancée but she's history and it's none of your business, he tells her silently.

After all, Ol' Blue Eyes here doesn't need to know that before he turned to exploiting his bachelorhood for fun and profit, he was doing a yearlong series of columns for *Urban Bride* magazine. Sort of an En Route to the Altar documentary from the groom's viewpoint.

The columns were wildly successful. Charlie was even inundated by fan mail. Little did he—or his editor at *Urban Bride*—suspect that once the altar was in sight, he'd find himself abandoned there.

So, Laurie's cruel and fickle heart resulted in Charlie's unemployment and a gaping hole in *Urban Bride*'s upcoming issue schedule.

When the dust had settled, he actually wrote the final piece, a raw and honest account of how it feels to be publicly jilted. Not only was it therapeutic, but it seemed socially relevant, given the television reality dating show craze.

His *Urban Bride* editor didn't want to run it. She was afraid it would be disturbing to her readership, which was, after all, made up of glowing brides-to-be. The magazine's job was to build up the fairy tale, not shatter the happily ever after myth.

Luckily, Charlie's friend Pork knew a friend of a friend of a friend who worked at *She*, and after a series of fortuitous events, Charlie landed his current columnist gig. So far, so good.

But that doesn't mean he feels like explaining it all to Margaret, who's still wearing that intrigued expression.

Hmm. There must be a way to change the subject unobtrusively.

He settles on, "How about you? Do you have a boyfriend?"

Both because it deflects the focus away from him, and because he really wants to know. He can't imagine *why* he wants to know, but it suddenly seems important.

"Yes," she says promptly—too promptly. "His name is Jason, and he's a pediatrician."

Charlie wants to point out that he didn't ask for the guy's credentials, but he's too busy marveling at the way she's suddenly gulping her beer with gusto—and at the frisson of disappointment running through him at the news that azure-eyed Margaret is spoken for.

Well, he's only human. A red-blooded, male human.

So . . .

Okay.

Now that he knows Margaret's off-limits, he can admit—if only to himself—that he's wildly attracted to her.

No, you aren't, his inner self argues. *You're repelled by her. She's everything you don't want in a woman.*

Except . . .

He suddenly wants it.

Make that *wanted*.

Past tense.

Yes, for a few fleeting moments, he actually *wanted* Ms. Wrong.

Naturally, he doesn't want her anymore, since she's taken.

And that's a good thing, he tells his errant libido.

It's a good thing because if she didn't have a boyfriend, he might feel obligated to go after her.

Just because he likes a challenge, and just because he likes her looks, and okay, her spitfire spirit.

And if he decided to go for it, he'd win her, because . . .

Well, because he always has. He's never met a woman he couldn't charm, at least temporarily.

So he'd charm Margaret, and then what?

And then they'd probably fall in love, and that wouldn't be good for anyone. Especially not for Charlie, who has sworn off love, and whose livelihood at this point depends on his *not* finding it. Until he finally finds the time—and okay, inspiration—to sit down and pen the great American novel, he's building a career around living a single guy's life and writing about it.

At least, that's what he keeps telling his father, who wants him to get over this silly "creative phase" and join the family business.

The last thing Charlie wants to be is a financial analyst. That his father and uncle accumulated vast wealth that way hasn't swayed him in the least. He doesn't need vast wealth.

Of course, Julie claims that's just because he's always had it.

She's right. If he didn't have his trust fund to fall back

on, he'd hardly be able to devote his time and energy to writing magazine columns. He'd be miserable, living his life according to somebody else's schedule.

Like Margaret probably does. Not that she looks miserable.

He asks, "Are you and your boyfriend serious?"

"What do you mean by serious?"

"You know . . . are you getting married?"

"Maybe when he gets back," she says.

"Where is he?"

"South America. But he'll be back soon."

"And then you're getting married?"

"I don't know. We haven't been dating for that long. But he's, you know . . ."

"A single doctor in Manhattan. They're hard to come by."

"I didn't say that."

"No, but I'm saying it, and believe me, I know."

"How do you know?"

"Reader mail," he says with a shrug.

"Oh." She seems to be contemplating that. Then she tells him, "Well, what I was going to say about Jason is that he's perfect for me."

"Nothing's perfect," Charlie says darkly.

"Maybe not, but my relationship with Jason is as close to perfect as you can get."

"What makes you say that?"

"It's obvious. Everybody thinks so."

Everybody but you? he wonders, watching her carefully. There's something hesitant about her expression and her body language; an almost blatant contradiction to her forthright tone.

That's the interesting thing about her, he concludes. She's a bundle of contradictions. She says she doesn't like sports, then she bursts out cheering like a hard-core fan. She says she doesn't like beer, then she chugs it. She's dressed to the nines, but you can't miss those freckles of hers. Freckles that make her seem girlish, approachable, almost cute. Freckles that should go hand in hand with a laid-back personality and a nickname to go with it. Like Peggy. Or Meg. Or—

"What are you thinking about?" she asks, watching him.

You.

I'm thinking that you might not be who—and what— you want me to think you are.

Aloud, he says only, "You know, things aren't always as they seem."

"Meaning . . . ?"

"Meaning sometimes, something that looks good on paper and in theory just doesn't work in real life."

"What's that supposed to mean?"

"It means that maybe everything about this guy Jason is right—maybe he's a great guy, good-looking and nice to you and he makes a lot of money to boot. But maybe you don't love him."

"I do love him," she says quickly. Too quickly.

Charlie's heart attempts to soar. He tamps the pesky thing down firmly, and says, just as firmly, "I think you want to love him because he's everything you *think* you should want."

"And I think *you* like to think you're a relationship expert, but you're not."

"I'm not? Don't tell my editor. She might take me off the payroll."

"Whatever." Margaret waves a hand at him and shakes her head.

Clearly, he's been dismissed.

Too bad. It's been a while since he engaged in a round of harmless flirtation. He was enjoying himself for the first time in ages, particularly once he realized that this can't go anywhere, and she doesn't want it to.

It's refreshing to meet a woman who doesn't have ulterior motives. From where he sits, it sometimes seems as though the city is crawling with predatory females, and most of the time, as soon as he sets foot out of his apartment, he can't help feeling like prey.

"Listen," Margaret says, shifting gears abruptly, "Dom and Julie will be back any second, and I think we have to make sure they get some quality alone time together after the game. I'm going to say I've got a big client presentation in the morning—which I do—and that I want to go home to bed. What are you going to say?"

"Oh, I don't know. Maybe I'll tag along with them," he says, just to get her back up.

Wow. Instant results.

Her gaze turns stormier than Sea Bright, New Jersey, in a full-blown nor'easter.

"Uh-uh," she snaps. "You can't tag along with them."

"Why not?" he asks, all innocence.

"Because a third wheel will ruin their date, that's why not."

"But I'm hungry. I want to go out to eat."

"I'm hungry, too. That's why I told them to bring me a hot dog."

"Well, I told them to bring me two hot dogs."

"Exactly. Which is why you aren't going out with them after the game."

"What if I want to? Not for the food, but for the human contact?" he asks, thoroughly enjoying her blatant vexation.

"Don't you have something better to do?"

"Nope."

"Well, pretend that you do."

"I know! How about if you and I pretend that we've fallen for each other and leave together to go back to your place?" he suggests, because he can't resist.

"That's sick," is her retort.

But he can't help noting an intriguing undercurrent in her tempestuous expression.

It's enough to send a torrent of fresh arousal through him even as he asks, keeping a straight face, "Why is that sick? Don't you think we'd make a cute couple?"

"No!"

He fights the urge to burst out laughing at her horror. "Oh, come on, Margaret, tell me you honestly wouldn't be attracted to me under different circumstances."

"That's exactly what I'm telling you. I can't think of any circumstances that would make me be attracted to you."

"I don't believe you."

"You're the most arrogant—"

"Not arrogant," he interrupts. "Just honest. If you didn't have Jake—"

"Jason," she inserts haughtily.

Of course, Jason. He knew it was Jason. He deliberately said Jake, to prove . . .

What?

What the hell is he trying to prove, here?

That Jason is insignificant?

That Charlie's right, and she's wrong?

That as much as she wants to believe she's found Mr. Right, she hasn't?

"Right, Jason," he says affably. "So you're saying that if you didn't have Jason and we were alone together in some romantic spot, you wouldn't give me a chance?"

"Exactly."

"Because . . . ?"

"Because you're not my type."

"Fair enough. You're not my type either. But that doesn't mean I'm close-minded. And you shouldn't be, either."

"I'm not close-minded."

"Sure you are," he says, and is gratified to see her eyes darken yet another shade.

He'd be willing to bet that old Jason never stands up to her this way. He probably lets her tell him what to do.

"You're obnoxious," Margaret informs him. "Who died and made you the ultimate authority on me?"

Talk about arrogance. She's the one who thinks she knows everything there is to know about . . . well, everything. Especially love.

"I'm really good at reading people," Charlie says mildly. "I bet in another time and place, under different circumstances, you and I could have hooked up."

"I bet you're wrong."

"Then prove it."

"How?"

"I'll kiss you, and you'll tell me whether you feel a spark."

She stares at him.

He stares back.

Especially at her luscious red mouth.

"That's the stupidest thing I've ever heard," she says, looking around nervously, licking her lips.

It's also the stupidest thing he's ever *said*.

He doesn't want to kiss her.

Sure you do.

All right, he *does*.

But he's not supposed to want to, and anyway, he can't kiss her, because she has Jason and Charlie has . . .

Okay, he no longer has a fiancée, but he does have an aversion to bossy women. Margaret is the epitome of what he doesn't want.

Which is why it makes absolutely no sense at all when, driven by pure impulse, he swoops in and kisses her.

He's doing it.

He's actually doing it.

Charlie's lips are on hers, and he's kissing her senseless; kissing her as she hasn't been kissed in months, or maybe . . .

Maybe ever.

Maggie's mind races alongside her pulse.

Pull away! Make him stop! Tell him to go to hell!

Shut up! screams a part of her she nearly forgot exists. The reckless, spontaneous, *If it feels good, do it* part of her that hasn't been this vocal since her college days.

Charlie's kiss takes her breath away, makes her hands crave a daring expedition into his needs-a-trim hair or across the broad expanse of his shoulders. Luckily, he pulls back just as her willpower is about to give way, leaving her trembling, shaken . . . hungry for more.

"Well?" he asks, his face the *Webster's* definition of smug.

"Well, what?"

"Aren't you going to admit you were wrong?"

"About what?"

"About me. About us. If we were alone together, and we were both available, you'd want me."

"You *are* available, and no, I don't want you."

Don't listen to her, bellows reckless, spontaneous Maggie, tired of being suppressed, bursting forth with shocking fervor. *I do. I want you. We're in the least romantic place on the planet, with thousands of people around, and I know she can't stand you, but* I *want you. And anyway, Jason agreed to see other people, so it's not like he's completely off-limits . . .*

"You're lying," he says with a maddening shrug.

"I am not."

Yes, she is.

It makes no sense, this sudden attraction to the most obnoxious man she's met since she left her hometown.

Why him?

Why here?

Why now?

Why not? demands her lustful inner self.

And with that, suddenly . . .

Of course!

Yes, it does make sense.

Jason's been gone for months. Maggie is, to put it bluntly, horny. She'd be attracted to *anyone* right now.

Anyone at all. This has nothing to do with Charlie the self-proclaimed romance guru and everything to do with good old-fashioned biological urges.

"We got you guys hot dogs."

Maggie blinks, then turns to see Dom and Julie standing on the aisle, loaded down with concession stand purchases. Charlie instantly scrambles back to his seat, and Julie slips past Maggie's knees into hers.

"Maggie, you can have two dogs if you want," Dom informs her, plunking a cardboard tray into her lap and sliding past her. "Julie doesn't feel like eating hers after all."

"Hey, Dominic, what did you just call her?" Charlie asks from his seat.

"Julie." Dom is momentarily confused. "That's her name, isn't it? Oh, crap, what is it, Judy? Sometimes I get confused about stuff like that."

Nice going, Dom, Maggie thinks, exasperated. *Way to admit you aren't even sure what her name is.*

"No, she's Julie. I meant *her*." Charlie points at Maggie, watching her with an intent expression that has her lower stomach fluttering.

It's just biology, she reminds herself. *Basic animalistic attraction. Nothing to worry about.*

"Huh?" a clueless Dom is asking.

"Did you just call her Maggie?"

"Who?" Dom asks.

"Her," Charlie says, looking frustrated and pointing again at Maggie.

"Yeah. Why? That's her name."

"Really." There's a gleam in Charlie's eye, and he seems to be assessing her with renewed interest.

"That's what Dom calls me," Maggie says pointedly.

"It's what everyone calls you," Dom says, sinking his teeth into a hot dog, devouring half of it in one bite.

"It's what my *friends* call me," she replies, more to Charlie than to Dom. As in, *You can continue to call me Margaret.*

"You look more like a Maggie," Julie tells her, smiling. "Margaret is too formal for you."

"Oh. Well . . . thanks." *I think.*

Realizing that Charlie is still gazing at her, Maggie sends him daggers. "What?"

"They call me Katherine that do talk of me," Charlie quotes, looking amused.

"What are you talking about. Who's Katherine?" Maggie asks as Dom, sitting between them and seemingly oblivious, munches his hot dog.

"Bonny Kate and sometimes Kate the curst . . ."

"Did somebody put something in your beer?" Maggie asks, wishing, in the wake of their kiss, that her pulse wouldn't quicken every time he so much as glances in her direction.

"No, I'm just quoting Shakespeare," he says with a shrug.

Talk about pretentious.

It figures.

"Why?" she asks him.

"You just reminded me of somebody."

Maggie wracks her brain, trying to recall English Lit 101, hardly her favorite college course. Who the heck is Bonny Kate?

"Hey, Maggie, take your dogs and pass the box down there, so Charlie can get his," Dom says.

"Yeah, *Maggie* . . . I'm getting hungry," Charlie comments.

Her gaze drops from the devilish twinkle in his brown eyes to his broadly grinning mouth.

Mere minutes ago, those lips were doing incredible things to hers.

How can she possibly be so incredibly turned on by that mouth and just as incredibly turned off by everything that comes out of it?

"Did you get any ketchup?" Charlie asks Dom and Julie.

"Ketchup?" Dom asks.

"For my hot dogs."

"Ketchup is for hamburgers," Maggie can't help but inform him. "Mustard is for hot dogs."

"Yeah, well, I like both on both," Charlie tells her.

"You would," Maggie mutters, not sure why the idea of ketchup on a frankfurter is suddenly so infuriating to her. She hands the box of hot dogs over to Dom. "Here you go."

"Don't you want at least one?"

"No, thanks," she says tersely. "I've totally lost my appetite."

Chapter Four

"That was some game, wasn't it?" Julie asks brightly, as the four of them make their way down the last escalator flight.

"Julie, they lost," Charlie points out glumly, zipping his parka in anticipation of the icy February wind that awaits them.

"They didn't just lose," Dom says, just as glumly. "They threw it away in the last minute of the game."

"That last call sucked," Maggie declares over her shoulder.

Naturally, she's leading the way down the escalator, just as she led the way out of the seats.

Charlie looks at her in surprise.

"The ref didn't know what he was talking about," she clarifies.

"I know. I just didn't think you knew."

"Don't let her fool you," Dominic says from the step above him. "Maggie knows a lot about a lot of things. And what she doesn't know . . . she thinks she knows."

"Yeah, I noticed that."

Ignoring them, Maggie steps off the escalator, wraps a

blue scarf around her neck, and gives an exaggerated yawn. "I'm exhausted. I can't wait to get out of this suit. I'm going home to bed."

Now there's an image. Maggie naked, in bed. Charlie feels a distinct stirring in the one part of him that doesn't give a damn whether she's the most annoying female on God's green earth.

"What about you?" Maggie asks Charlie.

"Me? I'm not wearing a suit. I dress for comfort." He resists the impulse to add, *You should try it sometime*.

"Not that. I mean, aren't you tired?"

"I am," Julie announces with a yawn. "Does anybody mind if I just call it a night, too?"

"I don't," Dom pipes up. "After a loss like that, I'm not in the mood for socializing."

Julie looks grateful. Dom smiles, looking pleased to be off the hook.

Charlie notices that Maggie's eying Dom with an *oh, no, you don't*, expression. Surely she doesn't think he and Julie are meant for each other? It's obvious to anyone that they have less in common than . . . than . . .

Than Maggie and I do, Charlie concludes.

He didn't miss Dominic checking out the buxom blonde two rows ahead, or the buxom redhead who kept tapping him on the shoulder from the row behind, wanting to know the score.

Dominic C. doesn't strike Charlie as the kind of man who's looking to settle down anytime soon. He's a nice guy, a Regular Joe kind of guy, but Julie needs somebody more . . .

Well, Charlie isn't sure what she needs, but he's certain it isn't Dominic.

Does Maggie honestly believe that the two of them are made for each other?

Judging by her fierce, "Oh, come on, the night is young—you two should go out to dinner," she honestly does.

Or maybe this isn't about Dominic and Julie at all.

Maybe Maggie is just hell-bent on matchmaking and refuses to give up.

Or maybe Maggie wants to ditch the two of them so that she can be alone with Charlie.

Yeah, and maybe the ref has come to his senses and is about to reassemble the Knicks and Lakers on the court for a do-over.

"I'd love to, really, but I'm beat," Julie says, looking at Charlie as if she wants him to come to her rescue.

"Yeah, you were up at dawn making Valentine's pastries, weren't you?"

She nods. "Maybe another time," she says, more to Maggie than to Dominic, who's looking at his watch.

"How about this weekend?" Maggie suggests.

"How about if I just call her?" Dominic says. "I have her business card. It lists her cell phone number. Can I do that, Julie? Call you on your cell sometime?"

"That would be fine." Julie smiles at him—a pleasant smile, not an *I can't wait until he calls me* smile.

"When's a good time to call you?" Maggie the aspiring social secretary wants to know.

Julie hesitates.

Charlie can tell she doesn't particularly want Dom to call her. He can also tell Dom doesn't particularly want to.

"Anytime is good," he informs Maggie on Julie's behalf.

The four of them step out into the glaring lights and

honking traffic of Seventh Avenue. It's still pouring, and a bitter wind is blowing.

Even if any of them—besides Maggie—wanted to stand there and prolong their good-byes, the weather won't let them. As Maggie puts up her umbrella, a gust of wind nearly rips it from her grasp.

Charlie instinctively grabs it and holds it steady, raising it over her head.

"Thanks," she says, looking up at him with startled blue eyes that precisely match the shade of her scarf.

"You're welcome."

There goes that pesky flicker of attraction again.

"Have a nice life with Jake when he gets back," Charlie tells her, as she takes the umbrella from his hand.

Their fingers brush.

He's getting better at resisting impulses, he notes, successfully fighting the urge to touch her hand, to hold it. Where the heck was this impressive willpower back in the arena, when he was grabbing her and kissing her?

"I will," she murmurs.

She will what?

Oh, right. She will have a nice life with Jake. Rather, Jason.

As she and Dominic head off into the night, Charlie watches her go . . . and realizes that this time, his mistake wasn't deliberate.

And that this time, she didn't correct him.

"Who's Jake?"

"Hmm?"

"Who's Jake?" Dom repeats, as Maggie sidesteps a puddle.

"Jake is my boyfriend," she tells him absently, wondering where Charlie lives and whether he's going to go home or—

"I thought his name was Jason."

"His name *is* Jason."

"You just said it was Jake."

Maggie looks at Dominic. "What are you talking about?"

"You just called your boyfriend Jake."

"I did not."

Did she?

It was Charlie, she realizes. Charlie called him Jake. The first time he said it, back in the arena, she almost suspected he'd done it on purpose. The second time, she's sure of it.

She turns to look back at the sidewalk where she left him, tempted to scream out, "His name is Jason, dammit!"

But Charlie and Julie have been swallowed up by the crowd and the darkness.

It's just as well.

The last thing Maggie wants is for him to realize that he—or that soul-rattling kiss of his—have gotten to her.

"What's wrong, Mags?"

"Nothing's wrong," she tells Dominic. "Get under my umbrella. You're getting soaked."

"Nah, my hood's keeping me dry."

"Well, come on, let's walk over to Sixth and get a cab uptown."

"By the time we do that, we could be there."

"Be where? Home in Queens?"

"No, the steak house. It's only a few blocks away."

"What do you mean? I thought you were beat. I thought you wanted to go home."

"Nah, that's just what I told them. I still want that steak."

"You ate three hot dogs, a popcorn, and a hot pretzel at the game. Plus two beers. How can you be hungry?"

"How can you not be? You didn't eat anything. Come on, let's go to the steak house. My treat."

She wants to protest, but suddenly, she's famished—and fully aware that there's nothing in her fridge but ketchup, mustard, and a container of yogurt with an iffy expiration date. She shouldn't eat a heavy meal at this time of the evening . . . but maybe if she just has a salad and a baked potato without butter . . .

"Okay," she agrees reluctantly.

Falling into step beside Dominic as they head uptown, she says, "You should be taking Julie out to eat, not me."

"Nah, I get the impression she doesn't eat much meat."

"What makes you say that?"

"She made a face when I ordered her a hot dog at the concession stand."

"Well, didn't you ask her what she wanted?"

"I thought a gentleman does the ordering."

"Maybe at Le Cirque. Not at a snack bar." Maggie shakes her head. "No wonder she couldn't wait to get away from you."

"She couldn't wait to get away from me?" He stops dead in his tracks. "What makes you say that?"

Clearly, this is new territory for Dominic Chickalini. Unless she's mistaken, Maggie has spotted a spark of challenge in his dark eyes.

"Oh, come on. You can't possibly think she was interested after the way you treated her at the game?"

They resume walking, but only for a few paces, stopping at the DON'T WALK light on the corner of Thirty-fifth and Seventh.

"How did I treat her?" Dom asks.

"Like she was invisible, for the most part. You talked more to Charlie than you did to her."

"That's because I had more to say to Charlie than I did to her. He's a great guy. Did you know he gave up the chance to make millions of dollars because he didn't want to go into his father's business?"

Millions of dollars? Charlie?

"Great guy? He sounds like a stupid guy," Maggie tells Dom. "Who in their right mind would give up millions of dollars?"

"Somebody who knows there's more to life than money."

Resenting the dig, Maggie haughtily informs him, "I know there's more to life than money."

"Yeah? Then why are you so hot for Dr. Do-Right? Because I've seen you with him, and let me tell you, Mags, he's not your type."

"Really? Then who is?"

She holds her breath.

As the light changes and they splash their way across the street, Dominic seems to be brainstorming for an answer.

Maggie waits until they're halfway up the next short block. Then she can't stand it any longer. "Don't you dare say that Charlie is my type, Dom."

"I wouldn't, because he's not."

"Good," she says, trying to ignore a stab of disappointment. "Because he's not."

"I just said that."

"I know. I was just repeating it, because . . . because it bears repeating."

Yes. If not for Dom's sake, then for her own.

She adds, for good measure, "That Charlie was the most overconfident, brazen guy I've ever met in my life."

Dom peers at her beneath her dripping umbrella. "I take it back. Maybe he is your type. Sounds like you have a lot in common."

She swats him on the arm. "Charlie is nothing like me."

"Yeah, well, his friend Julie's nothing like me."

"You didn't give her a chance. Things would have been different if you were sitting across from each other over candlelight and wine in a romantic restaurant."

Dom seems to consider this. "Maybe."

"Definitely. If Charlie didn't keep butting into your conversation with her, the two of you could have found plenty of common ground."

"I guess. She's a blonde, and you know how I like blondes." They stop for another light. "Oh, well. Easy come, easy—"

"Hold on a minute there, bub. You're not going to let her get away just like that, are you?"

"Aren't I?"

"No. You're not." Maggie's thoughts are racing. "I have a plan."

"So what else is new?" he grumbles. "You remind me of my sister Nina. Can't you ever just wing it?"

"People who wing it never accomplish anything. You may not believe it, but you're going to win Julie's heart, Dominic."

"Why am I going to do that?"

"Because you can. And because you want to."

"I don't know if I do. I don't think we're that compatible."

"Aren't you attracted to her?"

"Sure I am. She's pretty. Smart, too. And she bakes pies."

If the way to a man's heart were through his stomach alone, Julie the pastry chef would have Dominic's sewn up, Maggie concludes as they cross the street.

Unfortunately, there's more to love than that.

Just like there's more to love—and life—than making a good living. Or marrying somebody who does.

"Can I ask you something, Dom?"

"Sure, what?"

"Do you really think that I'm more interested in Jason's wallet than anything else?"

"Maybe not more than anything else," he admits. "Just . . . I don't think there's much about him that you're very interested in."

"How about the fact that he's smart, and caring, and stable? That he supports my career? That he'd make a good husband, and he loves children?"

"Is that enough?"

Her instinct is to dismiss him.

Unaccustomed to Dominic in the role of thoughtful advisor, Maggie forces herself to consider what he's saying.

The scary thing is, what he's saying is pretty much the same thing that Charlie was saying.

Geez, where the heck is Bindy when you need her? She'd slap some sense into Dom if she were here. She'd point out that there's nothing wrong with a woman seeking the very best in everything from shoe leather to hairstylists to men.

"I don't know, Maggie," Dom is saying, "I just think that sometimes, you're so driven to get where you think you should be going that you don't enjoy the scenery along the way."

Maggie frowns.

Dom blinks. "Wow, that was deep, wasn't it? I wonder if Charlie can use it for one of his articles?"

"Yeah, well, do me a favor and keep it to yourself, Dom. I don't need some cocksure columnist immortalizing me in print, okay?"

"Maybe that's exactly what you need."

"To be immortalized in print?"

"No, the cocksure columnist part. Somebody like Charlie would liven up your life, Mags."

"Somebody like Charlie would turn it upside down, then walk away, Dom."

"Sounds like you spent the last few hours thinking about something more than basketball." He winks.

"We're not talking about me," she says, nettled. "We're talking about you and how you should have been thinking about something other than basketball for the past few hours, Dom. We're talking about you and Julie and how you should go about getting her to go out with you again."

"Who says I want to do that?"

"You don't?"

"I didn't say that."

"Then I'll come up with a plan," Maggie says simply, stepping around a manhole cover. "And if it doesn't work, I'll . . . I'll . . ."

"You'll give me a turn to play matchmaker," Dom finishes for her.

"For yourself?"

"No, for you."

"I've already made my match," Maggie informs him.

"That's what you think. You're not going to wind up with Dr. Do-Right, Mags. I guarantee it."

They come to a halt at another intersection.

"How can you guarantee that?"

"Just a hunch. You're not the only one with intuition. The Chickalinis have intuition, too, you know."

"Then with whom does the Chickalini intuition tell you that I'm going to end up, Dom? Wait, don't say it."

"Don't say what?"

"Charlie."

"I wasn't going to say it," he says, watching her closely. "But this is the second time you have, Maggie. Are you trying to tell me something?"

"No!" She can feel her face burning.

"Are you sure? Because if you're interested in Charlie—"

"I'm not!"

"I think you are."

"Yeah, well, I know I'm not."

"Really? You also knew the Knicks were going to win the game tonight. You felt it in your bones, remember?"

"They almost did win," she points out. After all, unlike the so-called Chickalini intuition, the Harrigan intuition is rarely wrong.

"They lost."

"They almost didn't lose."

"But they did. You really hate to lose, don't you, Maggie? You can't stand being wrong."

"Do you know anybody who enjoys it?"

"I don't know anybody who resents it quite as much as you do."

"What does any of this have to do with Charlie?"

"Just that even if you were attracted to him, you wouldn't let yourself get involved, because he doesn't fit into the Maggie O'Mulligan plan of action."

"Well, that might be true if I were attracted to him . . ."

She might be talking to Dom, but for some reason, she's seeing only Charlie's face. Charlie's face, and Charlie's mouth. Her lips tingle at the memory of Charlie's kiss.

She forces herself to go on. "But since I'm not attracted to him, Dom, and since he doesn't believe in long-term relationships—which I not only believe in, but intend to have for the rest of my life, as in one, as in, marriage—it's really a moot point."

Sick of picturing Charlie, she closes her eyes.

Darn it, there he is again; his face an indelible imprint in her mind's eye. She has the feeling it will be there even when she crawls into bed tonight; perhaps even in her dreams. It's like he's haunting her, or stalking her, or whatever it is that opportunistic cads like him do to unwilling victims like her.

Opening her eyes, she sees that the orange DON'T WALK has turned into a white WALK. She steps off the curb.

"Maggie!"

Dom pulls her back as a cab whips around the corner, coming within a few inches of her legs.

"Geez, you didn't even look," he says. "What the heck are you doing, Mags?"

Trying to escape Charlie.

Heart pounding, she concludes that she was right about him.

He *is* dangerous.

Good thing she'll never see him again.

Chapter Five

"*When can I see you again?*" Charlie echoes. "That's all it says on the card?"

"No, there are a few lines of poetry, too," Julie tells him, her voice crackling with static. She's on her cell phone, presumably on her way to the subway after her lunch shift at the bistro.

If she were just across the hall at her place, she'd have run over here instead of calling. She knows he rarely answers the phone when he's working.

He almost didn't pick it up today. After last night's blind date fiasco, he woke in the wee hours, struck by inspiration. He's been at the computer since dawn, writing.

But not about Julie.

And not about Dom.

About none other than Margaret *Don't Call Me Maggie* O'Mulligan.

When he heard the phone ring, he didn't even bother to screen the call. He just snatched it up, needing a break from the high-maintenance character he's just created, and feeling a little like Dr. Frankenstein.

"Dom wrote poetry for you?" he asks Julie, shifting his attention away from his laptop screen, where the fictionalized version of Maggie is as uncooperative as her real-life counterpart. "What kind of poetry?"

"I don't know . . . the old-fashioned kind, I guess."

"What does it say?"

"It says, *If I could write the beauty of your eyes And in fresh numbers number all your graces, The age to come would say, 'This poet lies—Such heavenly touches ne'er touched earthly faces.'* Isn't it beautiful?" she asks breathlessly. "Do you think he wrote it?"

Charlie swallows a laugh. "Actually, it's a Shakespearean sonnet."

As it happens, Charlie's had the Bard on the brain today. For some reason, whenever he thinks of Maggie— and it's been often—he finds himself mentally casting her in the role of willful Kate in *The Taming of the Shrew*.

Last night, she didn't seem to place the passage he quoted to her. He was glad of that once he recalled that Petruchio's "bonny Kate" dialogue concludes with the words *Myself am moved to woo thee for my wife*. Charlie certainly doesn't want Maggie to think that he feels the same about her.

"Dominic didn't strike me as the type of guy who'd read Shakespeare," Julie is saying. "And I definitely didn't think he meant it when he said he'd call me."

"Well, he hasn't called you yet."

"No, but he sent two dozen red roses and this Shakespeare poem, and he says he wants to see me again."

"Do you want to?"

Dead silence.

For a moment, Charlie thinks her cell phone's lost the signal.

Then Julie says, "If you asked me this morning, I'd have said no."

"But now . . ." Charlie prompts, when she trails off.

"But now I think I do want to see him again. I think I was wrong about him. I thought we didn't have a lot in common since he didn't talk about much of anything—and when he did, it was about basketball. And hot dogs. But who knows? Sometimes still waters run deep."

Yes, and sometimes still waters are stagnant.

But Charlie isn't about to say that.

After all, he likes Dominic. He's the kind of guy Charlie would befriend: laid-back, funny, and into sports and food. He was a gentleman where Julie was concerned, too—except when he knocked her hat off her head. But that was entirely forgivable under the circumstances.

Yes, Dominic Chickalini seems to be an all-around great guy. Charlie isn't convinced that he and Julie have romantic potential. Nor is he convinced Dominic is the poetry-quoting type, but he could be wrong about that. He could be wrong about everything.

Dominic's only real drawback, as far as Charlie is concerned, is his connection to Maggie. Maybe if she'd keep her freckled, powdered nose out of Dominic's business, he'd be able to find a woman on his own.

"What should I do next?" Julie asks. "Should I call him and see if he asks me out? Or should I ask him out? I have his business card, so I could call him at his office."

"Give me a minute to think here," Charlie says, leaning back in his computer chair and rubbing his razor stubble. "Your next date with him is key."

If he's learned anything from his readers, it's that first dates are no indication of whether a relationship has a future. A first date can be a washout because of nerves and expectations, or it can be stellar because everything is new and exciting. Either way, it doesn't mean much. It's the second date that's a true barometer of what may—or can't possibly—happen.

Julie says, "Charlie, keep in mind that I was out of my element at the basketball game. This time maybe we could do something that's a little more up my alley. He should see me in my best light."

Bingo.

Pretty girls are a dime a dozen in New York. Dominic's eyes can feast on a beauty bonanza every time he sets foot on the street. But his taste buds . . .

Well, that's a different story.

"I've got a great idea, Julie," Charlie says, adjusting the brim of his "thinking hat"—the one he always wears when he's writing. It's a baseball cap with a three-dimensional duck's backside and tail feathers protruding above the brim. He and his buddies all bought them to wear to their friend Eric's—a.k.a. Bird Ass's—birthday party a few years back.

Charlie likes to twist the feathers around his finger when he's pondering something, and he does so now, before informing Julie, "You're not going to call Dominic at work."

"I'm not?"

"No. You're going to do something more interesting than that."

"I am?" she sounds suspicious.

"Yep. Just meet me in your kitchen in a half hour, and I'll tell you my plan."

Juggling an armload of charts, her trench coat, her umbrella, her briefcase, and a fresh cup of coffee—her third of the morning—Maggie heads toward Dominic's office in the account management department.

It's been one hell of a morning, and the afternoon promises to be even more intense, with a new business presentation on the agenda. Driven by her passion for her job—and every intention of making media director by her thirtieth birthday—Maggie has barely had time to breathe, let alone think about anything other than business.

Now, as she strides along the row of offices with open doors, she finds her thoughts wandering to the other night, and Charlie.

Aggravated that Julie's insolent friend—and his insolent kiss—can still flit into her distracted mind more than twenty-four hours later, Maggie shoves him firmly back out again.

Instead, she conjures an image of Jason's sweet, kind face.

Rather, she attempts to. But for some reason, she can't seem to recall what he looks like. For some reason, his features are superimposed with Charlie's.

Unsettled and resenting Charlie more by the second, Maggie resolves to start carrying a photo of Jason in her pocket until he comes home.

"Hi, Margaret," calls an account coordinator passing by with a stack of files.

"How's it going, Hugh?"

"Crazy," comes the harried reply.

Maggie smiles.

The frenetic pace of agency life isn't for everyone, but it certainly suits her. From the moment she steps off the elevator each morning, her adrenaline is pumping, and her mind is racing. Her job is perfect in every way.

Well, almost every way.

As always, as she makes her way through the account management department, she's nettled by the not-so-subtle office hierarchy, struck by the difference between this department and media—and the irony that here, the lowly assistants have better work accommodations than full-fledged planners do on the floor above.

Unlike her windowless cubicle upstairs, Dom's office has a door and a view. Granted, it's a view of a couple of Third Avenue office buildings, but at least there's a window. At least Dominic can have real plants, and not a dusty silk potted ivy like the one Maggie inherited from the cubicle's prior inhabitant.

Not that Dom cares for the philodendron and spider plants that line his narrow sill. A fellow assistant account executive tends to that task. Maggie would never have known it if she hadn't caught Lisa in action with a watering can one day.

Lisa wasn't the least bit embarrassed, nor was Dom the least bit apologetic when Maggie confronted him.

His excuse—"She offered to do it"—is a familiar one.

There is certainly no shortage of women who are willing to cater to Dominic Chickalini's every need.

Today, when Maggie walks into his office, she half expects to find him sitting behind his desk with his feet up, shoes being polished by his secretary and the voluptuous receptionist from Six fanning him with a palm frond.

But he's alone, and busy with his calculator and a yellow legal pad.

"Hey, what's up?" he asks, briefly looking up from the column of figures.

"I've got the CPMs the client wanted," Maggie tells him.

"Just a second. Have a seat. I'm almost done with this."

Maggie plops into one of his two guest chairs and punches a hole into the plastic sip lid of her coffee cup, noting—not for the first time—that her own office only has one guest chair.

Leave it to Dom to land the better job with a nicer office and a higher salary. If she didn't love him, she'd hate him.

After all, Maggie's the one who did an unpaid summer internship at Blair Barnett the summer before senior year, just to open the door to interviews after graduation. She was hoping for a job in account management, but was hired for media.

Meanwhile, Dom waltzed right in the door thanks to his connection to Maggie—and got a plum position thanks to his looks and charisma and a series of unattached female interviewers, all the way from Human Resources to the department head.

Figures. Next thing you know, he'll be account supervisor or move over to a brand manager's position at the client, while Maggie's still working her butt off in hopes of a promotion and a move to an office with a window.

To say that isn't fair is an understatement. In fact, Maggie doesn't allow herself to dwell on the harsh reality of office politics unless she can dash right off to a kickboxing class to take out her frustrations on the punching bag instead of on Dom.

No time for kickboxing today, though, so she forces herself to look on the bright side.

Just think, Maggie—when you can't see outside, you have no idea how crappy the weather is so it can't dampen your mood.

She shifts her attention to the rain-spattered window behind Dom's desk. She's got a client meeting across town in half an hour, and it's going to be impossible to find a cab in this downpour. Taking the subway will mean changing trains three times. Or she could always walk, since she has her umbrella.

Thinking of the umbrella makes her think once again of Charlie. She can't help remembering the way he helped her wrestle it back from the gusting wind as they exited the Garden, and how he gallantly held it over her head.

He did have a certain aura of breeding, despite his shaggy appearance.

Dominic said his family has millions. You'd certainly never know it.

Not that it matters.

Maggie wouldn't be interested in Charlie if he were a billionaire and begging for her hand.

If she hadn't just endured several months of forced celibacy, she never would have let him kiss her that way—and she sure as hell wouldn't still be thinking about it two days later.

"Okay, done," Dom says abruptly, turning off his calculator and pushing aside the yellow pad. He leans forward in his seat, elbows on his desk and fingers steepled beneath his chiseled chin.

Maggie can't help noticing how good-looking he is, in his dark suit, crisp white shirt, and maroon tie. He smells good, too. Like soap and cologne.

If only Julie P. could have seen him like this, instead of dressed down and guzzling beer . . .

"Has Julie called?" she asks him.

"Nope. I thought you said the roses were a sure bet."

"They are. Give her time."

"I don't think she's the type who will call. Maybe I should call her."

"If you don't hear from her by the end of the week, you can," Maggie concedes.

"Yeah, whatever," he says with a shrug. "But just so you know, I can't take her out this Saturday."

"Why not? Are you working at your dad's restaurant again?"

"No, Ralphie's home, so he's covering for me. I have plans."

"Plans with whom?"

"Somebody I met," he says cagily.

"Where?"

"On the seven train. She's a dancer."

"Terrific. You meet a stripper on the subway, and you'd rather see her than a nice girl like Jul—"

"She's a dancer, Mags. Not a stripper."

"You mean, like a ballerina?"

"I guess."

"Are you sure?"

He looks doubtful. "She just said she was a dancer."

"My intuition is telling me that she's the kind of dancer who uses a pole rather than a barre, Dom."

He snorts as though she just produced a crystal ball and

a magic wand. "You and your Harrigan intuition are full of—"

"Well, dancer or stripper, it doesn't matter. Julie's the one you want to focus on right now."

"I don't know, Maggie. I haven't heard from her, and it's been twenty-four hours since she got those roses. Don't you think two dozen was overkill? And that poem . . . I mean, I don't even know what it meant. What if she asks me about it? What if she expects me to go around quoting Shakespeare?"

"I'll help you learn a few lines, just in case," Maggie tells him.

"I don't know. I don't think that's my style, Mags. I think I'd be better off—"

"Dom? There's somebody here to see you," his secretary, Tonya, interrupts from the doorway.

"Who is it?" Dom asks, frowning and checking his appointment book.

"He says his name is Charles Kennelly, and he's out in the reception area."

"I don't know a Charles Kennelly."

"He says he knows you."

"Fine, whatever. Tell him to come in."

As Tonya nods and disappears, Maggie hands Dom the charts. "Look at these and call me back. I've got to get to a client meeting over on the West Side."

"Wait, let me just take a quick look now," Dom says, flipping pages.

Maggie waits impatiently, pacing around his office. His bulletin board is almost a duplicate of hers, dotted with invitations to parties and dinners thrown by various media suppliers. Pointing at an invitation to a celebration *Glam-*

our magazine is throwing in honor of Fashion Week, she asks, "Are you going to this?"

"When is it?"

"Tonight."

"Are you?"

"For a little while, if I'm not exhausted."

"I'll go with you."

She nods and moves on, pausing in front of a framed photo of his niece and nephew. Nina's children are adorable, Maggie decides, smiling back at their cherubic little faces.

Biological instinct kicks in as she studies Rose's silky black hair and Nino's precious first tooth poking into his shy smile.

Someday, I'll have a couple of kids of my own, Maggie promises herself. Jason will probably want at least three or four. And if she marries him, they'll be able to afford them.

Maggie tries—and fails—to picture a clutter of primary-colored plastic toys and crumbs littering Jason's East Thirty-eighth Street town house.

Well, that makes sense. Jason has live-in help. The place will never look like Maggie's married brothers' homes. She'll never be a carpool-driving soccer mom like her sisters-in-law, either. Nor will she ever be a media supervisor. Not if she's raising children in Manhattan with a doctor for a husband. She won't have to work—and she'll presumably be too busy—and content—to miss it.

Talk about a fairy tale come true.

All Maggie ever wanted, growing up, was to get out of Green Corners. She longed for glamour and excitement, romance and adventure. She longed for—

"Charlie?"

Jolted from her daydream, she looks up at Dominic to find him looking over her shoulder.

She turns around to discover the last person she'd ever expect—or want—to find standing in the doorway of Dom's office.

"What are you doing here?" she asks the man who's been haunting her for the last day and a half.

"I'd ask you the same thing, except in your case, I already know. You work at Blair Barnett, too, right? In the media department. On a cosmetics account."

Flattered that he remembers so many details about her, Maggie fights to maintain her expression of displeasure.

She also wonders why Charlie looks completely at ease in a corporate setting wearing faded jeans, work boots, a red flannel shirt, and navy pea coat, while she suddenly and inexplicably feels overdressed in her charcoal tweed suit, silk blouse, and pearls.

"I thought your secretary told you I was here," Charlie says to Dom.

"How was he supposed to know it was you?" Maggie asks before Dom can reply.

"You're not the only one in town, Margaret, who enjoys using their full name on occasion. Mine is Charles," he says, with a mischievous twinkle in his eye. "Charles Kennelly III, actually. Now you'll recognize my byline when you see it in *She*."

She tries to think of an appropriately clever response, but she's rattled by his very presence, dammit. He's so close she can smell this morning's shampoo wafting from his slightly damp hair, and it's all she can do not to plunge her fingers into it.

Luckily, Dom comes to her rescue.

"So, are you here to see Maggie, or me?" he asks, rising and shaking Charlie's hand—the one that's not gingerly balancing an oversize large white pastry box against his hip.

"I'm here to see you," Charlie replies quickly, as if there's not a chance in hell the other option would be the case. "And I've got to make it quick. My driver's double-parked."

His driver's double-parked?

Are we supposed to be impressed? Maggie wonders.

All right, maybe she is, a little.

Clearly, Dominic is, too. A lot.

"You've got a driver?" he asks Charlie. "Cool."

"It's just a car service I use sometimes." Charlie shrugs off Dom's unabashed admiration. "I wasn't sure I'd get a cab, and I didn't want to risk carrying this uptown on the subway."

"What is it?" Dom asks, gaping at the box.

"It's from Julie. I'm just the deliveryman."

"You can afford a driver but not a messenger service?" Maggie can't help asking.

"I wouldn't trust a messenger service with this." Charlie ceremoniously sets the box on top of a low credenza and gestures for Dom to open it.

Maggie can't resist the urge to stand on her tiptoes and peer over his shoulder as he does.

Inside the box is the most exquisite confection she's ever seen in her life. It's a cake, but it's designed to look like an engraved invitation on a creamy brocade background made of what looks like spun sugar. The icing letters are piped in painstaking calligraphy that must have taken hours.

"Julie made this?" Maggie asks, as Dom utters an awestruck profanity.

"She sure did," Charlie says proudly.

It's insane, but Maggie finds herself battling a wave of jealousy.

Listen, if Charlie were attracted to Julie, he wouldn't be trying to fix her up with another man, her inner voice points out. *Besides, what do you care? You already have a boyfriend.*

But she can't help feeling wistful. What would it be like to see Charlie beam with admiration over something *she* accomplished?

She fights back the ridiculous urge to tell him that she once took a cake decorating class as part of high school Home Ec. That she learned to make a cake that looked exactly like a wedge of Swiss cheese and that she won a red ribbon for it at the county fair.

Instead, she busies herself reading the message scrolled on Julie's magnificent creation, which bears zero resemblance to a hunk of cheese, Swiss or otherwise.

The pleasure of your company is requested for dinner on Saturday at eight o'clock in the evening. 21 Harcourt Street, Apartment 4E, New York City. Black Tie Optional.

"Harcourt Street?" Maggie asks. "Where's that?"

"In the Village," Charlie replies.

"Saturday night?" Dominic is shaking his head. "I already—"

"You already have a tux, right, Dom?" Maggie cuts in, elbowing him into silence. "From Rosalee's wedding? So you're all set."

"But I—"

"Is Julie cooking the dinner?" Maggie asks Charlie, loudly enough to drown out Dom's protest.

"She's cooking the dinner *and* the dessert."

Dominic looks thoughtful.

He's going to say he can't make it, Maggie realizes. *He's going to blow off a home-cooked dinner and a homespun sweetheart for a pole-dancing bimbo.*

She glances at Charlie.

As their eyes collide, she is reminded of exactly why she's had a hard time getting him out of her thoughts for the past thirtysomething hours. There's something about those brown eyes of his that makes her heart race a little faster.

But this isn't about her heart, or Charlie's. It's about Dominic's.

Thinking quickly, Maggie manages to jostle her friend's arm so that his fingers land squarely in the icing along the edge of the cake.

"Oops, sorry, Dom," she says sweetly.

"It's okay." He absently licks the frosting off.

Maggie holds her breath.

Dom's expression instantly goes from uncertainty to rapture.

Score!

"Is this almond icing?" Dom asks Charlie.

"I don't know, I'm just the messenger. You'll have to ask Julie when you see her on Saturday night."

"Yeah," Dom says slowly. "I guess I will."

Relieved, Maggie glances at her watch—and lets out a yelp.

"I've got twenty minutes to get across town," she announces, pulling on her coat. "Check those CPMs and get back to me by lunchtime, Dom."

"Yeah," he says, snagging another fingerful of icing.

"Where are you off to?" Charlie asks, as Maggie sails past him on her way to the door.

"Client meeting."

"Don't you want some cake?"

Yes, she wants some cake. She'd love to delve into that sugary rich confection and sate her sudden and fierce appetite for . . .

Well, for cake.

Breakfast was hours ago, and it consisted of a small bowl of whole grain cereal with skim milk.

But cake . . .

Well, cake is fattening. Cake is sinful. What makes him think she'd just casually indulge like that? What makes him think she doesn't have an ounce of self-control?

"No, I don't want cake," she tells Charlie firmly, buttoning her trench coat.

"Are you sure? Because it's really delicious."

"I'm positive. I don't want cake. Cake is . . . cake is . . . it's the last thing I want right now. And even if I wanted it—I have willpower, you know."

Okay, Maggie, are you really talking about cake, here?

"Really?" He seems to be doubting her willpower. "Are you sure you can resist it? Because I've tasted this before, and it's really, really delicious."

Is *he* talking about cake?

"Maybe we have different opinions about what's delicious and what isn't," Maggie informs Charlie, doing her best to ignore an undeniable craving for . . .

Okay, is *anyone* talking about cake?

"Mmm. This is great," Dominic announces, scooping another hunk of crumbly icing and shoving it into his mouth.

Dominic. Dominic is talking about cake.

"I have to go," Maggie says again. "I have a meeting."

Is that a flicker of disappointment in Charlie's eyes as he says, briefly, "Bye"?

Tucking her briefcase under her arm and giving a quick wave with her folded umbrella, she leaves him behind, grateful for an excuse to do so.

If she had to look at him for another second, she wouldn't be able to hold at bay the memory of that sizzling kiss at the game—nor was she certain she'd be able to hide her thoughts from him. The way he kept looking at her in there, you'd think he was trying to read her mind, as though he suspected he was on it.

Now, as she hurries past the secretaries' bay toward the reception area, the kiss comes back to her in a Technicolor rush.

Kisses like that just don't happen every day. Not when your boyfriend's in a different hemisphere.

Not even when he's in the same room and doing the kissing, Maggie reluctantly admits.

Which is precisely why she can never be in the same room with Charlie again.

Of course, if Dominic and Julie become a couple, she won't be able to avoid Charlie forever. She'll have to see him occasionally. Like at the wedding. And at little Maggie's christening.

What if they decide to make Charlie the baby's godfather? She'll have to see him then, since she's going to be the godmother.

Of course, by then, she'll probably be a real mother— to Jason's children, of course.

And Charlie will probably be there with a date. Maybe one of Dom's bimbo castoffs.

Maggie wonders what she and Charlie will say to each other when they meet again years from now at one of those blessed events. Will they laugh about how their friends got off to a rocky start at the Knicks game? Will they toast each other for their respective roles in making such a successful match? Will they drink too much champagne and confide that they were once, ever so fleetingly, attracted to each other?

No, Maggie concludes, as she presses the DOWN button at the elevator bank and efficiently belts and ties her trench. She will never, as long as she lives, under any circumstances, admit to Charlie—a.k.a. Charles Kennelly III—that she was actually attracted to him once upon a blind date.

The only thing she has any intention of saying to him, when she's a happily married doctor's wife, is *I told you so.*

Chapter Six

That Dominic is one heck of a nice guy, Charlie concludes as he rides the elevator down to the lobby five minutes later.

They have a few things in common, aside from their choice of sports teams to support and a mutual affinity for almond-flavored icing.

Dom lost his mother when he was a toddler.

Charlie lost his father around the same time—only Dad didn't die. He merely abandoned his family for the sake of his high-powered career.

Like Nino Chickalini, Charles Kennelly II is a self-made man.

Unlike Nino Chickalini, he's a wealthy one. His abandonment was purely on an emotional level, not a financial one. He made sure his children always had the best of whatever his money could buy. All they lacked was paternal attention.

Charlie swallows hard, wishing he were alone in the elevator. Not that he's going to burst into tears or anything. He's quite used to his family history by now. But sometimes, when he thinks about what he missed, growing up . . .

Well, he can't help feeling wistful.

Lucky Dominic. From what he says, Charlie can tell that his relationship with his father is close and affectionate.

As the two of them gobbled down large wedges of Julie's cake using plates and forks produced by an eager-to-please secretary, Dom told Charlie all about his father's small business off Ditmars Boulevard in Astoria. He said he always figured he'd take over the pizza parlor after he graduated from college—after all, it was what his father always expected of him. But Dom's social life was crippled when he worked restaurant hours; nor did he like spending all his waking hours in Queens.

When his sister Nina decided to stay put in the old neighborhood and marry a family friend, Dom had his out. Now Nina and her husband have virtually taken over Big Pizza Pie, and Dom only helps out in the restaurant when they're shorthanded.

Dominic's lucky, Charlie thinks once again. Lucky that he had siblings to step in and fulfill his father's expectations so that he could sidestep the family legacy without repercussion.

Not that Charlie doesn't have siblings himself. His three older sisters are married with children and living in the metropolitan area. But they're all estranged from their father.

So, in fact, was Charlie, until the old man came crawling back when Charlie was in high school. A two-pack-a-day smoker, he'd had a cancer scare and was worried that he'd die without ever getting to know the children he'd left behind.

Nobody else would speak to him. Not Mom, who was by then remarried to Charlie's stepfather, Art. Not his sisters, who were all either in college or settled down with husbands of their own.

But Charlie couldn't turn his father away.

Not even after he realized what a controlling son-of-a-bitch the man really is.

As the elevator doors slide open in the lobby, Charlie steps back to let the women out first. One of them, a pretty blonde, gives him an appreciative smile that lingers. Something tells Charlie she's admiring more than his gentlemanly manners.

He shifts his gaze to the drenching rain outside the plate-glass windows, not in the mood to encourage flirtation. Not with the blonde, anyway. Something tells him that she wouldn't hold a candle to Maggie when it comes to sassy repartee.

Flirting with Maggie—and regardless of her romantic availability, that *was* flirtation they engaged in upstairs—has left Charlie oddly energized.

Well, that should come in handy, as he's on his way over to Chelsea Piers to hit a bucket of balls. Golf is always therapeutic when he has writer's block—and he's had it all morning.

Of course, that might be because he wasted an entire day yesterday writing fiction when he should have been brainstorming ideas for his next column. Once the female character he had so impulsively created took hold, he couldn't seem to shake her off. She was as pushy as Maggie herself, demanding that he write about her when he should have been running errands, washing dishes, sleeping.

This morning, after a turbulent night in which the real Maggie melded with her fictional counterpart to invade his restless wakefulness and his erratic dreams, Charlie attempted to rein in the muse and focus, with little success, on his column.

He was grateful when Julie interrupted with her request that he hand-deliver her creation to Dominic's office. He never suspected that he might, in doing so, find himself face-to-face with the very object of his tension.

Now, as he pushes through the revolving door and out into the rain, he tells himself that seeing Maggie again in all her antagonistic glory should have banished her from his consciousness. If nothing else, he's been reminded that she's an uptight workaholic control freak.

But there's something else about her, some tantalizing quality he glimpses just often enough to whet his curiosity, that makes him wonder if she might not be—

Standing three feet away from him?

Yes, there she is under her dripping umbrella, poised curbside in the driving rain, just inches from his black Town Car's flashing hazard lights, her arm outstretched as she gazes futilely at the occupied taxis whizzing by.

"Can't get a cab?" he asks, touching her Burberry-clad arm.

Startled, she looks up at him. "What do you think?" she growls.

She darts a worried glance at her watch as his driver, Azim, spots him and steps out to open the back door.

"Come on," Charlie says, stepping back and gesturing at Maggie. "Get into the car."

She frowns, her expression riddled with uncertainty.

"Get in, Maggie," he urges again. "I'm getting drenched, and so is Azim. He'll drop you off at your meeting."

Maggie looks at the driver, who gives a little nod.

"Thank you," she says, mostly to Azim, as she lowers her umbrella and climbs past the two men into the backseat of the Town Car.

Charlie follows her, noting the spicy musk of her perfume already infiltrating the existing smell of new leather. How ironic that her scent takes over a space just as immediately and effectively as the woman herself does.

She deposits her briefcase, purse, and umbrella on the seat between them, effectively burying Charlie's small gym bag and the *New York Times* he was planning to read on his way across town.

As Azim closes the door behind them, he glances over at Maggie.

After fastening her seat belt and shaking a few stray raindrops from her hair, she reaches into her vast black leather bag and produces a compact, seemingly oblivious to Charlie's gaze.

"I'm going to West Thirtieth Street at Eighth Avenue," she informs Azim as he steers the car out into traffic.

"No problem, Miss."

Charlie watches her check her reflection before snapping it closed with a satisfied nod and storing it back in her bag.

When she glances up to find him watching her, he doesn't even bother to pretend that he isn't.

"You look great," he hears himself proclaim boldly, "in case you were wondering."

Clearly taken aback, she murmurs, "Thank you."

"You're welcome."

He watches her turn her head toward the rain-spattered window and is amused when, gazing at her profile, he sees the hint of a pleased smile quirk the corner of her mouth.

"Important meeting?" he asks.

She turns back to him. "They're all important."

"Sounds stressful."

She shrugs. "I don't mind stress."

He grins. "Somehow, I'm not surprised by that."

"What's that supposed to mean?"

"You just have a very intense personality."

"I'll take that as a compliment."

She *would*.

Yet maybe, Charlie realizes in surprise, that's how he meant it.

After all, you've got to admire a woman who knows precisely what she wants and goes after it with relish. You've even got to wonder what it would be like if she decided that *you were* exactly what she wants.

"Was that cake your idea?" Maggie asks him abruptly, effectively curtailing that dangerous train of thought.

"No," he lies. "It was Julie's. Were the roses your idea?"

"No. They were Dominic's."

"How about the poetry?"

"Also Dominic's idea. He has a romantic soul."

"Really."

The man Charlie just witnessed ingesting a hunk of cake the size of a tissue box doesn't strike him as particularly romantic or soulful, but he decides to take Maggie's word for it—for Julie's sake, if nothing else.

"Julie loved the roses," he tells her. "And the sonnet."

"I figured she—I mean, Dominic really hoped she would."

"So he likes her?"

"Who wouldn't? She's everything a man would want in a wife." Maggie's eyes suddenly narrow at Charlie, and she asks the question he's asked himself countless times. "In fact . . . why don't you want her yourself, Charlie?"

"Because we're just friends."

"Friendship is the best foundation for romance," she informs him with her trademark omniscience.

"Really? Then why aren't you involved with Dominic?"

"Me? With Dominic?" She laughs. "I'd never get involved with him. He's too—" She breaks off suddenly, then shifts gears.

"He's too family-oriented and ready to settle down," she informs Charlie, who doesn't believe that for a minute. "I'm a hundred percent committed to my career right now."

He opens his mouth to ask her about her boyfriend—and marriage. If he's not mistaken, she mentioned both as part of her future plans.

"Speaking of work, you know what?" she breezes on. "I have to check through my paperwork to make sure I have everything I need for my meeting."

"Be my guest," he says, glad the conversation is, for the moment at least, over.

He's beginning to wonder if he should have advised Julie to stick the roses in a vase, toss the card, and forget all about Dominic. Something tells him the guy isn't nearly as eager to marry himself off as his pal Maggie is.

So why is he going along with it? Dominic doesn't particularly strike him as a pushover of a guy, and he shouldn't have any trouble finding a woman on his own, especially here in New York, where the single woman/straight bachelor ratio is severely unbalanced.

Charlie looks over at Maggie. She's intent on the contents of her briefcase, frowning slightly as she shuffles through a packet of papers, rearranging their order with dogged determination.

Charlie gets the distinct impression that Maggie doesn't do anything halfway—nor does she tolerate half-heartedness in others. Clearly, she's decided Dominic needs a wife, and she's going to find him one. Her sights are set on Julie, for whatever reason.

And, truth be told, Julie could do a lot worse.

A guy like Dominic will be good for her—Charlie can't deny that. And if he isn't exactly a willing candidate for domestic bliss, he will be once he tastes Julie's home cooking.

Persuading her that the ideal second date entails her slaving over a hot stove wasn't any harder than talking her into baking Dominic an edible invitation. Julie's more than willing to give him a second chance, and who knows? Maybe without the distraction of Maggie's presence—okay, and Charlie's—Julie and Dom might actually get to focus on each other this time.

Maggie mutters a satisfied "There," and tucks her papers back into her briefcase, zipping it closed.

"Find what you were looking for?" Charlie inquires.

"Yes." She looks anxiously out the window at the traffic crawling past. The streets of midtown are jammed, as always.

She pulls out a cell phone and begins to dial.

"Who are you calling?"

"My voice mail."

"At home?"

"No, in the office. I need to check my messages."

"You just left."

Ignoring him, she presses a series of keys, listens, presses more keys, listens again. She disconnects the call, puts the phone back into her pocket, and removes an electronic organizer from her bag.

Charlie watches her deftly use the stylus to enter information and wonders what the heck could be so important that it couldn't wait. In Charlie's world, few things—other than a column deadline, a ravenous appetite, and okay, a full bladder—can't be put off indefinitely.

After returning the Palm Pilot to the depths of her bag, Maggie checks her watch, then asks Charlie, "What time do you have?"

"I don't."

"You don't what?"

"Have the time." He lifts his arm to reveal his bare wrist.

"You don't wear a watch?" she asks, wearing an expression that says he might as well have told her he doesn't wear underwear.

"Rarely."

She just shakes her head and looks out the window again. He notices her right foot flexing against the carpeted floor, as though she's gunning an imaginary gas pedal.

"In a hurry?" Charlie asks her, amused.

"I'm always in a hurry."

"I rarely am," he returns, with a deliberately exaggerated leisurely stretch as he leans against the back of the seat.

"Where are you going now?"

"To play golf at Chelsea Piers."

"Sounds fun," she says tersely, sounding as though she'd rather jump into the icy Hudson River.

"Do you play?"

"No."

"I didn't think so."

Her eyes flare. "Why not?"

"Just a hunch. Something tells me golf isn't your sport."

"What does something tell you *is* my sport?"

"Oh . . . I don't know. Sky diving? Or horse racing. Lacrosse, maybe. Something fast-paced and dangerous, or cutthroat."

"I'm feeling insulted," she says, but she's smiling.

"Don't. I admire your energy." He yawns lazily. "I just can't relate."

"Really. Well, I can't relate to your . . . *relaxation*."

Azim pulls the car to a stop at a traffic light and flicks on the turn signal.

Maggie promptly leans forward and taps the driver's shoulder. "You're going across town here?"

"Yes, Miss."

"I think it would be better to go down a few more blocks. It's Fashion Week, and the garment district is jammed. And there's a show in Bryant Park this afternoon, so it's crazy over there, too."

Azim casts a dubious glance at Maggie, then at Charlie.

"It's fine. Go down a few more blocks," Charlie instructs him, then turns to Maggie. "Fashion Week?"

"You know—where all the designers show their clothes for fall? You should know about it."

"Why should I know about it? I wear the same thing every fall. Every winter, spring, and summer, too."

"That is so not surprising," she comments, flicking her blue gaze over his attire.

He sits up straighter in his seat, noting that her perusal isn't exactly unappreciative. Unless he's mistaken, Miss Silk-and-Pearls isn't entirely opposed to a man who favors the rumpled, lived-in look.

Meanwhile, rumpled, lived-in-Charlie finds himself surprisingly captivated by her buttoned-up tweed and silk—rather, by a startlingly vivid fantasy about what's underneath.

"You should know about Fashion Week," she says, with her uncanny ability to stay on topic, seemingly oblivious to whatever it is that's sizzling between them, "because you work for *She*, and it's a fashion magazine."

"I told you, I'm a freelancer. And I write about relationships, not fashion."

"Oh, right. Because you're much more qualified to write about relationships than you are fashion."

He merely grins and looks out the window as Azim slows the Town Car at an intersection, prepared to make the right-hand turn.

"Not here," Maggie pipes up. "Go two more blocks, and you should be able to sail across until you get to Seventh—then you'll want to turn down again and go down another two blocks and then cut over."

This time, Azim doesn't even bother to look askance at

Charlie. He simply follows Maggie's commands, and within moments, they're sailing across town, just as she predicted.

Charlie just stares at her, impressed, against his will.

She turns and catches him watching her. "What?" she asks, self-consciously rubbing her cheek. "Do I have newsprint on my face or something?"

"No, it's just . . . never mind."

She shrugs and stares back out the window, ostensibly thinking about the important meeting that lies ahead.

When, a few minutes later, Azim pulls up in front of a corporate building and steps out to open the door for Maggie, Charlie notes that her driving instructions were right on target—and can't help wishing they hadn't been. Not just because it would be nice to know that she isn't right about absolutely everything, but because he wouldn't mind prolonging the ride just a little bit longer.

Sharing a backseat with Maggie was more pleasant than he anticipated. Not, he reminds himself, that he anticipated that it would be the least bit pleasant.

"Thanks for the ride," Maggie says, poised to climb out of the car.

"No problem. Good luck at the meeting."

"Good luck with golf. And . . . everything."

"You, too," he says, noting—and hating—the finality of her wave and the car door's slam.

He wonders if he'll ever see her again.

Chances are, he won't.

Unless, of course, Julie falls madly in love with Dominic.

Stranger things have happened.

Gazing after Maggie as she disappears into the building, Charlie smiles to himself.

Yes, stranger things indeed.

"I win," Carolyn announces, holding out her hand, palm up, in front of Bindy as Maggie drops gratefully into a chair at their table in a crowded midtown cafe two hours later. "Pay up."

Bindy fumbles in her quilted Chanel bag and delivers a ten-dollar bill into Carolyn's hand.

"What was the bet?" Maggie asks, amused, reaching for a menu.

Bindy flashes her recently professionally whitened smile. "That you wouldn't show again."

"Guys, that's not fair. I tried to call you yesterday and tell you I couldn't make it, but neither of you answered your cell phones. And I couldn't help getting hung up at the office."

"Maggie, you get hung up at the office every day," Bindy points out.

"Yeah, no wonder you're so skinny," Carolyn says, with a wistful glance down at her own pudgy figure. "You never eat lunch."

"Well, I'm going to eat today," Maggie informs her, scanning the menu. "I just came out of a horrendous meeting and I'm starved and I have to go to a magazine party tonight."

"I thought they always have amazing food at those parties," Carolyn says.

"They do, but this one's for *Glamour*, and who can eat with all those supermodels around? So, what should we get?" When she and her friends lunch together, they tend to order several different entrees and share.

"We already ordered," Bindy informs her.

"You didn't wait for me?"

"I wanted to." Carolyn casts an *I told you so* glance at Bindy. "But . . ."

"But we both have to get back to work at a reasonable time," Bindy points out, sipping her glass of red wine. "And you're twenty minutes late, Maggie."

"I am n—oh, I guess I am," she realizes, checking her watch. "Sorry. I couldn't get a cab, and I had to change subways three times to get back over here."

I probably should have just canceled lunch again, she decides, scanning the menu. She's going to have to eat and run if she wants to make it back to the office with plenty of time to prepare for this afternoon's presentation.

When the waiter materializes with her friends' orders—a grilled lamb and spinach salad and a platter of grilled vegetables—she orders a turkey-and-sprout wrap and an iced tea and prays it won't take long.

"Are you sure you don't want to order a glass of wine?" Carolyn asks. "You look like you could use one."

"No, I have to have a clear head this afternoon. But after this morning, I could use one."

"Rough meeting?"

"No, the meeting was fine. It was . . ."

Charlie.

But her friends don't know about him, and it's far too complicated to explain.

Or is it?

"Can I tell you guys something?" she asks, toying with the edge of her blue cloth napkin.

"Sure. Have some lamb," Carolyn pushes the plate toward Maggie, who takes a bite. "Is it juicy?"

"It's a little dry," Maggie says, chewing and swallowing.

"Not the lamb!" Carolyn giggles. "I meant the thing you want to tell us. Is it juicy?"

"Or is it about work? Because your work stuff is always way over my head," Bindy tells her. As an executive assistant in an architectural design firm, she often says that her main duty is to look fabulous. Which she does.

Willowy, dyed-blonde Bindy is the polar opposite of Carolyn, who works as an acquiring editor in a small book-publishing company and looks the part, with her dark ponytail, glasses, preppy red wool cardigan, tights, and sensible shoes.

"It's not about work," Maggie tells them. "It's about a guy."

The moment the words are out of her mouth, she wants to snatch them back.

Too late.

"A guy?" Carolyn asks. "You mean a guy who's not Jason?"

"Tell me you didn't cheat on him," Bindy says.

"It wasn't cheating. Jason and I agreed that we could see other people."

"But you made it this far without doing anything."

"Bindy, she didn't say she did anything," Carolyn points out. "Right, Maggie?"

She clears her throat. "Right . . . but I didn't say that I didn't, either."

"Maggie!" Carolyn's brown eyes widen behind her glasses. "What did you do?"

"And with who?" Bindy asks.

"With *whom*," corrects Carolyn the editor.

"It was just a kiss," Maggie tells them quickly.

"Just a kiss?" Carolyn shakes her head. "That's more action than I've had in months. Who was he?"

"Just a guy I met."

"Just a kiss is never *just* a kiss; just a guy is never *just* a guy." Bindy makes a tsk tsk sound.

"Did you meet him at work?"

"No, not at work. Why would you think that, Carolyn?"

"Because work is the only place you ever go these days."

"Not true. I do lots of things. I go to the gym—"

"An all-female gym," Bindy points out, spearing a grilled baby carrot with her fork.

"And I shop."

"Like you're going to meet an eligible man in Ladies' Suits at Macy's," Carolyn says. "We're waiting, Maggie. Who is he, where did you meet him, and—"

"And why did you cheat on Jason?"

"I didn't cheat. A kiss isn't cheating."

"It is by my definition—unless it was a peck on the cheek?" Bindy asks hopefully.

Maggie shakes her head.

"You cheated, Mag."

Maggie is grateful when the waiter sets down her iced tea so that she can busy herself with the straw.

Which takes all of two seconds to plunge into the drink.

"Maggie . . . hello! We're waiting."

She has no choice but to look up at her friends' expectant faces.

"His name is Charlie, and he's a pain in the butt, so I don't know why the heck I kissed him."

"Is he a cute pain in the butt?"

"Very cute, in a sloppy kind of way."

"What do you mean by sloppy?" Carolyn asks as Bindy makes a face.

"You know . . . he needs a haircut, and he doesn't tuck in his shirt, and he's just . . . casual."

"What's wrong with casual?" Carolyn wants to know.

"Everything's wrong with casual," Bindy comments. "This is New York. People tuck in their shirts, and they cut their hair."

"To be fair, he's self-employed," Maggie says, feeling an odd urge to come to Charlie's defense. "So I guess it doesn't matter what he wears."

"It matters to me," Bindy tells her. "And it should matter to you."

"What does he do?" Carolyn asks.

"He's a writer."

Carolyn's face lights up. "Books?"

"No, magazine articles. A column, really. In *She*."

"You're dating Bachelor at Large?" Carolyn exclaims, with a chunk of grilled eggplant poised halfway between the plate and her mouth. "Charles Kennelly III?"

"You've heard of him?"

"I love his columns. And I've seen his picture—they print it every month next to his byline. He's gorgeous. I can't believe you're dating him."

"I'm not dating him!"

"She's dating Jason." Bindy is all business. "Or did you forget about him, Maggie?"

"Of course I didn't forget about him."

Not more than momentarily, anyway, while she was kissing Charlie.

"I think Bachelor at Large is much cuter than Jason."

"That's because you always go for artsy, self-centered, irresponsible types," Bindy tells Carolyn. "And look where that gets you."

Carolyn shrugs. She's had a mad crush on her across-the-hall neighbor, a long-haired musician-slash-waiter, for more than a year now.

"Just because Judd doesn't know I'm alive doesn't mean that all artsy types are self-centered or irresponsible. In fact, I read this guy's column in *She* every month. He's obviously capable of making a deadline, so he can't be all that irrespon—"

"Hang on, it doesn't matter whether Charlie's irresponsible or not," Maggie cuts in, "because I'm not dating him. I just met him once, kissed him, and ran into him again this morning."

"Where did you meet?"

"And where did you run into him?"

Maggie sighs. No choice but to spill the whole sordid tale, beginning with Dominic's blind date at the basketball game and ending with this morning's trip across town.

"And you were still attracted to him when you saw him again today, then?" Carolyn asks.

"No," Maggie lies.

"Yes, you were," Bindy says, "or you wouldn't be bringing it up to us."

"I shouldn't be bringing it up to you, because that makes it seem more significant than it even is. I guess I just needed to get it out of my system."

The waiter arrives with Maggie's turkey-spout wrap,

which she promptly pushes into the center of the table to share. She's lost her appetite, thanks, once again, to Charlie and his kiss. How easy it is to blame everything that's wrong in her life on that.

In fact, if Blair Barnett doesn't win new business after this afternoon's pitch, it will be all Charlie's fault.

She's not certain why, exactly . . . she just knows that it will be.

"Maybe you should kiss him again," Carolyn suggests, as Maggie nibbles a bite of her wrap. "Just to get him out of your system."

"He's out of my system," Maggie assures her.

"Well then, maybe you can kiss him again so that I can live vicariously through you." Carolyn's eyes are twinkling. "Maybe I need to get him out of my system, too."

"Maggie, you can't kiss him again," Bindy says. "You have Jason. He'll be back soon, and, anyway, you can bet he's not down in South America kissing people behind your back."

"Only because there's probably nobody to kiss down in South America," Maggie can't resist saying. "In his last e-mail, he said he's surrounded by malnourished children and worried mothers and poisonous jungle insects and snakes. It doesn't exactly sound romantic."

"Poor Jason." Bindy shakes her head. "When he gets back to civilization, he's going to be in the nesting mode. You just might find yourself with a ring on your finger, Maggie."

"Bindy! We haven't been dating that long. Especially not if you count the time he was away."

"Yes, but when it's right, it's right."

And when it's wrong, Maggie tells herself silently, giving the old heave-ho to a mental image of Charlie, *it's wrong*.

There comes a time in every guy's life when he falls for Ms. Wrong . . .

Charlie frowns, stares at the sentence, and deletes the words **falls for.**

After a moment's thought, he replaces them with the more benign **meets.**

There.

That works.

It works, but it's blah.

The sentence needs some zing. Something sexy. Something like . . .

Kisses.

Okay.

Kisses has zing, and *kisses* is accurate.

Now he's back on track.

There comes a time in every guy's life when he kisses Ms. Wrong, a woman who is the polar opposite of everything he seeks in the opposite sex.

Oops.

Can't use **opposite** twice in the same sentence.

Charlie deletes the second one, replacing it with **fairer.**

No, that seems old-fashioned. He can just hear Maggie snorting—not that her opinion, real or imagined, matters in the least.

But, he concludes, there's nothing fair about her, and she's a member of the opposite sex. Therefore, he must delete **fairer**—which he does—and restore the second **opposite** to the sentence.

Meaning, the first **opposite** has to go, instead.

Charlie deletes that, then scowls at the screen, wracking his brain, then the software's thesaurus, for a replacement.

He can't find one.

Opposite is the only word that will do.

Maggie, after all, is the *opposite* of everything he seeks in the *opposite* sex. Period.

Yes, and opposites attract . . . which was going to be the theme of this column.

Charlie shakes his head.

This sucks.

The column. His life.

Why is he wasting his time writing about a woman whose path will never cross his again? At least, not if he can help it.

But when it comes to Maggie, he can't seem to help a whole lot.

The best thing to do, Charlie decides, backspacing furiously to obliterate the entire useless sentence, is focus his thoughts—and his columns—on other things.

Now all he has to do is come up with something more interesting to write about—and do—than kissing Ms. Wrong.

Chapter Seven

First thing Saturday morning, Maggie and Dominic meet at the gym to play racquetball. Afterward, she insists on going home with him to assess his tuxedo for the date with Julie.

As usual, the Chickalini home is bustling with activity.

Ralphie is home from college, holding court at the kitchen table with some of his old friends—most of them long-haired, long-legged girls with thick Queens accents and thicker eye makeup.

Dom's sister Nina and her husband Joey are in the process of moving Nina's old bedroom set from her father's house to their daughter's room across the way, while their two children scamper underfoot.

Dom's sister Rosalee, a week past her due date, is wedged into a recliner in the living room with her swollen ankles elevated. Her husband Timmy is on duty at the firehouse but is having cell phone problems, and apparently calls in every twenty minutes or so to make sure he isn't missing the start of labor.

Only Nino Chickalini, the family patriarch, is absent—

presumably busy kneading dough in his pizzeria around the corner. Or maybe he just had to escape the craziness for a while.

What with the frequently ringing telephone, a constantly barking dog, hip-hop emanating from a boom box in the kitchen and blaring television in the living room, and alternately ecstatic and sobbing toddlers, the place is, as always, a hotbed of multigenerational domesticity the likes of which Maggie hasn't encountered since—well, ever.

Having long ago mastered resistance to the innate urge to organize the Chickalini madhouse and its wayward occupants, she's learned to go with the flow whenever she's here. This morning, she ultimately finds herself sprawled on the living room floor entertaining little Rose and Nino with a Jack-in-the-box to keep them from tripping their parents as they move various pieces of furniture and bedding down the stairs and out the door.

"What the heck is my brother doing upstairs?" Rosalee asks around a mouthful of dry Cap'n Crunch, the box cradled on what's left of her lap.

"Trying on his tux. He's wearing it tonight for his date."

"Again!" Rose squeals, clapping her hands as the puppet pops out of the box for the fiftieth time.

"He's wearing a tux on a date? Where's he going? A wedding?"

"No"—Maggie cranks the handle again—"his future wife is cooking dinner for him."

Rosalee's plucked eyebrows disappear into her bangs. "You found a wife for him?"

"Yup. She's perfect."

"He didn't even tell me. Who is she?"

Maggie plucks an escaping child off the gate that separates the living room from the entry hall, where Nina and Joey are attempting to wedge a towering bureau through the front door.

"Her name is Julie, and she's just what Dom needs," she tells Rosalee. "Sweet, all-American, a great cook, very homey. She'd fit right in here."

"Good. When's he bringing her home to meet us?"

"Ow!" Nina howls from the hall. "Joey, that was my toe."

"I don't know . . . maybe he should wait until they've been dating for a while," Maggie tells Rosalee, as Jack pops out of the box and Rose shouts, "Again!"

"This thing is never going to fit through the door," Joey is saying.

"It has to," his wife protests. "They got it in. There must be a way to get it out."

"Well, there isn't."

"Well, there must be."

"I want my big girl bedwoom!" Rose wails.

"Shh, honey, you're going to get it," Rosalee reassures her niece.

As Nino attempts to scale the gate, Maggie goes after him, smothering his chubby cheeks with kisses when he howls in outraged frustration.

"How about you, Maggie?" Rosalee asks, crunching more cereal and popping a few pieces into her niece's beckoning hand. "Is your boyfriend still off saving the third world?"

"Yeah, but he should be getting ready to come home soon."

"I don't know how you do it."

"Do what?" She sets a writhing Nino on his feet again. He promptly goes toddling back toward the gate.

"Keep a long-distance relationship together. I'd go crazy if I didn't see Timmy every day. I can't stand it even when he has overnight duty at the firehouse."

"See? It still fits," Dom announces, coming down the stairs in an elegant black cutaway.

"Where's the tie?" Maggie asks, obediently cranking the box for Rose.

"I have to wear the tie? Cripes, Maggie, come on."

"It looks stupid without a tie, Dom," Nina reports from her post beside the wedged bureau.

"See? Get the tie," Maggie tells him. "And the cummerbund."

"This sucks," he complains, trudging back to the stairway.

"It'll be worth it when you're happily married to the woman of your dreams."

"Do you really think she's the woman of his dreams?" Rosalee asks Maggie. "Somehow, I can't see my brother settling down."

"Oh, I think all men reach a point where they crave stability," Maggie tells her, even as Charlie Kennelly barges into her thoughts.

"Almost all men, anyway," she amends, wishing Charlie would stay the heck out of her head. Every time he shows up there, persistent as old Jack the puppet, she's reminded of the kiss that rocked her world.

"I remember when I thought Timmy would never reach that point," Rosalee confides. "He clung to his damned bachelor freedom for so long I almost gave up. Good thing I didn't." She pats her enormous tummy.

"Yes, good thing," Maggie murmurs, wondering . . .

No. Absolutely not. No way. Some members of the male species just aren't cut out for marriage.

With a weary smile, she watches Nino sizing up the gate again.

"And you're coming with me *why?*" Dominic asks, as he and Maggie ascend the subway steps on Saturday evening.

"To help you find Harcourt Street." She feeds her Metrocard into the turnstile.

Dominic does the same. "I can find it. I have a map, and I have Julie's directions. I told you I wrote them down word for word when I talked to her this afternoon."

"I know, but you're terrible with maps, and you're not so good at directions, either." Maggie, of course, happens to be good at following both.

They climb the steps to the elevated train line. The subway runs above ground in Astoria, dropping into a tunnel only as it approaches the East River and Manhattan. There's a spectacular view of the glittering Manhattan skyline from up here on the platform, which Maggie pauses to admire, as always, as she and Dominic stop to wait for the train.

"So what, you think if you don't hold my hand, I'll never get there?" Dominic asks, adjusting his bow tie. "Like I'll end up in the South Bronx or something without your help?"

"It could happen." She leans toward him and tweaks the end of the tie.

"What are you doing?"

"It was crooked. You look terrific in that tux, Dom."

"I still think I could have worn a nice sweater," he grumbles.

"The invitation said Black Tie."

"It said Black Tie optional. I *opted* for no black tie."

"But I—"

"What you opted should have had nothing to do with it, Maggie. I haven't been this uncomfortable since my sister's wedding."

"But you look great," Maggie assures him, taking in his dapper head-to-toe elegance. "All you need is a top hat, and you'll look like you should be riding around in a limo."

"Like our friend Charlie?"

The name slams into her, leaving her more breathless than the chill February wind does.

"Charlie doesn't ride around in a limo," she tells Dominic.

"How do you know? He said he had a driver."

"Yes, but it wasn't a limo. Not the stretch kind, anyway."

"And you know this because . . .? Oh, I forgot." He smacks his head with mock recollection. "You know it because you know everything."

"No," she says, resenting the implication, "I know it because I rode in the car with him."

"With Charlie's driver?"

"And Charlie."

"When?"

"The other day, after he delivered the cake to your office."

"You didn't tell me that."

She shrugs. "You didn't ask."

"It was supposed to occur to me to ask you if by any chance you were riding around town in Charlie's limo?"

"Not around town. Across town."

"Same thing."

"No, it isn't. Around town is joyriding. Cross town is—well, it's not for fun. It's just to get where you're going."

"When it comes to you, everything is about getting where you're going, Maggie."

She frowns. "What do you mean by that?"

"Just . . . you should loosen up. Like me. Or like Charlie."

Charlie again. Is he going to haunt her for the rest of her life?

"You know, Mag," Dom goes on, "I think someone like him would be good for someone like you."

"Someone like me?" she echoes. "What do you mean, someone like me?"

"Somebody who . . ." He trails off, catching sight of her expression. "Forget it."

"You know what I think?"

"No, but I'm sure you're going to tell me," he mutters, gazing up the track for the train.

"I think Good Time Charlie needs somebody like me around to keep him on the ball, make sure he doesn't slack off."

"Well, at least we're in agreement," Dominic says. "Look, there's the train."

Maggie steps back from the edge of the platform as the train's headlights bear down on them.

"We're in agreement about what?"

"About you and Charlie being a good couple. Maybe if Julie and I hit it off after tonight, the four of us can double-date."

"Are you out of your—"

The rest of her words are lost in the shrieking of the subway's brakes as it rushes into the station.

They can't get seats together, and it's just as well. Maggie isn't in the mood to talk to Dom about why she and Charlie are—or, more specifically, aren't—the least bit interested in being a "good couple."

At least, *she's* not interested.

Is Charlie?

She can't help remembering how he looked at her across the backseat the other day in the car. Almost as if . . .

Well, as if he wanted to kiss her again.

Maggie promised herself—and, more importantly, promised Bindy—that she won't go around kissing anybody other than Jason.

Since Jason's away, that means no kissing until he gets back.

Which means . . .

She rubs her lonely, disappointed lips. Celibacy is harder than she anticipated. Not that she anticipated it being hard before her path crossed Charlie's. Until that happened, she was caught up in work, in errands, in planning and taking her Caribbean vacation with her friends. Even at the island resort, she wasn't tempted to stray.

Of course, that might have been because Carolyn inadvertently booked the three of them into a "family" vacation spot rather than one geared toward singles—a mistake the unwillingly unattached Bindy has yet to for-give.

Maggie and Dom ride the subway all the way down to the Village.

Maggie does her best to read the paperback she brought along, but she can't focus. She keeps thinking of things she wants to tell Dominic before he gets to Julie's place. Just pointers he should follow if he wants to win her over.

And he must . . . or he wouldn't be here. He'd be out on the town with that buxom dancer he met on the subway. Not that he said she was buxom, but Maggie knows. All of Dominic's handpicked dates are buxom.

Bored with her book, Maggie wonders whether, after she leaves Dominic off at his Harcourt Street destination, she should head up to The Strand to look for livelier week-end reading material. After all, an entire Saturday night and Sunday stretch emptily before her.

Too bad Bindy went skiing for the weekend with her sister, and Carolyn is on an editorial deadline. Maggie wouldn't mind having somebody to kill some time with.

She meets Dominic on the platform at the designated stop, only to find that his tie is once again askew.

"Stop touching it," she instructs him, as she straightens it again.

"I can't help it. It's strangling me."

The terrific thing about New York, Maggie notes, is that nobody gives them a second glance as they proceed along the platform and through the tunnel toward the exits, despite the fact that she's wearing jeans and sneak-ers and he's in a tux, and despite the fact that every few feet, she stops to manhandle him into keeping his hands off his bow tie.

"Enough already, Mags," Dom howls, swatting her away like a bug.

"I just want you to look handsome."

"I always look handsome."

True. He does.

"You know, a little humility would be a good idea," she tells him. "You might be great-looking, but don't forget that you have to work to win Julie's heart, Dom. She's not the kind of girl who's just going to take one look at you and fall swooning at your feet. If she were, she'd have done that already."

"Yeah, yeah, yeah. Whatever, Maggie. I know how to win a woman's heart."

"I don't think you do. Otherwise, you'd have settled down by now."

"Maybe I'm not ready for that."

"But you said you were."

They climb a flight of stairs toward the exit.

"No," Dom corrects her, "you said I was ready to settle down."

"But you agreed."

"True." He shrugs. "I thought I might be. But maybe . . . I don't know. Maybe Julie's a little too much on the wholesome side for me."

"Dom, that's ridiculous. Wholesome is good for you." That came out all wrong. It sounds like she's advertising a new cereal, for Pete's sake.

She opens her mouth to try again, but before she can get a word in, Dominic says, "Look, Mags, all I know is I'm going to go over to Julie's place and have some home-cooked chow and get to know—"

"Chow?" She rubs her temple wearily. "Dom, what-

ever you do, when you're with Julie, don't call food chow.
You're not an animal."

"Mags, leave me alone, will you?"

"I'm trying to help you."

He sighs heavily. "Which exit do we want?"

Women. Can't live with 'em, can definitely live without 'em.

Rereading the column's opening line for the fifth time
since he wrote it, Charlie nods. Good. This is a good
premise. A strong opening. A nice twist on the old cliché.

Clichés need a twist, he reminds himself, fingers
poised over the keyboard. That's why that Opposites Attract column opening didn't work the other day.

After all, everybody knows opposites attract.

Nobody knows that men are capable of living without
women.

But Charlie is going to tell them.

Warming to his subject, he types, **Until recently, the notion of lifelong bachelorhood was as quaintly archaic as . . .**

Okay, as what?

What is quaintly archaic?

Charlie brainstorms.

Chastity belts? Dowries? Hope chests?

Nah. Those are all quaintly archaic, but they conjure
feminine images. He isn't writing about women. He's
writing about men *without* women.

He rereads the opening yet again and sighs.

This isn't working.

What he wants to say is that in this day and age, plenty
of men willingly and contentedly stay permanently unattached.

That there's nothing wrong with—'or unusual about—a

perfectly attractive, red-blooded, heterosexual man remaining single for the rest of his life.

Okay, if he believes that, why is he having such a hell of a time writing it?

He's burnt-out. He's wasted too many hours today, working on that stupid piece of fiction—or whatever it is—about the fictionalized Maggie character.

What he needs is a break. A change of scenery.

He closes the document and pushes back his chair, remembering too late that he forgot to hit SAVE.

Oh, well.

That column idea was crap, anyway. Who is he to make social commentary based on nothing but his own quirky existence?

Charlie isn't riding a revolutionary wave of millennial bachelorhood. He's foundering in a sea of self-doubt.

Hmm . . .

That's an interesting column idea. Charlie as drowning man; Maggie as life raft . . .

Oh, please. Quit while you're ahead.

Taking his own advice, he makes his way to the door.

Maggie and Dom emerge on the street and walk west, according to Julie's directions and the map. By Maggie's calculations, they'll be at Julie's apartment building in less than ten minutes, which means she has to work fast.

"Listen, Dom, whatever Julie cooks for you tonight, make sure you have seconds."

"What if I don't want seconds?"

She smirks. "You always want seconds."

"Not if I don't like something."

"I'm sure you'll like whatever Julie cooks. She's a chef."

"A pastry chef. And one who doesn't eat meat."

"You don't know that for sure."

"Yes, I do."

"How?"

"I asked her on the phone. She's a vegetarian."

"Well, that's good," Maggie tells him, once again playing up the *wholesome is good for you* angle. Where Julie's concerned, it seems to be unavoidable. "It means she cares about her health and about animals."

"It means she's probably going to make something out of tofu and serve it to me. I hate tofu."

"It's—"

"Good for me. Yeah, I know. So are a lot of things I don't like," he says darkly.

Maggie rolls her eyes. "You're not going into this with the right attitude, Dom."

"Sure I am. I just happen to be a meat-and-potatoes kind of man."

"Well, you can skip the carnivore thing just for one night. Trust me, you'll survive. And while we're on the subject of your date, whatever you do, don't sleep with her."

"Why not?" He frowns. "She doesn't have some kind of disease, does she?"

"Of course she doesn't have a disease!"

"Are you sure? Have you seen her medical records?"

"Do you demand the medical records of every woman you date?"

"No, but . . . why wouldn't I sleep with her if she's perfectly healthy and perfectly attractive and perfectly willing?"

"Because it's too soon. You don't sleep with somebody on the second date."

"Sure you do."

"I don't."

"Well, I do," he says with a shrug.

"Maybe that's part of the problem."

"I don't consider it a problem, Mags."

"What I mean is, maybe that's why you haven't found the right girl yet. Maybe you keep choosing women who are too . . ."

"Slutty?" he supplies.

"Exactly. I would never sleep with somebody on the second date, Dominic, and I'm willing to bet that Julie won't either. But if she wants to—"

"Then why not take her up on it? I mean, if she's slutty, then she's not marriage material, according to you, so why not have a little fun? Especially since I went to all the trouble of putting on a tux. I might as well—"

"Whoa, keep your tux on, Bub," Maggie warns him. "You'll be glad you did."

"I doubt that," he mutters.

"And speaking of your tux, you can loosen your tie and take your jacket off as the night goes on, but don't roll up your sleeves, and don't take off your shoes."

"Why not?"

Maggie makes a face. "Because smelly feet aren't romantic."

"Who says my feet are smelly?"

"I do. Trust me, they are. And look, there's her building." She points across the street at a small brick apartment building that matches Julie's address. There's a pizza place on the first floor, just like Julie described.

"Okay, well, thanks for walking me over," Dom says with a wave, starting across the street.

"Don't you want me to come inside with you?" Maggie asks, falling into step at his side.

"No!" He looks horrified.

"I don't mean upstairs. I just mean I could walk you to the elevator."

"What am I, five? I can manage on my own, thanks, Mags." They've reached the front of Julie's building. "I'll call you tomorrow and let you know how it went."

"Make sure that you do. And call me before nine, because I go to mass then."

"Before nine on a Sunday morning?" He snorts. "I'll call you after noon, when I get up. I went to church this afternoon. Have a good night, Mags. Got any plans?"

"I, um . . . no."

For a moment, he looks as though he feels sorry for her.

"That's the way I like it," she assures him. "This was such a brutal week at work that all I want is to unwind with a cup of tea and a good book."

"Well, have fun."

"I will." She waves, watching him stroll into the lobby and speak to the doorman.

She takes a few steps away, turns to look over her shoulder, and notices that Dominic's conversation with the doorman seems oddly prolonged.

Maggie frowns and double-checks the address.

Is this the wrong building?

No, number twenty-one—it matches what's written on the piece of paper Dominic handed her earlier, but . . .

Who knows? Maybe he wrote it down wrong or something. Maybe it's really twelve.

Maggie steps into the warm lobby.

Both Dom and the doorman look up at her.

"What are you doing in here, Maggie?" Dom asks, looking incredulous.

"Just checking to see why you aren't on your way up yet." She glances from Dom to the doorman to the small television set tucked into a corner of the lobby. A college basketball game is in progress on the screen.

"Syracuse is playing, and I was checking the score," Dom tells her, clearly put out. "I'm going up in a minute."

"Why not now?"

"Because there's only a minute left in the quarter."

"Dom—"

"Maggie, go."

"All right, all right, I'm going."

She pushes through the doors out into the brisk winter wind once again. The warm smell of pizza wafts from the restaurant next door, making her mouth water.

It wouldn't hurt to stop in for a slice, would it?

She only had a cup of vegetable soup for dinner, and anyway, she played racquetball this morning and took a spinning class this afternoon at the health club. She can afford a few extra calories.

Besides, what else does she have to do?

You can have willpower and keep walking.

She inhales the savory air again.

Willpower on a Saturday night . . . that's no fun.

Irked by her lack of self-control, she decides, *I'll go in, but I won't get pizza. I'll just get the cold antipasto salad and a bottle of spring water.*

But when it's her turn to order, she finds herself asking for two slices with sausage and extra cheese and a bottle of Bud, unable to stave off a fierce and sudden craving for cold beer and spicy meat.

What is with me tonight? she wonders. *Where's my self-discipline?*

The pizzeria is bustling on this Saturday night. Mostly with NYU students and cozy couples, with a few young families sprinkled into the mix. Maggie sits in a corner facing the window and wonders how it's going with Dom and Julie upstairs.

He's only been there ten minutes. They're not even past the pleasant introductory chitchat phase of the date.

The early stages of a relationship are so hard, Maggie thinks, as her order arrives. So hard, but so exhilarating—if it's the right person.

You'll never have a first date—or a second date or a third—ever again, she realizes with a start. *Not if Jason is the right person for you.*

If he's the right person, she's already made her way out of the dating world.

Well, good. It wasn't all that great in the first place—going out, hoping to meet somebody, meeting somebody, hoping he'll call . . .

She can live without the turmoil. Her life is fulfilling enough as it is. And Jason . . . well, he's everything she always wanted.

Growing up on the farm, she fantasized about men like him—well-educated, well-heeled city men. Men who were really going places and would take her along for the ride.

But you're going places, too, she reminds herself now. *You don't need to ride anybody's coattails. You'll be media director in a few years, and after that, maybe move over into ad sales, where the money is. Then you'll never find yourself alone in some run-down pizzeria on a Saturday night.*

She eyes the beer, the sausage, the heap of melted cheese, thinking that anyone who didn't know better might conclude that you can take the girl out of Wisconsin, but you can't entirely take the Wisconsin out of the—

"Maggie?"

She looks up, startled by the sound of her name in this strange place.

"Charlie?"

Joy flits through her—utterly inappropriate joy, but undeniably real.

"What are you doing here?" To her own ears, her voice sounds more ecstatic than dismayed.

Maybe to his ears, too, because he plops down across from her in the booth. "Picking up my lunch."

"Lunch?" She checks her watch. "At this hour?"

"Okay, dinner. Whatever. I usually stay up until the middle of the night and sleep until noon, so this is lunch for me."

That *so* figures, Maggie thinks.

Aloud, she says only, "What I mean is, what are you doing here? Why aren't you . . . uptown? Or downtown? Or a borough?"

In other words, why, of all the places there are for him to be in the country's largest city, did he have to walk into this pizzeria? Does he have some kind of extrasensory instinct that allows him to home in on her territory, like a pesky fly perpetually crashing the same picnic?

"I live upstairs."

Okay, so maybe not *her* territory, but still . . .

"You live upstairs?" she echoes. "With Julie?"

Funny. She could have sworn Julie said she lived alone in a studio.

"No, across the hall from Julie. We're neighbors. And I eat here five nights a week, at least, so—are you wearing *jeans?*"

He stoops to look at her legs under the table, then pops up again to say, "You *are* wearing jeans. And sneakers."

"And that's significant because . . . ?"

"Because I didn't know you had it in you. Every time I see you, you look like you should be posing for a Talbots catalogue."

"Well, those were weekdays. What did you expect? Did you think I went around in skirts and pumps on Saturdays?"

"Absolutely." He bends over again to look under the table, then tells her, "You look pretty good in jeans. Like a whole new person."

He's trying to get your back up, Maggie tells herself. *Don't fall into his trap.*

She forces herself to calmly and politely say only, "Thanks."

He glances down at her plate. "How do you like the pizza?"

"It's good. Not as good as it is at Dominic's father's place, but close."

"What did you get on it? Did you get the mushroom?"

He peers at her remaining slice. "You should have gotten the mushroom. It's the best. They're marinated or something, and spicy."

"I got sausage. With extra cheese."

His eyes widen. "You're kidding."

"No," she informs him, "I'm not."

She wants to take a bite, but he's watching her so closely she feels uncomfortable. Part of her wishes he would just pick up his order and leave, and another part of her wishes . . .

Stop that! she scolds her inner self. *You don't want him to stay and eat with you. That would be awkward.*

"Mind if I stay and eat with you?" asks Charlie the mind reader.

"Um, well, I'm almost done, but—sure. Sure, that's fine."

After all, telling him not to stay would be rude, wouldn't it?

"Good. Thanks. My apartment tends to close in on me when I've spent the entire day in it, writing."

"Are you working on a column?"

He hesitates. "I'm supposed to be, but . . . I keep getting distracted."

"By what?"

"I'm not . . . sure. I think it's a short story. Or an essay. Or maybe a book."

"You're not sure?"

"I didn't plan to write it," he tells Maggie, looking—embarrassed?

"What do you mean?"

He shrugs. "It's just something that popped out and took over my life these past few days."

"What's it about?"

"I don't like to talk about works-in-progress," he says. "Especially not this one. Is that your beer?"

"Yes."

"It looks good. I ordered some, too, but I'm dying of thirst now. Mind if I have a sip?"

"Er—no."

She watches him tip the bottle back against his lips. He takes a drink, then hands it to her.

He seems to be waiting for her to drink, so she lifts it to her mouth, conscious of the fact that it's almost like kissing him by proxy.

Okay, it's nothing like kissing him at all, but she seems to have Charlie and his lips on the brain again.

She plunks the bottle onto the table and sees that one of the counter guys is approaching with a pizza box and a six pack.

"Your order's set, Charlie," he says. "Sorry about the wait."

"No problem, Dan. I'm going to eat it here."

"You found a friend?"

Dan smiles at Maggie, who feels compelled to say, "We're not friends, really . . . we just, um, met. Our friends are, uh . . ."

"Julie's computer match is a friend of Maggie's," Charlie tells Dan smoothly.

"Oh, yeah, she's cooking that dinner for him tonight, right?"

"Right."

Dan nods and waves, saying, "Let me know how that goes."

As he walks off, Maggie asks Charlie, "You told the pizza guy about Julie and Dom?"

"He's like family," Charlie tells her. "It's no big deal. He knows Julie. She's in here all the time."

"Oh."

Maggie finds herself envious, and she isn't quite sure why. Being a regular at a pizzeria is certainly no big deal. She's a regular at Big Pizza Pie, Dom's family's place in Queens.

But . . .

This is different.

There's something about Charlie—some casual sense of belonging, of fitting in wherever he happens to be—that makes her wonder what it would be like to be a fixture in his world.

It would probably be fun. Fun, in a decadent way. You probably wouldn't accomplish much, if you spent your days with Charlie.

"What are you thinking about?" he asks.

Maggie realizes he's watching her, and looking fascinated for some reason.

"I'm just wondering how you ever get anything done."

"What do you mean? I've been working all day."

"But not on your job, right? On something totally different. It just seems like you get distracted pretty easily."

"Not that easily. And anyway, what's wrong with that? It's better than being chained to a desk twelve hours a day, five days a week."

"If you're referring to me, I'm not chained to my desk. I love my job. It's diverse, and exciting, and—"

"Inflexible," he says around a mouthful of pizza. "I don't see how that doesn't bother you."

"Not being able to drop everything on a whim and drift off to do something that strikes my fancy? Trust me, it doesn't bother me in the least."

At least, it didn't until right now.

Charlie makes her sound like an uptight stick in the mud.

"No wonder you don't believe in marriage," she tells him.

"Huh? Who told you that?"

"You did. The night we met."

"Oh. Well, I don't."

"That's what you said. And I'm not surprised. I mean, if all you want to do is pick up and go wherever you want whenever you want with whomever you want . . . well, you should never get married."

"Trust me . . . I never will. I like living my life on my own terms. No rules. No nagging. No schedules."

"Everybody needs structure and responsibility," she informs him, hating that she sounds like Miss Engleberger, the spinsterish second grade teacher at Green Corners Elementary, but unable to help herself. She resents his assumption that his freewheeling lifestyle is the norm and hers is—well, abnormal.

"Everybody also needs spontaneity and freedom."

"But not all the time."

"Exactly."

"I'm perfectly capable of being spontaneous and free," she informs him.

"Really?" Looking less than convinced, he takes another bite of pizza. Then, his eyes light up and, without waiting to finish chewing and swallowing, he says abruptly, "I have an idea."

Uh-oh.

"What kind of idea?"

Something tells Maggie that it involves her proving her spontaneous and freedom-loving alter ego.

"Wait here. I'll be right back." He jumps up and heads for the door.

"Where are you going?" Maggie calls after him.

"To make a phone call. I need to check something. Just don't go anywhere."

"I have to leave," she says, more to herself than to him.

But only because he's already gone.

I really should get home, she decides, checking her watch. It's already eight-thirty, and she's going to church first thing in the morning, and—

And you really do need to get a life, she concludes, feeling oddly restless. *Just because your boyfriend happens to be away doesn't mean you have to live like you're confined to a convent.*

She'll wait until Charlie gets back, then she'll get out of here. Maybe she can stop at The Strand and pick up a good book to read when she gets home. Or at Blockbuster, for a video. Or even both. The night is still young.

Woohoo, she thinks flatly. Some weekend. Books, videos, and church.

It's almost tempting to throw caution to the winds and see what Charlie has up his plaid flannel sleeve.

No. That wouldn't merely be throwing caution to the winds, it would be sailing a rowboat into a category-five hurricane.

There's simply no denying that Charlie gets under her skin in more ways than one. Yes, he grates on her nerves, but he also makes her heart beat a little faster every time she catches him looking at her like—

Like he wants to kiss her.

God, she hopes the expression isn't mutual. For all she knows, he can tell at a glance that she's still attracted to him.

If she knows what's good for her, she'll blow out of here before he even gets back.

No. That would be rude. She should at least wait and tell him good-bye.

With a sigh, she reaches for the remainder of her second slice of pizza and washes down a big mouthful of gooey cheese and sausage with a gulp of beer.

Mmm.

The thing is . . .

Sometimes, things that aren't good for you are pretty damned hard to resist.

She spies Charlie's distinct cocky swagger at the door, and her heart skips a beat.

Taking a deep breath, she steels herself against another pesky wave of attraction.

Whatever you do, don't let him talk you into anything stupid, Maggie.

Chapter Eight

"Come on, Lucky Seven!" Maggie bellows, as the roulette wheel clicks into motion. "Let's go, Lucky Seven!"

Charlie grins, rubbing his sore right arm. That he persuaded Maggie to hop on a chartered private plane to Atlantic City was a miracle in itself. She had a million excuses, all of them countered by reasonable arguments on his part.

She agreed to his proposition only after he assured her that he did this sort of thing all the time and that his trust fund was more than adequate to cover the extraordinary—in her opinion—expense. He also had to promise to teach her how to gamble; promise to provide her with a hundred dollars—and no more—in gambling funds; promise to depart Atlantic City the moment she lost it; promise to have her home in plenty of time for early mass if she didn't lose it promptly.

Of course, he also had to provide her with his private pilot Adam's credentials, a complete rundown of the small plane's safety features, a meteorological forecast that proved there was no freak blizzard in the offing, and the guarantee that he would from this evening on stop accusing her of being a fuddy-duddy.

Considering all of those rules and regulations—and the fact that she spent much of the plane ride down the Jersey coast staring out the window wearing a grim expression of resignation—he never expected her to have this much fun once they got here.

But the past few hours have unleashed a side of Maggie that he never imagined lurked beneath that oh-so-civilized exterior. Even in her jeans, sneakers, and wool sweater, she exuded a certain sophisticated inaccessibility. And even on the plane, she was the quintessential back-seat driver, venturing into the cockpit more than once to speak to Adam.

But once they landed, she deferred to Charlie, who had arranged for a black stretch limo to take them directly to the row of casinos lining the snowdrifted boardwalk.

Maggie is a quick learner. All it takes are a few pointers before she is winning at craps and poker, smacking him on the arm every time she wins. He'll have a nice purple bruise by morning.

As for Maggie, her dark pageboy is tousled from all the jumping around she's done, her cheeks are flushed, and her voice is getting hoarse from shouting "Hit me" at the blackjack dealer at the previous casino.

Then again, he probably should have guessed that gambling would be right up her competitive, winner-takes-all alley. She's good at it, too—up a few hundred bucks and the wheel is click-click-clicking to rest on . . .

"*Seven!* All right, *seven!*" With a shriek, she launches herself into Charlie's arms.

Nearly knocked off-balance by the human rocket, he

steadies himself and grins, looking down into her ecstatic face.

"Did you see that, Charlie? I won. I won!"

"I saw. You did. You won!"

Her excitement is contagious; his heart is racing, and his knees are feeling a little wobbly.

Or maybe it's not excitement sweeping over him at all. At least, not the kind that comes from winning at roulette.

It takes a few moments for her joy to subside. Charlie spends them trying to get hold of himself, trying to remember that they're here in Atlantic City together only so that he can prove a point.

What is that point again?

Oh, yes. That she needs to learn to lighten up and live a little.

Not that he, Charlie, is the man she's been searching for all of his life, and that Maggie—at least this new and improved version of Maggie—is the woman he's been—

"Let's try something new," she interrupts his disconcerting thought process in that throaty voice that doesn't sound the least bit like her own.

That sexy timbre, Charlie concludes, is why it's so easy for his subconscious mind to initially misinterpret her words.

Because when she continues, "I'm thinking slots," extracting herself from his arms and looking around the casino, it takes a moment for him to process the information.

Slots?

She's thinking slots?

Oh. Of course.

He was thinking . . . well, what he was thinking was far riskier than anything the casino has to offer.

"Come on, Charlie." She grabs his sore right arm and hauls him away from the roulette table.

He finds himself wishing she'd drag him right into the adjoining hotel lobby, book a room, and have her way with him.

"Do I need quarters for the slot machines?" she asks, surveying her fistful of chips.

"I have quarters." He produces a roll from his pocket.

"I'll pay you back."

"Stop saying that."

"But I want to pay you back," she says. "I never expected you to just hand me a hundred dollars to gamble away. When I said that I thought—"

"You thought I'd conclude that you were a mercenary wench who only wanted me for the Kennelly fortune?"

"Who says I want you at all?" she shoots back with an impudent jerk of her chin.

A few hours ago, her words might have wounded him. But now her blue eyes are alight with flirtatious mischief and a gleam that tells Charlie she does want him, whether she realizes it or not.

It's enough to make him pull her against his chest, and say, low, in her ear, "I say you want me. And I say it's mutual."

She gasps when he says it, and again when he leans toward her face. But the moment his lips meet hers, any hint of protest evaporates. Her mouth melts into his, and she kisses him back, matching his passion with unexpected fervor.

Then she pulls back, looking a little dazed, to glance

around, and say, "I think we should find the slot machines."

"I think you should quit while you're ahead," he advises her.

And so, he reminds himself, should he.

But Maggie isn't the kind of woman who willingly heeds unsolicited advice.

No, she's the type of woman who greets unsolicited advice with some of her own:

"I think you should be quiet and let me decide how to run this show."

"But—"

"Look, Charlie, I agreed to this crazy scheme of yours. As long as we're here, let me have some fun."

"You've had nothing but fun since we got here, Maggie. At least, that's how it seems to me."

"The night's still young," she retorts, and plows her way over to the nearest slot machine.

Charlie has no choice but to grin and follow her, making room in his pockets for her winnings.

"Who would ever think that plain old bacon and eggs and white toast with grape jelly could taste this good?" Maggie asks around a mouthful of the very breakfast she secretly detested every morning of her life on her parents' farm.

"Who would ever think that it wouldn't?" Charlie asks, devouring a strip of bacon.

"I would," Maggie confesses, her voice still hoarse from hours of joyful squealing and hollering at the pit boss. "I don't think I've had eggs in five or six years. At least, not fried. Omelets, maybe. And hard-boiled in spinach salad. But not plain old sunny-side up."

"Why not?"

She shrugs. "I got sick of them. When I left Wisconsin, I never wanted to see another egg. It was my job to go out to the henhouse at the crack of dawn to gather them."

Charlie shakes his head. "Somehow, I can't picture that."

"What? Me up at the crack of dawn?"

"Well, actually, you are now, but . . ."

Maggie checks her watch, marveling that it's the first time she's bothered to do that since the digital date rolled over to Sunday. Startled by the time, she glances out the hotel restaurant window—the first transparent glass they've encountered since they set foot in the casino about seven hours ago.

Upon their arrival, Charlie told her that casinos don't have windows so that people won't be aware of time passing. They'll just keep playing, and playing, and playing, forgetting all about the world beyond the casino doors.

At the time, Maggie thought that was a ridiculous notion, wondering how anybody could be irresponsible enough to lose track of time that way.

Who would have guessed that she herself could fall victim? Or that she'd just keep winning . . . and winning . . . and winning?

Charlie called it beginner's luck. Maggie calls it the Harrigan intuition, which has never come in handier than in Atlantic City.

Whatever the case, Maggie figures she'd probably better not return anytime soon. Not if entire evenings evaporate in the blink of an eye. Gambling until dawn with a man she vowed to avoid certainly isn't the most productive—or wisest—use of her time.

Now she's captivated by a glimpse of the sky over the ocean, etched with streaks of pinkish coral light. It's not the first sunrise she's seen since she left the farm—not by a long shot. But it's the most beautiful.

"Let me guess—you get up at dawn every day?" Charlie asks, generously buttering another triangle of toast.

"Pretty much," she informs him. "I like to jog along the river when it's nice out. And I like to get to the office early when I'm in planning, to get a jump start on my day. And when I fly, I always take the first flight of the morning. That's the best way to avoid delays. I can't stand waiting around airports."

"Yeah, I'll bet. Anyway, imagining you up at the crack of dawn wasn't the thing I couldn't picture, Maggie. It's the farm part—you know, the whole henhouse scene—that I just can't fathom."

Wondering if she should be insulted, Maggie finds it difficult to muster her usual Charlie-inspired antagonism.

She says only, after a sip of coffee, "I guess that's just as hard for you as it is for me to picture you born with a silver spoon in your mouth."

"But I wasn't."

"What about the trust fund?"

"The money came later," he says. "When I was born, my parents were trying to raise four kids in Brooklyn on a middle-class income."

"You grew up in Brooklyn? But I thought—"

"My father made his first killing in the market right around the time I was taking my first steps at my first birthday party. He missed that."

"Your first steps?"

"And the party. And every other milestone I had. When my mother insisted on moving to the suburbs because the schools were better, he kept an apartment in the city so that he wouldn't have to commute. He didn't want to waste two precious hours a day on the train, let alone more hours a day on us."

"So he didn't even live with you full-time?"

"He didn't live with us at all by the time I turned three. He left my mother—and us—because we didn't fit into his business plan."

"I'm sorry." Maggie reaches across the table to touch Charlie's hand. "That must have been hard."

"Yeah." He looks down at his cup of coffee, stirring it purposefully although it must be lukewarm by now, and he hasn't added cream or sugar. "He was completely out of my life—and my sisters' lives—until I was just about grown. My mother always said he was an all-or-nothing kind of guy, so I guess he felt that if he couldn't give us everything, he wouldn't give us anything. At least, not when it came to his time. His money, we had."

Maggie thinks about her own father, who never missed a first step or a school play or an appointment with the tooth fairy, much less years' worth of birthdays and Christmas mornings and graduations and weddings. To think that she used to be embarrassed when he showed up in the school auditorium in his threadbare clothes with soil caked under his nails, flashing that wide Irish grin that revealed the broken front tooth he could never afford to have fixed.

She swallows a bitter lump in her throat along with a mouthful of tepid coffee and promises herself that she'll call her parents later, just to say hi. She doesn't do that often enough these days, what with her hectic work schedule and the time change and their early-to-bed, early-to-rise lifestyle . . .

"Would you like more coffee?" the waitress asks, materializing with a copper-colored plastic carafe and a world-weary smile.

Charlie looks up expectantly at Maggie, who shakes her head. "I'm fine."

Normally, she doesn't turn down a java refill. Her busy days are generally fueled in part by a liberal caffeine dosage. But the coffee is subpar here compared to the gourmet beans she favors, and anyway, despite having been up all night, she's feeling strangely energized.

"We'll just take the check," Charlie tells the waitress. He looks at Maggie. "Should I page Adam?"

She glances out the window again, where the sky is growing brighter by the minute. "You know what I'd like to do before we leave?"

"Hmm?"

"Take a walk on the boardwalk. Or the beach."

He glances dubiously out at the winter landscape and the wind-whipped surf. "Are you sure? You're not really dressed very warmly."

She shrugs. "I'll use part of my winnings to buy a hat and mittens and scarf for each of us before we go out. I wanted to stop in the gift shop anyway to get some lozenges for my throat."

"Maybe you shouldn't go out into the cold, then. You don't sound so good."

"Well, I feel fine. It's not like I'm sick. Come on, Charlie. I grew up landlocked, and I never get to the beach even now that I live on the East Coast."

"I thought you said you had a share in the Hamptons last summer."

"I did, but it was a half share, and I had to work on two of my weekends, and it rained on two others. I never got my fill of the ocean."

"Well, I hope you're not planning to dive in now, because I can't guarantee I'll go in after you if you get a leg cramp."

She laughs. "I promise."

"Here you go, sir," the waitress says, depositing the check in front of Charlie.

Maggie reaches across the table to grab it as she departs.

"What are you doing?" he asks, snatching it out of her reach.

"Since you keep refusing to let me give you back your gambling money—even the original hundred—I'm treating you to breakfast."

"No, you aren't."

"Yes, I am. It's the least I can do. Give me the check, Charlie."

"No."

"Yes."

He shakes his head and reaches into his pocket for his wallet.

Maggie glares at him, Harrigan temper flaring. "I want to pay."

"Why?"

"Because . . . I just do."

"Well, I want to treat you."

"You just treated me to a private plane ride and a night out on the town, Charlie. And anyway, it's not like this is . . ."

She trails off, suddenly uncomfortable.

"It's not like this is what?"

"You know . . ."

"No, I don't," he says, but she can tell by his expression that he does know. He's daring her to go ahead and say it.

Never one to turn down a dare, Maggie takes a deep breath and she does. "It's not like this is a date, Charlie."

For an endless few moments, he's silent, but his gaze never wavers from hers.

She forces herself not to look at the window, or at her empty coffee cup, or the few crumbs she left on her plate.

"Really? It's not a date?" he says at last. "Because it sure felt like a date back there in the casino when you were kissing me."

"When *I* was kissing *you*?" she asks incredulously. "Try switching that around."

"Uh-uh. I might have thrown the pass, but you grabbed it and ran with it."

She folds her arms indignantly. "That's absolutely—"

True.

You know it's true, Maggie. You kissed him back, and you enjoyed every minute of it. You didn't want to stop, and if you hadn't suddenly remembered that you were in the middle of a public place, you sure as hell wouldn't have.

"You're saying you didn't kiss me back?" Charlie asks.

"Maybe I got caught up in the moment," she admits.

"But that was obviously a big mistake. I don't want you to think that tonight is anything other than what it is."

"Yeah, well, I've got news for you. Tonight is this morning—"

"You know what I mean."

"Yeah, I know what you mean, but—"

"And just because I kissed you doesn't mean you can go around thinking that—"

"I hate to break it to you, Margaret, but in this country people are free to go around thinking whatever they want."

Exasperated, she grabs her jacket off the back of the chair, and says crisply, "Go ahead and call Adam, Charlie. I need to get home in time for church."

"Not yet. I promised you a walk on the beach, remember?"

"Well, you weren't crazy about that idea in the first place. And anyway, I changed my mind."

"Well, so did I," he says with a maddening glint in his eye. "Come on. Let's hit the beach."

There's something exhilarating about sea air, even in the dead of winter, Charlie concludes as he and Maggie stroll along the beach.

That is, *he* strolls.

Maggie's idea of a stroll is to stride a dozen paces ahead of him, stopping every so often to look over her shoulder and call over the wind and surf, "Are you coming?"

The sand is scattered with icy snowdrifts left over from the last storm, and the air has to be below freezing this morning.

Charlie is grateful for the knit cap and gloves she bought for him in the hotel gift shop. She bought some for herself, too—only they didn't have gloves for women; only red mittens. From a distance, she looks like a little girl in them, Charlie thinks, smiling as he watches her pause to look out at the horizon.

The February sun is more milky than golden, and the sky more gray than blue. There's a speck out on the horizon; some kind of boat or ship, Charlie surmises.

Maggie turns to look back at him. "Wouldn't it be great to be out on the water on a day like this?" she calls raspily.

"I don't know—it's not exactly pleasure cruise weather," he tells her, reaching the spot where she stands and half-expecting her to start walking again.

She doesn't, just shields her eyes with her hand and gazes at the sea.

"I don't mean a pleasure cruise," she tells him, bending and picking up a smooth, flat rock. "I mean sailing across the ocean to Europe, or Africa. Wouldn't it be exciting?"

"Sure," Charlie agrees, having been to Europe and Africa many times—but always via an airplane. His thoughts stray to the unused tickets to the French Riviera. In a few more weeks, they'll be as useless as the diamond engagement ring Laurie still has.

"Have you ever been abroad?" Maggie is asking as she hurls the stone into the ocean. It skips four times. "Wow, did you see that? Four skips."

"Nice," he comments, bending to pick up a stone of his own as he answers her question. He's beginning to notice that it's impossible not to multitask when you're with Maggie. "Yes, I've been abroad. How about you?"

"No, never. I never even had a passport until last

month. The only time I ever left the country was to go to Jamaica a few weeks ago."

"With Jason?" He skips his stone. Three times.

"No." She looks startled by the mention of his name, and pauses a moment to skip another stone—this time five times—before adding, "I went with a couple of friends of mine."

"Female friends?"

"Of course, with female friends," she says, starting to walk again.

"Well, it could have been with Dominic. He's a male, and he's your friend." He falls into step beside her, determined to keep up this time.

"He and I could never travel together," she says with a dismissive wave of her red mitten.

"Why not?"

"He'd drive me crazy. I'd probably have to do everything for him, from packing his luggage to reminding him to wear sunscreen. And he'd never want to do anything but sit in a chair on the beach with rum drinks."

"Sounds pretty good to me."

"Yeah. It would."

"Well, isn't that what you did in Jamaica?"

"Sure . . . but not the entire time."

"What else is there to do there?"

"Loads of stuff."

"Like . . . ?" He's picturing her following the hotel maid around showing her a more efficient way of organizing her cart.

"I climbed Dunn's River Falls a few times and I toured a couple of museums and a sugarcane plantation and I snorkeled and sailed and went horseback riding and did a lot of shopping in the markets."

"And you still had time to sit on the beach with a rum drink?"

"Of course."

"And your friends kept up with you?"

She shrugs. "Not the entire time. I did some stuff alone." She pauses. "Okay, I did most of that stuff alone."

"Weren't you lonely?"

"Alone and lonely aren't the same thing, Charlie," she informs him.

"You're right. They're not." After all, he spends his work days in solitary seclusion and is never the least bit lonely. But growing up in a household filled with women—and a father who never showed his face—well, that was loneliness.

They fall silent, walking along the beach.

Charlie mindlessly keeps up with her this time, his thoughts on his difficult childhood, where they often seem to stray.

Growing up in an all-female household was certainly easier for his sisters than it was for him. They didn't seem to miss much about not having a father, except when the annual Dad and Daughter dance rolled around at school. But an uncle or a neighbor—or later, their stepfather, Art—always stepped up to the occasion. For the most part, Deborah and Candace and Anita emerged from those fatherless years unscathed.

Not Charlie. Not only did he lack a father, but he might as well have had four mothers. His sisters fussed over him when he was little and drove him crazy as he grew up. Their inherent bossiness untempered by a paternal voice of reason, they were forever on Charlie's case, nagging and nudging and nosier, even, than Mom.

Then there was the whole sports thing. He was on the baseball team and the basketball team, but Mom firmly vetoed football, hockey, and lacrosse even when all his friends were playing. She said those sports were too violent and dangerous.

Charlie always felt that if his father had been around, he could have overridden that maternal veto—along with countless others. Worst of all was his mother's refusal to let him get his learner's permit when he turned sixteen. She was spooked by a tragic fatal car accident involving a couple of boys from his school and didn't allow Charlie to learn to drive until the summer before college. She only relented because his stepfather was in their lives by then and talked some sense into her.

"What are you thinking about?" Maggie asks Charlie, touching his arm.

"Bossy women," he admits without hesitation.

She frowns.

"I'm not talking about you," he tells her.

At least, not this time.

"Then, who?"

"Long story. Forget it."

She looks like she's going to protest—then, to his surprise, nods and changes the subject to speculation about how many people would be on this beach at this hour in the height of July.

Charlie's relieved. He doesn't feel like being pressed for details on his past.

Laurie thrived on getting him to talk about it. She was

very into therapy and believed in discussing just about everything ad nauseum. Especially the past.

And the future.

Back before they got engaged, she was on a mission to get him to commit. The moment the ring was on her finger, the wedding was planned right down to the first song to which they would dance as husband and wife, and the color of bow tie on Charlie's tuxedo—neither of which was a decision that allowed for any input from him.

Now that the dust has had months to settle, he's grateful that he's not on the cusp of his first wedding anniversary with Laurie. He's not even certain they'd have made it this far if she had gone through with the wedding.

Like Laurie said when she left him, Charlie just isn't cut out to be a husband. He's too selfish, too independent, too sloppy. He isn't capable of changing—at least, not as far as Laurie is concerned.

His friend Butts told him he'd heard that Laurie's seriously involved with a Wall Street type. Charlie isn't surprised about that. In fact, the only thing that's surprising is that he isn't the least bit jealous. He's long over being angry and hurt by Laurie's rejection. Thank goodness one of them had the guts to call off the wedding before it was too late.

"Thanks, Charlie."

Startled, he looks over to see Maggie smiling up at him, and he realizes they're back on the deserted boardwalk.

"Thanks for what?"

"This night. And the morning. I hate to admit it, but it was just what I needed."

"Why do you hate to admit it?"

"Because . . ." She hedges, biting her lower lip.

"Because . . ."

"Because you were right," she says at last, not meeting his gaze. "I do need to be more spontaneous. My life has been so rigid lately that I forgot what it was like to do something on a total whim."

Stunned that Margaret-Know-It-All-O'Mulligan has actually deferred to him, Charlie fights the temptation to gloat.

He merely shrugs, and says, "You should do it more often."

"Come to Atlantic City?" She frowns. "I don't know. I think I could be a dangerously compulsive gambler, Charlie. I have an addictive personality. If you hadn't dragged me away from that last craps table, I might have started to lose."

"Yeah, well . . ." He shrugs, then finds himself stifling a yawn.

Maggie yawns, too. Loudly.

They've come full circle, he realizes.

They're right back at the spot in front of the restaurant entrance, where they began their journey as the sun was coming up.

Now it's climbing in the sky, and it's time for Charlie to page his pilot for the trip back home. Unless . . .

"I don't suppose you want to stick around here for a while longer?" Charlie asks.

"And do what?"

He brushes a strand of windblown hair back from her eyes. "I don't know . . ."

We could get a hotel room . . .

But he doesn't dare say it.

She yawns again.

So does he.

"We should get back," she says.

"We should."

But neither of them moves.

He welcomes the wind that blows her hair into her eyes again and the chance to stroke her cheek gently as he brushes it away again.

"Thanks," she says.

"You're welcome."

He leans closer; her eyes flutter closed.

He kisses her.

"We shouldn't be doing this," she murmurs against his mouth.

"No," he agrees, "We shouldn't."

He kisses her again, pulling her up against his chest, frustrated by the layers of denim and wool that separate their bodies.

"We should go," she tells him, when he forces himself to pull back again.

"Where?" he asks, knowing full well what she means.

They should go . . .

Back to the city.

They should go . . .

Their separate ways.

They should go . . .

"Someplace warm," she whispers, shivering a little.

"We can do that."

She yawns again. "Suddenly, I'm so sleepy."

So is he. Too weary to fight off his attraction to Maggie.

"Should we go someplace?" he asks, knowing full well what he's really asking.

Maggie hesitates, then nods.

"Where?" he asks, just to be sure. After all, the restaurant will be warm. So will the plane. Maybe that's all she meant.

"Do you think we can get a hotel room?" she asks, and his heart launches like one of Maggie's pebbles skipping into the surf.

He gestures at the towering luxury hotels along the boardwalk, his casual attitude belying the thundering pulse and giddy fantasies that have taken over. "I don't think there's a shortage of places to stay, do you?"

"No, I meant that it's morning, Charlie. People check out of hotels at this hour, not into them."

"This is Atlantic City. You can get anything you want at any hour." He pulls her closer, scarcely daring to ask, "What do you want, Maggie?"

"The same thing you do, I think," comes the reply.

This time, Maggie's the one who initiates the kiss, and this time, it's more intoxicating than the last.

"Let's go," he says finally, wrapping an arm around her shoulder and walking her toward the nearest hotel.

Maggie drops onto the king-size bed and sinks back against the pillows with a sigh.

"This feels so good, I could close my eyes and drift right to sleep."

Through half-closed eyes, she watches Charlie deadbolt the door and walk over to the window.

"Hey, don't go to sleep yet," he says, sitting in a chair and bending to take off his sneakers. "Wait for me."

"Mmm," she says, closing her eyes and smiling.

She has every intention of waiting for him. Those kisses on the beach stirred something to life deep within her; she has no intention of trying to quell the increasingly urgent need that's been building from the moment she agreed to stay here with him.

How shockingly easy it is to forget everything else. Just like in the casino—it's as though somebody blocked out all the windows in her mind so that she won't accidentally glimpse a reminder of where—and who—she's supposed to be.

For the first time in her life, there are no shoulds. For the first time in her life, right here, right now, is all that exists for Maggie. Right here, right now . . .

With Charlie.

She opens her eyes to gaze at him—just in time to see him turn his shoe upside down and pour sand onto the carpet.

"Charlie!" she scolds, and he looks up guiltily. She can't help laughing at his expression.

He looks for all the world like a little boy who's just been caught smearing grape jelly on the piano keys.

"I can't help it," he says. "They're full of sand."

"There's a wastebasket two feet away."

"Yes, but there's also a vacuum-cleaner-toting maid who's going to get a big fat tip from me."

This, Maggie thinks—or rather, the old Maggie would have thought—would potentially be a major obstacle, were she considering any kind of relationship with Charlie. She has a zero tolerance policy when it comes to lazy sloppiness.

But the new Maggie—the Maggie who also happens to

have sand in her sneakers, in the dead of winter, no less—
is somehow merely charmed. And anyway, this new Maggie has other things on her mind—like what's going to
happen when Charlie leaves the chair and the shoes and
the sandy rug behind.

For her sake, apparently, he deposits the contents of his
second shoe into the plastic-lined wastebasket, then gives
her a smug look.

"Nice work," she says with an approving smile.

"I thought you'd like that. I'm not a total slob, you
know."

"Glad to hear it."

Should she be this relaxed? This casual? It's as though
they've done this a hundred times before when the truth
is, they've never even been alone together in private until
this moment.

Seeing Charlie walk to the window, she asks impatiently, "Now what are you doing?"

"Closing these." He fumbles around in the heavy
brown brocade drapes for a moment before he finds the
cord. The drapes rattle closed, plunging the room into
darkness.

Maggie hears him padding across the floor; feels his
weight sinking the mattress beside her as the bedsprings
creak.

"Where are you, Maggie?"

"I'm here," she whispers softly, and his hands encounter her shoulder. He pulls her close.

His lips graze her hair, her cheek, her mouth.

He breaks off to ask, "Are you okay?"

"Very okay."

Her hands wander into his hair as he nuzzles the hollow at the base of her throat. Twining her fingers through his thick locks, she wonders how she ever could have thought he needed a haircut.

When his mouth slides over to the sensitive valley beneath her earlobe a little moan escapes her. How on earth does he know exactly where to kiss her, exactly how to do it?

He rolls away only long enough to undress himself quickly, rustling fabric and clanking his belt buckle in the dark before he sinks down beside her once again.

Her breath catches in her throat when her wandering fingers encounter broad, naked masculine shoulders leaning over her. She wishes, briefly, that he had left the curtains open so that she could see what he looks like this way. Then his hands slip beneath her sweater, followed by his hungry mouth, and all coherent thought vanishes from her mind.

Maggie's clothes fall away piece by piece until she's naked in his arms, yet craving closer contact still. She quivers with impatient need as Charlie trails over her exposed flesh with gentle fingers, caressing lips, a warm tongue. He's everywhere—everywhere except the intimate spot where she needs him the most.

Just as she thinks she can't wait another instant, he pulls back, bedsprings creaking as he rolls away abruptly.

She cries out in dismay.

Chuckling softly in the dark, he whispers, "Relax, Maggie, I'm not going anywhere."

"Then what are you . . ." She hears him fumbling on the nightstand, realizes he's hunting for his wallet, comprehends why.

Only then does a flicker of indecisiveness dart through

her. For one wild-eyed, frantic moment, she wants to tell him to stop, to forget it.

Then she hears the telltale tearing sound and the distinct crinkling of latex unfurled.

When he leans over her again, kissing her neck, she pulls him close. There's no turning back now; nor does she want to.

She wants only this. Only him.

Her name escapes his lips on a sigh as he sinks into her; then again, with a second thrust, on a gasp of pleasure.

She clings to his shoulders, riding wave upon wave toward an elusive destination.

"Maggie," he grinds out as his movement crests within her, sending ripples of pleasure to sweep her home at last.

Finally, he collapses beside her, pulling her across his chest and the quilted hotel bedspread over them both. Gradually, their frantic panting subsides and passion ebbs, leaving in its wake sleepy contentment.

Maggie's last thought, before she drifts off, is that she has only one regret: that sooner or later, reality is bound to intrude once again.

Chapter Nine

"Hey, where were you?" Dominic demands, sticking his head into Maggie's office at twenty after nine on Monday morning.

She looks up from the latest issue of *Mediaweek*, which she doesn't usually allow herself to read until the subway ride home.

Monday mornings typically start off with a bang. She likes to be in the office before eight, delving into her work and a light breakfast simultaneously.

Today, however, she's in the mood to ease into the work week—with frequent breaks for daydreaming about Charlie. She arrived an hour past her usual time, and instead of picking up a low-fat yogurt to eat at her desk, she bought a Krispy Kreme donut.

All right, *two* Krispy Kremes—and they were worth every last finger-licking sugar-glazed calorie.

"I was out getting another cup of coffee," she innocently informs Dominic, lifting the steaming cup from Starbucks.

Today, instead of her usual traditional blend with skim

milk, she found herself ordering the mocha. *Not* skim. *With* whipped cream. It was so good she had to run down the street a few minutes ago to get a second one.

"No, not just now," Dominic says. "I meant where were you yesterday."

"Oh . . . that." It's impossible to keep a tiny smile from playing on her lips as she sips her coffee.

"I tried to call you all day. Didn't you get my messages?"

"I did . . . but I got home too late to call you back."

"The first time I called, it was Saturday night. The last time I called, it was ten o'clock last night. On a Sunday," he adds for effect.

"Right." She smiles pleasantly.

"So you're saying you were out?"

"That's what I'm saying."

"Till when?"

"I think it was around one or two this morning when I got in," she says cheerfully.

He peers suspiciously at her.

"You don't look exhausted."

"That's because I'm not exhausted."

She slept better yesterday, in Charlie's embrace, than she has in ages. They woke up once, in midafternoon, long enough to make love, order outrageously expensive, outrageously fattening fried chicken and mashed potatoes from room service, eat, and make love again. Then they slept well into the evening, leaving Maggie refreshed for the short plane ride home.

When she crawled into her bed and set the alarm, she never expected to fall soundly to sleep, but the next thing she knew, she was waking from a bizarre and semierotic dream about Charlie.

In it, they were lounging naked on the deck of a yacht on the Mediterranean, warm sunlight beaming down from a blue summer sky. The erotic part of the dream involved sun-bronzed skin and tanning oil; the not-so-erotic part involved a chicken that kept squawking around the deck, laying more eggs than any chicken is capable of laying in a lifetime. Maggie kept telling Charlie she should go collect the eggs, but he kept kissing her, distracting her. Pretty soon a storm rolled in and the yacht was bobbing on whitecaps and eggs were rolling everywhere, cracking, breaking, oozing . . .

And then Maggie woke up.

The dream has been on her mind ever since.

Sometimes, when a dream seems particularly relevant, she jots down notes upon awakening, lest the details slip away as the day progresses. When a dream is as vividly spicy as the one about Charlie, notes are superfluous. The steamy—and the strange—details have been flitting in and out of her consciousness all morning.

"Are you on drugs or something?" Dominic asks, still watching her.

"No! Why?"

"You look different. More . . . I don't know—mellow."

"Really?" She shrugs. "Well, I guess the weekend did me a world of good." She waits for him to ask her where she was, wondering how much of the truth she'll admit when he does.

But he doesn't ask.

He paces the few steps it's possible to pace in her

cramped office, and says, "I know why you avoided my calls."

"You do?" How the heck does he know? Can he tell just by looking at her that she spent a decadent weekend in Charlie's arms?

He nods. "You heard about what happened with Julie, right? What, did she call you?"

She gasps, pressing a hand to her mouth.

How could she have forgotten?

How could she *and* Charlie have forgotten? In all the hours they spent together, the subject of their friends' second date somehow never came up.

"No, Julie didn't call me, and I have no idea what happened," Maggie tells him, reminding herself that she has a vested interest in Dom's budding relationship with Charlie's friend. She's supposed to be overseeing every detail of the courtship, not launching one of her own.

"Well? How did it go Saturday night, Dom?"

"From bad to worse," he says darkly.

Uh-oh.

"We had a fight."

"A fistfight?" she asks, in a weak attempt at humor.

Really weak.

He doesn't even crack a smile. "You know what kind of fight I mean."

"Well . . . what was it about?"

"Meat."

She waits for elaboration.

When it doesn't come, she echoes, "Meat?"

"Yes, meat," he says impatiently, as though she should have known. "I knew this was going to happen. I told you she was a vegetarian."

"But Dom . . . what happened?"

"She cooked me a steak."

"Oh. Well, that's . . . that's good, right?"

"When I told her how I like it rare, she acted like I expected her to slaughter a cow on her kitchen floor."

"She wanted to cook it well-done?"

"She didn't want to cook it at all. It was obviously torture for her even to handle red meat. When I told her to take it out of the broiler after two minutes, she made this face . . ." He shakes his head, obviously disgusted.

"You can't blame her for that, Dom."

"It's not just that. I asked her to try it—you know, just take a little bite. I don't see how anybody can resist filet mignon. But she wouldn't."

"Well, she's a vegetarian! She doesn't eat meat. Not because she doesn't think she'd like it, but probably . . . you know, based on principle."

"Whatever. She took one look at the blood running out of my meat and accused me of being a murderer."

"*What?*"

"I'm not kidding. She was crying and everything, saying something about feeling like an accomplice to murder."

"That's a little extreme," Maggie admits.

"She's a nut job," Dom tells her flatly. "I can't believe you thought she was right for me. I mean, wholesome and healthy is one thing, but this was—do you know what she was planning to have for her dinner?"

"What?"

"Weeds."

Maggie shakes her head. "*What?*"

"You heard me."

"She was going to smoke weed?"

"No. She was going to *eat* weeds."

"Huh?"

"She threw a bunch of weeds into a pot and cooked them."

"Actual weeds?"

"That's what she said when I asked her what they were. She tried to force them on me, but I told her she was crazy. I mean, what is she, a goat? That's what I told her. I said, 'Animals graze on grass. Humans eat real food.' "

"Like animals."

"No, animals graze on grass, humans—"

"Eat animals. Real food. Right?"

"Right! That's exactly what I mean. How come you understand me and she doesn't have a clue? Am I that complicated?"

Maggie shakes her head, biting back a smile.

"What?" Dominic asks. "You think this is funny?"

"I don't. Trust me, I've got other things to worry about, Dom."

"Like what?"

Like the fact that when Charlie deposited her on the doorstep of the two-family house where she lives in Queens and asked to see her again, she agreed. He wanted to know which night, but she's got several business parties to attend this week and wasn't sure when she'd be free without looking at her schedule. He's supposed to call her this afternoon.

Why did you agree to that? Why didn't you just say thanks for the memories and leave it at that? Why didn't you remind him that you have a boyfriend? Hell, for that matter, why didn't you remember that you have a boyfriend?

Jason.

Jason, Jason, Jason. Perfect-for-Maggie Jason.

She closes her eyes, trying to conjure his face, but seeing only Charlie's.

You've got to stop this. You can't go sneaking around with him, acting as though nothing matters but being with him. He's distracting you from your work, and you're losing sleep—okay, not really, but that will eventually go with the territory with a guy like Charlie. . . .

"Are you sure you're not on drugs?" Dominic is asking.

Her eyes snap open. "Of course I'm not on drugs. What are you talking about?"

"You look like you're sleeping."

"I'm not sleeping. I'm thinking."

"About why you got me into this computer dating mess in the first place?"

"No, but . . ." She frowns. "I didn't exactly twist your arm, Dom. You agreed to do it."

"You did so twist my arm," he protests. "You literally twisted it, dragging me over to Matchmocha, Matchmocha every day. You know what? I can find women on my own. I don't need some computer, and I don't need you to tell me what to look for."

"You can find women on your own," Maggie tells him, "but not the right kind of women. Not the marrying kind."

"Who says I want a wife?"

"You did. And I do. You need a wife, Dom. You love to be taken care of. You need a woman like Julie, who knows how to cook and bake and sew and do all of the things you'd expect your wife to do for you."

"I'd expect my wife to know how to cook a steak," he counters. "I'd need a wife whose idea of fine dining doesn't involve a grassy meadow."

"Dom—"

"I'm finished with Julie, okay?" he says, heading for the door. "I never want to see her again, or hear about her again. Okay?"

"Okay."

The problem is . . . Maggie has a feeling she's not finished with Julie's friend Charlie. Not by a long shot.

By Monday afternoon, Charlie still hasn't a clue what his next column is going to be about, but his fictionalized Maggie piece is twenty pages longer than it was before Atlantic City. It's not a short story, and it's not an essay— that much is certain. Defining what it *isn't* is much easier than defining what it *is* . . . or what it may become.

Breathing life into the character he created is more compelling than any literary challenge he's faced to date. She has taken on a three-dimensional depth that leaves him wondering what she'll do next, where his journey with her will lead. It's as though the character is in charge and he, Charlie, is merely the scribe elected to chronicle her thoughts and actions.

For whom, he has no idea.

He's never written anything for his eyes alone.

When he was young, he wrote stories and verses for his mother and Miss Furnell, his favorite teacher. In high school and college, he wrote love poetry for girls he dated. Ever since, he's written for his editors and his readers.

But this . . .

Well, this piece doesn't need an audience. Which means it's a colossal waste of his time, something Maggie—both real and fictional versions—would decry as perhaps the ultimate sin.

He's in the midst of a well-deserved break—sprawled on the couch in his sweatpants and his thinking hat, munching Fritos and guzzling Pepsi, thoroughly enjoying Tom and Jerry on Cartoon Network—when somebody knocks on his door.

Thanks to the building's security system, only two people are capable of knocking on Charlie's door without being buzzed upstairs first: the super and Julie. Since the super rarely ventures away from his television in the midst of *General Hospital*—and since *General Hospital* is on right now—it's safe to conclude that Charlie's knocker is Julie.

"Come in," he calls, having left the door unlocked earlier, when he went out for the papers.

"You forgot the bolt again," Julie chides him, materializing in the doorway wearing her chef's whites and clutching a white paper bag.

"I didn't forget. I just didn't bother."

"Laziness can be an open invitation to an ax murderer, Charlie."

"What are the chances that an ax murderer would happen to try my door today, Julie?"

"It's unlocked all the time."

"Right, and I'm still alive. Do you actually think that an ax murderer goes around the city trying doors, hoping to find one that's unlocked?"

"I hope not, because if that's the case, your days are numbered."

Charlie grins and holds up the bag of Fritos. "I'd hate to think this is my last meal. Want some?"

"No, thanks. I brought you this." She hands him the white paper bag.

"What is it?"

"Day-old apple turnovers from the restaurant. Listen, Charlie, we need to talk." She plops down on the couch next to him.

"About what?" He trades the corn chips for a big mouthful of flaky apple turnover.

"Saturday night," she says simply.

His jaw drops. "You know? Who told you?"

"Know what?" she asks, looking puzzled. "And you're chewing with your mouth open. Close it."

He actually wasn't chewing at all, just staring at her with a sodden lump of apples and pastry on his tongue. Apparently, news travels faster than he thought. He hasn't told another living soul about his fling with Maggie—or the fact that he's seeing her again.

He chews, swallows, and tries again. "You know about . . . Saturday night?"

"*What?*" She looks blank.

Okay, clearly, she doesn't know.

Clearly, something else of earth-shattering significance happened while he and Maggie were falling for each other in Atlantic City.

Clearly . . .

"Oh! I forgot all about your date!" he realizes. "You and Dominic . . . how was it?"

"He's a psychopath."

"A psychopath?" Okay, that's not good. "In what way?"

"In the usual psychopathic way," she says tartly, sounding nothing like her sweet and sunny self. "I can't believe you left me alone with him."

"What did he do?" Charlie asks, alarmed. "Did he hurt you?"

"There are bloodstains all over my white silk blouse and my beige Berber rug," Julie informs him, "and if you don't think I'm going to be sending him the dry-cleaning and carpet-cleaning bills—"

"Bloodstains? Julie, what the hell happened? Did you call the police?"

"No, but I called my shrink. I haven't had to see her since before Jean-Louis, but this pretty much pushed me over the edge. I swear, I don't think there's a normal man left in New York, Charlie."

"I'm normal."

She appears to be considering the hat, the Frito breath, the apple pastry crumbs, the cartoons.

"Not to be mean, Charlie, but not really," she says, adding diplomatically, "At least you're not psychopathic like *him*."

"What the hell did he do?"

"He chased me around my apartment trying to stuff a hunk of meat down my throat, that's what he did."

"You mean . . ." He swallows hard. "Julie . . . did he rape you?"

"No! Geez, Charlie, I'm talking about filet mignon."

Like that makes it any better? Okay, it does, but . . .

Charlie doesn't know whether to be outraged or incredulous, so he settles for a bit of both. "My God! Was he trying to kill you? Or . . ."

Or what?

What earthly reason could a man possibly have for chasing a woman around trying to stuff a hunk of filet mignon down her throat?

"Who knows?" She shrugs. "He just went crazy. One minute I was cooking him dinner, and the next, he was shouting at me like a madman, with blood dripping from his mouth."

"But . . . whose blood?"

"The cow's blood. From the steak *you* insisted that I cook for him, instead of a nice vegetable lasagne like I wanted to make."

Charlie shakes his head, trying to clear it.

"So this is my fault?" he asks Julie. "Trust me, he wouldn't have liked your vegetable lasagne. Even I don't like it, and I like everything."

She gasps as though he slapped her.

"I'm sorry, Julie . . . it's just that lasagne should not be green, and it shouldn't have spinach and tofu in it."

"Who says?"

"I say. And I'm sure Dominic says. I mean, he's Italian. If you served him lasagne, he'd be expecting regular white noodles and regular red sauce with meat and sausage. Not . . . vegetables. Yich."

To his dismay, Julie bursts into tears.

"Julie, what's wrong?"

"You're taking his side!"

"What? I am not. I'm not taking any side. I don't even know what happened."

"I told you, he chased me. He tried to stuff bloody meat

down my throat." Her shoulders are heaving with sobs. "He . . . he told me I had to learn to eat animals and like it."

"He said that?"

"In so many words." She sniffles loudly. "And he made fun of me, Charlie. He made fun of my dandelion and collard greens saute. And he . . . he . . ."

She trails off, crying too hard to go on.

Charlie shifts the pastry to the opposite hand and pats her back. "It's all right, sweetie. What else did he do?"

"He called me a . . . he called me . . ."

"Calm down." He strokes her shuddering shoulders. "Deep breaths, Julie. Come on. In . . . out. Good girl."

She sniffles.

"What did he call you?"

"A sheep." She goes off on a fresh gale of tears.

"He called you a *sheep?*" Charlie is seething now. "How dare he?"

"I don't know," she wails. "I don't look like a sheep, do I?"

"No! Of course you don't look like a sheep." He strides to the bathroom to look for tissues, finds that the box is empty, and returns with a wad of toilet paper.

He hands it to her, and she blows her nose and wipes her eyes.

"Julie, I'm so sorry. I can't believe I set you up with such an insensitive clod. I picked him out because I thought he was an old-fashioned guy, not . . ."

"He is an old-fashioned guy," she says glumly. "A Neanderthal man. You can't get any more old-fashioned than that."

"Well, I'm going to talk to him," Charlie decides, standing. "He can't get away with this."

"Charlie, you can't! What if he . . ."

"Chases me around with meat? Calls me a sheep? Trust me, Julie, I can take anything he has to dish out."

"But—"

"Don't worry, Julie. You just go get your blouse and your rug."

"My . . . my rug?"

"Never mind, I'll go get it. How big is it?"

"Five by seven."

"Good. I can carry that."

"Carry it where?"

"Didn't you say it has bloodstains on it because of Dominic?"

"Yeah, but, Charlie—"

"I'll take care of everything," he assures Julie, heading for the door.

Striding out of the elevator on the account management floor, Maggie tells Dominic, "I still think that we need to convince the client not to put all that money into Prime. Cable is a better option for the new launch."

"But you heard what Ted said, Maggie," Dom replies, inserting his card key and holding open the glass door into the reception area. "They don't want—what the—?"

He breaks off, comes to a sudden stop just in front of the receptionist's desk.

Puzzled, Maggie looks from Dom's horrified expression to the receptionist's apologetic one to the object of everybody's attention.

Charlie.

Charlie is standing in the reception area, wearing sweats and sneakers and some kind of ridiculous hat, a rolled-up carpet balanced over his shoulder like a Minuteman's musket.

He may be oddly dressed for a corporate setting in midafternoon, but that matters very little, considering that Maggie instantly undresses him with her eyes. Winged creatures flutter in the pit of her stomach, too persistent to be gentle butterflies.

Sunday in the hotel room comes back to her in all its decadent glory, and she realizes that despite her earlier intention to slow things down, she wants nothing but full speed ahead when it comes to Charlie.

"Mr. Kennelly is here to see you, Dom," the receptionist says efficiently, only her wavering smile betraying her perturbation.

"Charlie . . . what are you doing here?" Maggie asks, going over to him.

And why is he here to see Dom and not her?

"The cake was delicious," Dominic says with a smirk, offering his hand to shake Charlie's. "But a rug . . . really, it's too much."

Charlie ignores Dom's hand, depositing the rug at his feet with a grunt, then reaching into the pocket of his sweats for a wadded-up white object.

"Here"—he thrusts it into Dom's outstretched hand—"that's for you, too."

"What is it?"

It's a woman's silk blouse, Maggie realizes. And it's covered in some kind of . . .

"Bloodstains," Charlie says curtly, addressing only Dominic. "Have them removed and the blouse returned to Julie by the end of the week."

"What? You've got to be . . . she's the one who dropped the meat!" Dom tells him.

"She dropped it? I don't think so."

"Okay, she didn't exactly drop it, she just . . . she spit it out all over the place. I had nothing to do with that. I didn't—"

"You didn't chase her and force-feed it to her?"

"No!" Dom looks at Maggie. "Are you hearing this, Mags? Do you believe this crap? He thinks I chased Julie and shoved meat down her throat? What am I, some kind of lunatic?"

"That's exactly what you are," Charlie tells him. "Julie said—"

"Don't you want to hear what I have to say?" Dom cuts in.

"Not particularly," is the reply.

Dom glowers, then storms away.

"Where are you going? You forgot the rug," Charlie calls after him.

"You know what you can do with that rug?" Dom's last few words are unintelligible, but the meaning is made clear by his parting gesture.

Maggie looks at Charlie, who until now has ignored her presence.

"Hey, babe," he says with a smile. "How's it going?"

What?

Babe?

And . . .

He's suddenly going to act as though what just happened didn't just happen?

Befuddled, Maggie says, "What are you doing?"

"Come get a cup of coffee with me, and I'll give you a heads up. Julie says your friend is off his rocker."

"Really?" Temper flaring, she tosses her head. "Then I guess the feeling's mutual, because Dom said the same thing about her."

"What, exactly, did he say?"

She gives him a capsulized account of Dom's version of the nightmarish date. But it's a struggle to stay on topic when all she wants to do is hurl herself into his arms and ask him when they can be alone together again. She wants to tell him that she got an invitation to the party *She* magazine is throwing next week, and she wants to ask him if he'll be there—or if, maybe, they can go together.

She's staring at his mouth, remembering the magic it was working on her just twenty-four hours ago, when she sees it moving and realizes he's talking to her.

It takes a moment of mental backtracking to figure out exactly what those luscious lips are saying—and when she does, it doesn't matter how luscious they are, because she wouldn't allow them to touch her again if he were the last bachelor in New York and she were totally available. Which she isn't—and he isn't, though he has every intention of becoming just that—and she'd be wise to remember it from here on in.

"How dare you call me a liar?" she snarls at Charlie, who merely shakes his head in a maddeningly noncommittal *if the shoe fits* kind of way.

"You're saying that you believe Julie and you don't believe me?" Maggie asks.

"I'm saying that I believe Julie, and I don't believe Dom, and if Dom's where you're getting your information—and obviously, he is, since I know you didn't witness the scene because you were off creating an alibi with me—"

Stung, she cuts in, "Is that what you call it? Creating an alibi?"

"No, Maggie, come on, don't be mad at me. This doesn't have anything to do with you. Or me. Let's stay out of it."

"It's a little late for that." She glares pointedly at the rolled-up rug at their feet.

"Okay, so I got a little carried away. I couldn't help it. Julie's a wreck."

"Why? Does she feel guilty for calling Dom a murderer just because he likes a good steak once in a while? And anyway, nobody forced her to cook it or eat it, so—"

"He forced her to eat it."

"No, he didn't. He asked her to taste it. There's a huge difference."

"She didn't want to taste it, Maggie, and he wouldn't take no for an answer."

"He offered it to her, and she took it and threw it at him, Charlie," she says, shooting daggers with her eyes, wondering how just moments ago she could have contemplated throwing away everything—her boyfriend, her ideals, her morals—on this person.

"That's his story."

"Why would he lie?"

"Why would she?"

Maggie glares at him. "I can't believe that I wasted an entire weekend on you when I could have been . . . accomplishing something worthwhile."

"Like what? Alphabetizing your bookshelf? Watching

CNN? Every minute doesn't have to be productive, re-member?"

Conscious of the receptionist eavesdropping, Maggie hisses, "Yes, well, being productive is a hell of a lot better than being stupid."

"Are you calling me stupid?"

"No," she retorts, stalking toward the elevator. "I'm calling *me* stupid for ever getting involved with you."

Chapter Ten

"It's a good thing your birthday is only once a year," Charlie informs Prairie Dog Friday night, "because I have a feeling I'm starting to get too old to do this more often than that."

Prairie Dog, whose flushed cheeks almost match the shade of his hair, asks, "Too old to do what? Have a few drinks with friends?"

"You know . . . all of this." Charlie waves a hand around the crowded nightclub filled with beautiful people.

Beautiful people dancing, and drinking, and laughing, and talking, and sneaking off to the bathrooms in pairs to do whatever it is beautiful people do when they're alone together behind closed doors.

His role in the club scene has always been more observer than participant in rampant debauchery, but Charlie just isn't in the mood to be here at all tonight. In fact, he *shouldn't* be here, and if it weren't his closest friend's birthday, he wouldn't be.

He should be home working on his column. He hasn't accomplished a thing this week, other than brooding and playing a lot of golf. He kept hoping he'd have a brainstorm while staring out the window or hitting a bucket of balls at Chelsea Piers, but inspiration for the column has yet to strike.

Meanwhile, he's lost any inclination to work on the Maggie-inspired piece now that Maggie's no longer in his life.

Which, of course, is for the best.

Maggie in his life was nothing but trouble.

But . . .

Maggie *out* of his life is troubling, too.

He keeps reliving that day in the ad agency, wondering what he could have—or should have—done differently.

To make matters worse, Julie isn't speaking to him now, either. She wanted him to get her rug and her blouse back, but there was no way he was going to go crawling back to Dominic's place of employment and run the risk of seeing Maggie again.

As for Julie, she has stubbornly refused Charlie's repeated offers to buy her a new blouse and a new rug. She told him he never should have taken it upon himself to dump her belongings at Dominic's feet in the first place.

"We're not that old, Charlie," his friend Butts is telling him, his eyes uncharacteristically serious behind his new glasses. "We're in our prime."

"We are?" Pork asks, looking ruefully down at his generous beer belly. "If this is my prime, I'm afraid to see what's next."

"You know what's next," Prairie Dog says, swallowing some Scotch. "You marry Daniella and you buy a house in Jersey and you have a couple of kids and you spend the next fifteen or twenty years commuting on weekdays and coaching soccer on weekends."

"Cripes, does it have to be Jersey? Her parents are there. I want a bridge or a tunnel between me and my in-laws."

"That's the only part you have trouble with?" Charlie asks Pork, dumbfounded. "Moving to Jersey?"

"I gotta admit, the rest of it sounds pretty good."

This, from the guy who mere months ago—or was it years—was regularly guzzling beer from a hose connected to a funnel and sleeping with three different women simultaneously.

"Yeah, it does sound good, doesn't it?" Butts asks. "Susie's been bugging me to get engaged since Christmas. I'm thinking of doing it for her birthday. It's in April. Did you know April's birthstone is a diamond?"

No, the guys murmur, they didn't know that.

"Well, it is. Susie told me."

Charlie, who has long been convinced Susie's only dating Butts because he's a bond trader with a bright future, is tempted to roll his eyes. He manages to refrain, for Butts's sake. If the guy is somehow blind to the fact that his girlfriend—and possibly future wife— is a manipulative gold digger, it's not up to Charlie to enlighten him. He probably wouldn't believe it, anyway.

When Charlie was dating Laurie, his friends tried more than once to warn him that she was all wrong for him. Did he listen? No.

Who was there to pick up the pieces, getting him drunk on his would-be wedding day with nary an *I Told You So*? His friends.

"You know, we guys have to stick together," Charlie informs them, after a generous swig of bourbon. "When you come right down to it, we're all we have."

"Yeah," Pork agrees. "I, uh, I also have Daniella."

"And I have Susie," Butts declares. "And Prairie Dog has . . . what's her name again, Dog?"

"Kat."

"How could you forget?" Pork asks. "We were there the night he met her. We figured it was meant to be. Dog and Kat."

"No, you didn't," Prairie Dog puts in. "You thought it couldn't last. You thought we'd be fighting like . . ."

"Cats and dogs." They all say it in unison.

Only Pork laughs, then stops and looks at the others. "C'mon guys, where's your sense of humor?"

"I don't think the idea of me fighting with Kat is funny," Prairie Dog tells them.

"And I don't think it's all that funny, either," Butts says. "I mean, it's not like her real name is Kat. It's Katherine."

"It's Kathleen," Prairie Dog corrects. "And we don't fight. Ever."

"Never?" Pork asks in disbelief.

"Well, only when we go to weddings."

They all nod in solemn recognition. Other people's weddings, Charlie recalls, can be the death of a relationship. Back when she desperately wanted to get engaged and he desperately wanted to preserve his bachelorhood—not that he doesn't now—he and Laurie had many a fight on the edge of a dance floor.

"Yeah, me and Susie keep having the wedding fight, too," Butts says. "We have another wedding to go to next month, and I'm dreading it."

"Then why wait till April to give her the ring?" Prairie Dog wants to know.

"Because, you know how it is . . . I'm not quite ready."

They all nod soberly.

They all—including Charlie—know how it is.

He sighs, wondering when their lives got so serious. Prairie Dog's birthday used to be about all-night drunken revelry. Now, though the setting is the same, they might as well be sitting around a shrink's office for a group therapy session.

"You know, don't you, that we're going to fall like dominoes once you give her that ring," Pork tells Butts.

"Yeah, all except Charlie." Prairie Dog looks at him. "You can be our token bachelor. You know, keep us posted on what we're missing."

"What if I don't?"

"Keep us posted on the single life? It's what you do for a living," Butts says in a *duh* tone.

"I know, but . . . you guys think I'm going to be single forever?"

They nod resolutely, all three of them, without hesitation.

"But what if I meet someone next week and fall head over heels in love with her?"

Or what if I met someone last week and fell head over heels in love with her?

"Never happen."

"Uh-uh."

"You're not cut out for that, Charlie."

Their responses are so certain that he wonders what the hell he was thinking. He doesn't want to be in love with anybody. No way. Just look what being in love does to a guy.

He glances around at his friends.

At Pork, whose girth has widened by the week thanks to Daniella's home cooking.

At Butts, who checks his cell phone every five minutes to make sure he didn't miss a call from Susie in all the din from the crowd.

At Prairie Dog, who used to wear regular jeans and tee shirts like the rest of them until Kat got into his closet. Now he's in pressed chinos and a chambray button-down.

No, Charlie doesn't want to be in love with anybody.

And certainly not with Maggie.

Not that it matters, because Maggie doesn't want to be in love with him, either. She wants to be in love with some doctor she never sees.

What's wrong with her?

Why can't she see that Jason is all wrong for her?

Oh, like you have any clue what Jason's like, Charlie tells himself. *For all you know, he's perfect for her.*

He's probably the kind of guy who likes to be buttoned-up and busy—the kind of guy who wakes up early and gets plenty of sleep and flosses daily and would never, ever, dump sand from his shoes onto a hotel carpet.

Yeah, chances are, Jason is perfect for Maggie.

But if that's the case . . . why did she spend the weekend with Charlie?

Why, when he kissed her, did she kiss him back?

Why, when they made love, did she cling to him as though she never wanted to stop?

Charlie is certain he's never going to get any answers

to those questions. Not the ones he'd want to hear, anyway.

"I still don't see why I have to come with you," Maggie tells Dominic on Saturday morning as they step off the number six train. "If Charlie could carry that rug all the way up to midtown, you can carry it back down again."

"Charlie probably took a limo," Dom says, grunting under the weight of the rolled-up Berber carpet. "We don't have that luxury."

"A cab would've been better. Then the driver could've helped you get the stuff out while I went to the health club like I was supposed to."

"Mags, I spent a fortune on having this stuff cleaned, and there's another whole week till payday. I can't afford a cab all the way downtown and the kind of tip I'd need to give the driver to help me manhandle this rug."

"Looks like you're doing fine on your own, Dom," she points out.

"Yeah, but I need you to carry that so it doesn't get wrinkled or drag on the ground."

He gestures at the plastic-shrouded blouse on a dry-cleaner's wire hanger in Maggie's hands.

"Plus," he adds, "you're the one who got me into this mess in the first place."

"Me? I didn't tell you to spatter blood all over Julie's blouse and carpet."

"No, you just convinced me to go out with her."

As they climb the stairs, Maggie is reminded of taking this same journey on Saturday night. How different things were then. Those were her last moments as a normal person. Normal as in untainted by an affair with a man who bears no resemblance to the person she envisions as her life partner—whether or not that person turns out to be Jason.

She can't help noticing that his e-mails this week have been more distant, more filled with boring descriptions of the scenery and medical procedures and less filled with romantic longing for her.

Is it her? Does he sense, somehow, that she's cheated on him? Or has their relationship begun to run its course?

Strangely, that possibility is less unsettling to Maggie than the thought that she'll never see Charlie Kennelly again, other than as a postage-stamp-sized head shot looking out from the pages of *She*.

If only things hadn't ended so abruptly on Monday. If only she'd had the chance to explain to him that she couldn't go on seeing him—which, she has managed to convince herself in the days since, she surely would have done when he called her.

But Charlie had to go and barge into her workplace wearing that stupid hat and toting a carpet, of all things, spouting ridiculous accusations, forcing her to come to her senses on the spot instead of in a more gradual and natural process.

That, she concludes, is why she's feeling so unnerved. She didn't have time to properly extricate herself from their entanglement in a levelheaded way. She couldn't plan what to tell Charlie, and she couldn't list for him all the reasons he's wrong for her.

She had to content herself with writing them down, these past few days, in her Palm Pilot. Every time one of Charlie's glaring faults strikes her, she stops what she's doing and pulls out her stylus to make note of it.

Funny, how some of those faults can almost seem endearing in retrospect, when she scans the long list.

"You remember which building it is on Harcourt Street, right, Maggie?"

"Of course."

She helps him push the rug through the gated turnstile at the exit, and together they emerge onto the street. It's another gray, drizzly morning in a string of gray, drizzly mornings—the kind of day when it's necessary to keep the lights on when you're inside and a hooded water-repellent jacket on when you're out.

Maggie struggles with her hood while trying to hold the hanger aloft, lest the long sheath of plastic wrap drag through a dirty puddle. Finally, she gives up. Why not get rained on? She's only going to the gym when she's finished helping Dominic. In fact, she's wearing her workout clothes under her parka, her face is scrubbed free of makeup, and her hair is back in an elastic. Normally, she wouldn't set foot in Manhattan in this condition, but Dominic waylaid her at her door, and here she is.

"Listen, when we get there, I'll wait on the street"—or preferably in a deserted alley—"while you give the stuff to the doorman," Maggie tells Dominic.

"No way. You're coming in with me. I need your help getting in the door."

"The doorman will help you."

"You'll help me," Dominic says.

When she opens her mouth to protest, he shushes her, saying, "I'm not in the mood to argue about this, Maggie. I'm trying to do the gentlemanly thing, here. Be a sport and help me out."

"Fair enough."

He is being a gentleman. She was surprised when she learned that he'd carted Julie's stained blouse and the rug all the way to Wong Lee Chin in Astoria. It made her wonder if by chance he'd exaggerated Julie's shrewish behavior on their date—or his own innocence.

Maggie's hair is getting damp, and her shoulder blade is beginning to ache from holding the hanger so high above her head.

As they round the corner onto Harcourt Street, her heart begins to beat a little faster.

There's no chance you'll run into Charlie, she assures herself. *No chance at all.*

After all, he sleeps in on Saturday mornings. Till noon, didn't he say? That's still a few hours away.

Still . . .

"Are you sure I can't wait out here?" she asks Dominic in front of the building.

"Positive."

A different doorman is on duty today. He looks up from this morning's *New York Post* to say, "Can I help you?"

"We have a delivery for Julie Purello in Apartment 4 E," Dominic says briskly, leaning the carpet against the wall beside the elevator.

"Okay." If the doorman finds them an unusual delivery team, he doesn't let on.

Encouraged, Maggie hangs the blouse on a mail slot as Dominic says, "We'll just leave the stuff here, and you can—"

"Whoa, hang on a second there," the doorman says, lifting a telephone. "I have to check with the resident to make sure she's expecting you."

"She isn't," Dom says, two steps behind Maggie en route to the door, "but it's fine."

"Wait a second, buddy," the doorman says. "I can't let you just dump this stuff in the lobby."

"But it's hers."

"I'll just check." The doorman holds up an index finger, and says into the phone, "Yeah, hi, Ms. Purello, it's Don. I've got a delivery here for you . . ."

Maggie and Dom look at each other.

". . . looks like a rug and a shirt."

"It's a blouse," Maggie corrects him.

Dom shoots her a dirty look.

"There's a difference," she tells him. "A blouse is dressier and has buttons; a shirt is—"

"Who cares?" he hisses. "Let's just get out of here."

"She says she's coming down," the doorman tells them. "She wants you to wait."

"But—we're kind of in a hurry," Dom protests.

Don the Doorman gives him a look that says they're not going anywhere until Julie has accepted the carpet and blouse.

"I can leave," Maggie informs Dominic. "After all, this has nothing to do with me."

"Why can't you stay?"

Truth be told, it's because she's not exactly eager to see Julie again—or rather, to have Julie see *her* looking like she was just rescued from a storm drain.

She can just hear Julie saying to Charlie, "I saw Dom's friend Maggie in the lobby today. What the heck did you ever see in *her?*"

Then again, maybe Julie doesn't have a clue that anything happened between the two of them.

Dominic certainly doesn't.

Maggie came close to confessing to him a few times this week, whenever he gave her a probing look and asked her what was on her mind.

But it's bad enough that she told her female friends about her fling. Every other phrase out of Bindy's mouth has been "I told you so," and every other phrase out of Carolyn's has been, "You're crazy to give him up."

Apparently Carolyn has edited one too many romance novels lately, and has seized the fanciful notion of Maggie and the Bachelor at Large as star-crossed lovers. She insisted that Maggie tell her every last detail of her weekend in Atlantic City with Charlie, which meant Maggie had to relive aloud the very memories she was trying to banish from her mind.

Now that it—whatever *it* was that they shared—is over, she can pretend that she's not attracted to Charlie all she wants, but the truth is, she was. Desperately attracted. So attracted that if he stepped into this lobby right now, she can't guarantee that she won't hurl herself into his arms at the slightest hint of invitation.

"I'll wait outside," she tells Dom, unable to spend another moment in this building knowing that Charlie's asleep somewhere under its roof.

But before she can step out onto the street, the elevator arrives in the lobby with a *ding* and doors that slide open immediately.

Maggie freezes.

It's going to be him, she realizes intuitively.

It's going to be Charlie.

So certain is she that she's about to come face-to-face

with him that her mind races frantically for something, anything, to say.

Should she suggest that they go someplace and talk? Or should she wait for him to make the first move?

Should she apologize?

For what?

Should she tell him that she expects an apology?

For what?

Her thoughts are so muddled that suddenly, she can't even remember what, exactly, went wrong between them.

Then the elevator's lone occupant steps out . . .

And it isn't him.

It's Julie.

Maggie exhales, waiting for relief to wash over her.

To her shock, it doesn't happen. There's no relief— only a flicker of disappointment and the realization that sometimes, the old Harrigan intuition is way, way off.

"Let me get this straight." Charlie rubs his eyes and gapes at Julie, who less than a minute ago materialized over his bed, startling him out of a pleasant dream.

Not that he has any idea what it was about. His dreams tend to vanish from his thoughts the moment he sits up. Which he just did . . . and much too quickly after all that Scotch he drank last night.

Collapsing against the pillows again, his stomach roiling, he says, "You're speaking to me again?"

"I was never not speaking to you. I was angry. But I'm over it." She sniffs the air and looks around the darkened room. "It smells like a distillery in here."

Ignoring her, he goes on, "So you're over being angry at me, and you're over being angry at Dom, and you want me to help you get back together with him? Is that what you're saying?"

"That's what I'm saying. Would you?"

"But . . . why?"

"Because, Charlie . . ." She sits on the edge of the bed, jolting him.

He gulps as another wave of nausea sweeps over him. He never should have had that fourth Scotch.

Or was it his fifth?

And he sure as hell never should have eaten those suicidal chicken wings on the way home. Does he have any Alka-Seltzer in the medicine cabinet?

He opens his mouth to ask Julie to go check for him, but she's talking about something else, and her tone sounds urgent. Charlie can't imagine what can be more pressing than finding something to settle his stomach, but he tunes back in just in time to hear her say, "—and he was just here, and I realized I might have made a big mistake."

"Who was here? The super?"

"No, *Dom*. Are you even listening to me, Charlie?"

"Dom was just here?" He frowns, his gaze darting as far around his studio as it can go without necessitating a throbbing head-turn. He half expects to see Dom lurking behind a curtain, though why he'd be doing that is beyond Charlie. Nothing makes sense today, and he hasn't even set foot out of bed yet.

"No, he wasn't *here*," Julie tells him. "Just . . . here. You know. Downstairs. In the lobby. With Maggie."

"Maggie?"

Potent as last night's liquor, the name slams into him

with as much force, scrambling his already incoherent thoughts.

Maggie was here? Why?

"She and Dominic dropped off my rug and my blouse," Julie is saying.

The rug. The blouse. Dom. Maggie. It's all coming back to him now, along with his dream.

She was in it—that much he recalls. In it, and un-clothed, and not the least bit angry at Charlie. In fact, quite the opposite.

He closes his eyes, longing to drift right back into that sensual, blissful place, but Julie just keeps talking, dammit.

"And, Charlie—he had the stuff dry-cleaned for me. He said the place had to do the rug three times before the stains would come out. But you know what, Charlie? He made sure they came out. My rug looks brand-new. And I couldn't think of anything to say to him except 'thank you.'"

"What's wrong with thank you?" Charlie rubs his pounding skull. "Thank you is polite. It's what you say when somebody does something nice for you. In fact, Julie, what he did wasn't *nice*—it was necessary."

"Not really."

"Julie, if somebody ruins something that doesn't be-long to them, they need either to fix it or replace it. That's just common courtesy."

"But maybe . . ."

"Maybe what?" Something tells him there's more to this than she's letting on, but he isn't in the mood to ana-lyze anything at the moment.

"Maybe . . ." She shifts her weight, jostling the mattress again.

Dammit, he really needs that Alka-Seltzer. He opens his impossibly dry and foul-tasting mouth to ask for it, but she's saying, "I don't know . . . it's just, what if the blood on the rug wasn't entirely his fault?"

"How can it not be?"

She shrugs. Hedges just long enough for him to realize that Julie's earlier version of the date—the version that sent him careening into a midtown advertising agency like a madman, alienating Maggie in the process—might not have been a hundred percent accurate.

"Julie . . . You did tell me the truth, didn't you?"

"Of course I did. But I don't know, you know . . . even if it *was* his fault, I should forgive him. Right?"

"It sounds like you already have. Which doesn't explain why you found it absolutely necessary to burst in here at this hour."

"This hour? Charlie, it's morning."

"Morning, what time?"

"I don't know . . . almost ten?"

He groans and rolls over. He could have sworn he just crawled into bed five minutes ago. "I was out past five, Julie. I need to sleep a few more hours. But first I need Alka-Seltzer. Can you check my medicine cabinet? Please?"

The great thing about Julie, he notes, and not for the first time, is that she's got that sympathetic, nurturing nature.

She promptly heads to the bathroom, where he hears her rummaging around in his medicine cabinet. Finally, she comes back to the bed.

"No luck."

"I could have sworn I had Alka-Seltzer in there."

"You did, but it expired back in 2002. I threw it away."

"You *what*? Go get it, Julie, please. I need it."

"It's expired. Expired medication can be dangerous."

"So can what's about to come out of me if I don't take something right away. Trust me. Do you have any Alka-Seltzer at your place?"

"I only use holistic therapy now, remember?"

Nope. That must be another one of those details he's always forgetting about Julie—and everybody else. He really needs to pay more attention when people tell him things.

You could be like Maggie and go around jotting things down all day in an electronic organizer.

Maggie.

Maggie, again.

His stomach churns. Not just because of Maggie, but the thought of her isn't helping.

Plus, he's seized by a sudden and vague memory of telling Prairie Dog, Butts, and Pork about her at some point in the wee hours of the evening. Not just mentioning her in passing, but going into rhapsodic detail about how he had fallen head over heels for a woman he couldn't stand.

With any luck, he's hallucinating the memory.

If he's not, his friends will never let him live it down. Not after he spent the first half of the evening whole-heartedly going along with the widespread assumption that he's immune to women and their charms—not to mention mercilessly teasing his buddies for being down-right whipped.

"Julie," he pleads, "I feel sick. I really need something for my stomach."

"Charlie, I'll make a deal with you. I'll run down the street to Duane Reade for some Alka-Seltzer if you help me out with Dominic."

He groans. "How can I do that?"

"Just tell me what to say to him."

"You're on your own this time, Jul'. I don't want to get involved."

"You already *are* involved . . . and besides, you have a way with words. I need your eloquence."

"And I need something for my stomach. Some sleep, too."

"Okay, okay, I heard you the first few times. God, I never realized you were such a whiner."

"I'm not whining. I'm in pain."

"Look, I'll be right back. Just remember our deal."

"What deal?" he grunts. "I didn't agree to anything."

Too late.

The apartment door has already closed behind her.

Too late in more ways than one, Charlie realizes, rushing for the bathroom as the volcanic contents of his stomach erupt at last.

Someday, Maggie thinks as she walks back to her apartment just off Ditmars Boulevard, *I'll live in Manhattan in a doorman building with laundry facilities on every floor.*

No more taking the subway back and forth from Queens; no more pungent cooking odors drifting up through the floor vents to scent her closet and everything in it; no more lugging a sackful of freshly folded, hot-from-the-dryer clothes two long blocks in the pouring rain.

By the time she reaches the front stoop of the tidy brick two-family house, she realizes she'll have to drape her formerly dry laundry over the shower rod when she gets upstairs.

She unlocks the front door and steps into the dim vestibule that separates the stairway from the first-floor apartment of her elderly landlords, Mr. and Mrs. Mylonas, who speak little English and think her name is Margie. As usual, she can smell their Sunday dinner—an unidentifiable roasted meat—and hear stringed instrumental Greek music emanating from behind their frosted glass door.

She climbs the stairs and steps into the four small rooms that are her haven. Not much of a haven, given the cracked linoleum in the kitchen, the plumber-defying leaky tub in the bathroom, and the bedroom that lacks a door. But who needs a door when you live alone?

She painted the entire apartment—at her own expense—when she moved in. Prior to a fresh coat of white, the rooms were a mishmash of peeling pastels and stained orange floral wallpaper circa 1975.

The paint brightened things considerably, as did several plants and some pretty curtains and slipcovers she bought at the Macy's white sale last month. But the best thing about the place—other than no roommates and low rent—is that Dominic lives right around the corner. Without him, she'd be lonely.

What if Dominic falls for Julie, gets married, and moves away? Then Maggie will be abandoned in Queens.

The only way she'd be able to afford Manhattan on her salary is to get a roommate, or married. Until the latter happens—God willing—here she'll stay. She doesn't want to live with strangers, and her closest friends aren't willing to move. Carolyn, whose publishing salary is even lower than Maggie's media planner one, commutes from her parents' house on Long Island. Bindy has a precious rent-controlled studio on the Upper East Side.

As Maggie deposits the bag on the floor just inside the door, the phone starts to ring.

She shrugs out of her wet coat and shoes before hurrying into the living room to answer it. That's another problem with this apartment, she thinks, reaching for the receiver. No phone jack in the kitchen or the bedroom. If she were planning on staying here indefinitely, she might pay to have them put in. She might do a lot of things.

"Hello?"

"Maggie. It's me!"

At the sound of a male voice, her heart skips a beat.

"Charlie! I'm so glad—"

"Who's Charlie?"

Oh, no. Oh, God.

What a cliché, she thinks, as she fumbles to correct her mistake.

"Jason! I'm sorry, the connection is so clear I, uh, I thought you were . . . someone from here. From work. Someone from work. Here."

Shut up, Maggie.

"Nope," he says, "it's just me."

"I'm glad it is."

"How are you, Maggie?"

"I'm good. How are you?"

"Homesick. I'd kill for a bagel and lox."

"What, no lox in the jungle?"

He chuckles. "No lox in the jungle, but in a few more days there will be no *me* in the jungle."

"You're coming home?"

"I'm coming home. I—well, I've got a lot to share with you."

"That's—that's great! I can't wait to see you!"

Does her voice sound as hollow to him as it does to her?

"When will you be here, Jason?"

"Next weekend. I'll e-mail you and let you know for sure."

"Okay."

"I've got to go, now, Maggie . . . I've got to call my parents and let them know, too."

"Okay."

He called her first. Before he called his parents.

She should be exhilarated. He called her first, and he's coming home. Why isn't she exhilarated?

Is it her imagination, or was their conversation . . . stilted? And not just on her end. He didn't say anything particularly intimate. Like *I miss you*, or . . .

Well, he certainly isn't going to tell her he loves her now if he didn't say it while they were together in New York.

Nor would she expect him to, or even want him to. They're not at that stage yet.

But we can be.

Is that—is *he*—still what she wants? What if it—if *he*—isn't? What then?

You're putting too much pressure on yourself, Maggie. You'll be glad to see Jason when he gets here. Just wait and see.

* * *

Pain is good.

Charlie nods, and continues typing.

If there were no pain, there would be no . . .

He stops typing.

No pain, no . . .

Gain?

That he actually considers the obvious should be a warning that he's not going to get anything worthwhile written today.

He's been at it for hours, doing his best to write a meaningful column about broken hearts—namely, his own.

Not that his heart is technically broken. After all, what he and Maggie shared was nothing more than a fling. He never expected it to last. He never wanted it to last.

Still, the fact that it crashed and burned so quickly caught him off guard—and so has his profound reaction.

This is almost worse—okay, it is worse—than when Laurie jilted him.

Why this is worse is beyond him, but he doesn't remember feeling this emotionally shattered after that breakup.

Maybe he was just too busy undoing wedding and honeymoon plans to notice.

Or maybe he wasn't really in love with Laurie in the first place.

But if that's true, then it would logically follow that he is—or was—in love with Maggie.

Nah.

You don't fall in love overnight.

Or do you?

Love hurts.

Is Charlie in love?

He's certainly in pain—not just physically, from his skull-throbbing hangover, but mentally, emotionally, spiritually. And it's all Maggie's fault. Everything. Including the hangover.

He looks back at the computer screen.

Pain is good.

Bull.

Pain is *not* good. Pain sucks.

Shaking his pounding head, Charlie deletes the three words that were to comprise his new column, then crawls back to bed.

Chapter Eleven

Another Monday—and this time, thank goodness, Maggie's week starts out on the right footing, which, according to the Harrigan intuition, bodes well for her future.

Today, there are no indulgences. No hitting the snooze alarm, no Krispy Kremes, no mocha or whipped cream in her coffee.

She's right back into the self-disciplined swing of things: at the office by seven-thirty, latest issue of *Mediaweek* stashed in her bag to read later, up to her eyeballs creating a programming deck by mid-morning.

When Dominic sticks his head in her office just before noon, she assumes he's touching base before this afternoon's conference call with the brand manager.

"Maggie? You busy?"

"I'm always busy. What's up?"

He shoves a sheet of five-by-seven card stock under her nose.

"What's this?" At first glance, it looks like an engraved invitation—several lines of flowing text on a cream-colored background.

"It was just delivered by a messenger service. Read it, Mags."

"Who's it from?"

"You'll see."

She does see, by the first line.

> *There once was a lady named Julie Purello*
> *Who cooked dinner one night for a very sweet fellow*
> *They were getting along*
> *Until things went all wrong*
> *She still owes him dessert, and it won't be mere Jell-O.*

Beneath the last line is a phone number.

Maggie grins. "Cute limerick."

"Do you think she wrote it?"

"I don't think she copied it from a poetry anthology, if that's what you're asking," she says dryly.

"Well, now what? Do I call her?"

"That depends on how you feel about dessert," Maggie tells him. "And about Julie."

"You know how I feel about dessert, Mags. I love it. Even Jell-O. I mean, it's kind of boring, but it's . . ."

"Comfort food?"

"Exactly. When I'm in the mood for Jell-O, it hits the spot. Especially when you jazz it up with whipped cream. But sometimes . . ."

"Sometimes you want chocolate fudge cake or crème brûlée or something that's more . . . sinful."

"Yeah."

Maggie nods, fully aware that they're not just talking about dessert.

"Sounds like Julie wants a chance to show you that she can make crème brûlèe."

"Yeah," he says again.

"Are you going to take her up on it?"

"Well . . . it's not like I don't want to call her. I mean, she was pretty nice the other day when I gave her the dry-cleaned stuff back. But . . . do you think I should? What if she's got a thing for me, and I don't feel the same and I break her heart?"

She lays a hand on his rolled-up shirtsleeve, saying, "That's a chance you'll have to take, Dom. You've got nothing to lose."

"I guess."

"So you're going to call her?"

"Yeah. I am."

"Good. Just remember, if you marry her, you have to name your first child after me."

"You're jumping the gun, Maggie," he says ruefully. "I'm just hoping we can get through another date without a food fight."

Two days later, Charlie is once again staring at his blank computer screen when he hears footsteps in the hall outside his door.

Good. Julie's home from work.

He desperately needs a break from the column he's supposedly writing. When Kayla, his editor, called this morning, he thought she was checking up on him and assured her that this month's piece will be his best work yet—a funny, upbeat piece about . . .

Well, he's not sure. But he didn't tell that to Kayla. He

merely said, when she inquired about his funny, upbeat topic, "I want to surprise you this time."

She seemed satisfied with that and went on to the real reason for her call—which, as it turned out, had nothing to do with his failure to hand in a column outline and everything to do with his failure to RSVP to an invitation that is most likely at the bottom of the pile of last week's unopened mail.

Now, hearing keys jangling in the hallway, Charlie tosses aside his thinking hat—which doesn't seem to be working these days anyway—and pads in his bare feet to the door. He throws it open in time to see Julie sticking her key into her lock.

"Hey, what's up, Charlie?"

"I am, since nine o'clock this morning. I actually found my alarm clock and set it so that I could get an early start. It still works."

"The clock?"

"Yeah, I wasn't sure that it would."

"You have no idea how lucky you are that you use an alarm clock once a year and that nine o'clock is early for you. Try starting your workday at four-thirty and making a hundred strawberry tarts before sunup."

"Try starting your workday at nine with every intention of writing a hundred pages—or at least two—by sundown."

"How's the column coming?"

"Don't ask. That's not why I'm here."

"It's not?"

"Well . . . ?" he asks expectantly, joining her in the hall, then in her apartment as she steps over the threshold.

"Well, what?" She hurls her keys in the general direction of a small table and shrugs out of her down coat.

"How'd it go last night with Dominic? I heard him leave after midnight, so I'm assuming there was no bloodshed."

Julie kicks off her shoes and deposits a paper grocery bag from the health food store on the counter. "You heard him leave? I'm surprised you didn't hightail it over here for all the details then."

"I wanted to, but I was watching that new Adam Sandler movie on Pay-Per-View. By the time it was over, I figured you were probably asleep."

"You figured right." She yawns, then reaches into the grocery bag, unpacking a carton of organic milk, a pound of organic butter, a container of bulk granola, and some kind of whitish stalks with greenish-purplish leaves on the end.

It never ceases to amaze him that Julie knows how to cook vegetables he's never seen or heard of in his life, and manages to make most of them taste pretty decent.

Speaking of which, "What did you make for Dom?" he asks, leaning on the counter and watching her stash her purchases in the fridge.

"Just dessert. I did what you said and I told him that I'd make him absolutely anything his heart desired. You know what he asked for, of all things?"

"Cherry pie?"

Cherry pie, for God knows what reason, makes him think of Maggie.

"No, not cherry pie," Julie says.

Then again, these days, everything makes him think of Maggie, so it's not surprising.

Plagued by the knowledge that Dom was right across the hall last night, Charlie had to fight the urge to drop in at Julie's place and strike up a conversation, just so he could casually inquire about Maggie.

For all he knows, her doctor boyfriend is back in town, and she's engaged. Which would probably be the best thing for everybody.

"*Strufoli*," Julie says.

"*Gesundheit*."

She laughs. "No, that's what Dominic wanted me to make. You know . . . Italian honey balls?"

Charlie doesn't know Italian honey balls.

"My grandma always makes *strufoli* on Christmas Eve," Julie informs him. "And Dom says both of his grandmothers did, too. But one died, and the other one is senile in a nursing home, and he hasn't had it in a while."

Charlie nods, getting the picture. Obviously, feeding poor *strufoli*-deprived Dominic appeals to Julie's nurturing instincts.

"I called my grandmother, and I got a recipe, and I made it for Dominic."

"Do you have any left?" Charlie asks, noting, with just a hint of platonic jealousy that she's never made *strufoli* for *him*. Not that he ever heard of it before, but still.

"Just this." Julie retrieves a silver-wrapped plate from the fridge and sets it in front of him.

Charlie peels back the tinfoil to see a measly cluster of sticky-looking golden nuggets the size of gum balls, covered in bright-colored sprinkles.

He attempts to pop one into his mouth, but it doesn't want to leave its comrades behind on the plate. He winds up polishing off the leftovers in a single bite.

"It's good," he tells Julie, after chewing and swallowing. "Did Dom like it?"

"Dom loved it. You know, I have to say, he's a nice guy. He's taking me out to dinner on Friday night."

"That's great, Julie. Do you think he's Mr. Right?"

"I don't know . . . Don't you think it's too soon to tell?"

"What, no sparks?" he asks, reading volumes in her delayed reply.

"I didn't say that," she tells him, opening a bottle of springwater and guzzling some. "It was only our second date."

"Your third." He takes the bottle from her hand and takes a swig, then hands it back.

"Technically, maybe, but we decided not to count that last one."

"Good idea." He stretches, brushes the crumbs from his thermal undershirt, and runs a hand through his hair. "I'd better get going. I think I'll get a haircut before tonight."

"What's tonight?"

"Some party my editor wants me to go to. It's at a nice place off Park Avenue South, so I guess I'd better not show up looking like Twisted Sister meets Jesus. Maybe I'll even shave."

"And dress up?"

He glances down at himself. "No flannel?"

She shakes her head. "Too sloppy."

"You think?"

"I *know*. Trust me," Julie says. "Wear that nice sweater you have."

"Which one?" asks the man who has a closetful of nice sweaters from his mother and sisters—most of them with the price tags still attached.

"The black cashmere turtleneck you wore on New Year's Eve."

Oh. *That* nice sweater. Laurie gave it to him two Christmases ago, when she was still deluded enough to think she could make him over into somebody fit to be seen with her on his arm.

He normally wouldn't have bothered to wear it on New Year's Eve, since his only plan was to watch the ball drop in Times Square with his buddies, per their usual tradition. But as December 31 wore on, Prairie Dog, Pork, and Butts called one by one with excuses, feigning everything from the flu to fears of terrorism.

Facing the knowledge that after all these years, his friends had chosen to blow him off in favor of midnight kisses with the women in their lives, Charlie went out to pick up Chinese and ran into his new pal Julie in the lobby. She didn't have plans either, and she wasn't in the mood to battle the crowds in Times Square, so they went out to a nice dinner.

That was when Charlie first tried to talk himself into falling for Julie—and when he first realized that it wasn't going to happen. If they didn't wind up in each other's arms after their respective bitter breakups, mutually lonely holidays, and two bottles of vintage Cristal, it wasn't meant to be.

Is there a column in there someplace? Charlie wonders, leaving Julie's apartment and reentering his own.

He grabs his thinking hat, plunks it on his head, and sinks into his desk chair to consider it.

After a few minutes, he reaches for his laptop and types the opening line.

You can't make yourself fall in love.

Nor, he acknowledges, pausing with his fingers on the keyboard as Maggie's face pops into his head, can you make yourself fall *out* of love.

Where the hell did that come from?

He's not in love with Maggie. He barely knows her. One intimate weekend does not a relationship make.

No, Charlie doesn't love Maggie. He's merely attracted to her.

So wildly attracted that it's incredibly easy to fantasize about falling in love with her—and almost as tempting to write about it.

You can't make yourself fall in love. It just happens. It happens when you least expect it to happen, and it happens when you least want it to happen. It happens when you're doing everything in your power to make sure that it doesn't happen.

He stops typing. Leans back in his chair, twirling the feathers above the brim of his cap, and reads what he's written.

Rereads it. Deletes the last *happen*. Puts it back in. Deletes it again and italicizes doesn't.

Then he aims the mouse at the SAVE button, ready to click.

The movement is automatic, an every-other-paragraph habit honed the first time he lost several pages' worth of work because he forgot to back it up.

Wait a minute. What are you doing?

You're not in love. Who are you to write about it?

Frowning, Charlie moves the mouse again, this time highlighting the text.

He hesitates only for a moment.

Then, pushing Maggie firmly from his mind, he presses DELETE.

Chapter Twelve

There's nothing like holding your own in a roomful of supermodels, Maggie decides on Wednesday night, catching sight of her reflection in one of the restaurant's many mirrored walls. It's good for the soul, good for the ego, and good for her willpower whenever another delectable hors d'oeuvre passes temptingly by on a silver tray.

She's wearing the slinky black cocktail dress she wore to her boss's wedding last March with a pair of Bindy's Jimmy Choo stilettos and rhinestone drop earrings. Her shoulders are bare, her hemline is short, and her hair is up in a kittenish tumble-down topknot. She went with a pale lipstick and matching manicure, glad she opted for softly feminine pink over siren red. It sets her apart from the rest of the women at the *She* shindig, most of whom are either bold fashionistas, buttoned-up agency types, or some eclectic hybrid of both.

"How come you look so hot tonight, Maggie?" Dominic asks, snagging a grilled basil-wrapped shrimp from a passing waiter's tray.

"I don't know . . . do I look hot?" she asks, as though

her appearance isn't as calculated as Dominic's strategic position halfway between the bar and the kitchen, the better to capture the most succulent hors d'oeuvres before they're circulated to the room at large.

"Very hot," Dominic assures her. "If you were my type, I'd be all over you in a heartbeat."

"I don't think Julie would appreciate that."

"I don't know, Maggie . . . she might not mind. I talked to her on the phone before I left the office, and I can't tell if she's into me or not."

"Are you into her?"

"Sure. She's cute."

"Puppies are cute. Toddlers are cute. Cute isn't . . ." She trails off, noticing the look on his face. "What's the matter?"

"Isn't that Julie's friend Charlie over there?"

Her heart leaps into her throat. She turns her head, only slightly, in the direction Dominic indicates—just far enough to see a man who most definitely isn't Charlie.

Disappointment courses through her.

Did you really think he might show up here? she asks herself.

Of course you did. Why else would you go to so much trouble to look—to use Dominic's word for it—*hot.*

After all, Charlie works for *She* magazine. True, he's a freelancer, and the party is being thrown by the advertising sales department and has nothing to do with editorial, but most of the editors are here, and quite a few models. You'd think the writers would also be invited.

You'd think . . . and you'd hope.

Maggie turns back to Dominic, carefully keeping her expression neutral. "No," she says, "that's not him."

Dominic has lost interest already. He's too busy sidling up to a gorgeous blonde waitress carrying crab puffs.

"We have to stop meeting like this, darling."

Maggie looks up to see John DiMaio, a former media supervisor at Blair Barnett. She was relieved when he landed an assistant director job at a smaller agency last summer. He asked Maggie out a few times, and didn't get the hint when she turned him down.

Unfortunately, she keeps bumping into him at parties and lunches, and he can always be counted upon to ask when they're going to get together for a drink.

"Hi, John." She pastes on a smile just pleasant enough to be polite, but not encouraging in any way.

"You look gorgeous."

"Thank you." She shifts her weight from one uncomfortable high-heeled shoe to the other, wishing the room were less crowded so that he wouldn't have to stand so close. From this vantage point, he can just about see down into her cleavage.

While making idle small talk with John, she scans the room for Charlie. No sign of him, but there's Dominic across a sea of people, looking awfully cozy with the blonde du jour.

"Will you excuse me for a second?" Maggie asks John. "I see somebody I have to talk to."

"Only if you promise you'll be back."

"I promise," she lies.

Trying to make her way over to Dominic is like trying to grasp a beach ball in the outgoing tide. She's moving closer to Dom's side of the room, but he and the blonde are drifting farther away in the ever-thickening crowd.

Frustrated, Maggie pulls out her cell phone and dials.

She watches Dom pull his out of his pocket.

"Hello?" his voice says in her ear.

"What are you doing?"

"I'm at the party. Where are you?"

"I'm at the party, watching you."

He looks around the room, spots her, and scowls. "Then why are you asking what I'm doing?"

"Did you forget about Julie?" she asks, pushing back a few wisps of hair that have escaped from her topknot.

"You're a real pain in the butt sometimes, did you know that?"

"I'm just looking out for your best interests, Dom."

"Then hang up, Maggie."

"But Dom—"

He disconnects the call, holds up his phone in her direction, and waves.

"You didn't get cut off, you big loser," she mutters, hitting REDIAL.

Terrific. The phone goes directly into voice mail, which means he's turned it off.

Scowling, she puts her own phone away and takes a sip of her Pinot Grigio.

Oh, well, she concludes philosophically, if he and Julie are meant to be, Dominic will eventually lose interest in other women.

Shouldn't that be true for you, too? she demands of herself.

Why are you running around in a little black number on the off chance that you might run into Charlie?

Because, dammit, she misses him. Because she'd give anything to see him just one more time before . . .

Before Jason comes home. She might as well admit it. This might be her last chance to—to—

To clear the air. That, she promises herself, is all she wants to do. See Charlie, and clear the air. Nothing more. No kisses, no jaunts to Atlantic City, no falling into bed together.

If she can just see him again, she might be able to resolve this awful, unfinished feeling—this ridiculous sense that something worthwhile might have developed between them.

Deep in her heart—no, more importantly, in her *mind*—she knows that nothing serious could ever have come of their attraction.

And anything less than serious simply doesn't fit into her plans.

Her life, after all, is built on precision.

His life is built on whim.

There's no way to meld the two—no such thing as whimsical precision or precise whimsy. They'd drive each other crazy. They already have. And her Palm Pilot contains a list of his faults that's longer than her list of business contacts.

Just let it be, Maggie. Stop thinking about him. You're never going to see him a—

"I don't believe it. Margaret O'Mulligan. What are you doing here?"

Spinning around, she finds herself face-to-face with the man she glimpsed across the room. The man who isn't Charlie.

Except . . .

He *is* Charlie.

He's Charlie with a haircut. Charlie with a clean shave.

Charlie with a dark suit and tie. Charlie looking like he stepped out of *GQ* magazine.

Wow.

Every thought Maggie had about forgetting him just flew right past the rhinestone drop earrings.

"What are *you* doing here?" she manages to say.

"That was my line. Yours is supposed to be a reply."

"It's an industry party."

"It is?"

"Don't you know where you are?"

He shrugs. "I guess I lost the invitation. All I know is that my editor called me up and told me I should be here, so I came."

Maggie is as struck by the fact that he would show up at an event without knowing exactly what the event is for as she is by just how damned good he looks when he's not slumming.

Not that he doesn't look good when he's slumming. But it's a different kind of good. This—this is—

"What'cha looking at, Margaret?" he asks with a cocky tilt of his head, as though he knows damned well what she's looking at.

"You. You're less . . . hairy."

Oh, geez. Is that the nicest thing she can think of to say?

No, but it's the most appropriate thing in this setting.

And anyway, she's not about to let on just how appealing she finds his clean-cut look, lest he somehow manage to seduce her to an Atlantic City hotel again.

"Yeah, I'm less hairy," he says with a laugh.

But . . .

Is that a flicker of disappointment in his brown eyes?

Well, what does he expect her to say? Or do? Throw herself into his Brooks Brothers–clad arms?

"So . . . what is this? Bachelor at Large goes corporate?" she asks, forcing a light tone, stepping aside as yet another group of newcomers squeezes past her to get to the bar. The noise level seems to have risen a few decibels since she ran into Charlie, forcing her to stand close in order to hear him.

"I'm only corporate till midnight," Charlie tells her. "Then I turn into a slob again."

"You're not a slob!"

"Sure I am. Just not tonight."

"You just like to be comfortable. I mean, why not? You work at home. It's not like you have to wear a suit every day. In fact, I can't believe you even own one."

"I forgot that I do. I found it when I opened my closet. I bought it for Prairie Dog's mother's funeral last year. I was a pallbearer."

"You were pallbearer at a canine funeral?" She's heard about that sort of thing. There's even a pet cemetery up in Westchester where people bury their dead dogs and cats.

But Charlie is laughing, saying, "Not a canine funeral. Prairie Dog is human, and so was his mother. He's a friend of mine. I met him when we were seven. His real name is Peter Dwight, but his parents always called him P.D., and when people asked him what the initials stood for, he said Prairie Dog. It stuck."

Maggie smiles. Of course big-hearted, laid-back Charlie is the kind of guy who would keep a friend he made when he was seven. He must have been like one of the family to Prairie Dog's mother. Maggie can see how that might happen.

She finds herself imagining Charlie on her parents' farm. She pictures his strapping frame tilting back one of the hand-hewn chairs around the dining room table, pictures him passing platters and taking seconds and swapping sports stories with Dad and her brothers.

Which, of course, is never going to happen.

It's just not hard to imagine, that's all.

"So, you're here with people from work?" Charlie asks, rocking back on his heels, looking around the room like he's bored stiff.

"Just Dom." She looks around. The spot where her friend was standing is jammed with people, none of them Dom or the pretty waitress.

"Where is he?" Charlie asks.

"Who knows? He's probably taken off with the blonde du—"

Oops.

Too late, she remembers that Dom is dating Julie.

Not exclusively, but Charlie is Julie's friend. He shouldn't be privy to any Chickalini Casanova action.

"Blonde du—? Huh?"

"Blond dude," improvises Maggie, shoving another escaped strand of her own hair from her eyes.

"Which blond dude? And why would Dom take off with a dude? He's not . . . does he, uh . . ."

"What?"

"You know—swing both ways?"

"No!" She might as well tell the truth, which is far less damaging to Dom's reputation than what's obviously running through Charlie's mind at the moment.

"I was going to say he's probably taken off with the blonde du jour," she admits.

"Blonde du jour?" Charlie echoes. "I thought Julie was the blonde du jour. Or du month. Or, hopefully, du lifetime."

"Yeah, I think she might be. Dom really, really likes her. She wrote him a limerick."

"I know. She—uh, told me. She loves poetry. All kinds of poetry."

"Really? Because Dom is, um, writing a poem for her."

"Oh? I thought he was taking off with the blonde du jour."

"I didn't mean he's doing it right this minute. The poetry. The blonde, he's um—"

"Doing right this minute?" Charlie quirks a brow.

"No! Charlie, you know how guys are. You're a guy. You're the ultimate guy, right? Bachelor At Large. You know how guys like to flirt when they see an attractive woman. It doesn't mean anything."

"I just don't want to see Julie hurt again," he says, stepping closer to her as a waiter passes behind him with a tray full of drinks.

The room is getting crowded. Hot and crowded, and was that Charlie's arm that just grazed her ribs?

"Sorry," he says. "Someone bumped me."

"It's okay."

She tries to focus on anything but her proximity to Charlie.

What the heck were they talking about?

Oh, yeah.

"I don't want to see Dom hurt, either," Maggie tells Charlie, and is promptly jostled into him by somebody trying to get by. It's all she can do to stay on her feet. He puts a hand on her arm to steady her. "You okay?"

"Fine," she says, her voice sounding almost shrill with panic.

Don't let him touch you. If he touches you, it's all over. You know what happened on the beach.

Deep breaths.

Focus.

Focus on the conversation.

Right. What was it about?

Oh, yeah.

Dom.

But she doesn't really feel like talking about Dom. She doesn't feel like talking, period.

"How's your wine?" Charlie's mouth is so close she can feel his warm, cinnamon-scented breath stirring her hair.

"It's, um . . ." She draws a complete blank.

"Good?"

"Yes. It's good." She laughs nervously and gulps some wine. "You must think I need to borrow your thesaurus, huh?"

"To tell you the truth, I always was attracted to vocabulary-challenged women."

Oh Lord, Maggie thinks. *He really does think I'm a blithering airhead.*

If he comes any closer, she'll probably lose the ability to converse altogether. She'll be consumed by trying not to let any part of her body accidentally touch any part of his.

Yes, or maybe she'll be consumed by trying to think of ways to let her body accidentally on purpose touch his.

"Do you want another glass?" Charlie asks, gesturing at her dwindling Pinot Grigio, then at the bar.

"Of wine?"

"Nah, just a glass. I can stick them both in my jacket and smuggle them out of here for you so you'll have a pair."

She laughs.

So does he.

It feels good to laugh with him, and even better to be jostled up against him by somebody else squeezing past her.

"Oops. Sorry," she says, feeling her cheeks flush as his arm brushes against her side.

"It's okay. This place is jammed. Are these parties always like this?"

"Usually."

"How often do you come to them?"

"All the time. It's part of my job."

"Maybe your job isn't as bad as I thought," he comments. "Listen, do you want another wine? Because I'm going to grab a beer."

She shouldn't.

She really, really shouldn't.

She always sticks to one drink at business affairs, then switches to seltzer. It's not a good idea to mingle with colleagues unless she has her wits fully about her.

And it's certainly not a good idea to mingle with Charlie Kennelly unless she has her wits fully about her.

"Sure," she finds herself telling him, good ideas be damned. "Another wine sounds . . ."

"Good?" he asks, his eyes twinkling.

"Exactly." She allows hers to twinkle right back at him.

"You know," Charlie says into Maggie's ear, "I wondered if I was ever going to see you again."

"I wondered the same thing."

Almost an hour of witty conversation, a relatively isolated and less crowded corner of the room, and a second glass of wine have obviously relaxed her. She's been laughing at his jokes and making a few of her own, and has stopped stepping back every time he steps closer to her.

At this point, Charlie feels confident enough in her mood to ask, "Did you want to?"

"Did I want to what? See you again?"

He nods.

She tilts her head, as if contemplating the question. Another wisp of dark hair slips from the clip on top of her head, begging his fingers, just as the others have.

"I did want to see you again," she admits.

That does it. This time, he allows himself to reach out and brush the strand of hair away from her face.

She flinches, only slightly, but for a moment, he's positive she's going to tell him to back off.

Instead, she says only, "Thanks. It keeps getting into my eyes."

"It looks pretty on top of your head like that. I've only seen it hanging down."

She shrugs. "I never wear it up, really. Not unless I have someplace fancy to go."

"Well, that makes two of us. Although in my case you can substitute wearing it up for cutting my hair—or even just combing it."

"I like your hair cut and combed," she informs him

with her characteristic Maggie decisiveness. "You should always wear it short. It makes you look . . ."

"Smarter?"

She laughs. "No."

"Stupider?"

She laughs again. "No, not—"

"Sexier?"

This time, the laugh doesn't reach her eyes.

"Bingo," he says, as a little thrill zings through him. "You think I'm sexy with short hair."

"You had shaggy hair in Atlantic City," she says flippantly. "Remember?"

"So you thought I was sexy then?"

"What, you couldn't tell?"

He smiles, remembering. He could tell, all right. "But now you're not attracted to me?"

"Did I say that?"

"So, you are attracted to me now?"

"Did I say *that?*"

"You didn't have to. I can see it in your eyes," he says teasingly. "Go ahead. Admit it. You want me. You think I'm irresistible." He leans toward her, closing his eyes, as though he expects her to kiss him.

She pushes him away laughingly. "You're crazy."

"Crazy about you," he says in a movie-star-deep voice.

She laughs again.

"You think I'm kidding, don't you, Maggie." He rests a hand on the wall behind her shoulder, leaning in to say, in a low voice, "You don't believe me. Do you want me to show you?"

"No!"

"Come on. Just one kiss."

"Here? You're kidding, right?" The smile is fading from her lips. She looks around. "This is a professional event, Charlie, not a rec room full of teenagers."

"Then let's leave."

She rolls her eyes, laughs, shakes her head.

But she doesn't say no.

"Leave and go where?"

"Wherever you want to go."

"It's getting late," she says, "and my feet are killing me. I want to go home to bed."

"Fine." He takes her hand. "Let's go."

"Charlie—I can't."

Of course she can't. It's not as though he expected her to go along with it.

Well, not really.

It's just . . .

There's something about her—some sense of longing that she can't quite seem to mask with amusement or irritation.

"I know you can't," he tells her, nodding. Then he asks, "Why can't you, again?"

She smiles. "Because. This is a work affair, not a—"

"I know, not a basement rec room."

"Or a pickup joint. If we left together, people would talk."

"Who cares? We don't even know them. The only person in this room that I know is my editor, and last time I saw her by the bar she was getting bombed."

"Well, I know a lot of people here," Maggie tells him. "They're my colleagues, and I can't have them thinking that I'm, um . . ."

"Sexually active?" he supplies dryly.

She swats his arm. "That's not it. I just can't—"

She breaks off suddenly and reaches into her bag.

"What's wrong?"

"I've got a call." She produces a small cell phone.

"How'd you hear that ringing?"

"Because I have great hearing."

"Of course you do," he mutters, as she answers it.

Never in his life has he met a woman with as much self-confidence as Maggie has.

It used to get on his nerves, but suddenly, it seems to be one of her most attractive and refreshing qualities.

There's something ultrasexy about a woman who believes in herself. When Maggie wants something, she goes after it, and it never occurs to her that she might not get it.

If she wants him—

And something tells him that she does, despite her protests to the contrary—

Well, then, it's only a matter of time before she'll have him wrapped around her little finger.

And that, Charlie reminds himself, is the last place he ever expected—or wanted—to be.

"Maggie? Do you know where Dom is?" asks a rushed-sounding female voice.

"Who is this?" Maggie presses the receiver tightly against her right ear and covers her left with her hand to shut out the noise, turning toward the wall.

"It's Nina. I tried his cell phone, and he's got it turned off. We've got an emergency here, and we need him to get home right away."

"What's wrong?" Maggie asks, her stomach turning over.

"Rosalee's in labor, and Pop drove her to the hospital a while ago."

"Oh, that's so exciting!"

"It is, but Timmy's at work, and nobody can reach him. There's a big fire somewhere out in Flushing, and Joey went to try to track him down. Rosalee called just now and said the baby's coming faster than they expected. She's frantic without Timmy. I promised her I'd get over there right away to coach her in case he doesn't make it in time. I talked to Pop, and he's a mess—he can't be in the delivery room after—well, after what happened with Mom. And with me."

Maggie nods, fully aware that Dom's mother died in childbirth and that Nina almost met the same fate. No wonder she sounds so concerned about her sister, and no wonder Rosalee is desperate to have somebody there to help her through it.

"Do you have any idea where Dom is?" Nina asks. "Because I need him to get here and watch Rose and Nino so that I can get to the hospital. There's no one else I can ask. My in-laws are still in Florida, and—"

"Nina, it's okay. I have no idea where Dom is, but I can grab a cab and be there in fifteen minutes," Maggie promises, thankful that the restaurant is only two blocks from the Queensborough Bridge.

"Oh, Maggie, would you? I'd be so grateful. I just really need to be there with Ro."

"I understand. Just tell her to hang on and I'm on my way." Maggie disconnects the call and starts to bolt for the door.

"Whoa, wait! Where are you going?"

Charlie. She forgot all about him.

She explains the situation as briefly as she can, and is stunned by his response: "I'm coming with you."

"What? I just told you that I have to baby-sit for two little—"

"I know, and I'm going to help you. There's no telling how long you're going to be there. It could take all night. It did every time one of my sisters gave birth."

"But I don't need help." She strides toward the door, pushing her way through the crowd with Charlie dogging her steps.

"Maybe you don't need help, Maggie, but you probably could use the company."

"I'm sure the kids will keep me plenty of company."

"Yeah, well, so will I. And I happen to love kids. I'm great with them. Did I ever tell you I'm an uncle?"

"No, you never did."

"Sure I did. You weren't paying attention. I just told you that my sisters have given birth. That makes me an uncle, right?"

She sighs, smiles, elbows her way past two waiters and a couple of tipsy businessmen.

"I guess it does make you an uncle," she agrees. "How many nieces and nephews do you have?"

"No nephews. My family doesn't do boys. I have three nieces, and they all love me."

"I bet they do." Despite her hurry and the worry over Rosalee, she can't suppress a widening smile at the thought of Uncle Charlie romping around with three little girls.

"Well, the oldest two love me," he goes on, as Maggie reaches the coat check line and fishes her ticket out of her purse. "We play circus. The baby, Molly—she's not even two yet—she thinks I'm an actual lion. She screams when she sees me coming."

"Well, maybe the haircut will help," Maggie tells him, handing over her ticket, grabbing her coat, and tossing a couple of dollars into the tip bowl. "You can show her that you got rid of your mane, and you're a regular human being underneath."

"Right. It worked on you."

"Right." She can't help grinning.

He takes her black velvet swing coat from her and helps her into it.

Surprised by the gentlemanly gesture, she says, "Thank you. I guess I'll see you—"

"I'm coming with you. Remember?"

"But—"

"No arguments, Maggie."

"But—"

"I'm not ready to say good night yet," he says firmly. "Come on, let's go."

"What about your coat?"

"I didn't wear one."

"But it's twenty degrees out there."

He shrugs and gestures at his suit coat. "One jacket at a time is enough."

"Charlie—"

"I'm coming. So let's go."

Together, they push their way back through the crowd. This time, Charlie's in the lead. She has no choice but to follow him to the door since it's where she's going anyway.

She can't believe he's serious, but apparently, he is.

Why he'd want to spend the rest of the night as a makeshift nanny is beyond her.

All right, no, it isn't. He's hoping he's going to get lucky.

If Maggie were wise, she'd hold her ground and absolutely forbid him to come with her.

But apparently, her wisdom has gone the way of Charlie's wavy locks, leaving in its place a burgeoning reckless desire to see where the evening takes them.

Outside in the relative quiet of First Avenue, she turns to him, saying, "Look, Charlie, you don't even know where I'm going, and—"

"It doesn't matter. I'm going with you."

"What if I told you Dom's sister lives out in Jersey?"

"I love Jersey," he says, stepping to the curb and raising his arm to flag a cab. "Springsteen, *The Sopranos*, the Miss America Pageant, and the Meadowlands. What's not to love?"

"Nina doesn't live in Jersey."

"You just said that she did."

"No, I just said what if she did."

"What, you figured I wasn't willing to transport you across a state line again?"

Spotting an on-duty yellow cab barreling up the avenue, he steps farther into the street and waves his arm.

"How about across a river? Because Nina lives in Queens."

"Frankly, Jersey would've been better. Shea Stadium is in Queens and I hate the Mets. But since it's preseason, I'll deal."

The taxi pulls over. Charlie promptly opens the back door for Maggie.

She hesitates only a moment. "You're really coming with me?"

"You betcha."

She sighs and climbs into the backseat, giving the driver the address as Charlie climbs in after her.

As the cab hurtles them up First Avenue toward the Queensborough Bridge, Maggie looks at Charlie.

His face is alternately cast in light and shadow from the street, but she can see enough to realize that he's wearing a smug grin.

"Charlie, if you're thinking anything is going to happen other than diaper changing and bottle-feeding, I'd better warn you right now that it isn't."

"Are you sure? Because I'm great at wrestling around on the floor."

Again picturing fun-loving Uncle Charlie and his nieces, she allows her stern expression to soften. "Actually, it's so late that I doubt the kids will even be up."

"Then maybe you and I can wrestle."

"Charlie . . ."

She trails off.

"Yes?" he asks pleasantly, putting his arm along the back of the seat, against her shoulders.

"Just . . . don't. Okay?" She squirms a little, but the weight of his arm remains. "Don't make this hard for me."

"I'm trying to make things easier for you, Maggie. That's why I'm coming with you."

"Your coming with me makes it hard for me to remember that I wasn't supposed to want to see you ever again."

"Yeah, well, that's only fair, since I already remembered that I wasn't supposed to want to see you ever again, either, let alone want to—"

"Don't say it."

"What? Kiss you?" His lower arm slips down past her shoulder, pulling her close. "Because I do want to, and I'm willing to bet that you want to, too."

She turns her head to look out the window at the passing girders of the bridge. "Wanting to do something doesn't mean you automatically allow yourself to do it."

"Sure it does."

"Haven't you ever heard of self-discipline? It's good for the soul."

"Haven't you ever heard of self-indulgence? That's good for the soul, too."

She shakes her head and turns back to him. "Charlie—"

He captures her mouth with his.

Her fingers rise to his shoulders, meant to push him away; yet somehow, instead clutching his lapels, she pulls him to her.

She's as powerless to stop the kiss as she was to keep him from coming with her.

No.

Somewhere in the back of her mind she knows that isn't true. She could have stopped that, and she can stop this, if she wants to.

The trouble is, she doesn't want to.

The trouble is, she came to the party tonight looking for him, hoping against hope for the chance to see him again before Jason comes home. Because once Jason is home, her life will be full speed ahead. Not just her professional life; but her personal one as well.

He breaks off the kiss with a sigh, his lips streaking

across her cheek, her jaw, her hair. He brushes it back from her eyes again, and she looks at him solemnly in the dark.

"I just want you to know," she says, "that this is as far as it's going to go tonight."

"Why is that?"

"Because—"

"Because you have a boyfriend? I have to tell you, Maggie, that argument is getting less convincing over time. If this boyfriend is so crazy about you, where is he?"

"He's on his way home, actually. And he's not the only reason I can't be with you, Charlie. In fact . . . maybe he has nothing to do with it."

If that's a bombshell revelation to him, he doesn't let on.

Meanwhile . . . it sure as hell was a bombshell revelation to Maggie.

All this time, she's been telling herself that she has to choose between Jason and Charlie, and that Jason is the sensible choice.

The truth is . . . right now, Jason isn't even a choice.

Admit it, Maggie. Your relationship with him is in limbo. You were free to see other people while he was gone. Jason wasn't standing in your way of getting involved with Charlie.

You *were* standing in your way.

Well, there was a good reason for that—and there still is.

Charlie is all wrong for her, as wrong as—well, as ketchup on a hot dog.

Charlie stands for everything she doesn't want her life to be. When she's with him, she doesn't know what's going to happen next—and that bothers her. You don't feel your way through life, taking whichever path suits you at the moment. You map out a course with specific destinations, and you stick to it.

Otherwise, you could find yourself stuck on a farm in Wisconsin—or worse.

But Charlie's not in Wisconsin. Charlie's in New York.

Yes, Charlie's in New York—for now. There's no telling where he'll be tomorrow, or next year. He's a writer. He can live wherever he wants to live.

So that's it, Maggie? It's about New York? That's why you don't want to get involved with Charlie?

Of course it isn't. It's far more complicated than that. It's about compatibility. It's about commitment. It's about being with somebody who wants and needs the same things that you want and need.

From the time she first began to plot her future, Maggie always envisioned the kind of man who would complete her.

And he isn't Charlie.

Maybe he isn't Jason, either—but Jason comes a hell of a lot closer to fitting the bill.

Jason has a stable career.

Charlie's a freelance writer.

A freelance writer with a large trust fund and a penchant for car services and chartered planes.

Okay, so this isn't about money, either.

It's about . . . lifestyle.

It's about being with somebody who enjoys doing the same things you enjoy.

Things other than sex, which everyone enjoys, so that, Maggie assures herself, doesn't count.

Then again—never in her life has she met a man who made her feel as sensually charged as Charlie does. Which explains a lot.

Including the fact that she isn't pushing him away as he leans over to kiss her again as the cab races up Thirty-first Street beneath the shadow of the elevated tracks.

This time, she allows her mouth to open, allows his tongue to slip past her lips to caress hers. Acute longing stirs to life in the pit of her belly, beginning as a tickle and rapidly building to an almost painful ache that she knows can never be sated.

She can hear his breath coming hard and fast as he lifts his lips and cups her face in his hands.

"You can't tell me you're not feeling anything, Maggie."

She swallows hard, her own breathing as ragged as his. "It doesn't matter what I'm feeling because even if I were feeling something"—the most intense something she's ever experienced in her life—"I wouldn't act on it. I didn't get where I am by following my every whim."

"You didn't get where you are by denying them, either. You'd be a farm wife in the Midwest if you denied your desires."

She opens her mouth to argue, but clamps it closed again. He's right, dammit. Her thoughts are whirling with the skewed logic of his argument.

She thrives on taking risks.

But they've always been calculated ones.

Even when she was gambling in Atlantic City, she understood the stakes. She never bet more than she was willing to lose—and in the end, she didn't lose.

If she takes a chance on Charlie, she might lose everything—including her heart.

That, Maggie concludes, sliding out of his embrace, is a chance she simply doesn't have the guts to take.

Chapter Thirteen

Lying beside Maggie, holding her in his arms as she sleeps, Charlie concludes that he could do this every night for the rest of his life and be utterly content.

Well, not *this*, exactly.

In an ideal world, they'd be in a king-size bed instead of on a stranger's couch, and they'd be naked, and she'd have drifted off after a night of lovemaking.

But this is good, too.

This, Charlie reminds himself, is more than he anticipated when he spotted her across the room at that party.

A sneeze tickles his nose. His gaze falls on the vaseful of cut flowers on the Materis' coffee table. Apparently he's allergic to them, because his nostrils have been twitching ever since he and Maggie sat down here a few hours ago.

He purses his lips, wriggles his nose, dips his head toward his shoulder to press his nostrils into his shirt—anything to hold the sneeze at bay and keep Maggie from waking up. He just wants to hold her for a little while longer so that he can pretend this is more than it is.

The urge to sneeze passes, and Charlie gazes unseeingly at the television. The late-night talk shows that kept him and Maggie occupied for the first couple of hours of the evening have long since given way to a series of increasingly ridiculous infomercials, but Charlie can't reach the remote on the coffee table to change the channel.

Not that it matters.

He hasn't been watching TV anyway. He's been watching Maggie, and wondering if there's any way he can stretch these precious moments together into something more. Say, a lifetime.

Or even just another date.

Maybe he's just being ridiculously optimistic, but it actually seems possible. The date, not the lifetime.

That's because Maggie asleep is far less formidable than Maggie wide awake and in full barracuda mode.

Maggie asleep fills him with dreamy possibility; Maggie wide-awake riddles him with fervent need—and equally fervent doubt.

Maggie asleep is a vision of innocent beauty; Maggie wide-awake, a potent firestorm that ignites within him the need to challenge her—and to challenge himself.

Does he really intend to remain single for the rest of his days?

Of course you do. You know better than to waver when it comes to that. Your marital status is nonnegotiable.

All right, but that doesn't mean relationships with the opposite sex are entirely off-limits. Even if they can't lead anywhere remotely domestic.

He looks around the comfortable living room, trying to envision himself settling down in a place like this.

The family-friendly decor is interchangeable with

Charlie's sisters' homes. The furniture is kid-friendly with presumably washable slipcovers. The coffee table and end tables' edges are rimmed by a bumperlike cushions, the kind that are sold in child safety catalogues to protect toddling children from bumps and bruises. There are baskets of bright-colored plastic toys and framed photographs everywhere you look.

The thing is, even if he attempts—and succeeds at—picturing himself in this setting, he sure as hell can't see Maggie here. She spent the first half hour straightening the place after Nina left: wiping crumbs from surfaces, retrieving elusive Lego pieces from beneath the furniture, organizing the stack of catalogues on the end table.

When he told her to stop, she simply said, "I can't help it. Chaos drives me crazy."

Well, with marriage and children comes chaos. That much, Charlie understands. He doesn't want it—not that kind of chaos—and she doesn't, either.

Who knows? Maybe we're perfect for each other after all.

Which brings him back to square one.

That he wants Maggie in his life in some nondomestic capacity is a given.

That he *needs* her in his life is not.

What he *needs* is, quite simply, to find out whether she's willing to give a relationship with him a shot. If she isn't, he needs her out of his life, once and for all.

No more tantalizing chance encounters, no more steamy kisses that lead merely to steamier kisses and unfulfilled desire, no more wondering, no more *what-ifs*.

Only when Maggie's out of his life for good will he be able to focus on what really counts: experiencing the joys of bachelorhood so that he can get back on track with his writing.

He looks down at her, wondering how, in a vast city that's positively teeming with available women, he managed to entangle himself with the planet's most complicated and high-maintenance female specimen.

As though the weight of his gaze has awakened her, Maggie stirs in his arms. The sooty fringe of lashes flutter open, revealing a glimpse of that pure, startling blue. For a moment, she stares serenely up into his eyes, a tiny smile playing at her lips.

Then, as though she's abruptly realized where they are, she bolts into an upright position and demands, "What are you doing?"

"Me?" He shrugs innocently. "I'm watching TV."

Her gaze flits to the screen, where a bland and smiling hostess is demonstrating the joys of a suitcase that converts into a rollaway guest bed.

"You're watching this?"

"Yup. I'm thinking of getting that."

"Yeah, right."

Marveling at the rapid transition from beautiful dreamer to chops buster, he can't resist asking, "What makes you think I wouldn't buy that? It's nifty."

She smirks and looks around, rubbing her eyes, unwittingly smudging her makeup. "What time is it?"

"I have no idea. Probably almost four."

She checks her watch. "It is. Nobody's called?"

Between the expression of surprise and the smudged eyeliner, her eyes look bigger than ever—like one of those Precious Moments figurines his sister collects for his oldest niece.

"You were sleeping on my lap, Maggie. Do you think I'd have been able to answer the phone without your knowing it?"

She's silent, probably wondering how she landed on his lap.

He contemplates explaining that she started out leaning on a pillow, then slumped against his shoulder, then gradually grew cuddlier as drowsiness overtook her, slipping lower and lower until she was prone.

But why not leave all that to her imagination? He's rather enjoying the befuddled expression on her face—and his own position of control, for a change.

"I'm worried about Rosalee," she announces.

"I'm sure she's fine."

"She's not fine, she's having a baby."

"People have babies every day. Every second. It's not that big a deal."

"Of course it's a big deal. Especially in Dom's family."

She tells him, then, about Dom's mother dying while giving birth to his younger brother, and about Nina's brush with death when she had her daughter.

Charlie nods, understanding why Maggie's making such a big deal out of this. It is a big deal.

"Why hasn't anyone called?" she asks, pacing.

"Nina did call, before. Remember? She said her husband still hadn't found her brother-in-law and that the labor was progressing."

"I know, but that was hours ago. Why hasn't she called since?"

"Probably because there's no baby yet. These things can take days," he says with the reassuring expertise of a seasoned uncle.

"*Days?* I have to be at the office in a few hours."

"Well, you can go, and I'll stay here and watch the kids."

She snorts. "You? You don't even know them. Nina would freak out if she came home and found a strange man in her house, and the kids would freak if they woke up and—"

She breaks off, and he hears a howl from somewhere upstairs.

"Terrific," she says. "One of them's awake. Now what?"

"We go upstairs and check, what else?" He shakes his head, already up and headed for the stairway, stepping over her neatly placed high-heeled sandals at the foot of the flight. "I thought you said you have nieces and nephews, too."

"I do, but . . . I mean, I don't see them very often."

"So in other words, you're damned lucky I'm here."

"Shh! Don't swear in front of the kids, Charlie," she hisses, following him into the upstairs hall, where all is now silent.

"They can't hear me," he whispers, and gestures at the two semiclosed doors out of the four that line the hallway. "Which kid was crying?"

"I have no idea. I guess we'd better check them both. You take that door, and I'll take this one. Just be quiet."

He tiptoes toward the door opposite the one she's opening. The moment his fingers brush against it, it swings open with a loud creak and bangs the wall inside the room.

All hell breaks loose immediately.

"Look what you've done!" Maggie wails above the bloodcurdling shrieks that fill the hall.

"I didn't do anything," Charlie protests.

He strides into the room, lit by the glow of a clown night-light, and plucks a sobbing little footed-sleeper-clad fellow out of the crib.

"Hey there, buddy, what's the problem? It's okay, little guy. It's okay."

"Don't cry, Rose," he hears Maggie saying across the hall. "It's me, Maggie. Uncle Dom's friend. Remember me?"

Apparently Rose doesn't, because she screams even louder.

"We did Jack-in-the-box together, Rose, remember?" Maggie launches into a frantic-sounding rendition of "Pop Goes the Weasel," substituting "Da-da-da-das" every time she doesn't know a lyric. Which is often.

Grinning at her hapless efforts and off-key singing, Charlie bounces the baby boy on his hip. He turns on the lamp, shows the tot his reflection in the mirror, and makes a silly face. In a matter of moments, Nino's sobs turn to sniffles, then to giggles.

Maggie emerges in the hallway just as Charlie does. She's given up on singing, and her hair has come completely free of its pins, tumbling past her flushed face to her shoulders. She's clutching a tousle-headed little girl who's writhing and wailing hysterically in her grasp.

"Wose is sad," Nino tells Charlie solemnly, watching his sister elbowing Maggie in the cheek.

"Here, take him, and I'll calm her down," Charlie tells Maggie.

"How? She's out of control."

"I'll handle it," he says, so firmly that she trades kids

without further protest and carries the little boy down to the living room.

"I want my mommy," little Rose cries, flailing in his arms.

"Hey, it's okay, sweetheart. Your mommy and daddy went to the hospital to get your new baby cousin out of Auntie Rosalee's tummy," Charlie informs the little girl. "Do you think your new cousin will be a boy or a girl or a puppy?"

That gets a smile and an abrupt pause in the flailing action.

"A puppy!" Rose says decisively.

"Oh, yeah? A puppy with a tail?"

"Yeah! A puppy with a tail."

Moments later, he's got Rose giggling as he gives her a piggyback ride downstairs.

Maggie looks up in surprise from the storybook she's reading to the little boy on her lap. "What did you do?"

"Nothing," he says with a shrug. "I told you I'm great with kids."

"What's your name?" Rose asks, tweaking his hair.

"Charlie. What's yours? Oh, wait, I know. You're named after a beautiful flower. It's Daisy."

She screams with laughter. "No!"

"It's Lily."

"No!"

"It's Petunia?"

"No," Rose shouts gleefully. "I'm Rose!"

"Your toes?"

"No! I said I'm Rose!"

"You said tickle your toes? Well, all right, if you insist." He deposits her on the couch beside Maggie and tickles her bare feet.

"Mine, too! Mine, too!" Nino shouts, wriggling in delighted anticipation.

Charlie tickles his toes, too.

"Hers, too!" Rose demands, pointing at Maggie's hose-clad feet.

"Don't even think about it," Maggie warns him, laughing.

"Don't worry, I won't. I'll just . . . *do it!*" He reaches for her and within moments has her giggling and squealing helplessly on the couch with the kids.

Finally, limp with exhaustion, Rose declares herself "hungwee," and Nino pipes up, "me, too!"

Maggie smooths her hair, straightens her dress, and looks with uncertainty at Charlie. "They're hungry."

"Let's go feed them," he says, swinging Nino onto his shoulders and heading toward the back of the house.

There, he finds pretty much what he was expecting: a high chair, a booster seat, and a refrigerator covered in magnets and children's artwork, fully stocked with apple juice, milk, and yogurt.

In a matter of minutes, the kids are settled with sippy cups, yogurt, and Goldfish crackers Charlie found in the cupboard.

"Well?" he asks, looking at Maggie. "Am I good or am I good?"

Spooning coffee grounds into the filter basket on the counter, she shakes her head with admiration. "I hate to admit it, but . . . you're good."

He flashes a smug smile and retrieves Nino's dropped sippy cup as it rolls beneath the table.

"Did it spill?" Maggie reaches for a sponge.

"No, it's spillproof. See?" He tips it upside down, laughing when she flinches.

"Wow. I guess you learn something new every day, huh?"

"If you're lucky."

Smiling, she replaces the carafe in the coffeemaker and turns it on.

He's certainly learned something new today, he thinks, watching her absently shove her hair back from her face, marveling at this new and improved—i.e., relaxed—Maggie.

Relaxed, that is, until the phone rings suddenly, just as she's pouring two cups of steaming coffee.

"Get it!" she commands Charlie.

"Where is it?" He looks around.

"Never mind, I'll get it."

She's already got it, moving at lightning speed across the kitchen to snatch it from its wall cradle and blurting, "Hello?"

She listens a moment, then breaks into a big smile. Turning to Charlie and the children, she announces, "It's a boy!"

"A boy puppy?" Rose asks hopefully, as Maggie retreats to the next room with the phone cradled between her shoulder and her ear.

"A boy baby," Charlie tells her, tweaking her freckled nose with one hand and plucking Nino's precariously perched yogurt from the table's edge with the other. "But don't worry, Petunia, babies are cute, too."

"They don't have tails," Rose pouts, on the verge of tears. "I wanted it to be a puppy! You said—"

"I'll be your puppy. How about that?"

She breaks off, tilting her head dubiously, as if considering the offer. "How can you be my puppy? You don't have a tail."

"Tail!" Nino echoes, banging his spoon on the table.

Charlie removes his already loosened necktie from his collar and tucks one end into the back of his waistband.

He's down on all fours, scampering around the kitchen and begging for Goldfish crackers, when Maggie returns.

"Nina says—" She stops short in the doorway and laughs.

"Look, Maggie! See my new puppy?" Rose shouts.

"Me, too!" Nino trills. "Puppy!"

"You're crazy," Maggie says, as Charlie pants at her feet.

He barks and wags his tail.

Giggling, Maggie pats his hair. "Nice doggie. Nice crazy doggie."

The children are delighted and insist that he sit up and beg so that Maggie can pop crackers into his mouth.

Only when he's ingested more Goldfish crackers than any adult should be force-fed at any hour of the day, let alone predawn, does he manage to divert the kids' attention back to their own snacks.

"How's everything at the hospital?" he asks Maggie, sitting at the table as she sets a cup of coffee, a creamer, and a sugar bowl in front of him.

"Timmy made it there just in time to cut the cord, and everybody's happy. Nina said Joey's on his way back here now, so I don't have to worry about getting to work."

"That's good."

But it isn't.

His all-nighter with Maggie is drawing to a close.

"You can go now if you want," she says, with that quirky mind-reading talent of hers. She sits across from him with her own coffee and takes a sip, then adds, "I think I've got everything under control for the next fifteen minutes until their dad gets back from the hospital."

"I'll stay with you," he says, as though he's doing her a favor when in truth, he can't bear the thought of saying good-bye just yet.

"You don't have to."

"I know I don't, but I want to. You never know when they'll need a command puppy performance."

"I can be a puppy," Maggie protests.

He takes in her sparkly earrings, her plunging neckline, her panty hose.

"I dare you," he says with a grin.

She lifts her chin and indicates the kids. "I'd only do it for them."

"Do you two want Maggie to be a puppy?" Charlie asks Rose and Nino.

They clap their hands.

"Puppy!" Nino shouts.

"No, she's a kitty cat," Rose says. "A pretty kitty cat. Be a kitty cat, Maggie."

Shooting a triumphant glance at Charlie, she sets down her mug.

He watches, fascinated, as she lowers herself onto the floor, and transforms herself into a sex kitten. At least, as far as Charlie's concerned. As an extraordinarily sylphlike Maggie stretches languidly and purrs beneath their feet, the children giggle and laugh.

Nobody seems to notice that Charlie is utterly mesmerized by her performance until Maggie slides over to rub her shoulders against his legs.

"Pet the pretty kitty, Charlie!" Rose demands.

Charlie is only too willing to oblige, leaning down to stroke Maggie's silken hair with gentle, slightly trembling fingers.

She jerks her head upright at his touch, her startled gaze colliding with his. Her face instantly flames redder than the cherry-sprigged wallpaper overhead.

"That's enough kitty cat," she says abruptly, getting to her feet and brushing off her dress.

Charlie watches her return to her seat and go about adding sugar and cream to her coffee, though as he recalls, she takes it with neither.

Pleased that she's as outwardly rattled as he feels inside, he asks, "Do you live far from here, Maggie?"

"Around the corner," she replies, and her eyes, when she allows them to meet his, are alight with possibility. "Why?"

"No reason," he says with a shrug. "No reason at all."

Fumbling with the keys, it takes three tries before Maggie fits the right one into the lock. She turns it, jerks the door open, and steps into her apartment, lit only by the first light of winter dawn spilling through the windows.

Charlie kicks the door closed behind them and takes her into his arms, kissing her hungrily at last.

Maggie gasps at the intensity of his lips on hers, his insistent hands that strip off her coat, his touch that sears her flesh as he takes hold of her shoulders and backs her against the door. The length of his body is pressed into hers, leaving no room to doubt his masculine urgency.

Maggie allows herself to melt into his arms, knowing full well—and not, for the moment, the least bit concerned about—where this is leading.

He breaks off kissing her long enough to ask, "Where's your bed?"

"In there," she says, pointing.

He sweeps her into his arms like a movie hero, carrying her to her bedroom and depositing her on the neatly spread comforter.

"Why am I not surprised?" he murmurs, in between nibbling her ear, her neck, her throat.

"Surprised about what?"

"You make your bed."

"You don't? Why am *I* not surprised?"

"Why bother to make it when you're just going to mess it up again?"

She opens her mouth to tell him why, but his ravenous lips have claimed hers once more.

Time falls away as swiftly as their clothing, spinning Maggie into a far-off place where nothing matters but the exquisite sensations playing over her flesh.

Their lovemaking is a lust-saturated frenzy the first time; sensually languid the second, when they awaken after a brief doze in each other's arms.

"That was incredible," Maggie whispers, her head cradled against Charlie's bare chest.

"It was." His fingertips lazily trace her spine, sending shivers up and down.

He kisses her hair, and she yawns, utterly content. It's as though she's floating off on a rosy cotton candy cloud to some magical Neverland . . .

Until the alarm clock on the bedside table goes off abruptly.

Falling back to earth with a jarring thud, Maggie doesn't even have to turn her head to see what time it is. Her alarm is set to go off at five-forty-five every morning.

"I have to go to work," she tells Charlie, who still hovers above her, elbows propped on either side of her shoulders. She reaches over to jab at the snooze alarm button, something she never allows herself to do when the alarm wakes her.

"Call in sick."

"I can't. I have a meeting."

"You always have a meeting. Come with me instead."

"Come with you where?" she asks, laughing.

He kisses her neck. "Come with me to Europe."

"Sure, as long as you have me back in time for my meeting."

"I'm serious, Maggie." He lifts his head to gaze down at her. "I have two plane tickets I have to use by this weekend. Let's take off and go away together."

Why does he make it sound so damned tempting, so damned . . . possible?

"I can't," she says weakly, as he goes back to kissing her neck. "I have to work."

"You need a vacation."

"Mmm . . ."

He nuzzles the hollow beneath her ear.

He's right. She does. She needs a—

Wait a minute.

"I just had a vacation," she informs him, pulling back slightly. She can't think clearly when he's kissing her like that.

"Not with me."

"Yes, but—"

"You need a vacation with me."

"Charlie, I get two weeks off a year, and I just used one of them to go to Jamaica with my friends."

"That leaves you with a second week off. Spend it with me."

"I can't. I need to save it."

"For what?"

"I don't know . . . Christmas with my family?"

"That can't be as much fun as Europe with me."

"Charlie, you know that I can't just drop everything and fly away with you."

"Why not? You did it before."

True. She did do it before.

"Well," she retorts, "that was my first mist—"

Her words are lost as he kisses her mouth again. And again.

By the time they come up for air, her snooze alarm is bleating once more.

This time, Maggie turns it off completely. "I've got to get up, Charlie."

"Just a few more minutes," he croons, his breath hot against her ear.

"I can't," she says reluctantly. "If I don't go now, I never will."

"So never do."

She laughs, pushes him off her, sits up. "You make it sound so simple."

"It *is* simple."

"I don't have a trust fund to fall back on, Charlie. I have to go to work."

"Okay, then go to work and come right back here. I'll be waiting for you and we can pick up where we left off."

"We can't."

"Why not?"

"I have a movie screening to go to tonight. Our client is sponsoring it, and I have to be there."

"Can I come?"

Probably. She was invited with a guest.

Still, she hesitates. "That wouldn't be a good idea."

"Why not?"

Taking a deep breath, Maggie says, "Because I don't think we should see each other after this."

"Well, I don't either."

She blinks. "You don't?"

"No. We're obviously all wrong for each other."

Disappointment shoots through her. He thinks she's all wrong for him?

She wraps herself in a sheet and swings her legs over the edge of the bed, aloud saying only, "I know we're all wrong for each other. I've been saying that ever since Atlantic City."

"To whom?"

"Hmm?"

"Have you told anybody about us? Dom?"

"No! Have you told Julie?"

"No."

"Good. We wouldn't want anyone to get the wrong idea."

"Exactly."

"Especially since Jason is coming back to New York this weekend."

Charlie's expression darkens. "He is?"

Maggie nods.

"So you're going to pick up where you left off with him?"

"I don't know, Charlie. Maybe. I won't be able to figure that out until I see him. But it shouldn't matter"—It shouldn't, but it does—"because you just said that we're wrong for each other. We both know it."

"Right. And I think the smartest thing we can do is make plans for tomorrow night."

"What kind of skewed logic is that?"

"It's like giving up beer for Lent."

"*You're* Catholic?"

He nods. "Sure. Are you?"

"Please. With a name like Maggie O'Mulligan, you have to ask?"

He laughs.

She doesn't. She finds the fact that they share a religion oddly unsettling.

It means that if she brought him home, Mom and Dad would have one less potential objection.

Not that she's going to bring him home, and not that she has any intention of marrying him, because she doesn't. No way. Nuh-uh. No, sir.

But still . . .

"I don't drink beer," she reminds him, forcing her thoughts back to the matter at hand. Which happens to be, for God knows what reason, Lenten sacrifices.

"I've seen you drink beer."

"But I don't usually."

"Okay, then . . . how about chocolate? Do you like chocolate?"

"No."

He frowns. "What kind of person doesn't like chocolate?"

She shrugs. "A person who gets a headache when she eats it."

"Oh, for . . ." He looks exasperated. "Well, what do you like?"

"To eat?"

"To eat, drink, do. You know . . . what are your guilty pleasures?"

Other than him? Let's see . . .

"I like fresh raspberries."

"Fruit? That's the best you can do?"

"What? I love raspberries."

He follows her to the bathroom, where she plucks her toothbrush from its holder. "Do you ever give them up for Lent?"

"No. That would be cheating. They're out of season during Lent."

"Well, what *do* you give up for Lent?"

"What are you, an undercover rep for the Vatican? Why do you care?"

"Just tell me, Maggie."

She sighs, squirting Crest onto her toothbrush and turning on the water. "Last year, I gave up sugar."

"You mean, sugar in your coffee?"

She turns off the water. "I mean, all sugar in any form."

"You gave up all sugar for six weeks?" He looks incredulous. "Isn't that a little extreme?"

She removes her brush from her mouth long enough to spit, and ask, "Are you going to tell me why you care?"

"Because I'm trying to prove a point, here. Okay, look,

Maggie . . . what did you do to prepare for giving up sugar?"

"What do you mean?"

"Okay, before I gave up beer, I went to a Mardi Gras party and deliberately drank so much of it that it was the last thing I wanted to see the next day—or for a long time after that."

"That's either brilliant," she says, around a mouthful of bristles, "or really, really stupid."

"So you didn't O.D. on sugar before you gave it up?"

She hesitates, remembering. "Maybe I ate a few sweets."

More specifically, a bag of Twizzlers and an entire carton of Marshmallow Peeps washed down with Pepsi.

"A few?"

"All right, quite a few," she admits, and turns on the water briefly to wet her toothbrush again.

"Exactly. And that's what you need to do now, Maggie. Think of me the same way."

What is he talking about? He wants her to think of him as a Peep?

"We have to get each other out of our systems, right? So all we have to do is spend so much time together that we never want to see each other again."

"That's the most flawed reasoning I've ever heard in my life," Maggie informs him, brushing vigorously.

"What? I can't understand you when you have that in your mouth," he says.

Somehow, somewhere between the last bristle swipe of her molars and turning on the water again to give her brush a final rinse, she changes her mind.

"Maybe you're right," is what she says, and she has no idea why.

Because she's weary of arguing with him?

Because she's not ready to say good-bye?

Because she wants an excuse—any excuse—to keep on seeing him?

"Of course I'm right. You're not the only one who can be right, you know." He reaches out to grab her hand on the faucet. "Stop doing that, will you?"

"Doing what?" She frowns at his reflection beside hers in the mirror.

"Stop turning the water on, then off, then on, then off. It's driving me crazy. Just leave it on until you're done."

"I *am* done. And that would waste water. Don't you care about the water crisis? Wait, let me guess. You had no idea there even *was* a water crisis."

"I didn't, but I have a perfect solution. Let's shower together."

"Charlie!"

"What? That way, we can conserve water."

"Charlie . . ."

"Maggie, I'm just trying to be a concerned citizen and do my part. Come on . . ." Standing close behind her, he lifts her hair and kisses the nape of her neck. "What do you say?"

Maggie, who decides that she is nothing if not a concerned citizen, says yes.

Chapter Fourteen

Friday night at six-thirty, Maggie steps out of a cab on Harcourt Street—and finds herself face-to-face with Dominic, who just did the same thing.

"Maggie!" he calls, clearly startled, as both cabs pull away, leaving them on the sidewalk together in front of Julie's—and Charlie's—building. "What are you doing here?"

"I—what are you doing here?" she asks, wondering how she could have forgotten that she might run into Dom here.

Just yesterday, he mentioned—not for the first time—that he's taking Julie out to dinner tonight. Naturally, the blond waitress from the *She* party is history, and he's ready to resume courtship of his possible future bride.

"I'm picking up Julie for our date," he says in a *duh* tone. "Don't tell me you're thinking you're going to chaperone us, Mags, because I swear to God, that's not going to happen."

For a fleeting moment, she contemplates seizing the logical alibi he just provided.

But if she does that . . .

What about Charlie?

She's spent every nonworking moment with him for the past two days—ostensibly in an attempt to rid herself of any feelings for him. Their plan isn't succeeding—at least, not for her. And Charlie, when she left him in her bed this morning, showed no signs of aversion when he kissed her good-bye, and said, "See you tonight."

So here it is, tonight, and here she is, eager to see him again—and here's Dominic, giving her the evil eye, assuming she's here for an entirely different reason.

She can either go along with his assumption, or come clean and risk making the fling—or affair, or whatever it is that she and Charlie are having—official.

Opting for the latter, she prefaces her announcement with, "If you tell anybody, I swear I'll kill you."

He rolls his eyes, his breath puffing white in the frosty night air as he says, "Yeah, yeah, yeah, I've heard that before. So what's going on, Maggie?"

Clenching her gloved hands into fists, certain she's going to regret this, she admits, "I'm going out with Charlie," and waits for him to look dumbfounded.

"Charlie who?"

"Charlie Kennelly!"

"Julie's Charlie?"

His phrasing—even if it's purely platonic—sparks a ripple of envy in the most illogical part of Maggie's brain.

"Julie's friend Charlie, yes."

"Why are you going out with him? Let me guess . . . the two of you have some crazy scheme to spy on us?"

"No! We're going on a date."

"Why?"

"Because . . ." Good Lord, does she have to spell it out?

Apparently she does.

Exasperated, Maggie asks, "Why do people usually go out on dates, Dom?"

"Because they're interested in each oth—oh!"

At long last, the dumbfounded expression she anticipated crosses his features, chased by a smug grin.

"You're into Charlie, Mags? I don't believe it."

"Why not?"

"It's just—and you're trying to tell me that he's into *you?*"

Insulted, she scowls. "I'm not *trying* to tell you; I am telling you. Is that so impossible to believe?"

"Yeah," he says with a shrug. "It is. The two of you are just so . . ."

"Different?" she supplies when he can't seem to find the word he's looking for.

He snorts. "That's an understatement. I wouldn't be more shocked if somebody told me Bill O'Reilly hooked up with Hillary Clinton. Then again . . ."

"What?"

"Opposites do attract. Right?"

"So they say. Hey—where are the flowers?"

"What flowers?"

"The flowers I told you that you should bring to Julie when you showed up tonight."

"Oh . . . I'm bringing her this instead." He holds up the latest issue of *Sports Illustrated* with the Knicks on the cover. "Since she's a fan, I figured she'd like this better."

"You figured wrong, Dom. No woman would rather have a magazine than flowers."

"That's your opinion."

"And it's a sensible one." Maggie grabs his arm and hauls him across the street toward a Korean market.

If Charlie had his way, he and Maggie would be alone together, preferably unclothed, and in each other's arms.

He's begun to notice that he rarely gets his way—particularly where Maggie's involved—and thus finds himself at a table for four in a cozy Italian restaurant, listening to Dominic Chickalini wax enthusiastically about his newborn nephew, Timothy Jr.

It was Julie's idea that he and Maggie accompany her and Dom on their date, and he could hardly refuse. Not when she elbowed him into silence when he tried to protest.

He knows his friend is as reluctant to spend the evening alone with Dominic as Charlie is eager to spend it alone with Maggie. Not that Julie had any clue about Maggie until Dom told her, presumably moments after his arrival in her apartment.

"This is perfect!" Julie announced. "The four of us can double-date!"

Charlie—who has always subscribed to the theory that being capable of doing something doesn't automatically mean that you *should* do something—didn't have the heart to let her down. Not after she spent the afternoon telling him about the sexy new French sous chef at the bistro, and how much easier it is for her to talk to him than it is for her to make conversation with Dominic.

Charlie's beginning to suspect that Julie and Dom are as lost a cause as . . . well, as he and Maggie are. The difference is, Julie and Dom are trying their hardest to be attracted to each other—and Maggie and he are doing the opposite.

Now, as Dominic reveals that his new nephew's baby toe is smaller than the sliver of garlic on his fork, Charlie catches Julie stifling a yawn and Maggie checking her watch.

"He sounds like a cute kid, Dom," Charlie says, popping a last heaping mouthful of ravioli into his mouth and noting that he still has room for the spumoni he's been craving all week. "I'll have to get a look at him one of these days."

"Rosalee's bringing him over to Pop's for dinner on Sunday afternoon. You and Maggie should come over."

"Yeah? Maybe we will."

"I can't on Sunday," Maggie says, suddenly very busy buttering a roll.

"Why not?" Dom asks. "You got plans?"

"I—kind of." Maggie sneaks a look at Charlie, whose stomach turns over as he comprehends what those plans must entail.

"What plans?" Dom asks, oblivious to the look that passes between them.

"Just . . . there's some stuff I have to do."

Stuff, Charlie knows, that involves her boyfriend being back in New York.

Well, what were you expecting? You knew he was coming back, and you knew this couldn't last forever.

"Would you like to see dessert menus?" the waiter asks.

Charlie shakes his head, having lost his craving for spumoni—and everything else—everything except the one thing he can never, ever have.

Back in Charlie's apartment, Maggie looks around as he turns on lights and lowers the blinds.

Earlier, she was too distracted by the change in their dinner plans to focus much attention on her surroundings.

Now she wanders around the single room, taking note of the bed—unmade, of course; the heaps of wrinkled clothes on every surface; the laptop on a desk surrounded by piles of papers and books. There's a flat-screen television on one wall that's bigger than the window on the opposite wall; a Play Station; a complicated-looking stereo system with speakers that must annoy the hell out of the adjoining neighbors. Other than the clutter—which is everywhere—the place is bare.

"You know what you could use?" Maggie asks Charlie.

"I thought you'd never ask." His head is in the fridge, but he turns it to give her a lascivious grin.

"No, I meant curtains. Curtains and rugs, and some cute throw pillows."

"Cute throw pillows? What, shaped like ladybugs or flowers or something?"

"No, but maybe a nice floral print to jazz up the beige sofa. Know what I mean?"

"Not really. You want a glass of wine?" He sniffs a half-full bottle. "I'm pretty sure this is still good."

"No thanks, I'll just have water." On her way back to the couch, she brushes against a table and collapses a tower of mail. Picking it up, she sees that it's unopened. "You really should go through this, Charlie. What if it's important?"

"I'll get to it. I'm on a deadline."

"But doesn't the clutter make it impossible for you to

work in this place? You should go through it with a big
trash bag. I'll help you if you—"

"You want to throw away all my stuff?"

"Just the junk. You're a pack rat. I could help you get
organized."

"Thanks, but no freaking way."

She sighs, kicks off the pumps she's had on since six-
thirty this morning, and collapses on the couch with a
sigh. Wiggling her aching toes, she says, "I've been dying
to do *this* all night."

"I've been dying to do this all night," Charlie informs
her, setting two glasses of ice water on the coffee table,
sitting next to her, and taking her in his arms.

As he dips her back against the cushions and his mouth
claims hers, Maggie sighs with pleasure, lost in the moment . . .

Until he breaks off raggedly to ask, "Now what, Maggie?"

"Hmm?" She closes her eyes, raining fluttery kisses
along his jaw, relishing the stubbly scratchiness of his
cheek against the silken skin of her own, the contrast
sending delicious shivers down her spine.

"Now what?" he repeats, pulling his head back to look
at her.

She laughs, allowing her fingers to lightly dance their
way up his arms until her hands meet at the nape of his
neck, and she tugs his head down again, murmuring, "I
think you know what's next."

He breaks off the kiss too soon, saying in a voice that
sounds hoarse with passion—or with something else—
"That's not what I mean, Maggie."

Uh-oh. "Then what do you mean?"

"I mean, what's next for us? Now that he's coming back."

Uh-oh again.

Jason.

You knew this was coming, Maggie reminds herself. *It was obvious at the restaurant. His mood changed the moment you mentioned your plans for Sunday.*

That he recovered in time to drink an espresso and insist on paying the entire check fooled her into believing he was over his momentary jealousy—if, indeed, that's what it was.

"He was always coming back, Charlie," she says gently. "You knew that."

"So did you. Why did you let this go so far? The last few days—hell, the last few weeks—are nothing but a waste, Maggie."

Her Irish temper flaring, Maggie shoots back, "You're the one who convinced me that we should keep seeing each other. You said we'd get sick of each other. And don't you dare try to deny it because you know it's true."

She braces for an argument, but he merely shrugs. "It is true. I did say that. And I thought it would happen. I never thought . . . I never wanted . . ."

"I never wanted this either," she says when he trails off. "I just thought we could get each other out of our systems and move on."

"But now you don't think that we can?"

She hesitates; stubbornly refuses to say what he wants to hear. "I think that if we stop seeing each other, we can forget about each other."

He dismisses that with a wave of his hand and a sardonic, "That'll never work."

"What do you mean that'll never work? It makes more sense than your theory, which is the equivalent of telling a person that if they want to lose weight, they should eat everything in sight."

"Exactly."

"Exactly, what?"

"If somebody wants to lose weight, they should eat and eat and eat until they're so full they never want to eat again."

"But . . ." Maggie throws up her hands in exaggeration. "That's ridiculous, Charlie."

"No it isn't."

"Yes it is. Because sooner or later, they'll just be hungry again. And when they are, they'll eat."

"But not necessarily the wrong things. Maybe they'll be sick of fattening, junky, empty-calorie doughnuts. Maybe they'll want to eat broccoli instead."

"Are you comparing me to a doughnut, Charlie?"

He grins and brushes the backs of his fingers along her temple. "In the nicest way possible."

"Well in that case—you're a doughnut, too."

"Thanks. And your boyfriend . . . he's broccoli."

She hedges. "I wouldn't say that."

"Well, I would."

"You've never even met him."

"I don't have to. I know he's broccoli. And I also know that broccoli's not exciting, and its benefits are probably overrated, and personally, I think it stinks, but . . . it's good for you. Doughnuts every day . . ."

"They're not good for you," she says with a wry smile. "Is that what you're trying to say?"

"Yeah, I guess that's what I'm trying to say." He sounds sad.

"Well, it's a pretty creative way of telling me that you and I aren't meant to be together. Not that I didn't already know." She leans her head against his shoulder. "You must be a good writer, Charlie."

"Not lately. I spent the whole day trying to work and not getting anything done."

"Why not?"

"I don't know. Maybe I was too busy craving doughnuts."

She laughs. "I'm not sick of them yet. Are you?"

"Not yet." He leans down to kiss her.

She stops him, pressing a finger against his lips. "Just as long as we both understand that nothing's changed, right, Charlie? We're still clear on what we're doing here."

"We're just having fun," he says, his expression grim.

"Right," she agrees, suddenly feeling depressed. "We're just having fun."

Charlie glowers into his beer. "I hate this song."

"But you love Springsteen," Butts protests, above the noise from the jukebox on the opposite end of the bar.

"Not this song. This song is stupid."

"Yeah, a little," Butts agrees, lifting his own foaming mug to his lips.

"It's a lot stupid," Charlie informs him. "Not everybody has a hungry heart. What the hell is a hungry heart?"

"It's—"

"I know what it is."

"But you—"

"Not everybody has one, that's what I'm saying." Charlie drinks some beer and stares glumly into space, thinking about yesterday, and Maggie. And last night, and Maggie. And this morning, and—

"All right!" Butts elbows him in the ribs and points to the Knicks game on the television set above the bar. "Did you see that jump shot?"

"Nope."

"But you were looking right at it."

"I missed it, okay?" Charlie snaps.

"Okay," Butts says. After a moment, he asks, "What's wrong with you tonight?"

"Nothing."

"Are you sure, Charlie?"

No, he's not sure. He's not sure about anything right now, and he's not sure about anything he used to be sure about, either.

"Look . . . I understand. It's Laurie, right?" Butts says.

Charlie blinks. "What?"

"You heard she was getting married. I told Prairie Dog not to tell you. He's got the biggest mouth I ever—"

"Laurie's getting married?"

Butts gapes. "You didn't know?"

"No. And I don't care."

Butts pats his arm silently, obviously not believing him.

"Really, Butts. I don't care. This isn't about Laurie. It's about . . ."

He hesitates, not wanting to go there.

But apparently, it's too late not to, because the astonishingly intuitive Butts asks, "Who is she?"

"Her name's Maggie," Charlie admits, "and she's the biggest pain in the—"

"Aren't they all?" Butts cuts in. "So what's the problem? She's not into you?"

Charlie's thoughts drift over the last three nights in bed with Maggie, and despite his melancholy mood he can't keep a smile from touching his lips as he says, "No, she's into me. It's just . . ."

"She's married?"

"No!"

Maggie, married. The very thought of it makes him sick.

The thought of Maggie, married, to somebody else, that is.

And, of course, that's the only way to think of Maggie married because he, Charlie Kennelly, will never be anybody's husband. Not even hers.

In fact, he told her as much after that movie screening she took him to Thursday night. It was a romantic comedy about a series of wedding mishaps, and when it was over, Maggie turned to him to ask, "What did you think?"

"I think I made the right decision when I vowed never to be a groom," he told her.

He almost expected her to look disappointed, but she didn't. In fact, the knowledge almost seemed to energize her. It was as though his commitment phobia made him safer, somehow. Ultimately off-limits to a marriage-minded female the likes of Margaret O' Mulligan, whose marriage-minded broccoli head of a boyfriend is back in town.

He wonders whether Maggie would have rushed off to

meet Jason today if he, Charlie, hadn't said that about never being a groom.

Maybe she was just pretending to be okay with that. Maybe if Charlie was willing to make some kind of commitment, she wouldn't be, at this very moment—

"So if she's into you, and she's not married, what's the problem?" Butts asks.

You're not a promises kind of guy, Charlie.

"Listen, Charlie, you'd better tell me what's up, because I'm risking the wrath of Susie being here drinking beer with you in a dive bar on a Sunday afternoon instead of at her cousin's baby's christening."

"I appreciate it, Butts."

"Yeah, so do I. Christenings aren't my scene."

"You could have just told her you didn't want to go."

Butts snorts, shaking his head. "Yeah, right."

Therein, Charlie decides, lies the problem.

The problem being that men who fall in love lose control of their lives. The moment women show up with their silky hair and their silkier skin and their—their floral throw pillows, they take over. No sooner does a man declare himself smitten, than he must relinquish control of everything from how he spends his free time to what he can and can't wear in public.

Charlie, who is perfectly comfortable occupying a stool at the Stumble On Inn on a snowy Sunday wearing his oldest jeans and a gray hooded sweatshirt emblazoned with his college alma mater's seal, has no intention of relinquishing control.

Especially to a control freak like Maggie.

Which is why it makes absolutely no sense that he's drowning his sorrows—sorrows he has no business having in the first place—while she's out reconciling with her boyfriend.

Okay, not reconciling, per se. Maggie mentioned only that she was going to see Jason, who has apparently come marching back to town like a soldier returning from some distant battlefield back to claim his bride.

"Have fun," were Charlie's casual parting words when he left her apartment this morning, uncertain when—or whether—he'll be seeing her again.

Have fun.

Well, he sure as hell didn't mean it.

Nor, when Butts presses him for details now, does he mean it when he says, "Never mind. She's just some crazy skirt."

Crazy skirt?

He can just imagine what Maggie would say if she heard him calling her that.

She wouldn't stand for it, that's for sure. She doesn't stand for much.

Charlie raises his beer mug, toasting an imaginary Jason.

You've got your work cut out for you, pal.

"You sure you're okay?" Butts asks, watching Charlie carefully.

"I'm fine." He pushes her firmly from his thoughts—this time, he promises, for good. "Let's get another round."

Butts checks his watch.

Charlie is instantly reminded of Maggie. Well, that didn't last for long. So much for promises, even those he makes to himself.

"Wow, look at the time," Butts says.

"Put your watch away."

Charlie raises a hand to flag the bartender over.

"I should go," Butts protests. "It's getting late."

"Oh, come on, Butts. Another round. On me."

"I don't think that's a good—"

"Another round," Charlie repeats, this time to the bartender. "On me."

Shaking white flakes from her hair and stomping slush from her boots, Maggie greets the black Nehru jacket-clad Royalton Hotel doorman who quickly opens the door for her with a perfunctory "Good afternoon."

Yes. It's afternoon, all right. Whether it's going to be a good one remains to be seen, Maggie thinks, swallowing hard as she sweeps into the hotel.

The lobby's hushed interior is as monochromatic as snow-swept Forty-fourth Street was, but far more elegantly and deliberately so.

Given the choice, she'd have selected another spot to be reunited with Jason. Say, his place, or hers—or *any* place more private than this. The Royalton was his idea; it's where he took her for drinks before their first date.

Slipping her black leather gloves into her coat pocket, Maggie scans the lobby cocktail lounge for him. The place is relatively crowded for a stormy weekend afternoon: cozy couples, a random celebrity or two, and starry-eyed tourists whose clothing provides rare splashes of color in the room.

Maggie spots Jason on a distant couch with a cell phone pressed to his ear. Apparently caught up in his conversation, he doesn't see her.

Good. That will give her time to steel herself for the reunion she was so eagerly anticipating until it actually loomed.

Now that he's back in New York, she's willing to pick up where they left off . . . but only if the sparks are there—and only if they're stronger than the sparks she's been sharing with Charlie.

Sparks? Calling what she and Charlie share "sparks" is like calling a blowtorch a "flicker."

And anyway . . .

No more thinking about Charlie, she admonishes herself as she walks through the lounge, keeping her eye on Jason.

He looks tanned and handsome; far thinner than she remembers. Almost gaunt, compared to Charlie's healthy—

No more Charlie, dammit!

Okay, okay. I'll stop. I'll focus on Jason. It's just . . . hard.

She studies him as she walks closer, concluding that Jason probably lost quite a bit of weight while he was away. He could pass for a tourist—or at least, a suburbanite—wearing a pale pink Ralph Lauren button-down and khakis with a cream-colored sweater tied around his shoulders.

Maggie tries, and fails, to picture Charlie in similarly preppy clothing. In fact, the only way she's able to conjure him at all is stark naked against her tangled sheets—which is where he was when she left him this morning to go to mass.

"Don't you want to come with me to church?" she asked him, grinning and wriggling out of his grasp as he tried to coax her, fully dressed, back to bed.

"Not at this hour," he said, yawning. "When I go, it's

usually to a late-afternoon mass at my parish down in the Village."

At least he goes, Maggie thought then—and thinks again now. Her faith is important to her, and she's glad that he shares it.

Not that Jason doesn't. And Jason—not Charlie—is the focus of her attention today.

Being with him again will tell her everything she needs to know. At least, that's what she's counting on. The few stolen days with Charlie have made her question everything she ever wanted—or assumed she wanted.

Taking a deep breath, Maggie covers the last few feet of ground between them, arriving in front of him just as he disconnects his call.

"Maggie!" He stands and pulls her into his arms, giving her a bear hug before holding her back a bit to look down into her face. "You look gorgeous."

"Thanks. You look . . ." *Like a stranger.* "You look great, too, Jason."

"I do?" He laughs, shaking his head. "That's not what my mother said. She thinks I've lost too much weight. She had her cook send over a huge spread first thing this morning."

Reminded again that she and Jason inhabit different worlds—and that his is one she has long coveted—Maggie does her best to banish the image of unshaven Charlie in his boxer shorts, frying eggs in her kitchen, asking her whether she wants three or four.

Thanks to his contagiously voracious appetite the last few days they've spent together, the waistband on Maggie's black silk trousers feels uncomfortably snug as she sits beside Jason.

"How was your flight?" she asks him, steadying her trembling hands by clenching them in her lap.

"Late. Long. Turbulent. You know, the usual."

"Did they lose your luggage?"

"No."

"Then, hey, you're ahead of the game."

Could this conversation be any more trite? Maggie wonders, her fingernails digging into the palms of her hands. Three months apart, and this is all they have to say?

A waitress who could pass for Cindy Crawford appears to take their order—two glasses of red wine—then drifts away, leaving Maggie alone with Jason again—and once more fumbling for conversation.

The task seems to be hers alone, as he seems oddly preoccupied.

Discarding a number of topics that would tread dangerously close to what she's been doing with herself—rather, with Charlie—in Jason's absence, she settles on, "Is it good to be home?"

She doesn't expect the slight hesitation before he says, "Sure." Nor does she expect the serious expression in his eyes when she dares to meet them.

"What's wrong, Jason?"

Does he know, somehow, what she's been up to? Does he sense that she's fallen for somebody else? She'll deny it. She'll explain that it was merely a few dates; that they agreed to see other people, and she hopes he did, too.

"Maggie, I have something to tell you."

Uh-oh.

The Harrigan intuition revs into gear.

He's found somebody else, Maggie realizes, stung.

He's gone and fallen in love with some . . . some jungle goddess.

"You're in love with her?" she asks, wondering how she feels, knowing only that it isn't jealous, or regretful, or anything of the sort.

Jason blinks, looking around. "In love with whom?"

"Oh, I thought . . . I figured that was what you needed to tell me. That you've found somebody else."

Guilt flickers in his gaze, yet he says, "No, it's not that."

"Then what?" Maggie asks, wondering what's up with her sixth sense lately. Next thing you know, it'll be telling her that she has a future with Charlie.

Then you'll know for sure that it's out of whack, she tells herself ruefully.

"Maggie . . . I'm not staying in New York. I wanted to tell you as soon as possible, and I wanted to do it in person."

Relief washes over her like a tidal wave that, along with his bombshell, she never saw coming.

She feels weak, leaning back against the couch cushions for support.

Apparently, Jason interprets her reaction as crippling disappointment; he grasps both her hands in his and says fervently, "I'm sorry, Maggie. I know you weren't expecting this."

"No, I—I wasn't expecting it at all," she murmurs, utterly dazed as all her tentative plans, all that *potential* is swept away like lovers' heart-encased initials erased from the sand by the incoming tide.

"I want you to know that this has nothing to do with you."

She nods mutely, her thoughts spinning.

"Like I said, there's nobody else—it's nothing like that."

Guilt attempts to steal over her, but she pushes it away. They agreed to see other people. That's what she did with Charlie. That she has feelings for somebody else—and Jason doesn't—is a moot point.

He's leaving New York—that's what matters.

He goes on talking, telling her about the journey to South America, and how he truly believes that he's found his calling, and how his services are needed next in the war-torn Middle East.

As the news settles in, she finally grasps that Jason has chosen the desert wasteland and thousands of ailing, starving orphans over New York—and Maggie. Somehow, the comprehension brings her nothing but comfort.

For once, and quite inexplicably, Maggie—who thrives on being in control—gladly relinquishes it. Jason's decision has been made, thus leaving her with one less decision to make.

When their wine arrives, she smiles and holds up her glass.

"Let's toast your new beginning, Jason."

His eyes widen. "Are . . . you're sure? You're okay with this?"

"I'm fine with it. You're doing the right thing. I wouldn't expect you to stay here after all you've told me. It's obvious that you're meant to do other things."

"Maggie—"

"This will be fulfilling for you. I can tell."

"It will, but—let me finish. You can come with me if you—"

"No," she says quickly. "I can't, Jason. I've got too many things to keep me in New York. My career, and my friends, and . . . my apartment," she feebly substitutes for the forbidden word that came first to her mind.

The forbidden word, of course, being *Charlie*.

Charlie isn't what brought her to New York, and he sure as hell isn't what's keeping her here.

"I understand that your life is here, Maggie," Jason tells her, setting his wineglass on the table and squeezing her hand. "I honestly thought mine would be, too. I even thought we might end up together."

She smiles sadly. "So did I."

Good-bye, four kids and a housekeeper. Good-bye, East Thirty-eighth Street town house. Good-bye, Jason.

He tells her, "I figured taking this trip would be a unique experience—you know, something I always wanted to try before I settled down. But . . . it turns out I don't want to settle down anytime soon. I just . . . I can't. I hope you understand."

"I do, Jason."

He leans over to kiss her.

She knows, then, what her decision would have been had he not made it for her.

There are no sparks. Her feelings for Jason are in the past.

Suddenly, all she wants to do is tell Charlie that she's free . . . and that she's willing to take a chance on him. On them.

But that doesn't change the fact that he isn't, she reminds herself. *And you shouldn't be, either.*

Nothing's changed for Charlie. He still thinks you're all wrong for each other.

And they are. Charlie's as wrong for Maggie as he ever was.

She has to face the truth. Letting go of Jason merely relieves her of a future with him. It doesn't create one with Charlie. Nothing short of a miracle could accomplish that.

"Charlie! What are you doing here?"

"I'm home," he announces, leaning against the doorframe.

"What the—? No, you aren't," Julie says, rubbing her sleepy eyes and squinting out into the hallway.

"Yes, I am. What are you doing here?"

"I live here, and you're . . . you're stinking drunk."

"Broccoli stinks," he hisses. "Maggie's boyfriend is broccoli, and he stinks."

"So do you." Julie makes a face and takes his arm, leading him inside.

"Somebody redecorated my apartment while I was out," he accuses, looking around in dismay. "I bet Maggie did it."

"This is my apartment, you dope. I heard you trying to shove your key into my lock. You scared the heck out of me. I thought you were a burglar."

"Huh?" He looks around; recognition sparks. "You're right! It is your apartment, Julie!"

"Yup."

"What a relief. So Maggie di'n throw away my stuff?"

"Not that I know of." Julie shoves him into a chair. "Here, sit down. I'll make some coffee. You could use some."

"Got any doughnuts? I could use some a' those, too."

"Doughnuts? I'm fresh out."

"Damn." He snaps his fingers. "I love doughnuts. Doughnuts are good for you. You could live on doughnuts, you know that?"

"Charlie—"

"Maggie doesn't know that. I tried to tell her, but . . ." He shakes his head, wishing it weren't pounding and wondering why the heck Julie's face is so blurry.

"Maggie thinks she knows everything," he informs her.

"Well, so do you. I guess that makes you perfect for each other."

"What? I do'n think I know everything."

"Sure you do. You think you know what's best for me, and you don't even know what's best for yourself. You keep talking about how happy you are living the single life and writing about it, but Charlie, you're lonely."

"I'm not lonely!"

"Sure you are."

"No way. I have you. You wanna go to the French Riviera? I have to use my tickets in a couple of days, or I lose them."

"Charlie, I'm just your friend. You don't want to bring me. That was supposed to be your honeymoon."

"See? You're right. You're my friend. I'm not lonely. I have you, and I have Butts . . . that's two." He's counting off on his fingers. "I have Prairie Dog. I have Pork. That's four." He stares sadly down at his unclaimed thumb. "Maybe tha's not enough?"

"I don't think it is."

"Do you think I need five?"

"Could be."

"Okay, maybe I need Maggie. Maybe she can be my thumb."

Julie pats his arm. "That's the smartest thing you've said yet. I just wish you were going to remember it in the morning."

He bolts out of his seat. "Morning? Is it—"

"No, it's—"

"When iss morning, I have to work. I have to write my column. Iss late. What am I gonna write about, huh, Julie? Should I write about Maggie and how she can be my thumb?"

"I don't know . . . your readers might not get it."

"But I want to write about Maggie," he says fervently. "I want to because—oh, man. I knew it. I knew it."

"What did you know?"

"I love her. Did I ever tell you that, Jul'?"

"No," Julie says, smiling. "You never did."

"Well . . . I do."

"That's great, Charlie. Maybe you should tell her."

"No!" he protests, horrified. "I can't tell her. No way. 'Cause Maggie doesn't love me. She loves broccoli instead. 'Cause broccoli's good for you, even though it stinks."

"Just when I thought you were making perfect sense . . ." Julie sighs. "I'll go make the coffee."

Chapter Fifteen

Another Monday morning, and Maggie drags herself to her desk on a few hours' sleep at most.

Why didn't Charlie call her back last night?

She left him a message when she got home from the date with Jason.

When hours went by and he didn't return the call, she started wondering if he ignores his answering machine the way he ignores his mail. So she called again, late, knowing he'd be up, since he told her he never goes to bed before midnight.

She got the machine again and left another message, concluding that he was either out, or screening his calls. Then she hung up and obsessed about it for the rest of the night.

What if he was out trolling the town for women?

What if he was screening his calls?

Neither scenario allowed her to rest easily—hence, scratchy, burning eyelids, an aching back, and the sense that this day is going to drag on forever.

After an interminable department meeting, she meets

Carolyn for lunch at a crowded coffee shop on Lexington Avenue.

"Why didn't you want me to invite Bindy?" Carolyn asks, as Maggie slides into the booth opposite her.

"Because I'm not in the mood to have her tell me I'm making a big mistake again."

"What big mistake are you making this time?"

"The same one I made last time, according to Bindy. Letting Jason escape my clutches."

She quickly explains the situation to Carolyn, whose expression is sympathetic behind her owlish glasses.

"Well, it's not like you have a choice. You have to let him go. I mean, what else can you do? Follow him to the Persian Gulf?" Carolyn asks.

"He asked me to go with him, but . . ."

"You said no?"

"Of course I said no." She hesitates, uncertain whether she should bring up Charlie.

Of course she shouldn't. He has nothing to do with anything.

"Well," Carolyn says, "if you were in love with Jason, you'd follow him anywhere. You wouldn't care about anything but being with him. You'd make it work."

"You think?"

"I *know*. I've edited enough romance novels in my career, haven't I?"

"So that makes you an expert? That's like . . ."

"Like what?" Carolyn prods when Maggie catches herself and clamps her mouth shut.

It's like Charlie considering himself a relationship guru because he writes a column about being a bachelor.

But Carolyn has finally stopped asking her about Charlie every time they've spoken since Maggie admitted to kissing him. The last thing she wants is to trigger that whole line of questioning for another couple of weeks.

Carolyn is still waiting for a reply.

Thinking quickly, Maggie says, "That's like Bindy thinking she can build houses because she works for an architectural firm."

They order salads and coffee, and wonder aloud whether Bindy's latest fledgling romance—with a corporate attorney—will lead anywhere.

"If she weren't so damned picky, she could be married by now," Carolyn says. "Her standards are ridiculously high. She won't date anybody who doesn't make a certain salary, or live in a certain neighborhood, or wear certain clothes. She thinks she knows exactly what she wants, and she won't stop looking until she finds it."

"Mmm."

It suddenly occurs to Maggie that Carolyn might just as well be talking about her.

"Is that so bad?" Maggie asks. "You know . . . Bindy being so . . . choosy?"

"I think it is. She's ruled out a lot of options right from the start. What if she met a starving actor or a . . . a sailor, or a—I don't know, a kiddie party clown, who was perfect for her in every way that wasn't superficial?"

Maggie laughs. "I can't see Bindy with a clown."

"Neither can I, but you know what I mean. She would never give a guy like that a chance because he doesn't fit into the Bindy image."

Right.

Just as Charlie doesn't fit into the Maggie image.

Their salads arrive, both with ranch dressing on the

side, no croutons—just as Maggie requested. Carolyn's request for extra croutons and blue cheese dressing was apparently ignored, but she doesn't realize it until the waitress has left.

"Get her back here," Maggie says, trying to wave her over.

"No, it's okay. I'll eat it this way."

"Carolyn, that's ridiculous. You should get what you ordered."

"It's not that big a deal. I like ranch, too."

"It's fat-free."

"Well, I can stand to skip a few fat grams," Carolyn says, with a rueful glance at her ample figure.

"But—it's not what you wanted."

Carolyn shrugs and digs into her salad, saying, "Oh, well. You can't always get what you want."

Flummoxed, Maggie picks up her fork.

"Plus," Carolyn goes on, "now I can afford to have a Krispy Kreme when I stop for my coffee later."

Krispy Kreme . . .

Doughnut . . .

Charlie.

"What's wrong, Maggie?"

"Hmm?" She looks up to find Carolyn popping a grape tomato into her mouth, eyeing her with a curious expression.

"Aren't you going to eat?"

Maggie picks up the plastic cupful of fat-free ranch dressing and dabs a bit on the iceberg lettuce. Then she stares at it.

Carolyn clears her throat. "Okay. Spill it. What's up?"

"It's just that I think I might have made a big mistake after all."

"Letting Jason go?"

"No. That wasn't a mistake. I just . . . remember I told you about that guy Charlie?"

"Duh, of course I remember. Charlie Kennelly, Bachelor at Large." Carolyn grins. "He's so hot."

"He *is* hot," Maggie admits, the noisy coffee shop falling away as her thoughts drift to steamy nights in Charlie's arms . . .

"Maggie! You slept with him," Carolyn hisses.

Startled, Maggie looks up, feeling her cheeks grow warm. "Why do you think that?"

"I can tell by the look on your face."

"Don't tell anyone, okay?"

"Oh, please. Who am I going to tell?"

"I don't know . . . Bindy?"

"What am I, stupid? I'd never tell her. So are you seeing him?"

"Yes—No. I mean, not really. Not like that. We're just . . ."

"Friends?"

"No!"

Carolyn laughs. "Okay, I guess the 'f' word is offensive, huh? So you're more than friends, but less than . . . well, you're not less than lovers, obviously. So what are you?"

"I don't know. I didn't think we could be anything. He's about as wrong for me as anybody can possibly be."

"In what way?"

Hmm. Maggie considers Charlie.

How do I not *love thee? Let me count the ways.*

In fact, she already has. Thirty-three of them so far, itemized with bullet points in her Palm Pilot.

"He's sloppy."

"So am I, and you love me."

"But I don't live with you."

"No, but you said you were willing to."

"True."

"What's the difference between a slobby female room-mate and a slobby male one? Never mind—come on, what else?"

"He's lazy," Maggie says promptly.

"He can't be that lazy. He's disciplined enough to meet his magazine deadlines every month."

"Well, don't hold your breath for his next column. He's slacking off even as we speak." She looks at her watch. "In fact, he's probably still sleeping. Which is yet another fault. A huge one."

"That he sleeps in? So would I, if I didn't have to be in the office at nine, which he doesn't. So would anyone."

"I wouldn't."

"You're right, Maggie. You wouldn't. And from what you've told me, I can see why he's absolutely, totally wrong for you. I mean—if the two of you wouldn't even get up and go to bed on the same schedule, then forget it. No wonder you're going to tell him you can never see him again."

"I didn't say I was going to tell him that." An inexplicable wave of panic rises into Maggie's throat. She reaches for her water glass, bent on washing it back down into the fluttery pit of her stomach, where it belongs.

"Then you're still going to see him? Even though he's all wrong for you?"

"I didn't say that either." Maggie swallows some water. "But you can see what I'm saying, right? Why I think he's wrong for me?"

"No. I'm just trying to be agreeable." Carolyn spears a cucumber slice and pops it into her mouth, crunching, and saying, "I have to go back to the office and have a long, drawn-out editorial meeting, and I'm not in the mood to preface it with one of those long, drawn-out, can't-win arguments with you."

"Come on, Carolyn. I won't—"

"Sure you will. Because you're trying to talk yourself out of Charlie, Maggie, and you won't listen to reason. You're clinging to these superficial things about him— things that don't matter in the grand scheme of things."

"Sure they matter. To me." Maggie jabs her fork into a pale hunk of lettuce. "I can't believe any restaurant in Manhattan still uses iceberg in salad."

"What would you expect in a place like this? Mesclun greens?"

"Romaine, at least."

"But you're eating the iceberg. And it isn't so bad. Admit it."

"I know what you're doing, Carolyn."

"I'm talking about lettuce."

"No, you aren't."

"Sure I am. But you have Charlie on the brain, so . . ." She shrugs. "Oh, why bother? You already know what I'm going to tell you."

"No I don't."

"Sure you do. That's why you invited me here, and not Bindy. You know what she'd tell you about Charlie, too."

"That I should never see him again."

"Right. And you didn't want to hear that. You wanted to hear my infinite romantic wisdom. You wanted to hear me say what I said before. That you should give Charlie a chance."

"Maybe I did want to hear that," Maggie agrees slowly, nodding.

"Okay. I said it. You heard it. Now what are you going to do about it?"

Nursing his second hangover in as many weeks, Charlie tries to figure out where he went wrong.

Not just last night—because after all, that much is obvious. His misstep last night was allowing Butts to leave the Stumble On Inn without him, then switching from beer to Scotch. He'll never mix the two again.

In fact, he's fairly certain he'll never indulge in an alcoholic beverage again—which more or less proves that theory he was applying to his relationship with Maggie.

And that, my friend, is where you went wrong, big-time.

Attempting a relationship with Maggie—even a temporary, purely physical one—was a misstep the equivalent of stumbling over the edge of the Queensborough Bridge—and the damage is just as irrevocable.

Now that she's under his skin, he can't figure out why his handy dandy plan to get her out isn't working. Always before, if he spent enough time with a woman, he wound up feeling claustrophobic.

Well, except with Laurie. She had her faults, but they were faults he assumed he could live with. Their problem was that she couldn't live with his faults.

If Laurie hadn't jilted him, he'd be married to her right now.

Thank God, thank God, thank God he isn't married to her right now.

Marriage to Laurie would have been about as fulfilling and successful as—well, as his parents' marriage.

What little he remembers of the two of them together alternates between screaming, door-slamming fights and icy silence. It's a miracle, really, that Charlie was willing to get engaged to anyone in the first place, given his parents' track record.

Well, it's not like you're ever going to get engaged again. Been there, done that, over it. Period.

That he's jaded when it comes to love is a given. Yet . . .

Maggie called him yesterday. Twice.

He didn't get the messages until today, when he woke up and noticed the light flashing on his answering machine.

Why did she call him?

To tell him that she's marrying Jason?

Or to tell him . . .

That she *isn't?*

That she doesn't want to get married at all, which is why she'll be happy to hang out with him for a while longer, until they can get past this ridiculous, insatiable lust?

Okay, so maybe—just maybe—there's a tiny part of jaded Charlie that still believes in happy endings.

But that's probably only because he's a writer. A writer with a huge imagination and the ability to escape reality on a daily basis.

Not, he thinks, stretching and returning his focus to the blinking cursor on the empty screen before him once again, that he's supposed to be indulging his fiction writing as frequently as that—if ever. He can't let another day pass without getting something—anything—done on his new column.

Glancing at the clock, he realizes that the day is three-quarters over. He's been sitting here for a few hours, and all he's done so far is toy with the feathers on his thinking hat and fight the urge to open the document he was working on last week. The one about the character he's come to think of as Fictional Maggie.

Just knowing she's there, locked away in his computer's memory, is so distracting that the real Maggie's shadow might as well be looming over his shoulder.

He sits up straight in his desk chair, fingers poised on the keyboard.

Write.

Write, dammit!

Nothing.

He flings his thinking hat across the room in dismay.

Oh, for Pete's sake, just get something down.

In college, his creative writing professor used an exercise to get them started. He'd set an egg timer and they would have three minutes to do stream of consciousness writing. Content didn't matter—they could just write their own names over and over again if that was all that came to mind. The important thing was to get something down and trigger the creative process.

Okay, so do it.

Charlie starts typing.

M-A-G-G-I-E

With a curse, he backspaces over it just as the intercom buzzes.

Striding to the door, he presses the button and barks, "What?"

"Sorry to disturb you, Mr. Kennelly," the doorman says apologetically. "I've got somebody here to see you. She says her name is Mandy—"

The doorman's voice abruptly gives way to Maggie's. "Not Mandy. *Maggie*. It's Maggie, Charlie."

Dumbfounded, he can feel his pulse quicken at the sound of her voice.

"Excuse me, ma'am," the doorman is saying, "but you're not supposed to—"

"Just a second. Charlie, can I come up?"

His stomach flip-flops. "Yeah. Come on up."

He turns away from the door. The place is a mess. The place is a mess and—he catches a glimpse of himself in the mirrored closet door—*he's* a mess.

This is why you should never have short hair, he concludes, raking his fingers along his scalp in an effort to make it lie flat. The top persists in standing straight up like a little boy's July crew cut. At least when it's shaggy it doesn't stand on end.

He glances from the pile of still-unopened mail, to which he's added a new batch, to the kitchen, where the remains of his midnight snack and this afternoon's breakfast clutter the countertop. And there are the clothes he wore yesterday, strewn across the floor between the door and the bed in precisely the order he stepped out of them. Only his boxer shorts seem to be missing—until he spots them hanging on the bedpost.

Right now, he's wearing nothing other than a pair of flannel pajama bottoms, a day-old growth of beard, and a scowl.

What's Maggie going to say? he wonders, followed by a fierce, *Who cares what Maggie has to say?*

He dares her to walk in here like she owns the place—like she owns him—and start criticizing everything. He just dares her.

"Floral throw pillows, my ass," he mutters, running his hand through his hair again. Only this time, his goal is to make it as unruly as possible.

And anyway, he wonders as he paces away from the door and back again, what the hell is she doing here at this hour of the afternoon? It's not even five o'clock yet. Shouldn't she be working?

Shouldn't you? You don't have time to kill on this . . . this . . .

"Crazy skirt," he mutters, as a knock sounds on the door.

He opens it, coming face-to-face with Maggie. Maggie in a trim blue suit, a wool dress coat, and pearls. Maggie with her hair in a smooth chignon and a smile slowly freezing on her lipsticked lips as she meets his ferocious gaze.

"What's wrong with you, Charlie?"

"What's wrong with me? Nothing. Why are you here? Why aren't you working . . . or with Jason?"

"I left the office early. I needed to talk to you."

"You left work to talk to me? It must be important."

"It is. Can I come in?"

He wants to tell her no. She can't come into his apartment, and she can't come into his . . . his . . . his *life*.

But she's already here, stepping over the threshold like she owns the place—and him.

There's nothing for him to do but close the door after her.

"Aren't you going to lock it?" she asks, watching him.

"No. Why?"

"You should keep your door locked. It's dangerous not to. You never know who might be lurking."

"You mean like strange women on the lam from their midtown offices?"

She smirks. "Exactly."

Deliberately leaving the door unlocked, he sits beside her on his couch. His *beige* couch. The beige couch that always looked fine to him unadorned—until she had to go and suggest that he jazz it up. Ever since she said it, he can't look at his couch without feeling as though it looks a little . . . blah. As though something is missing.

How can something suddenly seem to be missing when he always thought it was perfectly adequate the way it was? It makes no sense—and it bugs the hell out of him.

"I hate floral print," he blurts.

"*What?*"

"Floral print. I don't like it. I just had to get that off my chest, before you say anything else."

"Okay," she says slowly, looking bewildered. "Whatever."

"The pillows. You said I needed pillows. Remember? In floral print."

"Well . . . I'm not here to redecorate. Charlie, are you okay?"

"I'm great. Never been better."

Her gaze falls on the computer across the room.

He wildly tries to remember whether he erased her name from the screen. He did, didn't he? Please, God, let him have erased her name because if old Eagle Eye here spots it, she'll know . . . she'll know . . .

She'll know that you know how to spell Maggie, that's all she'll know, he tries to reassure himself.

Uh-uh.

No, she'll know that he can't stop thinking about her, even now that Jason is back in town.

"So are you getting married?" he asks curtly.

Taken aback, she shakes her head slowly.

His spirits soar.

She's not getting married!

"Jason is going to the Middle East, and he asked me to go with him."

His soaring spirits come in for a crash landing . . .

"I told him that I can't do that."

. . . a touch-and-go landing, actually; he's taken off once again.

"Because of your job?" he asks cautiously.

"That and . . . other things."

"What other things?"

Say it, he thinks, holding his breath. *Please, Maggie.*

"You know," she says, looking at her shoes, at the coffee table, at the window—everywhere but at him.

If you just say it, I'll—I'll—I'll change. I promise I will. Say you're staying because of me.

If you admit that, then I'll admit that I might not want to be a bachelor forever. That lately, it isn't as much fun as it used to be. That I might even want to . . .

Gulp.

Settle down.

Not now, he amends quickly. *And not for sure, just maybe. Just . . . someday. In the distant, distant future.*

"Anyway," Maggie says, finally looking at him, "I told Jason that my life is here, and I have a plan, you know? I want certain things. I've always wanted certain things. Things I'm not going to get if I pick up and leave."

"Things like . . . ?"

"A promotion to media supervisor. With a raise."

"Mmm hmm."

"And, you know, the usual stuff. Stuff that everybody wants. You know. A husband, and kids, and a home," she says in a rush.

A husband.

Not . . .

Me, specifically.

Which is fine . . . because he doesn't want to be a husband, anyway.

He has a life of his own, dammit, and he doesn't want to change a thing.

"You know what I mean, Charlie?" she asks in a small voice. Smaller, that is, than Maggie's usual confident tone.

It's almost as though she's . . .

Insecure?

Maggie?

Maggie who-knows-exactly-what-she-wants-and-it-isn't-him?

"Actually, I don't," he tells her. "I mean, you said that everybody wants those things, but I don't think that's true."

Something flares in her blue eyes. "Of course you don't. You're the Bachelor at Large. How could I forget? Marriage, kids, a home . . . those things are all a big waste of time as far as you're concerned, right?"

No!

"Yeah," he finds himself saying. "Pretty much."

"That's what I thought."

He watches her fold her arms and lift her chin; her breath catching in her throat almost as though she's about to say something else. But she's silent; willful and silent. He can feel the tension emanating from her.

What was he thinking, a few minutes ago? That he'd change for her? That he'd be willing to compromise his lifestyle, his freedom, for her?

Yeah, right.

You don't do promises, remember?

"Well," she says brusquely, getting to her feet, "I just wanted to tell you that. About Jason. In case . . . you know. In case you were wondering."

"Yeah," he says, regret seeping into his thoughts—but not, thanks to supreme self-control, into his voice. "I was wondering."

"And now you know. Well, I'd better get back to work now."

"You've got a lot to do, huh?"

Her lips curve into something that bears precious little resemblance to a smile. "Always."

"Yeah."

For a moment, they just stare at each other.

Then, because there's nothing left to say, he tells her, "So I'll see you."

"Yeah. I'll see you."

With that, she's gone.

The moment he closes the door after her, Charlie is overwhelmed by the urge to throw it open again, to chase after her, to tell her that she's wrong about him. That maybe, given the time and opportunity to figure things out, he might just want those things after all.

But *maybe* and *might* wouldn't be enough for a woman like Maggie. She isn't willing to wait.

How do you know unless you ask her?

Maybe he should put it into her hands—give her the option of sticking around, just in case he was wrong about her patience—or lack thereof.

He reaches for the doorknob, turning it slowly.

After all . . . she cheered the Knicks, and ordered sausage on her pizza, and she went with him to Atlantic City. Maybe she'll surprise him again.

Maybe, if he just asks . . .

He pulls the door open.

He rushes out into the hallway.

"Maggie—"

He stops short, watching the elevator doors sliding closed after her.

"Here are the reach frequencies you needed." Maggie deposits a sheaf of papers on Dom's desk, nearly toppling his coffee.

"Geez, watch it, Mags. That's my first cup of the day."

"Lucky you. This is my fourth." She raises the half-filled paper hot cup in her own hand.

"What time did you come in?"

"Six." She yawns.

"Six? Why? We were here till after midnight."

"I needed to go through some paperwork," she lies.

In truth, she was here because after a night spent tossing and turning in her bed, she figured she might as well be productive. Work is supposed to be getting her mind off

Charlie, but so far, he's still there, morning, noon, and night. He's even in her dreams—dreams, God help her, about doughnut-shaped pillows, and flowered doughnuts, and . . .

Well, there are erotic dreams, too.

Feeling Dominic's gaze, she looks up and hopes that he can't read her thoughts. They've been so busy with work that she's managed to avoid the topic of dating Charlie— or the fact that she no longer is—for the past few days, ever since Monday afternoon.

Now, sensing that Dominic is about to ask her a question she doesn't want to answer, she blurts, "When are you going out with Julie again?"

"Why? Do you and Charlie want to come with us?"

"No!"

Bingo. Dominic levels a shrewd gaze at her. "What's wrong? Did you and Charlie have a fight?"

"Stop saying *me and Charlie,* okay?"

"I didn't say *me* and Charlie. I said *you* and Charlie."

"This isn't funny, Dom. There is no 'you and Charlie.' And we're not talking about me and Charlie, we're talking about you and Julie."

"Well, there's no 'you and Julie,' either," he informs her. "It just didn't work out."

"What do you mean it didn't work out? She's perfect for you."

"No, Maggie, she's not. And I'm not perfect for her, either."

"But I thought—"

"That's the problem, Mags. You thought. You were the one who picked her out for me."

"Because she was everything you wanted. What could

have possibly gone wrong? Did you—please tell me you didn't throw another piece of meat at her, Dominic."

"It was nothing like that. It just—the other night, after dinner, when we left you and Charlie"—He holds up a finger to shush her when she opens her mouth to protest his phrasing—"we realized that neither of us was interested in keeping up a relationship."

"But she's your type! She's a great cook, and she's . . . she's blond."

"Maggie, it takes more than that to make me fall in love."

"But she loves the Knicks, and she darns socks, and—"

"Whatever, Maggie, there were no sparks, okay?"

Sparks. Sparks, again.

"What's so great about sparks?" Maggie mutters. "Sparks don't last."

"Well, maybe I'm not interested in settling down after all, you know? Maybe I want to stay single for a while, have fun, date a lot of people. Just be free."

"Yeah, that figures," she mutters, shaking her head.

"What?"

"Nothing."

"Did you say 'that figures'? What's that supposed to mean?"

"Just that men are all alike. You all think freedom is so precious. You know what's precious? Belonging to somebody. Knowing that they're not going to leave whenever the whim strikes. Being . . . in love. That's precious."

Dominic stares at her. "Are you in love with Charlie, Maggie?"

"No!"

He frowns. "I don't believe you. It sounds like

you're—oh, for God's sake, please tell me you're not in love with Doctor Do-Right."

"Of course I'm not in love with . . . Doctor Do-Right."

Sorry, Jason, she says silently. *Sorry for calling you that, and sorry for not being in love with you. It would have made things a lot easier for me if I were.*

Loving a man like Jason would be simple.

Loving a man like Charlie—

Not that she loves him, but if she did . . .

Well, it would be anything but simple.

"You're not in love with Doctor Do-Right? Thank God. That guy was all wrong for you, Maggie. You're too special for somebody like that. I really think you and Charlie—"

"Stop that! There is no—"

"But why? Why is there no you and Charlie? Your decision, or his?"

"His," Maggie tells him, swallowing her pride along with her pain.

She gave him a chance—a few chances—to tell her how he felt about her. Rather, how she thought he felt about her.

Quite obviously, he doesn't.

When she showed up at his apartment, she was ready to hurl herself into his arms and tell him that she didn't need any of the things she thought she needed. That she needs only him.

Boy, would that have been a mistake. His hostility toward her was as palpable as his five o'clock shadow.

"Are you sure, Maggie? Because when I was with the two of you on Friday night, it was pretty clear that he was crazy about you. He looked at you the way my brother-in-law Joey looks at Nina. She can be in one of his old shirts with her hair in a ponytail and no makeup on, and you'd think she was a Bond girl, the way he's looking at her."

Maggie smiles faintly. "Are you saying I'm not Bond girl material, Dom?"

"Mags, you know I think you're a babe. But what I'm trying to say is that Charlie does, too. And not just on the outside. The guy is into you. At least, he *was*. How the heck did you manage to screw things up between Friday night and now?"

"What makes you think it was me?"

"Oh, come on, Maggie. I know you. You're stubborn as hell, and you can be a real pain in the—"

"Gee, thanks, Dom. You're making me feel a whole lot better. I've got to get back to my office. Let me know what the client thinks of those reach frequency numbers."

"Yeah, okay. Hang in there, Mags. I have a feeling everything's going to work out."

"Not with Charlie, if that's what you mean. He's Bachelor at Large, remember?"

Chapter Sixteen

On Friday afternoon, Charlie is staring at the blinking cursor on his empty computer screen—which has become a daily ritual for him—when Julie pops her head in his door.

"You're still not locking this, huh?"

He shakes his head. "I'm still not doing a lot of things you—and everybody else—think I should be doing. Come on in."

He pushes his chair back and takes off his thinking cap, raking his fingers through his matted hair, grateful for the distraction of Julie.

"Still having writer's block?" she asks sympathetically, closing the door behind her and locking it.

"Yeah." He gulps hours-old room-temperature coffee from the mug on his desk and makes a face. It wasn't very good to begin with; now it tastes like poison.

"Maybe a change of scenery will help," Julie suggests.

"Nah. I tried sitting on the couch with my laptop, but it just made me sleepy."

"That's not what I meant. Maybe you should get out of here for a few days."

"And go where?"

"You still have your plane tickets to Europe, right?"

"Yeah . . ."

"And the other night, you asked me to go with you."

He frowns. "I did? When?"

"When you stumbled home trashed out of your mind and thought my apartment was your apartment."

He has a vague memory of that—and of drinking coffee on her couch—but he doesn't recall anything about inviting her to go to France. All the more reason he should never, ever drown his sorrows in liquor again. It could be dangerous, inviting women to leave the country with him for the weekend. Good thing it was only Julie.

Who, if he's not mistaken, actually wants to go, he realizes, peering at her pretty face.

"Are you saying you want to go to Europe with me?" he asks in disbelief, so startled that he sloshes coffee into his lap—good thing it's cold—and accidentally knocks his thinking cap off the edge of his desk.

"I'd love to go to Europe with you, Charlie."

"What about work? I thought you were working all weekend."

"Nah, they're letting me have off. And I've always wanted to go to France. And I checked with my friend Dana at the travel agency," she adds in a rush, "and she said that if I bring her the ticket right away, she can have it rebooked in my name. We can fly out tonight."

"*Tonight?*" Normally, he'd jump at the chance to take off at the drop of a thinking cap, but . . . "I don't know, Julie. I have to write this column."

"So? You have a laptop. What better place to write than on an eight-hour flight across the Atlantic? I'll sleep, you'll write, and by the time we land in Nice, you'll be able to e-mail your finished column to your editor. We'll spend a few days hanging on the beach, and you'll be back to normal. Sound good?"

Actually, it does sound . . . well, if not *good,* then at least better than any alternative he can possibly conjure.

Getting out of New York—and away from constant reminders of Maggie—might be just what he needs to clear his head and get over her at last.

"Now what?" Maggie mutters as she makes her way past the row of darkened account management offices toward the light spilling from Dominic's open door.

She was just packing up her briefcase, preparing to call it a day—and a week—when he called her extension and said he needed to see her right away.

Probably yet another urgent change the management rep wants made in the new media plan before Monday morning's presentation to the client.

It's just as well, Maggie concludes, passing the empty secretaries' bay, where a cleaning lady is emptying wastebaskets and another is vacuuming.

She would just as soon spend the weekend working. What else does she have to do? Sit around and pine away for what might have been?

No, it couldn't have been, she scolds herself in what's become a familiar refrain. *You're deluded if you think you and Charlie had a chance to build anything lasting.*

Steeling herself against the wave of sadness that inevitably washes over her, Maggie hesitates outside of Dominic's office to pull herself together.

The cleaning lady abruptly turns off her vacuum and

suddenly Maggie can hear Dominic in his office, talking to somebody in a low voice. It takes a minute to realize he's on the telephone.

"I know it is," he's saying, "but we're doing the right thing. If the plan works, they'll be grateful to us forever."

So this *is* about the media plan. Although infinite gratitude from the client is a bit extreme, if Maggie does say so herself. Brand management at the cosmetics account has been anything but appreciative of the agency's efforts these days.

"And if it doesn't work out," Dominic is saying, "oh, well. What have we got to lose?"

What have we got to lose?

Maggie rolls her eyes. Is he serious? They can lose a multimillion-dollar account, for one thing. Their jobs, for another.

Then again, maybe Dom's cavalier attitude makes sense. Maybe, in the grand scheme of things, there's more to life than money and a fast-paced career.

Well, of course there is. And it's not as if you didn't know that, Maggie reminds herself. *You've always wanted it all—the money, the job, and the rest.*

The rest being marriage. A family. Love.

You were going to prove to yourself—and to everyone back home—that it is possible to have it all.

Come on, Maggie. Buck up. Just because it didn't work out with Charlie—

With *Charlie*? Shouldn't she be thinking, with *Jason*?

After all, Jason was the one she pictured herself marrying. Not Charlie.

Charlie doesn't believe in commitment. You knew that

all along. So what have you really lost now that he's out of your life?

Nothing, Maggie tells herself resolutely. *You've lost nothing but trouble and complications.*

"Yeah, she'll be here any minute," Dom is saying into the phone. "I've got to go. I'll call you later."

"She's here now." Maggie strides into his office as he hangs up the receiver. "What do they want from us now? Blood?"

"Maggie!" He bolts upright in his chair. "Cripes, what were you doing? Eavesdropping?"

"No. Well, yes."

"For how long?"

"Long enough to know that my weekend plans are shot."

"I didn't think you had any."

"I'm guessing that I do now."

He grins. "Yeah, you do. I've arranged for a car service to take you home. They're probably waiting downstairs already."

"Home? What are you talking about? I thought I was working."

"You are. You're just going home to pack. The car will wait while you grab your stuff, then you'll go straight to JFK."

"The airport?"

"No, the middle school." Dominic quirks a brow at her. "Of course, the airport."

She sighs wearily. "Why am I going to the airport, Dom?"

"The client needs you to present the new plan tomorrow."

"On a Saturday?" Okay, that's not so far-fetched, and she's used to being at the client's beck and call, but . . . the airport?

She narrows a gaze at Dominic. "Where, exactly, will I be doing this presentation?"

"In the south of France." Dominic hands her a packet. "You have a passport, right? Here's your plane ticket."

Charlie gazes out the rain-spattered window of the Town Car, brooding.

On the seat beside him: his hastily packed duffel bag and his laptop.

On his mind: Maggie.

Maggie, whom he's leaving behind for good.

Oh, he'll be back to New York in a few days. But by then, he knows, it'll be too late. If he wants to take back what he said to her—and if he wants to say what he didn't say—he should do it before he goes.

He *doesn't* want to, of course . . .

He just knows that if he *did,* it will be too late by the time he gets back. That's all.

Because he has a hunch that by then, Maggie will either have found somebody new, or will be chasing off to the Middle East with Jason after all. She's not the type to let grass grow under her feet.

"Looks like the Van Wyck is as backed up as the Grand Central Parkway," Azim says from the front seat, scanning the bottlenecked traffic ahead.

He's never going to make it. Between the traffic and all the security at the airport, he's going to miss the flight to Nice.

Julie is probably already at the gate, pacing and wondering if she's embarking on a solo weekend.

Well, that's her fault. Why she insisted on meeting him at the airport instead of going together is beyond him.

Okay, no it isn't. She said she had to go shopping first. Said she had nothing to wear on the French Riviera.

Women.

Women and shopping.

Charlie rolls his eyes. He, of course, plans to wear on the French Riviera exactly what he'd wear in his apartment, minus a layer or two, depending on the weather.

Women, he thinks again, shaking his head in exasperation. They're all alike. Even Julie. They're stubborn and they're fussy and they're downright impossible in every way.

Especially Maggie.

Azim honks as a yellow cab nudges its way in ahead of the Town Car, then shakes his head. "I don't think you're going to make this flight, Charlie."

"Sure I will," he says resolutely, glancing at the clock on the dashboard. "I have to."

Yes, he does. Or risk running back to Maggie, making promises he'll never be able to keep.

"Flight 8751, nonstop from New York's John F. Kennedy Airport to Nice is now boarding all passengers."

Clutching her ticket in one hand and her briefcase in her other, Maggie takes a deep breath and walks toward the gate.

This is the best thing for me, she thinks, taking her place at the end of the line of passengers.

Getting out of New York for a few days, focusing on

business, seeing the sun again . . . it will do her a world of good. When she gets back, she can regroup and make a fresh start without thinking about Charlie every minute of every day.

If only . . .

Stop it, Maggie. If only what?

It's just that if this business trip hadn't come up, she might very well have found herself calling Charlie, or even trying to see him. Because every time she replays their parting scene in her head, she finds herself wishing that she had done things differently. Wishing she'd had the guts to ask Charlie questions she probably has no business asking . . . but questions to which she needs answers all the same.

It's that damned Harrigan intuition . . . that's the problem, here.

Common sense—and everything Charlie ever said— have made it clear that there's no future for Maggie with a man who wears his bachelorhood as proudly as a Cub Scout with a new badge.

But somewhere deep inside of her, hope refuses to die.

She can't help thinking that sooner or later, Cub Scouts grow up and put their badges away.

Wondering whether, sooner or later, Charlie might do the same.

And whether, when and if he's ready and willing . . .

She can be waiting.

"Please have your tickets ready," calls the flight attendant in a lilting French accent.

Maggie glances down to make sure hers is in order, taking a step forward toward the jetway when every bone in her body aches to do the opposite.

You can leave the airport now . . .

Get a cab . . .

Go straight to Harcourt Street . . .

And then what?

Throw yourself at Charlie and demand that he give you a chance?

No.

No way.

Anyway, she has to get on the plane. It's part of her job; part of agency life. When the client says jump, you jump. When the client says fly to France on the spur of the moment, you fly to France on the spur of the moment . . . even if it means leaving behind your last chance to find happiness with the man you love.

Last chance?

Happiness?

Love?

Where did that come from?

Love.

She doesn't *love* Charlie.

Love is . . .

Love is . . .

Love is more than a few sparks, that's what love is. Sparks are exciting, but they burn out instantly.

Love is . . .

Remember, Maggie-girl . . . it only takes a single spark to start a raging inferno.

Oh, Lord, where did that come from? And . . . why now? Now, when it's too late to—

"Mademoiselle?"

"Hmm?" Maggie looks up to see the gate attendant beckoning. It's her turn to board the plane.

"Your ticket?"

"Oh . . . yes. It's right here." She holds the ticket out.

The attendant reaches for it.

"Wait," Maggie says, her breath catching in her throat, heart pounding.

Running through the airport, Charlie jumps over a pile of luggage like an Olympic hurdler, scanning the overhead signs for his gate.

Azim took back streets to get him here in record time, considering the Friday evening rush-hour traffic.

Now, with mere seconds to spare, Charlie tells himself that if he's too late—if the door is closed and the plane has pushed back from the gate—he can only take that as a sign.

A sign that he and Maggie are meant to be together.

Yes, if he missed the flight, then he'll call Azim from his cell phone, get him back here, and have him drive Charlie straight to Maggie's apartment, where . . . where . . .

Where what, exactly, will happen?

Where you'll get down on bended knee and propose marriage?

What the hell are you thinking, dude? You walk down the aisle, and there goes everything—your livelihood, your social life, your independence, your beige couch.

Yes, but if you stick to your guns and refuse to consider ever walking down the aisle, there goes Maggie.

Oh, who is he kidding? Maggie's already gone.

Panting, he spots the sign for his gate just ahead. With a final push, he sprints toward the finish line, not sure whether he's hoping that he made the flight—or hoping that he missed it.

*   *   *

I made the wrong decision, Maggie tells herself as the Harrigan intuition kicks into high gear.

Her head buried in her hands, she wonders what the heck she was thinking back there at the gate. She came so close . . .

Well, it's too late to change her mind now. There's nothing to do but go through this.

Heaving a loud sigh—of resignation, not relief—she lifts her head . . .

Opens her eyes . . .

And finds herself staring into Charlie's.

"Maggie?" Charlie blinks.

She's still there.

Sitting beside him.

On the plane.

Certain he's hallucinating, he shakes his head to clear it, then looks again.

Nope, still there.

"Oh my God . . . what are you *doing* here?"

Did he say that?

No, she did. He's still too stunned to speak.

When he dashed down the aisle to take his empty seat, he was so busy scanning the other passengers for Julie's face, scanning the row numbers for his assignment, that he never even realized she was here.

Maggie.

Maggie?

He's *got* to be dreaming.

"Why are you on this plane, Charlie?"

"Why are *you* on this plane?" he retorts to the dream

Maggie, who looks—and sounds, and smells—deliciously real.

"I'm on a business trip."

Okay, that was real, too.

So if she's real, and this isn't a dream, then . . .

Charlie looks around, wondering if he got on the wrong flight. Say, one to Chicago, or Boston—someplace boring and businesslike.

"Excuse me," he says to the middle-aged matron across the aisle. "Where is this plane going?"

"To Nice," she says in French-accented English, raising an arched brow and muttering, "Crazy American" as she turns her attention back to the latest issue of *Vogue*.

"You have business on the Cote d'Azur?" Charlie asks Maggie as the flight attendant comes down the aisle inspecting seat belts.

"Of course. Do you?"

"No. I'm going on a vacation with—"

Oh.

Oh, *crap*.

Now it makes sense.

Julie.

Julie did this.

Julie and—

"You can come clean, Maggie," he says, shaking his head in disbelief and unfastening his seat belt. "I can't believe you and Julie would cook up a scheme like this."

"Me and Julie? What are you talking about? What scheme?"

He's already getting to his feet—and nearly falling off them as the plane lurches into motion, rolling back from the gate.

"Monsieur, please take your seat," the flight attendant commands, rushing over.

"I can't. I have to get off this plane."

"Is there a medical emergency?"

"Not a medical one, no." He glares at Maggie.

"Please take your seat with your seat belt fastened!" another attendant commands shrilly—so shrilly that he has no choice but to drop down again beside Maggie, who's digging frantically through her briefcase.

Pulling out a sheaf of papers, she begins scanning them, muttering under her breath. Charlie catches something about Dom and about a presentation—and a few off-color words that bring icy stares from the elderly nun seated on her other side.

"What are you doing?" Charlie asks her.

"I'm looking through the materials Dominic gave me for the trip."

"What does he have to do with it?"

"He's the one who—"

Oh.

Oh, *crap*.

Now it makes sense.

Dominic.

Dominic did this.

There's no client presentation in Nice.

How could she have fallen for something so far-fetched? She cringes, remembering how he promised to fax the information about the meeting to the hotel, and she believed him.

Well, why wouldn't she? The advertising business is nothing but last-minute, fast-paced, hectic action.

"He's the one who what?" Charlie is asking, seated beside her as the plane taxis out to the runway.

"He's the one who sent me on this trip. He said I had to be at a client meeting tomorrow."

"And Julie said she was coming with me to the Riviera for a long weekend."

"Julie?" Stunned, Maggie shakes her head, trying to grasp the sequence of events leading up to this surreal moment. "Julie was involved, too?"

"It was her idea. I had the tickets, and she knew I had to use them by this weekend or lose them."

"These are the tickets to Europe you were talking about?"

He nods. "Welcome to my honeymoon. How's this for irony?"

"Your . . . *honeymoon?*"

"Didn't I mention that I was supposed to get married?"

"No," Maggie says coolly, as her stomach lurches along with the plane as it makes a turn. "I don't think you did."

Charlie?

Married?

"Oh, well . . . yeah. I was engaged. More than a year ago. And then she left me at the altar, so . . ." He shrugs. "You get the gist of it."

Yes—and the gist of it changes everything.

This explains—at least in part—why Charlie doesn't believe in commitment. Why he's so skittish whenever anybody so much as mentions the word marriage. Why one of the first things he ever said to Maggie was that he was *never* getting married.

"Why did she leave you?" Maggie asks, twisting the strap of her briefcase in her lap.

"She said I had too many faults."

Guilt seeps in as Maggie thinks of the list she made on her Palm Pilot. The list of Charlie's faults, all the way from number one—*sloppy*—to number *thirty-three—licks peanut butter from spoon and puts back in jar.*

"She said I was too sloppy," Charlie says with a shrug. Ouch.

"She didn't marry you because you're sloppy?" Maggie does her best to sound outraged. "Didn't she ever hear of hiring a maid?"

Not, Maggie reminds herself, that a maid would be the remedy to all of Charlie's faults.

A maid wouldn't be able to touch, say, number *sixteen—sings theme to* Gilligan's Island *off-key in shower—* or number *twenty-four—dumps sugar on all cereal, even presweetened—even sickening-sweet Frosted Flakes.*

Then again, there are always earplugs . . . and eggs.

"Ladies and gentlemen, we are next in line for takeoff," comes the announcement from the cockpit.

Maggie looks at Charlie.

He raises his eyebrows. "Looks like we're going to the French Riviera together."

Chapter Seventeen

"What do you mean I can't get on a return flight until tomorrow morning?" Maggie shouts at the smiling, barely-speaks-English ticket agent. "I have to get right back to New York. I have things to do."

"I don't think he cares," Charlie observes, standing behind her.

She turns around and glares at him, then at the ticket agent again.

"I'm not even supposed to be here, you know."

The man just shrugs.

"Maggie, cut it out," Charlie says. "You made it through Customs. You've got your luggage. You're here. You might as well enjoy it. Look." He takes her arm and pulls her out of the line.

"What are you doing? I just lost my spot."

He drags her toward the sun-drenched plate-glass window, where a dazzling sea and a dazzling sky beckon—both bluer, even, than Maggie's eyes. "Just . . . look. Okay? Look out the window. It's beautiful, isn't it?"

For a moment, she's silent.

Then she turns to him, her jaw lifted stubbornly. "Okay. It's beautiful. But what the heck am I supposed to do with that?"

"Check into the hotel and go to the beach. You brought your bathing suit, right?"

"No. This is a business trip, Charlie, remember? I mean . . . it *was*. It was supposed to be." She shakes her head in despair.

"There's a gift shop in the hotel. They sell bathing suits."

"How do you know? Oh, yes, I forgot. You know all about the hotel. This was supposed to be your honeymoon."

Supposed to being the operative phrase here, Charlie thinks. Being here—with the reluctant Maggie—isn't remotely like a honeymoon.

She spent the entire flight in stony silence, arms folded, gaze at the seat back in front of her.

Charlie considered taking out his laptop, but knew it would be futile. There was no way he was getting anything written with Maggie sitting beside him. Instead, he curled up beneath a scratchy blanket and pretended to sleep.

Somehow, somewhere over the Atlantic, as night became glorious day beyond the small window at the end of the row, his angst gave way to resignation. By the time they landed, resignation had yielded to a spark of . . .

Well, if it isn't *hope,* it sure feels suspiciously optimistic.

That he got on the plane to escape Maggie and found himself seated next to her is one big cosmic slap in the face, as far as Charlie's concerned. What he intends to do about it remains to be seen. He only knows that they can't stand around the airport arguing.

"Come on, Maggie." He picks up her leaden suitcase—which apparently contains everything she owns *except* a bathing suit—and his featherweight duffel, leading her out into the balmy, blossom-scented sea air.

Grumbling, Maggie follows him.

He takes that as a sign. Of what, he isn't sure.

Two minutes later, they're in a cab headed for the seaside hotel—the one where Charlie once intended to bring his bride. He chose it for the exquisite views, the spectacular service, and the romantic ambiance.

An earlier glance at Maggie's itinerary yielded precisely the information he anticipated: that Dom and Julie have left the room arrangements intact. Meaning, Charlie and Maggie are both booked in the hotel's scrumptious honeymoon suite.

"What were they trying to do?" Maggie asks, clearly on the same wavelength as she stares glumly out the window at the glorious scenery. "Why on earth would they pull something so sneaky?"

"They're playing matchmaker, Maggie."

"Well, they suck at it."

"So do we," he says with a shrug.

"What do you mean?"

"Just that you and I both know that the two of them are about as wrong for each other as . . . as . . ."

Don't say it.

He trails off, riddled with confusion.

Don't say it, Charlie. Don't say it, because . . . because . . .

Because he's no longer sure he believes it.

"As *we* are?" Maggie asks ruefully, searching his eyes.

He holds his breath.

Say it.

Go ahead.

Say it.

Say *what?*

That she's wrong?

Frustrated, his thoughts whirling with uncertainty, Charlie frowns.

What is this, anyway?

Don't say it; say it. He, a man who always knew what he wanted—and what he didn't—suddenly has no idea what to say or do.

"Charlie?" Maggie asks, still watching him. Everything about her is hesitant. He's never seen her like this.

It's as though her future—the precisely orchestrated future to which she has clung so proudly—suddenly depends on him.

He gazes at her, feeling as though he's teetering on the edge of the Queensborough Bridge. There's nothing to do but . . .

Take the plunge.

"I don't know . . . I don't think we're so wrong for each other, Maggie."

There.

He said it, okay?

It's out there.

He's out there, free-falling, his future suspended with hers.

Now she can laugh hysterically, or tell him that he's out of his mind, or to go to hell, or whatever it is that she's going to . . .

"I don't think we are, either," Maggie says quietly—so quietly he has to lean closer to hear her.

"You don't?" The breath he didn't realize he was holding escapes him in a sigh. "But you—you—you like things a certain way."

"I know." She looks wistful. "And you like your freedom."

He nods. "You're right. I do."

Freedom.

Freedom to . . . to . . . to what?

To have a beige couch without flowered pillows? To get stinking drunk in a bar on a Sunday afternoon? To go around looking like he belongs in the back of a patrol car on an episode of *Cops*?

Does any of that really matter?

Charlie takes a deep breath.

"You know, Maggie . . . there might actually be different kinds of freedom. Maybe freedom doesn't always have to mean . . . picking up and leaving."

"But you—you told me you don't believe in . . . in staying." Maggie's voice is scratchy—from lack of sleep? From the dry air on the plane? From emotion?

Whatever the cause, her raspy tone carries him back to Atlantic City, back to the night she screamed herself hoarse in the casino—then made love to him in what he suddenly realizes was the wanton gamble of a lifetime.

He swallows hard.

Their journey is almost over; the cab is pulling up in front of the hotel.

"You're right," he tells her hurriedly, "I did say that I don't believe in . . . in staying. And I did say that you and I were totally wrong for each other. But I'm not like you."

"I know. That's the problem."

The cab stops.

"No," he says, desperate to make her see. "That's *not* the problem. It's the solution."

The driver opens the door for them, removes their luggage from the trunk.

She climbs out, and he scrambles after her.

"What are you talking about, Charlie?"

He stuffs several bills into the driver's hand, saying, "That I'm not like you. You, Maggie—you know everything. At least, you think you do."

Anger flashing in her eyes, she opens her mouth to protest.

"Hang on a second, Maggie, I'm not done talking."

"But—"

"Just hear me out."

The cab pulls away. A bellhop gathers the luggage. The doorman approaches.

Charlie waves him away, taking Maggie's hand and pulling her to a secluded stone bench beneath a shade tree.

"What I mean is, you think you're always right about everything, Maggie—and, as much as I hate to admit it, you usually are. But me—I've been wrong about quite a few things. And when I am—I don't like to admit that, either."

She's silent, watching him. The only sounds are the surf crashing in the distance, birds chirping in the canopy of trees overhead, leaves stirring and rustling in a warm breeze that blows a strand of hair into Maggie's face.

Charlie can see her hand trembling as she reaches up to push it away.

Struck by her uncharacteristic vulnerability and silence, and, more than ever before, by her beauty, he summons the courage, at last, to . . . to . . .

Say it.

"I was wrong about you, Maggie. And I was wrong about me. Maybe . . ."

He takes a deep breath, closes his eyes.

"Maybe I can believe in commitment. In . . . you know. In long-term relationships."

"In marriage?"

"Honestly—I don't know." He opens his eyes and looks at her. "I was willing to give it a shot before, and she was all wrong for me. I can't lie, Maggie. I'd be scared out of my mind to do it again."

Maggie's spirits plummet.

Just when she dared to believe that she and Charlie have a chance . . .

Just when everything she ever wanted—but never realized she wanted—was within grasp . . .

"But . . ."

The word is barely a whisper. She freezes, certain she heard it.

But.

He said *But.*

One tiny, whispered three letter word that changes everything.

But makes everything possible.

"Maggie, I'm not saying that I won't do it. I'm just saying . . . I'd be afraid."

She exhales, swallows hard over a lump of emotion that threatens to spill from her throat. She manages to say only, "Well . . . I'd be afraid, too."

"You? Afraid? You're fearless," he says, shaking his head.

"No, I'm not, Charlie." She reaches for his hands, squeezes them, clinging to them like a life raft in a stormy sea. "I'm not fearless. I'm terrified."

"Of what?"

"Of everything. Of . . . failing. Of loneliness. Of losing my job. Of losing . . . you."

"Maggie . . . I had no idea."

"Neither did I," she says shakily, "until right this second."

A breeze stirs the blossoms on the branches overhead and whips Maggie's hair into her face again. She reaches up to push it away, but Charlie's hand is already there, his fingers tenderly tucking her hair behind her ear, lingering on her cheek.

"You won't lose me, Maggie," he tells her, his voice as soft as the sea air against her skin. "Not if you open up and let me in."

She wants to. She does. But that would mean taking a chance. Letting go of everything that mattered. Taking a different road.

"I'm afraid," she whispers, shaking her head, clinging to his warm hands. "I want to . . . but I'm afraid."

"See? We're exactly alike. A couple of cowards."

She tries, and fails, to muster a smile. "Charlie, you're asking me to take a huge chance on you."

"You gambled in Atlantic City, and look how that turned out."

"You said that was beginner's luck."

"Yes. And this is just the beginning for us, Maggie. I love you."

There it is.

There, at last, is love.

"I love you, too, Charlie."

But is love enough?

"Then come on, Maggie. Give me a chance. Give *us* a chance. What do you say?"

She holds her breath.

Looks into his eyes.

And glimpses a future. A dazzling, unexpected future, full of surprises.

At last, listening to the Harrigan intuition—*and* to a heart full of love—she says, "I will if you're sure—absolutely, positively sure—that you want to try to make this work."

"I do."

He kisses her, then pulls back suddenly, grinning.

"Did you hear that?"

"What?" She listens, hearing nothing but the surf, and the birds, and the breeze.

"Those words. The ones I never thought would come out of my mouth."

"What words?"

"*I do*," he says. "And it wasn't so bad, saying them."

"Really?"

"Really. In fact . . ."

He breaks off to kiss her again, holding her close.

"In fact what?" she murmurs, leaning her head against his shoulder, hearing his heart pounding in unison with hers.

"I have a feeling I might want to say them again someday."

Maggie smiles. "Then I have a feeling you will."

Epilogue

Seventeen months later

Checking her watch, Maggie quickens her pace, scurrying up Fifth Avenue despite the stifling August midday heat and humidity.

She's late.

She, Margaret Kennelly, who has learned to relax considerably in the last year and a half, but still prides herself on punctuality, is late.

In more ways than one, she reminds herself, a tiny secret smile playing on her lips as she halts at an intersection.

Waiting for the light to change, she checks her reflection in a plate-glass store window. Satisfied with her trim silhouette in her lightweight summer dress, she glances at the mannequins in their chic autumn business suits and smiles again—this time, though, with just a hint of wistfulness at the knowledge that she won't be wearing them. Not this year, anyway.

The light changes to WALK and she does, briskly, pushing a strand of dark, sweat-dampened hair from her forehead.

She's almost there. Only two more blocks to go—but after crossing the final intersection, she finds herself mired in a crowd. Pushing her way along the clogged sidewalk, she suddenly stops short, realizing that it's not just a crowd—it's a line.

A line that stretches from the corner to the bookstore— the bookstore being her destination.

It can't be.

But it is.

These people—countless people, most of them, she realizes at second glance, women—are here for the same reason she is.

Well, sort of.

"Excuse me," she says briskly, moving past them, through them, ignoring their outrage and their comments.

No way is she waiting an hour—or longer, judging by the length of the line—to see her own husband.

"Maggie!"

She turns and spots Julie in the crowd, waving. "Can you believe it?" she squeals. "Look at all these people! Isn't it amazing?"

"Well, he's amazing," Maggie tells her with a smile, checking out the good-looking guy at her side.

"Oh, Maggie, this is Gregory. Gregory, this is Charlie's wife, Maggie."

Charlie's wife.

It's been six months since they made it official. You'd think she'd be used to it by now. Will she ever hear those words without feeling a little thrill?

After chatting briefly with Julie's new boyfriend, she

excuses herself to shoulder and elbow her way into the bookstore, past the disgruntled women and the bustling employees and the posters.

Posters of Charlie. Her Charlie. Charlie, smiling, beneath the title of his just-released book.

Husband At Large.

It may not be the Great American Novel, but judging by the turnout for this, his first stop on a national author tour, Maggie has a feeling that there's one in his future.

At last, she reaches the table where Charlie sits, pen in hand, beside a towering stack of hardcovers. Behind him, Carolyn—his proud editor—shuttles more books from shelf to table.

He looks up with a relieved grin. "Maggie!"

"Hey . . . you're a star, Charlie. Look at this." She indicates the crowded store. "How does it feel?"

"Better now that you're here. I was worried."

She leans over to kiss him, conscious of envious stares from his female fans.

"Sorry I'm late, Charlie."

"Did you get hung up at the office again?"

"Not this time. Dom has me covered there. I'm late because I had an appointment."

"With the client?" he asks, scrawling his signature in an open book and handing it to its beaming new owner.

"No," Maggie says. "With the doctor."

"Oh."

He signs his name in another book—and then it hits him.

He looks up at her, startled. "The doctor? Are you okay?"

"I'm fine. *We're* fine. In fact"—she grins, leaning over

the table to say in a low voice—"I think you'd better get busy writing the sequel, Charlie. And I happen to have the ideal title."

"Yeah? What is it?" he asks, as a slowly comprehending grin breaks over his face.

Maggie smiles back contentedly, hand resting on her still-flat—for now—belly. "How does *Daddy at Large* sound?"

Tossing the pen aside, her husband stands to sweep her into a bear hug. "It sounds perfect, Maggie. And I already have a feeling it's got a happy ending."

About the Author

WENDY MARKHAM's first and last blind date took place twenty-odd years ago, when she accompanied a silent boy named Lenny to the movie *Xanadu*. She feels fortunate never to have seen the movie—or her date—again. Now happily married to Mark—whose father, in a cosmic coincidence, is named Lenny—Wendy lives, writes, and bakes chocolate desserts for her two young children in suburban New York. Wendy's alter-ego, Wendy Corsi Staub, is a *New York Times* bestselling author of suspense novels. Check out her website at *www.wendycorsistaub.com* or e-mail her at *corsistaub@aol.com.*

More
Wendy Markham!

❦

Please turn this page

for a preview of

HELLO, IT'S ME

coming soon

in mass market.

Chapter One

"Hey, you've reached Andre. You know what to do. Wait for the beep and don't forget to leave your number."

Clutching the phone between her shoulder and her ear, Annie pipes another stripe of red icing along a rectangular sugar cookie, wondering how many stripes an American flag has, anyway.

Not that it matters. There aren't fifty white dabs of icing on the square of blue to the left of the stripe. Who cares whether a flag cookie is historically accurate, as long as it tastes good?

Beep.

Annie sets down the tube of icing and presses a button to disconnect the call.

Someday, maybe she'll leave a message, just for the hell of it.

Or maybe someday, she'll stop calling her late husband's cell phone just to hear the sound of his voice. Yes, someday, she'll stop paying the bill just so she can do that.

After all, it's not as though she can afford it. She can't afford much of anything these days. The Widow Harlowe is in dire straits, reduced to decorating cookies for some wealthy Hamptonite's Flag Day soiree tomorrow night, just to earn enough cash to keep her kids in Fritos and Lunchables.

She's lucky, she supposes, that her friend Merlin's catering business has taken off so quickly. With the summer season about to kick into full swing, she can probably count on enough cookie decorating gigs to carry them through the summer.

Then what?

Come September, the rich New Yorkers will flee back to the city, leaving the eastern end of Long Island to the hardy natives once again.

As much as she cherishes warm days in the sun and surf, Annie has always preferred the off-season. She may not have grown up out here as Andre did, but she learned early on to resent the "outsiders" who clog the roads and restaurants and beaches from Memorial Day to Labor Day.

Now, she resents that they've become her livelihood.

Hell, what—and who—doesn't she resent at this point?

The summer people, the bill collectors who call incessantly, even her friends—especially those who are happily attached.

The Widow Harlowe can't help but notice that the world is one big Noah's Ark, made up of twosomes, which leaves her . . .

Alone.

You're all alone, Annie.

A tear drops into the icing stripe, bleeding red across the white buttercream background.

Annie is instantly reminded of Milo losing his tooth in an apple the day her world turned upside down.

The day that began as happily as the endless string of others before it, and concluded with sirens and a uniformed policeman at her door.

And now . . .

Well, now she's all alone.

Thud.

Annie looks up at the water-stained kitchen ceiling.

Okay, not quite alone.

In fact, never alone. Never, ever alone.

Being with her children twenty-four-seven has taken some getting used to. In fact, she still isn't accustomed to not having a minute to herself during the day; nary a reprieve from her maternal watch.

Andre always liked to take Milo and Trixie off on adventures, leaving Annie with some time to herself. She hasn't had that in almost a year now, but was too caught up in her grief to realize how much she craved relaxing solitude until recently.

"What are you doing up there, Milo?" she calls, even as she wonders whether the teardrop will make this cookie taste salty. She can always toss it aside . . . but then she won't have a full sixteen dozen, and Merlin—or his snooty client—are sure to notice.

Not that she's even met the man who's throwing the Flag Day shindig, but it's safe to assume that anyone with a waterfront estate in Southampton is snooty.

"I'm practicing, Mommy," Milo shouts down the stairs.

Practicing. Of course.

"Just be careful, okay?" she calls wearily, piping another slightly jagged red stripe on the slightly soggy cookie and concluding somewhat illogically that it'll serve the snooty Southamptonite right to taste the tears of the Widow Harlowe.

Thud.

"Be careful, Milo!" she calls again.

"I will, Mommy," comes the reply. "That time I almost did it."

Sure he did.

He almost flew.

That, after all, is what he's been trying to do for months. Blanket/cape tucked in at his neck, arms outstretched, he attempts to take off on a daily—all right, an hourly—basis. His mission: to fly up to heaven so that he can tell his dad about his lost tooth and his new Superhero action figures and his first year of elementary school and everything else Andre has missed in the dozen months since he died.

Annie hasn't the heart to tell her son that his mission is futile. How can she, when she herself spends every day longing for one last chance to tell her husband that she loves him?

With a trembling hand, she pipes another stripe of red frosting, this one more wobbly than the last, on the cookie. Oh, hell. It looks like a zig-zag, not a stripe.

Annie tosses aside the icing tube and reaches again for the phone.

She dials the familiar number and waits as it rings once . . .

He's not going to answer. You know that. Even when he was alive and remembered to turn on his cell phone, he never picked it up on the first ring.

Twice . . .

Usually, he didn't even grab it on the second. Remember how you used to picture him fumbling around, looking for it in his pocket, or the glove compartment, or at the bottom of his beach bag or tackle box?

Three times . . .

He's not going to answer it. Not ever again. Why do you keep doing this to yourself, Annie? Fifty bucks a month just so that you can hear his voice?

Four . . .

There's a click, and then the inevitable.

"Hey, you've reached Andre. You know what to do . . ."

She waits for the beep. This time, when she hears it, she doesn't hang up.

This time, heedless of the tears streaming down her face and plopping like raindrops onto the half-finished flag, Annie leaves a message.

"No, Andre," she wails, "You're wrong. I don't. I don't know what to do. I need you so badly . . ."

Unable to force another word past the aching lump in her throat, Annie hangs up and stares bleakly into space.

Raising a crystal flute to his mouth, Thom Brannock takes a sip of champagne. It's odd, he thinks, to be drinking champagne when the afternoon sunlight is still beaming through the tall paned windows of his dining room. Happy hour is a few hours away. But then, this isn't pleasure; it's business. These days, what isn't?

"What do you think? Too dry?" the stereotypically buff, good-looking and effeminate caterer asks, hovering at his elbow.

"Too fruity," Thom pronounces, biting back the urge to add, *no offense*. He sets the flute on the freshly polished surface of the eight-foot table that once graced his grandmother's Newport dining room. "Can I try the other one again?"

"Of course."

The caterer—Marvin? Myron?—flits back to the first bottle and pours sparkling amber liquid into a clean flute.

"Keep your menu in mind."

Thom nods, sipping the champagne. What is the menu again? By the time he's finished selecting the beverages that will be served, will he even remember? Or care? Did he ever care in the first place?

"Dry enough?" Marvin or Myron asks.

It isn't, but Thom declares it just right. If he doesn't stop now, he won't be able to focus on his work.

"You're working again tonight?" Joyce pouted earlier when he informed her that he couldn't join her for dinner after all. "I thought you were on vacation."

Vacation.

Yeah, right.

He might be spending long weekends at his sprawling seven bedroom summer house complete with tennis court, pool, and private beach, but his mind is rarely far from his Wall Street office.

He watches the caterer make a note on a clipboard, then look up with a brisk smile. "We'll do the red wine next."

"Actually, Marvin—"

"It's Merlin."

Oops.

"Actually, Merlin, I'll leave that up to you."

"But—"

"I'm sure you'll choose the right wine."

"But—"

"If you'll excuse me, I'd better get back to work," Thom says in his best *class dismissed* tone, pushing back his chair.

I could have been a teacher in another life, he thinks, watching as Merlin takes his cue and begins clearing away the wine glasses and bottles.

A teacher.

Sure.

That would have gone over well with Mother. About as well as Thom's sister Susan's temporary engagement to an actor a few years ago.

An Oscar nomination and a Beverly Hills mansion meant little to Mother. What counted more than anything, as far as she was—and is—concerned, is breeding.

Susan's former fiancé didn't have it.

The man she eventually married does.

And so, Thom thinks with a twinge of resentment, does Joyce.

Like him, she grew up on Park Avenue and in Southampton. Like him, she went to all the right schools, rubbed shoulders with all the right people. Like him, she's attractive and intelligent.

Unlike him, she's thinking that it's time to settle down.

As far as Thom is concerned, his whole life has been settled down. He can't help longing to . . . well, to *unsettle*.

"I'll just need to go over a few more details with you, and then I'll be out of your hair," Merlin announces, breaking into Thom's errant thought pattern.

Which is for the best, of course. There's little time for daydreaming when you're in the midst of a corporate takeover *and* hosting a political fundraiser for two hundred of your—make that your mother's—closest friends.

With a sigh, Thom dutifully shifts his attention from fantasies about *unsettling* to Merlin and his clipboard.

Annie sits at the kitchen table, sipping this morning's cold coffee and flipping through the stack of bills she hasn't a prayer of paying in their entirety.

The trick, she realizes after the third flip-through, is to prioritize. She sets aside the mortgage statement, the electric bill, and the health insurance bill. The money left in her account will cover these, and leave enough for groceries if she buys generic brands.

Okay, so far so good. A little caffeine goes a long way.

A little case would go an even longer way. Annie thinks again of Merlin's offer. He's short a waitress for the party he's catering tonight, and he wants her to fill in. It's tempting . . . but the last thing she wants to do is wait on a bunch of snooty rich people. Which is why she told Merlin it was absolutely out of the question.

Annie nukes the remainder of this morning's coffee, and while she's waiting in front of the microwave, she again goes through the bills still left in her hand. If she doesn't pay the minimum on the Visa card soon, they'll cut her off. And Andre's cell phone is past due. She can't let that lapse.

Can't you?

It makes no sense to keep paying it, just so that she can hear his voice on the outgoing message every now and then and pretend he's still there, somewhere, on his way home.

It makes no sense, and yet she can't seem to help herself. Try as she might, she can't let go of the foolish fantasy that someday, she'll dial the number and he'll answer and she'll realize that this whole thing has been a bad dream.

Rubbing her exhausted eyes, Annie sinks into her chair again. She sets aside the pile of bills and sips some coffee. It tastes acrid, but she needs the caffeine to make it through the day.

She lowers her head to the table for a few blessed moments, fighting off sleep, wishing she could crawl back into bed.

Yawning, she forces her eyes open and stands up, looking around the cluttered kitchen.

Her gaze falls on the telephone.

Instinctively, she reaches for it and begins to dial. Just this once, she promises herself. One last time. Then she'll have the line disconnected and throw away the bill.

One ring . . .

This time, of course, she'll hang up at the beep. She should never have left a messge yesterday. Milo overheard her talking and thought she had reached Andre.

Two rings . . .

She had to explain to her son that she was talking to herself, not to Daddy. He wanted to know why she was holding the phone if she was talking to herself, a question she found impossible to answer.

Waiting for the inevitable third ring, Annie reaches for the cell phone bill. This really is ridiculous. It's time. Time to get rid of the indulgent expense. Time to let go.

Then, as she's about to rip the invoice in half . . .

"Hello?" her dead husband's voice says in her ear.

THE EDITOR'S DIARY

Dear Reader,

No matter how hard you kick and scream, you may find that fate has a funny way of telling you who is the boss. For Cupid's arrow always lands in exactly the right place—just ask Shelby Simon and Maggie O'Mulligan in our two Warner Forever titles this March.

Susan Andersen says that she's "hooked on **Mary McBride!**" and it's easy to see why in Mary McBride's latest book, **MS. SIMON SAYS.** Shelby Simon is too busy giving people advice to get a love life of her own. As the author of "Ms. Simon Says," her weekly advice column, Shelby reaches thousands of readers each week . . . until a series of letter bombs blow widowed cop Mick Callahan into her carefully constructed single life. Sent in to protect Shelby from these dangerous threats, Mick takes her away to her family's country home. Here, in a secluded paradise called Heart Lake, the rugged but tantalizingly secretive cop must protect the enticing but ever-meddling journalist. But resisting her is another matter. As danger comes to Heart Lake, putting them both at risk, Shelby keeps telling herself she can't fall for the one man sent to watch over her . . . or can she?

Moving from the intrigue of undercover cops to the excitement of Internet dating, we are pleased to offer **ONCE UPON A BLIND DATE** by **Wendy Markham.**

Romantic Times raves that Ms. Markham's previous book is a "wonderfully touching romance with a good sense of humor," but they haven't seen anything yet. Maggie is the best friend of Dominic. Charlie is the best friend of Julie. Through the magic of an on-line dating site, Maggie and Charlie will do anything it takes to set their buddies up on the most romantic blind date ever . . . even if it means tagging along. But from the moment they meet, Dom and Julie fizzle while Charlie and Maggie sizzle. She's involved with someone else. And he's Manhattan's most committed bachelor. So what will it take for these two matchmakers to give into Cupid and accept that love doesn't always go according to plan?

To find out more about Warner Forever, these March titles, and the authors, visit us at www.warnerforever.com.

With warmest wishes,

Karen Kosztolnyik, Senior Editor

P.S. Forget that spring cleaning! We've got two wonderful reasons to put your mop down and relax with these two Warner Forever titles. **Annie Solomon** pens an edge-of-your-seat suspense about a woman who's determined to bring her father's killer to justice and the detective who's out to unravel her secrets in **TELL ME NO LIES**; and **Shari Anton** delivers a spellbinding tale of a fiery woman determined to protect her family's holdings and the roguish knight who stands in her way in **ONCE A BRIDE**.